Spiritual Burden

Lynde Miller

This book is completely fictional and any references to real people or places are used fictitiously. Names or places that may resemble real things are not intentional and are made by the author's imagination.

First Edition

ISBN: 979-8-218-87909-9
Cover art by Rama Al-saty
Border art by Devon Taylor

Acknowledgments

A special thanks to my parents for listening to me yap about this book for about six years. Their support seemed to be never-ending! I would also like to thank my friends for giving me ideas and reading along as I wrote this. I don't think this book would have played out the way it did without them. You guys mean a lot to me. I would also like to thank my dad's buddy, Paul Costoff, who's an author himself. He helped motivate and educate me while writing this. To those who were with me during this journey, my appreciation is immeasurable, and I love you all. Thank you.

Stanley Morris
1987

Stanley Morris moved to Linfort Iowa about a month or two ago, not knowing what would be lurking in the depths of his very own backyard. His mother, Rosanne, didn't have much money for an even halfway decent house, and his father was already long gone along with most of the savings. His mom was looking for a new place to live after a fallout with her previous boyfriend, living in an apartment complex near Dubuque with him for about three months before things went south. It wasn't a nice apartment by any means, but neither was the man living there. Rosanne met him at a bar, a place she seemed to find most of her suitors. Stan wasn't sure what the cause of the breakup was this time, but he didn't really care to find out either. He had his suspicions, and he didn't need anything else.

As he walked up to the house, he was able to see all the flaws at a closer level. The brown siding chipped away in most places, while the mahogany asphalt shingles were torn up and stained from years of weathering. The moldy gutters lay astray in the lawn, left untouched for years. Ground bees flew in and out of a hole near the cracked wooden stoop, buzzing wildly as they did. Stan was sure the house was infested with rats and creepy crawlies. He didn't mind the bugs much, but the thought of a rat running across his face while he slept gave him shivers.

The house itself was on the edge of town, engulfed by the woods that surrounded it. He didn't want to think about what the forest would be like at night. Anything could be in there, silent and unseen. He felt the overgrown grass tickle the sides of his legs, poking and prodding at him. His mom stepped up to the stoop and opened the rotting wood door, bugs scurrying around them as she did. The inside of the house wasn't much better than the outside, and immediately the two were hit with the smell of rotting animals. Dust and rat crap caked the surface of the floor as mildew and cobwebs crept their way up the walls. The sagging, water-stained ceiling tiles gave him a sense of dread, making him feel as though they would cave in at any moment.

SPIRITUAL BURDEN

"I don't know about this place, " Stan mumbled. He didn't like the idea of living in a rat city, along with the rat funeral home. The floorboards creaked beneath him, making a dreadful groan that echoed through the quiet house.

"What other choice do we have, Stanley?" Rosanne gave him a look that spoke for itself. *I'm tired, Stan. This is all we can afford and I'm tired. So please don't fight me on this right now.* Clouds streaked across the darkening as the moon took the sun's place, the day coming to an end. He didn't protest anymore. Stan looked around the house with soft steps. It was indeed fairly small. There were two bedrooms and one bathroom, each containing its own set of problems. Stan was just happy he didn't have to share a room with his mother, as he had many times in the past. The kitchen was also very tiny, along with the living room, which happened to have a rather plump dead rat in it. Stan guessed that was where the smell was coming from.

"God, this place is a mess," Rosanne mumbled under her breath. He silently agreed and turned to the kitchen to see cockroaches scuttle across the floor. Their tiny bodies moving at astonishing speed. "This house will need a lot of work," she sighed, glancing around at the dirty chipped tile flooring. Its original white coloring had turned into a disgusting brown from being used over the years.

"It gives me the creeps," Stan replied, staring at the rat in the living room. Its dead glazed eyes stared back at him. Would he die trapped in this house just as this rat did? He couldn't stand being inside anymore. He went to the kitchen and towards the back door, hoping the fresh air would help with the nausea. He fumbled with the dirty and torn-up screen door, trying to get it unstuck from the track. Grunting a little, he finally got it open and was welcomed by the cool evening air.

The sounds of crickets filled the atmosphere as a train called in the distance. It was surprisingly calming, and for a second he felt as if he might actually enjoy living here. He let in a deep breath and allowed himself to absorb his surroundings. It was very different from the dinky little city apartments with no yards that he used to live in. He watched as birds flew to their trees for the night when something caught his eye: an off-white thing sticking out of the ground. He found himself moving towards it, the air growing still as he drew closer. *What could that possibly be?* He crouched down to see what it was, curiosity getting the better of him.

The long grass surrounding it seemed to lean forward toward the object. He extended a finger and gave it a poke before pulling it out. It looked like a bone of some sort; it was larger than the usual rabbits or squirrels he expected to see around here. He rubbed its coarse texture, feeling its cold surface. He paused, sensing his paranoia kicking in before dropping the bone. *Oh my god.* He thought as he lost balance and fell backwards. *What if that's a human bone?* He stumbled back into the house, slamming the screen door shut. Dust flew into the silent, open air.

Bradley Moore

Bradley Moore poured himself a bowl of his favorite cereal in the sunlight of his kitchen. He grabbed the milk and unscrewed the cap, hastily dumping some into the little blue and white bowl, spilling a little on the counter as he did. He didn't have long, or else he would miss the bus once again, not really being in the mood for another one of Mrs. Wilson's stupid lectures. She would go on about "*how important education is*" and "*you need to stop being late or else you will end up being another junkie on the streets. Do you really want that, Bradley?*" Along with more mindless bullshit that he couldn't care less for. Just thinking of her raspy voice made him hurry along with his soon-to-be soggy meal. He grabbed his spoon and crammed as much cereal in his mouth as he could, oats flying out and bouncing off the end of the table. Cleaning it up wasn't on his mind though; not being tardy was.

Bradley quickly finished up the rest of his breakfast, feeling thankful that he had already packed everything the night before. *Sweet, maybe I really won't have to deal with that old hag today,* he thought as he began to put on his shoes. He fumbled with the laces, his fingers moving awkwardly as he formed the loops. He quickly tightened them before getting up and straightening himself out, preparing to leave before his mother stopped him.

"Don't forget your duffel bag, hun," she reminded him before handing over his pack. He sighed, upset with himself for forgetting, yet feeling grateful that his mom was there to remind him. Although he wasn't able to see her often, he was appreciative of moments when he did. He just wished he could spend more time with her, finding it difficult to see her when she worked nights as a nurse and slept for most of the day. He did what he could to help her out around the house, but most days just felt empty without her there.

"Thanks, Mom, I'll see ya' later," he replied quickly before grabbing his duffel bag and leaving out the front door. The sun peeked out between two large clouds as goosebumps pricked his arms from the cool morning air. He made his way across the yard and towards the street, feeling the dew from the grass sweep against his ankles. Although his bus stop was only a few blocks away, he figured that fast walking would be his best bet.

Normally, he would enjoy the scenery while walking down Little Main, but today his mind was preoccupied with the thoughts of Mrs.Wilson, her stupid face, and her even more stupid lectures. Even though he despised everything about her, another side of him didn't want her to ruin his day. *Are you really gonna let an old asswipe kill your mood?* He decided to listen to that side of him instead and whistled a tune that had been stuck in his head for a while.

He slowed his pace a little, enjoying his surroundings as he did. The sky was a beautiful gray-blue with fluffy white clouds scattered across its landscape. He was excited for the summer that was quickly approaching, long days and shorter nights. He just wished that he had friends to spend the summer with. He had Ivan Balakin, the Russian guy from across town, but he didn't talk much, and he happened to be quite boring. Surely someone would join him to start fires and build forts in the woods.

After a while, he finally approached the bus stop and joined Nicole Brown and Amanda Smith. They both shot him a glare and stepped away, clearly disgusted by his arrival. At this point, he became used to this behavior and didn't really mind it. He had Amanda in his English class, who was a loudmouth in school, but dead silent around him. Someone would soon notice his worth and eagerly become his friend, right? Bradley wouldn't meet Stan until a month later.

Annette Jones

Annette Jones slammed her bedroom door open, already pissed off that she was spending yet another day at school instead of literally anywhere else. She stomped past her little brother Arnold's room and towards the stairs, her long blonde hair flowing behind her. The door quickly swung open, revealing the drowsy yet wide-eyed Arnold, showing off his missing front tooth as he smiled.

"Sheesh, you must be on the rag!" He sneered as she barged past.

"Oh, you can just bite me," she snapped back. She loved her little brother dearly, but he could be such an ignorant little airhead sometimes. Although she thought most ten-year-old boys were like that. She trounced her way down the stairs and into the kitchen, listening as her brother suddenly rushed past her and raced down. Her parents didn't really pay her or her brother mind when they came downstairs, although they didn't really pay much attention to either one of them in general. Sometimes it seemed as if they were invisible, unable to get as much as a "*that's nice, kiddo*" out of them on most days. Her family was quite wealthy, and apparently, money was more important to them than their own children. She made her way over to the counter, grabbing two small bowls from the cabinets above. She pulled out a couple of spoons before snatching the dented box of cereal off the counter, walking back over to the table after. She preferred pancakes, but didn't want to take the time to clean up the mess that comes with making them.

She pulled out a chair for herself and then the chair next to her for Arnold, who did a little bow before sitting down.

"Thank you, m'lady," he said as he sat down next to her, a rather vainglorious look on his face.

"Will you quit saying that? Who the hell even says that?" She asked in bemusement. He looked up at her with a smug expression on his face. He was always saying things like that, stuff she assumed he probably learned in the graffiti-ridden textbooks that the school gave out like candy.

"Old fancy people say that, duh. Haven't you ever watched a movie before?" He questioned while raising his eyebrow in a sophisticated manner. He scooted in, the chair screeching as it scraped across the wooden floor.

"Don't talk about our parents like that, Arnold." She scoffed profoundly as she scooted her own chair in. It made the same screeching sound as his did. "It's rude." He let out a small giggle as Annette poured herself a bowl, passing the box over to Arnold.

"You almost ate all the cereal, you cereal hog!" He shouted as the last bit of oats fell into his bowl with a harsh clink. The sound of it rang in her mind like a gong.

"Take a chill pill, it's just cereal," she responded blankly. They ate their breakfast together, bickering as they did. Arnold talked about his new group project that he and his friends were working on together in school, while Annette mentioned her Biology assignment she had yet to even start. She finished up her breakfast with a clink before sticking her tongue out at Arnold. He stuck his out right back and blew a raspberry. "Ew, Arnold, don't do that." She scolded, wiping herself off as if she had been doused in spit.

"Then don't eat all the cereal," he quipped in protest. She rolled her eyes before going over to the door to grab her bag, quickly stuffing her denim jacket that was set on a coat hanger into her pack. She really wasn't mentally prepared for today, yet she still opened the door and swiftly walked out anyway. The cool air rushed towards her as she went down the stoop, her ponytail bobbing behind her. She took a deep breath and started her way down the street. Annette wouldn't meet Stan until a month later.

Linfort

Linfort was a small town, of course; most towns in Iowa tended to be on the smaller side, but Linfort also seemed to have an even smaller history. Although it was decently popular for its town fair, which they would have every August 6th, it would only attract a few tourists from neighboring towns. The fair was primarily focused on the horticulture aspect, with local farmers using it as a way to make a few extra bucks. A small petting zoo would be set up for the kiddos, even though there would only be mules there to pet with the occasional goat. It seemed to always bring the attention and money of the townspeople there. But other than that, Linfort was a plain and simple town, right? Of course, every town has its secrets and Linfort is no exception, but some secrets tend to be a little darker than others. No town is perfect after all. But Linfort's biggest secret happens to be lying just beneath Stanley Morris's house, a rotting old filthy secret. A secret that the entire town was in on in the summer of 1964.

The majority of the people who were involved have moved on or moved out of town completely. Only a small handful of the townspeople still lived in Linfort, one of them being John Charles, a seventy-seven-year-old man who just happened to live on the same lonely street as Stan. Oak Street seemed to be almost forgotten with fallen leaves and overgrown grass, silent in the day but alive and aware at night. It was almost as if it was a street guarded by a phantom, cold and quiet. The emptiness of the street didn't seem to scare John though, even though he of course knew the history of it. Every night he would drive over the very road where Richard Huxley was struck dead, almost as silent as the leaves passing over the muted street.

Everyone knew it was a homicide, even the cops. No one said a word, it was very much intended to keep things quiet. Richard was an awful man with even worse motives, and once he was caught luring the Collin's kid to his house, they decided it was finally time to get rid of him. He claimed he was just going to show him something neat he found in his backyard when being questioned. Everyone was able to see through his lies and the town wanted him gone. It wasn't very hard to do away with him, in fact, it was very easy. Richard didn't drive a car, his license had been revoked since 1959. His schedule was also very easy to figure out. The man didn't do much besides walk to the gas station, at least that's what it looked like on the outside. On the inside, his mind was crawling with rancid thoughts that bounced all over.

Killing him was the easy part, yes, but it was also hard to forget the chilling sound of his bones being crushed under the large Ford Falcon wheels, blood splattering over it like paint. Randy Adams, one of the many locals who was in on Richard's murder kicked his mangled body a few times just for good measure, even going as far as to spit on his disfigured corpse. Cleaning it all up also seemed to propose a problem. The blood was smeared all over the empty road, along with bits and pieces of his clothes, bones, and flesh. Surprisingly enough, this wouldn't even come close to what was found in his own home, which was only a few feet away from the whole scene.

The stench of the old house was enough to make anyone walk out and ralph the rest of their lunch onto the sidewalk, causing an uneasy feeling to drift over the group. None of them wanted to see what was inside, but they had to find out. They had to know what was going on. The inside of the house seemed to be devoid of furniture, the only thing able to be seen in the living room was a wooden chair that faced the wall. But Richard Huxley's own secrets would be hidden in the bedroom. The stench of something decomposing was definitely stronger here, causing the already frightened group to fear the worst.

What was in the damp and darkened bedroom was utterly disturbing. Human brains inside of jars with formaldehyde were discarded and scattered across the bare floor, miles away from their original carriers. John faintly remembered some leaving the room to throw up, adding to the already horrendous smell. It was a truly awful scene. It wasn't hard to figure out where he had gotten them from as many witnesses had spotted him walking to the town cemetery late at night, a figure amongst the shadows. They traveled across the room and searched the closet, finding the body of a small child. It was fresh.

Huxley's reign of terror was finally over. So to think.

Bradley Moore

Crack! The sickening sound of his glasses breaking rang in Bradley's ears, his head banging against the ground with a thud. This wasn't the first time it had happened, and he knew it wouldn't be the last.

"You're such a piece of shit!" Annette Jones spat out from above him. She stood over him with a glare, her hands balled into fists.

"At least I don't look like shit!" He yelled back, causing him to start laughing again. He couldn't help it; she looked so stupid when she was upset, her mouth curling into a tight snarl while her bright blue eyes gleamed with fury and frustration. She looked like an angry toddler. Bradley thought she acted like one too, causing him to break out into laughter again. She kicked him in the shin before walking away, her blonde hair waving behind her, almost in a mocking way. It swayed back and forth like a snake, the Medusa of Linfort high, turning anyone who testified against her into a social outcast instead of stone.

"Loser!" She yelled as she flipped him off, storming down the hall with Vicky Taylor, her childhood friend, right by her side. He continued to cackle, clutching his chest as he lost his breath. He could hear her stomp away, practically smoking from her head as he continued to laugh on the cold tile floor. He faintly realized that his nose was bleeding. It didn't matter, his mom would be more upset about the broken glasses than his bloody nose. Glasses weren't very cheap after all.

This wasn't his first run-in with Annette either. He had a long history with her, mainly because he couldn't keep his mouth shut. Insult after insult and punch after punch. He caused this brawl by telling her that her hair was as greasy as a Maid-Rite sandwich. She, of course, didn't take it well and sucker punched him right in the schnoz. Also, as per usual, the students who enjoyed a good fight surrounded them in a little crowd, egging them on with the classic chant of "fight! Fight! Fight!" They needed some form of entertainment after all.

He sat up, feeling dizzy as he stared down at the shards of glass as they twinkled faintly in the large hallway against the fluorescent lights. His mom would be livid. This was the third time this year, and she would probably stop buying them if his eyesight wasn't so bad. He was almost glad they had broken beyond repair, not wanting to go to school with tape on them once again, as it only caused more teasing. He slowly got up, feeling the sharp pain in his shin where Annette had kicked him. The pain in his nose was even worse though, the blood still steadily pouring out. He glanced around the empty hallway with squinted eyes.

Where the hell is Ivan? Shouldn't he have been helping me? He stared down at his broken glasses, his vision all blurry. *Shit.* Why couldn't he have just kept his mouth shut? He bent down to pick up what was left of them, feeling tiny shards prick at his fingers. Blood dripped from his nose and onto the floor beside the glass. *I need to clean this blood off my face before I go to class..* He stood there and scratched his head, using his other hand to wipe his nose, a streak of red smearing on his hand as he did. He heard the sound of someone slamming their locker door down the hall, someone who was also late and would get the same lecture from Mrs. Wilson or one of the other crabby-ass teachers. The thought of meeting the same fate made him hurry just a little faster.

He started to fast walk toward the bathrooms, holding his hands underneath his chin in an attempt to keep the blood from dripping onto the pale floor. He quickly made a turn into the restroom before closing the door behind him. He listlessly thought that there might be someone else in there skipping class or smoking, but was lucky enough to find out that wasn't the case. He shuffled over to the mirror and inspected his nose. It was bloody alright, but it would hopefully stop soon. He rubbed his face with his hand and sighed.

"Why did I have to say that?" He quietly whispered to himself as he began to wash his face, the cool water running over him. He looked up again with a now-wet face, his reflection slowly becoming more distorted. His hair and features moved in slow waves as if he were looking into water instead of the school bathroom mirror. *It's probably just because I don't have my glasses on. Yeah, it will all be better once I get my glasses fixed.* He thought as he rubbed his eyes. It felt strange seeing himself in that way, thinking he looked almost alien.

He was debating whether he should just slip into one of the stalls and skip class as the bell rang outside. *Then I won't have to listen to that bitch, Mrs. Wilson. Yeah, let's just go ahead and do that.* He swiveled his head towards the empty stalls, listening to the faint sound of footsteps just outside the bathrooms. He turned back to the mirror again, rubbing his eyes with water one last time before looking into his reflection. With blurry vision, he spotted something near one of the stalls, something that wasn't there before. He quickly spun his head around to get a look, his eyes fighting to see what it was.

A grayish-clawed hand slowly opened the stall door, creeping its long fingers against the stall, its movement similar to a spider. Long, sharp fingernails tapped against the door in slow, sluggish motion, a low clicking emitting from behind the stall. He felt his heart pound within his chest, hectic thoughts swirling throughout his mind. *What the hell is in there?* He slowly stepped back, feeling his back meet the cold edge of the sink. His hand searched for the frames of his glasses blindly as he continued to stare at the thing in horror.

It seemed to be getting closer. Bright yellow eyes glistened through the crack as Bradley's hand flopped around aimlessly for his glasses, completely forgetting they were broken. He finally felt them, frantically putting them on as he shook his head with squeezed eyes, even though they were useless. He opened his eyes and to his surprise, it was gone. Without a second thought, he stumbled away and quickly walked out, not wanting to look back into the dark and desolate restroom. The door shut behind him, lights flickering as he made his way down the hall to Mrs. Wilson's classroom, leaving the creature from the bathroom behind him.

Vicky Taylor

"Wow, I still can't believe he said that about you!" Vicky Taylor exclaimed as she walked beside Annette, exiting out of the school's large front doors. Groups of students swarmed around them and stumbled down the staircase. One of them jumped down almost all of the steps, a little too eager to get out of school.

"Yeah, I sure showed him though." She responded with a grin. Vicky definitely didn't agree with Bradley's statement, but she wasn't really keen on breaking the dorks' glasses either. There were other ways to deal with idiots.

"Do you think any teachers were watching?" She asked with a raised brow. They turned the corner as others made their way past them.

"Puh-lease, if any of the teachers were watching we would already be sitting in detention next to some future dropout, chill out, Vick," Annette countered as she elbowed her in the arm. Vicky sighed. She knew Annette was right, and Annette knew too. They continued to walk down the street, the sun warming them as they did when Annette broke the silence. "So, how are you and your little nerd boyfriend doing?" She asked with a wink as she nudged her lightly. Vicky sighed once again. She was becoming tired of this topic and just wished Annette would drop it.

"Oh. My. God. Annette, how many times do I have to tell you he's not my boyfriend?" She asked with an annoyed glare, Annette's smiling eyes meeting with Vicky's stern ones. Vicky and "her little nerd boyfriend" Jamie Anderson were the top students in their small town's high school, often studying together after school in Linfort's town library, but to Annette, that meant that they were going out.

"He obviously is if you'd rather hang out with him than go to the mall with me," she retorted while applying her cherry-scented lip gloss. She always had an extra in her pocket, ready to go whenever needed. Vicky rolled her eyes. Of course, she enjoyed shopping with Annette, but she knew that her education was more important than a couple of cute shirts.

"Annette, the school year is almost over! Aren't you even just a *little* worried about your grades?" Annette stopped and snapped the lipgloss lid closed, looking up at Vicky with a testing look on her face.

"Would my parents even care if I failed?" She asked, raising her thin, almost perfect brow. "Would they pay me any mind?" Vicky kept her mouth shut. She knew how Annette's parents were. Ignorant rich pigs. "That's what I thought," she started to walk down the street again, her long hair swishing back and forth as she did. Vicky snapped herself out of her daze, speeding up to follow Annette. Annette knew how to get control of people, there was no doubt about that, and although Annette was her best friend, she also scared her. She knew the tension wouldn't last for long, as it usually never does. In the meantime, she listened to the birds and watched the cars go by.

Vicky turned her head back towards the school to see everyone else leaving, some on skateboards, most on foot. Most places in Linfort were within walking distance so the only people who drove were the ones who lived across town. She spotted Bradley, that airhead from earlier, stumbling out of the school. Someone gave him a hard shove with a laugh, causing him to slip down with a thump. He still somehow managed to clutch onto his broken glasses. Vicky felt a pang of guilt, noticing Annette turn her head to look too, her eyes narrowing.

"I kinda feel bad, 'Net," Vicky confessed, looking forward again. Annette gave her a puzzled look.

"Why? Maybe if he wasn't such a ditz, he wouldn't get picked on as much," she objected, shrugging her shoulders with a grin. Vicky looked at her with a worried gaze, she knew about their history but she also knew that Bradley didn't completely deserve it. She decided to keep the peace instead.

"Yeah.. Yeah, you're right he is pretty lame," she stammered with a nervous giggle. Annette gave her an *I'm right and you're wrong* type of smile. She tended to use that smile a lot.

"See? The kid's mental, he got what was coming for him." She assured as they advanced down the street, walking together in unison. Vicky nodded her head and squinted her eyes from the sun. Summers in Linfort tend to have nice weather, but today was very hot with little to no wind. Lucky for them, their houses were coming into view. Days like this made it feel good to live on the same street as their school. It's also nice that they live right across from each other, one of the reasons for their long-lasting friendship. She took a deep breath, still hearing the distant chatter of excited students behind her. She continued to walk beside Annette as a car slowly drove past them.

Something in the window caught her eye, and she put her hands above her eyes a little to cover the glare of the sun, revealing what looked to be an inhuman face in the backseat of the little tan Chevette. Her eyes widened as she stopped in her place. Annette didn't seem to notice. The face smiled at her, long fingers tapping against the window as if it was waving at her. Its toothy grin shone in the sunlight, fingers scraping against the roughed-up glass. Just like Bradley, they reminded her of spider legs. She felt herself go cold despite the heat surrounding her, its eyes glistened in the sun as she grabbed for Annette.

"Annette- do you see that?" She frantically questioned, breathless and bewildered. Annette turned to look, but the car along with the figure was already gone.

"See what, Vick?" She asked, looking at the now-empty King's Street. Vicky shook her head, looking one last time to make sure.

"Never mind, it was nothing." She mumbled, rubbing her eyes and continuing down the sidewalk, her footsteps almost in sync with her heartbeat.

"God, you're almost as looney as that dip," Annette teased while looking at her with a smirk. Vicky peered down at the ground. She honestly wished Annette was right, she didn't want what she had just seen to be real. She would rather be crazy. Her ears rang as Annette continued to blabber on about something that happened earlier in class. Vicky couldn't pay attention, the image burning in her mind as she continued down the silent street.

Stanley Morris

Stanley wasn't sure if he was awake or asleep, but his eyes felt open, feeling as though he could see the dimness of the moonlight coming from his decrepit bedroom window. His was the one with the hole in it, large and angry. He had a small room, with an even smaller bed pushed up against the corner of it. A breeze came through the hole in the window, causing him to shiver underneath his thin blanket. They hadn't bothered covering it up yet. Blurry pictures played in his mind like a movie, adjusting and becoming distorted ever so often. It was almost like looking through a fishbowl. *Please get me out of this.* His eyes moved rapidly underneath the lids. He felt hot and itchy all over, jerking his arm at each movement, seeing a tall gray figure with long claws for hands.

He couldn't make out any details on the face except for large teeth, curved in the shape of a smile. He jerked his head away, trying to look in a different direction but it was no use. He was trapped in this state of being both asleep and awake. The feeling was almost painful, his body restless. Fear gripped him as the creature taunted him. Sunken eyes gleaming, it waved at Stan before turning away from him, facing a different figure. This one looking human.

A taller boy around Stan's age, with dirty blonde hair, came into view. The boy looked up, facing Stan and the strange entity. He couldn't make out any specific features because of how blurry everything was, along with how the images in his mind waved lethargically. He seemed to look right through Stan as if he were just a spectator in this world. The boy fell backward at the sight of the figure, staring up in fear. The creature stepped forward and the characters faded away along with the rest of the scene. He saw this same situation repeat, only with different people and different places.

One after another, it was the same thing. Despite the blurriness of this false reality, it almost seemed real. He felt the fear in all of them. Some screamed, some froze, others ran. After what seemed like a never-ending cycle, he was brought to a new place. This place was dark and empty, the only thing that was there was a single chair. His vision was perfect now.

"This is it." Stan heard something say. The gravelly voice seemed distant yet close. *What is it?* He thought, hearing his inner voice echo throughout the darkened area. *"This is your mind. Your home. Isn't it beautiful? Isn't it just wonderful?"* It replied. Stan didn't know what to think. He didn't know where he was. He didn't know who was even speaking, but it could hear his thoughts. He could speak to it. *It's quiet, it's dark. I don't want to be here, who even are you?* His voice echoed once again. This time the voice was closer. *"It doesn't matter who I am, it only matters how you perceive yourself to be. It's quiet because you make it quiet. It's dark because you make it dark. You haven't been exposed to those around you yet, to what they know. You only know what you know. Your mind is limited, perhaps even trapped. If you don't like what you see, fix it."* It bellowed, starting to sound more and more distant with each word. Stan didn't understand. Was this a dream? *I don't get it.*

This time two yellowish eyes appeared in the darkness before him. "*You will understand soon enough.*" It showed its large teeth, each one of them being stained and sharp. A hand with three large claws emerged from the darkness, grabbing Stan's shoulder with a tug. He jolted awake, soaked in his own sweat, gasping for air as if he were being held underwater. He looked around the darkened room frantically, praying no one else was in there with him. He thought about the chair and the voice when it finally struck him. There was something else connected to this house.

Richard Huxley

I showed myself to them all, as a little greeting per se. Perhaps even a warning. Maybe I just needed a little refresher. Everybody knew him, knew me. Especially John Charles. Now trapped in the mind of a poor homeschooled boy, never able to see far from him. That's alright, I think. I can stay in his mind and observe it. Just as I always craved. Who knew you only got what you wanted when you're dead. I think I can work with this. Yes, this will work out just perfectly in my favor. Thank you for letting me into your life, Stanley Morris, because now you're going to give me exactly what I need.

Bradley Moore And a Month Later

Bradley quickly walked outside and closed the door behind him, wearing his old spare glasses. He wasn't able to see out of these ones as well as his old glasses, but he decided it was better than nothing. His mother planned on getting him new ones, so in the meantime he would just have to deal with the teasing. He adjusted his duffel bag, hoping he didn't forget anything. Once he felt content, he pushed his glasses up and walked out the door.

He knew he had to be more cautious at school now; his mom was already upset with him for breaking his glasses, but she also didn't want him coming back home with any more black eyes and empty duffel bags either. He had to learn to keep his mouth shut. He started his way down the small cul de sac, breathing in the fresh air while feeling a slight breeze hit his face. He put his hand above his eyes to cover the glare of the sun, not minding the light blaring into his eyes or the intense heat radiating onto his skin. To him, it meant summer was close. He looked down towards the bus stop at the bottom of the hill to see that neither Nicole nor Amanda were there. *Am I early?*

"Bradley! Is that you, hun?" An old lady's shrill voice pierced his ears. He whipped his head to the side to see the tiny woman squinting her aged eyes at him from her porch. He recognized her as Mrs. Bury, an eighty-five-year-old elderly lady who was becoming more blind with age. Bradley gave her a soft wave and a smile. Her husband, Mr. Bury, had died only a year ago, causing the poor blinding woman to live on her own. Bradley would visit her often because of this, knowing how it felt to be alone. He enjoyed their afternoon conversations when he would join her for a ham and cheese sandwich on her porch. During the time they spent together, she would often tell him stories from her youth. According to her, she used to be quite the hellion before she met her husband, Gareth Bury.

"Good morning, Mrs. Bury!" He replied warmly. She smiled and returned the wave.

"Good morning, Bradley! You better behave yourself at school!" She yelled over to him with a soft chuckle. She still treated him like he was a child, but Bradley didn't mind too much. He supposed that in a way he never really grew up anyway.

"No promises!" He yelled before taking off down the desolate street, his beat up KangaROOS pounding against the cracked sidewalk. The feeling of being early, along with running, was energizing, it was almost as rushing as that time he rode his bike down the steepest hill in town two summers ago. He was lucky he got away with only a broken ankle that day. He ran all the way to the rest of his bus stop, skidding to a stop and almost falling from the sudden halt. He bent over with his hands on his knees, taking in deep breaths, pushing his glasses up as they slipped down. He didn't know why he decided to run, it was as if a strong urge had possessed his legs to move.

He looked up toward the sun and felt a wave of dizziness wash over him, his limbs beginning to shake as he let out a small groan. His vision waved in and out as he slowly lowered toward the ground, folding into a half-bent-over position as if he got socked in the stomach. Once he felt a little better, he took a deep breath in before straightening himself out, trying to regain balance. *I oughta start running more.* He thought to himself with a sigh. Although his vision was still a tad blurry, he looked to see if anyone else was around, and to his surprise, there was.

A very pale boy with scruffy dark brown hair that covered the majority of his eyes stood by himself. It reminded Bradley of when he used to refuse to let his mom cut his hair, old memories of even older arguments. He wore a white t-shirt and blue shorts, standing across the road waiting to cross. *Where was he coming from? No one lives down there except for that one old geezer.* Bradley stood there, watching him quietly while trying to keep his mouth shut.

The boy had a very anxious way of moving, looking around warily as if he were paranoid. He kept his hands up to his chest, fidgeting with them a little as he watched for cars. At last, he finally ran to the side of the street that Bradley was on. The boy seemed to just now notice Bradley, pausing when coming up to the bus stop. *Is this life's way of giving me a friend? Maybe that's why I had the urge to run here, yeah... Yeah!*

"Gee, I bet I can see better than you and I have to wear glasses!" The boy looked up at him with a puzzled look on his face, one that might even be close to shock. *Oh boy, there you go running your mouth again.* "God, sorry, I mean-" He bit his lip and tried to continue on with what he was saying. "I'm Bradley Moore, and what's your name, stranger?" He stuck out his hand, which was still sweaty from running.

"Stan," He mumbled quietly, giving his hand a weak shake. He looked at Bradley's hands with slight disgust, probably from all the sweat. Bradley didn't care, instead noticing how bony his hands were. In fact, it wasn't just his hands that were bony, it was every part of him. *Geeze, does he even get fed at home?* He tried to push any negative thoughts to the back of his head. For now, he just wanted to know where this guy came from.

"I haven't seen you around here yet, just move in?" He asked as Stan slowly started walking toward the gas station. (Stan was ordered to buy a pack of smokes for his mom, not to have small talk with some dirty blonde-haired boy with glasses.)

"Yeah, I live just down Oak Street," Stan murmured, quickening his pace from a slow walk to a normal pace. Bradley continued to follow him, keeping up pace and walking by his side, their footsteps almost in sync. *Oak Street? Isn't that where that one incident happened? He must have moved into that.. House.* He tried to hide his discomfort and changed the subject.

"Woa, really? Awesome! So uh, where are you headed?" He asked, completely forgetting about school and the bus. With a mind like Bradley's, this tended to happen quite a bit.

"Gas station, I need to pick up some cigarettes for my mom." He mumbled quietly, fidgeting with his hands once again. They continued walking in silence as Bradley's attention quickly shifted back to his hands, pale and frail. He looked so cold on this warm summer day. Stan must have noticed him staring, quickly stuffing his hands in his pockets as they walked through the gas station doors. They were greeted with Gus, the pretty much only worker at the Linfort gas station. Gus was a bigger guy and didn't seem to like his job very much, almost always being seen with eyebags and a blank expression. Bradley still found him to be pretty enjoyable to talk to though.

"Hey, Gus!" Bradley hollered with a quick wave.

"Hello, Bradley," he acknoweledged with a lack of emotion. "Who's your new friend?" Stan shot him a glance as Bradley looked over at him anxiously.

"Well this is Stan, he's new around here, lives down Oak." He explained, gesturing towards Stan. Bradley noticed Gus give a small look of concern when hearing about Oak Street. Bradley exchanged the same look, Stan giving a little wave as he stepped up to the counter. He was completely oblivious. Gus gave a pencil-thin smile and waved back, letting his large hand flop back onto the smooth, freshly cleaned counter.

"Oak Street, eh? Well, welcome to Linfort Iowa, kid. Hope your life wasn't too exciting before this because it's about to get real dull." He flashed one of his toothy smiles, exposing his yellowish snaggletooth. Stan gave out a nervous laugh and nodded his head, giving Bradley a confused glance. Gus let out a low chuckle before slamming his hands on the counter, causing the two boys to jump. "Well, whaddya need, kid?" He asked with that same toothy grin. "I don't got all day." Gus was a pretty big guy, and Bradley could tell that he intimidated Stan judging by how nervous he was. He quickly fished his pockets for the note his mother gave him, shyly handing it to Gus.

He snatched it out of Stan's fingers and quietly read it. "Smokes for ya mom, eh?" He eyed both of them up suspiciously. "Well, I doubt either of you's would be lying to me, so I'll trust ya on this." He stated before getting a pack of cigarettes from behind him and setting it on the counter. Stan searched his pockets again before pulling out the money for it, handing it to Gus promptly. He counted it and looked at Stan with a scorn. "You're a quarter short, kid." He grunted as he counted through the money again.

"But my mom gave me the money, it has to be enough," He spat out quickly, his voice cracking. Bradley went through his own pockets before pulling out two dimes and a nickel, handing it to Gus quietly. Stan looked at him with surprise before flashing him an appreciative smile. Bradley nodded, giving him a quick thumbs up. When he finished recounting, he handed the pack to Stan. Gus gave Bradley a look of respect and a nod.

"You's two be good now, behave yourselves," he bellowed with a small smile, this time without the tooth. Bradley gave a little nod back, saluting

Gus who did the same. The two pushed the doors open and walked out, advancing back down the street and into the heat of the day.

"Thank you," Stan said without looking up. He stared at his feet, stuffing the pack into his back pocket.

"Hm? Oh yeah, totally, it was no big deal." He replied with a smile. Bradley was starting to really enjoy Stan's company. He glanced at Stan's hands again.

"Hey, what if you came over this Friday?" He asked, stopping just before the bus stop which was still empty, but now because he was late. Stan stopped as well, squinting his eyes from the blinding sun.

"Like tomorrow?" He asked, tilting his head to the side slightly.

"Yeah, uh, if you don't have any plans that is." He stammered, his voice cracking a bit. Stan seemed to think about it for a second before nodding his head, causing his bushy hair to bop up and down slightly.

"Sure, I can't see why not," he replied calmly. Bradley felt his body lift. Finally, someone who could be his friend, someone willing.

"Bitchin'! Here, I'll write down my address for you." He exclaimed as he quickly dove into his duffel bag, grabbing a pen and paper to write it down. He hastily wrote his address in neat writing before handing it to Stan. He hoped he could understand his writing, but judging by his smile and him setting it into his pocket, he could guess that he was able to.

"See you tomorrow, Bradley." He said with a wave, walking back down his street again. *See you tomorrow, Bradley.* Those words rung through his mind like lyrics to a catchy song. *See you tomorrow.* He missed the bus, but he didn't care. *See you.* He finally had a friend. *Tomorrow.*

Stanley Morris

Stan crossed the barren street, holding the note in his hand. He pinched the paper between his fingers as the wind gently lapped at it. He didn't know why he accepted the invite, but he was happy he did nonetheless. Bradley was an interesting person to say the least. He seemed to speak his mind, which was all over the place, something Stan couldn't understand as his own thoughts were very simple. Or at least he thought so. He tried thinking about past friendships he had, but just couldn't. Everything was a blur, cut out from his mind. The most he could remember from his childhood was empty bottles and cans.

Unlike Bradley, who also struggles to make friends, Stanley has just simply never had any. For the majority of his childhood, he would refuse to talk to anyone his age, all the way up until he was eight that is. He was able to talk to his teachers before his mother forced him to become homeschooled right before freshman year, isolating him from the outer world once again. But even before that, he still couldn't seem to make any friends. Although it was very hard to make friends in general when you were constantly moving from house to house. At least Stan has always lived in Iowa, never straying far from the endless corn fields and farms.

He didn't mind Iowa one bit, personally enjoying the countryside the most. He loved to see the large intricate farmhouses, along with the cows and desolate barns. The way the tall grass swayed with the leaves of a nearby tree in unison. Farmcats snoozing in the shade after a long day, he loved it all. He only ever lived in a few homes in the country, but those houses held some of his favorite memories. Those were the homes where it was just Stan and his mother, no drunk boyfriend of hers to stumble into the house in the middle of the night. However, the majority of the houses Stan lived in happened to be small towns just like this one. He liked living in town, sure, but it didn't hold the same feeling the way living in the country did. Nothing would ever be able to compare. He just really missed those country nights, sitting in the cool air under the light of the yellow moon.

He continued down the empty sidewalk, kicking rocks occasionally as he did. Still reminiscing on his childhood, he suddenly felt a cold shiver.

You don't need him, he'll just use you. Stan paused, shocked by the whispery voice that seemed to come from his head. He stopped in the middle of the sidewalk, looking around to see if anyone else was around.

"Huh?" He wasn't even sure if he had audibly said anything or not. He felt very dizzy, the world around him starting to slowly spin in gradual lethargic waves. *You don't need Bradley Moore.* Stan suddenly recognized the voice, the one from the dream-like hallucination. He felt like throwing up, but he could barely move. He didn't think he could even take one step forward if he wanted to. "Go away, I don't want to talk to you," Stan stammered promptly, trying to hide the shakiness in his voice. *Soon enough you will understand and listen to me, but I can only be patient for so long.* The voice hissed. Stan frowned. *Understand what?* "I said go away, why won't you listen?" He stood there, waiting for a response but was left with silence.

His vision went back to normal as if it were nothing. He shook his head before slowly starting to walk again. He wasn't afraid of the voice, but he didn't quite know what to think of it either. He also really didn't like the reaction that came with it, the blurry vision and vomity feeling wasn't very ideal. He thought back on what the voice said before. *Bradley wouldn't use me, he gave me money for the cigarettes.* But he also seemed desperate for friends, which isn't bad- right? He sighed. Stan remembered when all he wanted was at least one friend, just one person to talk to instead of his mother. No. No, it isn't bad at all. He stepped over the cracks in the sidewalk, causing tiny insects to retreat in a hurry. Leaves blew around carelessly throughout the street. He was able to see his house now, worn down from the years and weather. He put his hands on his face before rubbing his eyes tiredly.

He wasn't ready to step into that mucky house yet. Out of all the houses he's lived in, this one was the worst by far. He and his mother had tried to clean it up to the best of their ability, but despite their efforts, it still smelled of rot and mildew. He dreaded every second of being in that house, the thought of being able to go somewhere clean for the night excited him. *Well hopefully clean, I'm not very sure how clean Bradley's place will be.* He passed the only other house on his street, an older man sitting on the porch stared him down. His dark eyes looking into his own. He turned his head away and quickened his pace, feeling the old man's eyes burn into the back of his head. *Tomorrow*. He thought. *Tomorrow will be better, a fresh start. Tomorrow.*

Annette Jones

Annette flopped down on her canopy bed with a huff. She couldn't believe that Vicky was hanging out with that stupid little nerd rather than her. Just couldn't believe it! She was even starting to think that maybe she liked that barf bag *more* than her. She let out an aggressive sigh, listening to the music on her little pink boombox which neatly sat on her white dresser. *What if I went over to that shitty little library and told her exactly how I feel.* She rolled over on her side and stared out the window, glaring as she did as the sun quietly poured a soft light into her room. Biting her lip, she thought about how she had been friends with Vicky for years, since kindergarten for crying out loud! Could Jamie Anderson really top all of those years?

She stared at Vicky's house through the window, watching as Vicky's little sister Jennifer made chalk drawings on the driveway while her father mowed the lawn nearby. Annette lived almost directly across from her place, that's how they were such good friends, after all. That and money. Both of them came from wealthy families, living in big houses on King Street (also known as Mule Street as Bradley and others call it). Their large rooms being covered with nice white furniture and lush shag carpets. The only difference being the arrangement and the fact Annette has a small Madonna poster above her dresser. Her parents didn't care enough to make her take it down, they actually didn't even notice until three months after she put it up.

Her parents didn't care about most things Annette and her little brother did. It was the only reason she and her brother were able to get away with practically anything. Annette suspected the only reason they had kids in the first place was so they could fulfill the classic American dream and uphold the image of a "happy family." But they really only cared about themselves and status, leaving Annette and Arnold to take care of themselves, forcing them to grow up a little too fast. Nothing happy about that.

She sighed once again, getting up to look through her window, sunlight continuing to beam through it. She perked up as a sudden thought passed through her mind, that thought being of her brother Arnold. He skipped school often, and she knew that today he had been planning to go out by the railroad tracks to smash coins with his friends. In fact, he was probably out there right now screwing around with those little twerps. Just as that thought ran through her head, the front door slammed open with a large thud. Startled, she jumped up with a gasp before opening her bedroom door to see what caused the commotion.

"Annette!" Her brother yelled while running up the stairs, gripping the wooden banister. She stepped outside her room into the darkening hallway, giving him a puzzled look as he stumbled over. "I ran all the way here," he panted quickly as he wheezed. "I ran so fast you wouldn't even believe it! You just wouldn't!" Arnold put a hand on the wall and took in another deep breath. His face was flushed and he looked like he had just finished running a marathon.

"Well spit it out already! What is it?" She asked with her hands on her hips. He put a finger up, signaling for her to wait and when he finally caught his breath, his eyes lit up.

"Oh Annette, you won't believe what we found!"

Vicky Taylor

Vicky sighed and stretched as Robert Hill picked up the last of his things and made his way towards the library doors, giving a quick wave as he did.

"Thanks for the help, Vicky!" He shouted as he opened and then closed the large library door behind him.

"Cya next week!" She exclaimed, giving him a small wave and a smile, watching him leave. She heard Jamie Anderson sigh beside her.

"Finally," he grumbled, slamming his book closed. "He was a real dumbass." Vicky rolled her eyes but her grin still remained. He had been waiting for her to get done with Robert so they could pack up and leave, but he was surprisingly patient about it today, unlike most days. She and Jamie often helped tutor students at Linfort's small little library that sat next to the high school. Vicky didn't think that Jamie enjoyed it very much, but nonetheless, he still joined her every afternoon to do the job anyway.

He started putting his large textbooks into his duffel bag, grumbling as he did. Jamie was a short, heavyset Hispanic fellow with a temper. He almost always dressed in some type of formal wear, constantly trying to present himself nicely. He seemed to care a lot about stuff like that, always trying to keep on top of his grades and appearance. Although many others in Linfort didn't like him that much (including her best friend Annette), Vicky had always felt a good connection with him, even if he did seem a little full of himself.

"Yeah, I guess he was kind of a dip," she agreed with a small giggle, his face seemed to lighten up a little at the sound of her laugh. She quickly shoved her stuff into her bag and got up from the small wooden circle table, pushing her chair in as she did. Jamie got up and did the same, his chair letting out a small screech. "You ready to get out of here?" She asked with a huff as she adjusted her bag strap.

"I guess, I'm not ready for the heat though," he noted jokingly.

"Yeah, I suppose it did warm up a bit out there, didn't it?" She and Jamie walked up to the large double doors, pushing them open together, walking side by side, and into the hot Iowa summer air. Vicky's street was just to the right of the Library, but Jamie lived further down Linfort, next to the local dentist's office where his stepdad worked. Normally, Vicky would just go up her street and straight home, but sometimes she would walk with Jamie down to his house. Today was one of those days. Jamie, who was already sweating profusely, seemed to notice the fact she didn't turn down her street.

"Walking with me today, are we?" He asked with a slight smile. She returned the grin.

"I guess so," she said, nudging him a little as they continued down the cracked sidewalk. His face flushed as his eyes quietly lit up. At that moment, she really couldn't understand why nobody liked him very much or why Annette despised him. She felt her cheeks get a little red as her heart fluttered, a small smile appearing on her dark and tired face. They didn't speak much on the way to Jamie's house, and if they did it was about school. Jamie wasn't too much of a talker, but Vicky didn't mind too much. It was a nice change from the usual talkative Annette. She was very comfortable in the silence, listening to the sounds of their footsteps and the distant sound of a train.

When they finally reached Jamie's house, both of them were soaked with sweat, breathing heavily with tired and sunbeaten eyes. Birds flew above them on gentle wings. She looked up, watching them with a small smile and squinted eyes. She found herself enjoying sunny days like this, no matter how disgusting it made her feel after. The sweat was worth the warmth.

"Hey, Vick?" Jamie asked in a tired yet curious voice, looking up at her cautiously.

"Yes, Jamie?" She looked down at him with a puzzled look, the sun beating on their backs.

"Would you, I don't know... Want to come inside or something? Maybe to hang out?" He asked while shuffling his feet, looking like a nervous little kid asking a girl out on a date. She smirked before grabbing his hands, startling him a bit.

"Look, you're really sweet, but I'm gonna have to decline your date offer," Vicky professed jokingly. She didn't actually mean it, she just wanted to mess with him. She actually thought she might even have a thing for him, despite Annette's constant protesting. The expression on his face wasn't the one she expected it to be though, he looked surprised and hurt.

"What?" He questioned in shock, his face red in embarrassment.

"Awh c'mon Jamie, I was just messing with you." She jested with a nervous laugh, crossing her arms across her chest as his confusion and embarrassment turned to anger.

"Yeah alright, whatever." He grumbled, tugging his hands away from hers before turning to his house, sulking off towards the wooden front door with a scowl on his face.

"Jamie wai-" But before she could even finish her sentence, the door slammed closed and she was left alone outside with the hot summer air.

Jamie Anderson

Jamie Anderson slammed the door shut before being left alone inside the cooled house. He advanced into the dim living room, fuming as he did. His face burned as his head raced with thoughts. He always thought he might have feelings for Vicky; there was just something about her that stood out to him. Maybe it was her kindness or her smarts. Her dark skin and beautiful, coiled ebony hair definitely made her stand out from everyone else at the shitty little high school. She was a goddess. Just thinking of all these aspects made the situation hurt even more. He couldn't bear it.

He gritted his teeth before grabbing a decorative pillow from the sofa. His gaze burned into it, anger beginning to consume him. He suddenly tossed it across the room, hitting a glass that was sitting on the living room table, causing it to fall to the ground and break into a million pieces. He sat down, putting his face in his hands. How could he be so stupid? He was supposed to be smart, he was supposed to be perfect. He didn't want to be angry, but he just couldn't help it. His stepfather, Chris Anderson, rushed into the living room from the sound of the glass breaking.

"Is everything alright in here?" He asked worriedly, eyes wide with surprise and fear. He timidly made his way to where Jamie was sitting, searching for the source of the noise. Chris was an anxious man, along with being a people pleaser, the complete opposite of Jamie's deceased Navy father. Chris married Jamie's mother, Rosa Romero, seven years ago, having two children together, Jessie and Carolyn Anderson. Both of whom Jamie grew to hate.

"Stay the hell away from me, I'm fine." Jamie spat out with a dismissing wave, his other hand still holding his face. Jamie hated his stepfather most of all. Chris always tried too hard to be a good dad to him, but Jamie didn't really care. Why would he after all? He would never be his real dad, he's a replacement. He also happened to be a very pathetic man, so pathetic that he was afraid of his own stepson.

Chris paused before giving a look of disappointment, slumping back into his room presumably to go back to his reading. After he heard the door close, Jamie got up and quietly walked into the kitchen, using the heels of his feet to sound quieter, not that Chris would come out to see what he was doing anyway. He glanced around before opening the fridge door. The small luminescent light inside blinked on, revealing his stepfather's Coors beer, a ritual that was all too familiar to Jamie. He didn't want to, but he found himself slowly grabbing a can and holding it there in his hand, his thirst quickening as the coolness touched his fingers. He snapped the tab open, listening to the soft *pst* that emitted from the can. The sound of it made him forget about Vicky. He stared at it, mesmerized. Although this definitely was not his first time, it still had him entranced nonetheless.

He finally took a swig of it, the flavor hitting his tongue like a bullet. He knew it was bad, but it made him feel so good. He always did this when he felt bad, and he felt bad quite often. He savored it, taking in little sips so it would last longer. He had a feeling that Chris knew about his little secret, but Jamie also knew that he was too much of a pussy to say anything about it. He also knew that his mother wouldn't believe him if he decided to rat him out. Jamie was the golden child after all, the bratty little golden child who looked down on the world.

When he was finally finished, he shoved it deep in the trash can below some of the other garbage. Washing his hands, he thought about taking another one but decided against it. He didn't want to start a problem he couldn't fix. He leaned forward on the kitchen counter, rubbing his eyes while watching the sun make its way down the horizon from the small square window. He knew his siblings would be home soon, and that's when he would retreat to his room for the rest of the day. He also knew that he had some time for himself right now. He knew he could relax, and until his obnoxiously loud half-siblings came home, that's what he did.

Bradley Moore

Bradley Moore made his bed while the sunlight quietly danced through his window. He was preparing for Stan to come over, humming a song he heard on the radio as he did. He found it difficult to contain his excitement, this being the first time he had a friend spend the night in a long time. Of course, he had invited Ivan Balakin, but he was never able to stay for very long. He didn't seem to like being inside very much either, always looking out of windows while stuck inside. His parents also seemed to be very strict, and he didn't think his father was too fond of Americans, especially ones like Bradley.

Before Ivan there was Jamie, his best friend until he decided that he became too good for Bradley. They had been friends for years, doing everything together. Bradley didn't know exactly what changed, but at some point Jamie thought he was too immature and embarrassing to be seen with, so he left. They had a big fight about it, leaving Bradley in tears afterward. Deep down, he knew there was another reason Jamie didn't want to be friends anymore and it killed him inside. But that was the sixth grade, something to be left in the past. Stan wouldn't leave him the way Jamie did.

His mother seemed almost just as excited as he was. She knew how lonely Bradley had been throughout the years, only talking to the elderly around the town. He's always struggled for company; however, she feels that things might have been different if she hadn't had that miscarriage when Bradley was only seven, causing the family to break apart and his dad to leave. Neither one of them could figure out why he would leave. He never saw him again after that, and he never got the answers he so desperately craved. Maybe their marriage was already frail, or maybe Bradley himself was the problem. That feeling ate at him, a crawling sensation of guilt and unease. If it was his fault, he would never be able to find out.

He grabbed an old stuffed rabbit from his bed, holding it tenderly in his hands. Its original dark gray color had faded into a lighter one, it was slightly tattered with a few strings poking out of tiny limbs. He shamefully but gently set it under his bed, not wanting Stan to see that he still slept with a stuffed animal. Bradley had always been a little childish, part of the reason he didn't really make friends all that well. He was aware of this, but didn't quite understand how to grow up. How could he when he was never given the chance? His mom didn't really treat him as his age, seeming to miss the child he once was. Or maybe she was missing the child she never got the chance to have. He tried not to think about it too much, having other things to worry about at the moment.

Staring down at the ground, he wondered if there would be enough space for him to sleep, wondering if Stan would even *want* to sleep on the ground. He thought of even more problems, problems that could cause Stan to leave. Panicky thoughts flooded his mind, making him feel breathless. He shook his head and came to the conclusion that he would just put some sleeping bags in the living room along with some pillows; that way both of them would be sleeping on the floor. He swiftly went to the closet before opening it, grabbing his dark blue nylon bag that contained his worn-out sleeping bag.

He pulled it out and held it up with a smile, the sleeping bag evoking many old memories of dozing off in his backyard with an old friend he once had. He rolled it up nice and neat, going from the dim hallway and into the bright open living room. His mother quietly sat on the couch watching the news before getting ready for work. She turned her gaze from the television to him, watching wordlessly as he set up his sleeping bag on the shabby carpeted floor in front of the couch. She spoke up as he rose to his feet to examine his work.

"Getting ready for your friend?" She asked with a gentle grin. He plopped down on the worn-down, yet comfortable couch next to her.

"Yup! I was thinking about showing him around town, maybe picking up a movie on the way back or something." He explained, clearly trying to hide his excitement.

"Oh yeah? Well, that sounds like a fun time. If you'd like, I have a frozen pizza in the freezer if you two want that for dinner tonight," she offered smoothly. Bradley's eyes lit up at the sound of her proposition.

"Yeah! That way, I can do my stellar combo," he mentioned as she ruffled his hair a little.

"Mhm, I'll also make sure to leave some money on the kitchen counter in case you want to get anything extra for you and-" She paused for a moment, "what's your friend's name again?" A large grin appeared on Bradley's face.

"Stan, my friend's name is Stan."

Stanley Morris

Stanley looked out his broken window, the warm summer air blowing through it. He slowly got up, raising his arms in the air to stretch, letting out a big yawn as he did. He didn't get much sleep last night, but he hadn't been getting much sleep in general. He knelt down, taking a deep breath before searching under his bed for his sleeping bag. He was thrilled to leave this filthy house, but a little embarrassed for Bradley to see what condition his sleeping bag and clothes were in. He dragged out the raggedy sleeping bag, holes and dirt contaminating it. It was a hand-me-down from one of his mother's nicer ex-boyfriends, who he guesses wasn't a total douche compared to the many others she's had. Too bad he didn't stick.

He searched under the bed a little longer before pulling out his dirty old duffel bag, blowing the dirt and dust off of it. He stuffed the sleeping bag inside of it, starting his search for some clothes. He remembered that he happened to have a decent pair of loose PE shorts from his old school in Brandon, back when he used to attend school, that is. His mother wanted him to stay home with her, thinking that school wasn't good for him. Stan never understood why, but he didn't object either. He searched the decrepit closet for the shorts, finding an old white t-shirt as he did. When he finally found the shorts, he crammed them in the duffel bag along with the t-shirt. He sighed, sitting there for a second, taking in the dust and different smells emitting from the duffel bag as he did. *He'll laugh at you, you filthy little poor boy.* There it was, that voice again. Stan paused.

"Shut up, I don't want to talk." He waited for a response but was again left with nothing. He got up, still staring down at the much too-crammed pack. He picked it up and quietly left the room, making his way into the dirty kitchen where his mother sat with her head down, her long dark brown hair hanging over her face. He could tell she had been drinking again.

"Hey, Mom," he started to say, keeping his distance. She looked up, her tired eyes meeting his.

"Yes?" Her voice was crackly and quiet. He stepped a little closer to hear her better.

"I'm going to a friend's house tonight, I'll be back tomorrow." Her eyes flashed as she stared at him. He didn't like that.

"Come here, Stanley." She muttered weakly. He did as she asked and came closer, bending down a little so they were level. She reached up and held his face in her hands, pushing the hair out of his eyes with her fingers. "I'm proud of you Stan, and I trust that you will stay safe tonight, okay? Promise me that you will be safe tonight and come home to me tomorrow, alright?" She commanded sternly, staring into his deep brown eyes that were mostly covered by hair. He nodded his head. He knew that she was happy he made a new friend so quickly, but he also knew she wasn't herself when she would drink.

"I promise." He said quietly. She gave him a weak smile before lowering her hands from his face.

"Good, now I want you to enjoy yourself tonight," she mumbled, giving him a light pat on the shoulder.

"I will, Mom, love you." He gave her a brief hug, smelling the alcohol on her breath as he did. The smell nauseated him.

"I love you too," her voice cracked. He quickly left before her tears could stop him, opening the hard wooden door and feeling the immediate heat beat onto him. The inside of his house was so much darker than it was outside, it felt like a breath of fresh air, even if that air was hot and muggy. Anything to be free of that house. He grabbed the note Bradley gave him from his pocket and checked the address again, pushing the hair out of his eyes so he could read it better.

"Just up the street and to the left I guess," he mumbled quietly to himself. He stuffed the note back into his pocket before adjusting his duffel bag, setting off down the street. He knew that this would be a very tiring trip, wishing he had a bike or a skateboard, or anything to get him out of this heat faster. After a little while of walking, he soon passed the only other house on the street, the old man from before still sitting on the porch. His dark skin made him somewhat hidden in the shadows of the shade. He stared Stan down, same as last time. Silent and watchful. Although it made him uneasy, Stan pretended not to notice, continuing down the silent street, with the occasional call of a crow making him jump.

Around five minutes later he passed Bradley's bus stop, watching kids race down the hill on their bikes, speeding past Stan as if he were invisible. He listened as they laughed and screamed on their way down as he stopped to check the address once again. *It's just the cul-de-sac to the left. Only a little bit further.* He stuffed the note in his pocket again, continuing down the sidewalk for a few minutes, turning left when he spotted Maple Street, the small little cul-de-sac that Bradley lived on. The sun seemed to endlessly beat upon him, only stopping when he entered the soothing shade of a tree, wiping the sweat from his forehead when he finally spotted Bradley's house.

It was a pale blue color with a single-car garage, a large oak tree sitting neatly in front of it. A cat was laying in one of the windows, obviously enjoying the sunny spot of the house. Stan smiled and picked up the pace a little. *He's going to laugh at you for being so foolish and then send you right back home.* The voice hissed once again. Stan groaned and waved his hands in the air as if he could blow the voice away. He stepped up to the front door and knocked two times, enjoying the cool shade that the house provided. A few seconds later, the door opened, and Stan was met with the wild-eyed Bradley Moore. His face had a masked expression of surprise when he spotted Stan's raggedy bag, causing him to shamefully try hiding it a little more by putting his arm over it.

"Hey, you actually came!" Bradley was beaming ear to ear. "Come on in man! I betcha it's a lot cooler in here than it is out there," he exclaimed with an amused look.

"Uh yeah, it's pretty hot out here," Stan agreed awkwardly, stepping into the cooled house timidly. He let out a small gasp. It was the cleanest house he'd ever seen.

"Sorry if it's a little messy, I tried cleaning it up the best I could," Bradley apologized quickly as if the gasp was from disgust.

"No, it's perfect," Stan marveled in awe. The house didn't smell of rot and decay but rather smelled of faint cinnamon. They were immediately met with the living room, which had a comfy-looking brown cotton sofa set in the middle of it. A decent-sized television rested on top of a small wooden table that was pushed against the wall. To the right of the living room was the kitchen, bright and comfortable looking. In between the sofa and TV was a sleeping bag and a pillow, Stan assumed that this is where

Bradley had been planning for them to sleep. Bradley noticed him looking at the sleeping bag, his expression turning into worry.

"I planned for us to sleep there if that's, uh, if that's okay with you." He stammered quickly, stumbling over his words. Stan looked at his own bag with a nervous glance. *He'll see and laugh at you.* The voice jeered, this time from inside his head.

"Oh, would you just shut up already!" He shouted, completely forgetting that Bradley was standing right there, a horrified look appearing on his face.

"I'm sorry, I know I'm a bit of a blabber mouth," he apologized awkwardly, looking down trying to hide his hurt expression. Stan winced, immediately trying to think of something to say, something to fix this.

"No it's not you, it's uh," he glanced around the room, remembering the TV in front of the couch which just happened to be turned onto one of the news channels. "It's this stupid news anchor, can't stand the guy," he spat out quickly, gesturing towards the TV. Bradley looked up and towards the television, a look of relief washing over him.

"Ohhh, yeah that James guy is a real loon," he jested with a laugh. Stan smiled and nodded his head, relieved that Bradley believed him. "Here, let me take your bag and show you my room," he offered as he grabbed Stan's raggedy old duffel bag, placing it next to the couch before motioning for Stan to follow him. He noticed how easily excited Bradley was, along with being half-witted, but he thought that was alright. Smiling, Stan followed him down the hallway and into his room.

The sunlight poured through his non-broken window and onto his clean rug. The neat, nicely made bed looked much more inviting than his rickety old broken one, loose springs puncturing his back every time he turned over.

"Oh Smudge, there you are!" Bradley shrieked in excitement, grabbing a large white and brown cat from his closet. "Smudge, this is Stan, Stan, this is Smudge," he said while making the cat mimic a little wave.

"Wow, is it friendly?" Stan asked as they both sat down on the bed, the cat adjusting itself in Bradley's arms with sleepy eyes.

"Oh yeah, he's super friendly, most of the time at least- wanna pet him?" He asked as Smudge purred quietly. Stan nodded his head, slowly offering his hand to the cat. Smudge gratefully took up his volunteer, butting his head against his hand. A small grin appeared on Stan's face as he started to pet the cat, feeling an overwhelming wave of happiness wash over him. He felt so safe here, so at ease.

"So I got an idea of what we can do today," Bradley proposed with a shine in his eyes, straightening himself up.

"Really?" Stan did the same as their eyes met, both with the same excited look.

"Yeah, so I was thinking I could give you a tour of Linfort since you're new and stuff? And maybe stop to get ice cream and a movie for tonight." Smudge yawned and snuggled closer as if in approval of the plans. "My mom is also at work right now and won't be back until later tonight, she gets weird hours as a nurse so we won't really have to worry about being bothered either." Stan nodded his head excitedly.

"Yeah, I think I would really enjoy that," Stan exclaimed with a beam.

"Great, sounds like a plan!" Bradley yelled, raising a hand in the air for a high five, which Stan happily smacked in return. They rushed into the kitchen and grabbed the money Bradley's mom left them on the counter, leaving the house before setting off into the street, the sun beaming down on them harshly. Where Bradley guided him was back down towards Stan's street. He shot Bradley a look of confusion.

"Why are we going back this way?" Stan asked timidly.

"Welll, I wanted to start you off at the beginning, I'm also assuming you haven't seen the park yet." He responded promptly as they crossed the street. A flock of birds flew above them, crying out to each other in the sunlight.

"Park?" He thought for a second and it came to him, there was a park behind the treeline of the old man's house. "Oh yeah, a park," he stated after figuring it out.

"It's a really awesome place when you want to just sit outside and take in your surroundings," Bradley noted while they turned left towards the park, a soft breeze flowing through their hair. He looked at Bradley who was breathing in the fresh air with closed eyes. Stan did the same, finding himself to finally be at peace. When they got there, Stan noticed that the park itself had many trees along with scattered wooden benches and a decently sized pond in the middle. There were only a few people there, including some kids trying to fly a kite despite no wind along with a taller boy sitting on one of the benches near the pond. Stan thought he recognized the boy from somewhere, possibly from the gas station or something. Bradley squinted his eyes, wiping the sweat from his brow before smiling, pointing towards the boy on the bench.

"That's Ivan Balakin, he's one of my *many* friends from school," he stated matter-of-factly. "HEY IVAN!" He yelled while cupping his hands over his mouth. "OVER HERE!" He started waving manically, causing a small snicker to escape from Stan as the kids who were trying to fly their kite turned their heads in confusion. Ivan's head jolted up in shock as he looked around frantically until he finally spotted Bradley and his crazy waving.

"C'mon Stan, you should totally meet him," he coaxed as he started walking fast towards the pond. Ivan got up with a blank look before heading towards them. That's when Stan noticed how tall he really was, when they finally reached him, he towered over them. He had a blonde curtain hairstyle that was a bit longer in the back, and he wore a striped long-sleeved polo shirt even though it was almost summer. His light green tired-looking eyes rested above his long nose.

"Hey, Ivan, this is Stan! He's new around here so I'm showing him around." He exclaimed while looking up at him. Ivan looked from Bradley to Stan, who gave a small awkward wave. Looking at him this close made Stan sure he had seen him from somewhere before.

"Hello, Stan," he said monotonously, along with a slight accent of some sort. *Is he Russian?*

"Ivan here doesn't talk much," Bradley stated, nudging him a little. Stan looked up at Ivan, feeling a little intimidated by his silent stare. "But all you really need to know about him is that he likes nature and bugs." He jabbered quickly, patting Ivan's back as he continued to stare.

"Oh, bugs are cool," Stan added promptly, causing Ivan's blank expression to change to a subtle look of surprise.

"So Ivan, do you want to join me and Stan? We were gonna go get ice cream at Tastee Freeze later," Bradley asked with an excited grin. Ivan looked at the bench he was sitting on earlier and then back to Bradley. He sighed.

"Sure, why not." He agreed quietly. *Definitely Russian.* Bradley's grin widened.

"Bitchin'!" He exclaimed with a jump and a fist pump. Ivan gave Stan a slightly amused look at the sight of Bradley, Stan snickered again as Bradley excitedly motioned them out of the park.

The three of them went down the street and to the right, crossing Little Main. As Bradley continued to blabber about anything and everything, Stan noticed how quiet Ivan really was. He was in his own little world, yet still listening patiently to Bradley. They walked on for about an hour and as they did, they passed many interesting places that Bradley eagerly pointed out. Places like Dave's Bakery and the local flea market. Bradley also pointed out Irna's Diner, a small family-owned restaurant that looked like it had seen better days. He explained that one of the girls who worked there was a senior at their school and how he was surprised that she never dropped out. He said that she had this "totally gothic style" and that she didn't talk to many people. Bradley suggested that they should go there for lunch one day.

The sun's harsh light dimmed as they continued down the street. They walked for about fifteen more minutes before finally reaching Tastee Freez, which was right across from Linfort High. A rush of cool air came at them as they entered the small little shop. Walking up to the counter, Stan was shocked by all of the different options.

"Ivan, do you want anything?" Bradley asked as he pulled out the money his mom gave him, counting it out with his fingers on the counter.

"No, thank you," he declined quietly as he looked out the sunlit window.

"Your loss," Bradley shrugged as he finished counting out the money, ringing the small bell on the counter. An older lady with her eyes squinted shut hobbled out of the back room and towards the counter, adjusting her glasses as she did. "I'll have one scoop of bubble gum," Bradley told her, adjusting his own glasses. "Stan, what about you?" He looked for just a bit longer before responding.

"I'll probably just have chocolate." He replied, straightening himself up.

"Alright! Aaand one scoop of chocolate, if you may," Bradley told the lady who was struggling with the scooper, her hands shaking from years of arthritis. Stan glanced back at Ivan who was still looking out the window. Bradley slid the money over after she passed him two ice cream cones, melty cream already thawing over the side a little. He handed the chocolate one to Stan who thanked him and quickly licked the parts that dripped down the side. They then left the small building, Ivan being close behind with one hand in his pocket. The sun was slowly setting but the heat still remained, of course, a lot cooler than before.

"Over there is the burn pile," Bradley noted, pointing towards the front of the school and across the street while he licked his ice cream.

"Why is it called the burn pile?" Stan questioned, licking the chocolate that melted onto his hand.

"Every year when school ends, all the students from Linfort High will pile up their notebooks and assignments and set that shit on fire," he stated proudly. "It's basically like a ritual around here." Ivan nodded his head in agreement.

"I participated only once," he spoke up, looking towards the decently sized dent in the Earth where the fire would be set.

"Yeah, but wasn't it fun? Didn't you get some kind of thrill out of it?" Bradley asked with wild eyes, ignoring the ice cream that was melting down the cone and onto his hand.

"It was fun, yes," said Ivan with a small smile. Bradley smiled too, nudging him a little.

"So you do know how to have fun," he jeered teasingly. Stan followed from the rear, enjoying his ice cream while listening to them talk about school. He suddenly heard something else during their conversation though. The sound of fast footsteps slapping the concrete behind him was loud enough to be heard over Bradley's boisterous laugh. Before he could even turn around to see what it was, he was shoved out of the way and onto the ground, just barely saving what was left of his ice cream. His head wasn't as lucky, as it hit the ground pretty hard.

"Watch it, airhead!" He heard a sharp female voice call out from in front of him. He looked up dizzily to see three figures running down the street, two of them looking to be around his age and one of them being younger, possibly a middle schooler.

"You watch it, you mental bitch!" Bradley hollered back, flipping them off. Stan clutched onto his head as Ivan reached a hand down to help him up. He grabbed Ivan's strong hand, quickly being pulled up.

"Are you alright?" Ivan asked, looking down at him with worry. Stan nodded his head which now ached with pain.

"Stan, you alright man?" Bradley asked, turning towards him, grabbing his arm and checking for any possible injuries.

"Yeah, I'm okay," he remarked, wincing at the sharp pain in his head. The sky danced with color as the three of them stood in silence, watching the others run down the street.

"That was Annette Jones, biggest whore in Linfort," Bradley snapped, fuming from the head. "And I think the other two were her younger brother, Arnold, and her wannabe friend Vicky Taylor." Stan rubbed his head once more as Ivan looked up at the sky, squinting his eyes from the slowly dropping sun.

"I should probably go home now before it gets dark." He stated, looking back at Stan and Bradley.

"Yeah, and Stan and I still have to go get a movie," Bradley noted with a nod and a sigh, seeming a lot more calm now. They both waved goodbye to Ivan, who did the same before turning back around and making his way home. The two of them headed off down the street in the opposite direction, side by side, quietly talking as they did while leaving the heat from the day behind them.

Ivan Balakin

Ivan slowly made his way home, taking in the view of the small town as he did. He enjoyed the time he spent with Bradley and Stan, but he was happy to be by himself once again. It was a lot quieter without Bradley's constant talking and high energy. Ivan thought Stan seemed pretty nice, he was definitely a lot quieter than Bradley. Maybe even someone who he could relate to. He wasn't particularly interested in making any new friends, but he also wouldn't mind the company every once in a while. Maybe, just maybe, he could even get used to it.

He continued down the cracked sidewalk, knowing he had a long way to go but not minding it at all. He lived across town, but that didn't stop him from walking to the park every day. It made for a comforting environment, a lot better than what his home life offered. He thought of all the times Bradley had invited him over, wanting so badly to accept the proposal but knowing he couldn't because of his father. He needed an escape, so nature had become his outlet.

He became fascinated with insects and dedicated most of his time researching them with books he borrowed from the local library. His favorite insect was the stick bug; its ability to camouflage and mimic its surroundings captivated his interest. However, he also had a large soft spot for ants, even going as far as to own an ant farm. He took care of his harvester ants every day before and after going to school, watching them while being stuck at home. His father thought his interest in insects was pointless and that he should be focusing more on his education. Ivan didn't care, continuing his research anyway. He soon found that going to the park would be his best bet out of the house, whether it be to read or to just observe his surroundings.

He was a familiar and warm face at the park, but school tended to be different. At school he was an outsider, he would be told he was too "intimidating" or too "quiet" by others, but because of his height and strength, he wasn't pushed around too much. Not like he would do anything if he was anyway, he was pretty timid and wasn't one for confrontation. He looked up and watched as birds darted across the sky as he walked, being careful with each step as he did. He enjoyed every second he was outside, the fresh air clearing his brain from any negative thoughts he might have had.

The sky began to darken as gloomy clouds rolled into the horizon, looking as if it was going to rain. The thought of rain made him pick up speed. Normally, he enjoyed the rain, but he was afraid to pass the park on the way home. He knew it wouldn't happen, but he still feared that the rain would sweep him out from under his feet and drag him into the dark, murky water from the pond. He shuddered at the thought of it. Ever since he had almost drowned back in primary school, he had been terrified of the water, causing him to steer clear of the pond. He understood that the fear was irrational, but he didn't care. He didn't want to be near the water if he didn't have to. As his shoes quickly kissed the pavement below, tiny drops began to fall all around him. Looks like he would have to walk home in the rain anyway.

Annette Jones

Annette's heart pounded as she followed her brother down the street, the sun beating on her back as sweat ran down her forehead and into her eyes. They had been running for a while now, and she knew she needed a break. She didn't even know why they had to be running in the first place. Couldn't they have just biked? Or even used the car? She sighed, doubting he even thought of that in the first place.

"Hey, Arnold, I need a break!" She yelled, slowing down while taking in deep breaths. She sat down on the sidewalk with a huff as Arnold jogged over to her. "How do you have so much energy?" She asked in between breaths.

"C'mon, Annette! We don't have time!" Arnold whined. Annette rolled her eyes.

"I'm sure whatever you have to show me can wait for a few minutes," she panted, putting her hands over her eyes to hide the sun. Arnold sat down next to her with a groan, holding his head with his hands. "How much longer anyways?" She asked, looking over at the disappointed Arnold.

"It's behind the house where that one guy died like twenty years ago," he explained, looking at her as if she should already know this.

"So all the way across town? Ugh, Arnold you're such an airhead!" She spat out with a snarl, her eyes gleaming with anger.

"It will totally be worth it once you see what it is." He exclaimed with a smug look on his face.

"Yeah, this better be worth- " She started to say before she was caught off guard. She saw Vicky sulking down the street with her head down, looking tired and defeated. "Vicky!" Her head jerked up and she looked around, squinting her eyes from the sun. "Over here!" Annette yelled. When Vicky finally spotted them, she quickly walked over, watching for cars as she did.

"Hey! Didn't expect to see you here," Vicky said quickly, glancing at Arnold.

"I didn't expect to see you here either, I thought you would have been home by now," Annette noted with a raised eyebrow. Vicky's eyes fell, looking to the side away from Annette.

"Yeah, I walked Jamie home today. I think I really upset him," she explained with a guilt-ridden face, plopping down next to Annette.

"Isn't Jamie that short little nerd?" Arnold asked, raising his eyebrow just as Annette did.

"Yeah, you're still hanging out with him?" Annette questioned, her heart filled with jealousy, upset that Vicky would be hanging out with someone so lame instead of her.

"I mean, yeah, I guess so, but that doesn't matter right now. What are you two doing out here drenched with sweat? Did you run here or something?" She asked, changing the subject. Annette wondered what Vicky had said to make her so upset, but decided to not push the Jamie topic any longer.

"Yeah, we did run all the way here," Annette hissed, shooting a glare at Arnold who stuck his tongue out at her. "Arnold dragged me out here to show me something behind that one dead guy's house, Victor Huckley, or whatever his name was." She replied with a slow shrug.

"Yeah, do you want to come with us?" Arnold asked with excitement. Vicky looked in the direction of her house and then back at them.

"Sure, why not," she listlessly agreed.

"Awesome!" Arnold crowed, getting up quickly. Annette groaned and followed suit, along with Vicky. They took off down the street once again, feeling the wind on their sweaty faces. They continued to run for a long time, going down street after street. Bikes and cars zoomed past them, making Annette wish even more that they would have used the bikes instead of running.

At some point, Annette bumped into a raggedy-looking boy who looked to be around her age. It wasn't until Bradley yelled something, making her turn her head around, that made Annette realize he was there too, along with the tall Russian guy. All three of them had a look of shock on their faces. Annette didn't care and kept on running as the sky darkened with angry-looking clouds.

By the time they finally made it, rain had started to fall. Fat raindrops falling onto their sweaty heads as the summer air had cooled down. Arnold took them behind the decrepit house, slowing down just a little as he did. Glancing inside she noticed the lights were on. *I thought that place was abandoned, is someone seriously living in that dump?* She didn't have time to think about it much as the three of them ran in the rain until they made it to the train tracks.

"What took you so long!" One of Arnold's friends yelled, crouching over something next to the tracks.

"Yeah, we were worried someone was going to spot us back here!" Mitchell West complained. Mitchell was Arnold's best friend, they practically did everything together. They were on the same baseball team, something Arnold was very proud of. Annette didn't like him too much, she thought he was very obnoxious, but she could care less for who he was friends with. They stepped up to the tracks, where four of Arnold's little friends were swarming something on the ground near the rails.

Arnold moved them aside so Annette and Vicky could see, a gasp escaping them as they looked down at the tracks. His limbs were contorted and mangled, one of his legs completely detached from the rest of his body. A boy a little older than Arnold lay lifeless next to the tracks, his clothes were soaked with blood, and his bag sat just a little further down the rails. His mouth was left agape as his jaw was dislocated. The side of his head was exposed, revealing a bit of his skull which shone through blood and hair. As flies buzzed around his body, Vicky put her hand up to her mouth in disbelief, Annette turning her head to the side to throw up.

"It's that missing kid, Peter," Arnold marveled in awe. Peter Smith had been missing for about a week now. Apparently, he ran away from home one night after a fight with his parents, being declared missing the next day. He was only fourteen, a tragedy for the entire Smith family. The rain slammed against their bodies just as the sun did an hour ago as they all quietly huddled around the lifeless, Peter Smith.

"Oh my god," Vicky spoke quietly, just as stunned as Annette was. The strangest part of this entire situation was his split-open head and missing brain, as if it were taken out. It was just gone. Vicky seemed to notice it too, exchanging looks of concern.

Maybe he wasn't even hit by a train. The rain poured on.

Bradley Moore

Bradley started up the oven, humming as the rain poured on outside. Stan sat quietly on the couch looking out the window watching the raindrops roll down the glass. Bradley did a little dance throughout the kitchen as he searched for the pizza inside the freezer, kicking the door closed upon finding it. He placed the frigid pizza on the counter before peeking his head around the corner to the darkened living room, checking in on Stan.

"Are you excited to have the three P's?" He asked with a large grin. Stan turned his head, surprised by Bradley's sudden question, sitting up a little.

"Huh?" A puzzled look appeared on his face.

"The three P's! Pop, pizza, and popcorn, I made it up myself." Bradley explained with a proud look.

"Yeah, that sounds pretty nice." Stan smiled and then looked back out the window again. Bradley noticed how quiet Stan was, but at the same time, most of his friends had been like that, so he didn't really mind. He was definitely a lot more talkative than Ivan, that's for sure. He danced his way into the kitchen again before sticking the pizza in the oven, setting it carefully on the oven rack with his mom's old raggedy mitts. He set the timer and then made his search for the popcorn. The storm began to progress outside as he did, thunder rumbled quietly in the distance as it crept its way toward town. He reached up into one of the wooden cabinets and found the microwave popcorn, smiling as he grabbed it.

"Sweet," he flipped it up in the air but failed to catch it, watching it fall to the ground awkwardly. He picked it up quickly as if it never happened and stuffed it into the microwave. He pushed the worn-down buttons to set up the time again, just as he did for the oven. He continued his little boogie, making his way into the living room, plopping down on the couch next to Stan. He grabbed around for the remote, turning on the small TV upon finding it. Stan turned his head and looked towards Bradley.

"Are we starting the movie now?" He asked timidly, shifting in his seat a little. They got their movie from the gas station after it started raining, running back with their hands over their heads, laughing as they did. It was some R-rated movie about camp counselors. Gus told them not to tell anyone he had let them rent it, which they happily agreed to.

"Yeah, I thought we could start it while we wait for the pizza and stuff," he suggested, getting off the couch and sticking the movie in the dusty little VCR. After messing with the VCR for a little bit, the microwave beeped as he switched the TV onto the movie. He bounced up quickly and ran over into the kitchen and to the microwave, the smell of popcorn filling the air. He grabbed a large plastic blue bowl and some salt before opening the greasy paper bag and pouring it in, sprinkling the salt on a little after.

He tossed the bag into the trash with a swift motion and carried the bowl into the living room, shaking it a little as he did to mix the salt in. He set the bowl between him and Stan and then sat down, already stuffing some of the popcorn into his mouth. Stan grabbed some too as the movie started, quietly crunching on the freshly salted popcorn.

Ominous music started playing as the opening credits slowly emanated onto the screen. About ten minutes after the movie started, the oven beeped, causing Stan to jump a little. Bradley groaned, pausing the movie before getting up to check the oven. He put on the old oven mitts and pulled out the steaming hot peperoni pizza, the smell mixing in with popcorn as the cheese quietly sizzled from the heat. He waited for it to cool down a bit, grabbing two cans of cold pop from the fridge before bringing it all into the living room, setting it next to the popcorn.

"I present to you, the three P's," Bradley announced while presenting the food. "Also be careful, it's pretty hot," he warned, licking the grease off his fingers. Stan nodded as Bradley started up the movie again.

Bradley watched as Stan finished off the last of his pop, setting it on the floor next to his sleeping bag. Or at least, his new sleeping bag. Bradley had switched Stan's raggedy old sleeping bag with a spare one that was probably much more comfortable while Stan was in the bathroom. He didn't think Stan noticed it yet. Bradley's thoughts broke when he heard screams coming from the TV along with Stan's whispers.

"Was I not supposed to set it down there?" Stan asked quietly.

"Huh?"

"You were staring at that pop can for a while, would you like me to throw it away now?" Bradley shook his head and waved his hand in dismissal.

"No man, you're fine, I was just lost in thought I guess." He returned his gaze back to the bright screen where a group was sitting around a campfire. Grabbing a slice of pizza, the scene switched over to a girl standing naked in a lake, presumably taking a late-night swim.

"Awh c'mon! The number one horror movie rule is to not separate from the rest of the group!" He barked at the screen angrily, taking a bite of the greasy pizza afterward. Stan silently agreed with Bradley's complaints but stayed fixated on the movie, watching as the masked killer closed in on the unsuspecting victim.

"The dumb blondes almost always die first," Bradley noted with a shrug as the killer stabbed her in the chest. Bradley thought about the girl being Annette and laughed, making Stan glance over at him in confusion. Bradley shook his head and continued to laugh a little, finishing off the last of his slice.

"Why was she swimming alone at night anyway?" Stan questioned in obvious confusion.

"Ever heard of skinny dipping?" Stan nodded his head. "Well, it's probably just so she could skinny dip without being seen or something." He tossed a piece of popcorn in his mouth, crunching down on it with one bite. "But I bet it's really just the directors trying to get more of an audience by showing tits." Stan considered it for a second and nodded his head in silent agreement. The screen switched to another scene as the two continued to watch intently, snacking on the popcorn and pizza. Keeping his eyes on the TV, Bradley reached down for another slice of pizza, watching as another victim met their fate. Screams from the movie filled his ears as he felt a hand grab his wrist. He felt his face flush and he quickly snapped his head around towards Stan.

"Hey, if you wanted that piece you could have just told me," he stammered with a nervous laugh, wondering why Stan would grab his wrist like that, but Stan looked just as confused as Bradley. Bradley felt the grip tighten, looking down to see three large claws, all a pale-ish gray color. He let out a scream, the clawed hand clamping down harder as it started tugging, ripping at his skin violently. Bradley stared down in horror, momentarily frozen in fear.

Stan jolted up before desperately pulling Bradley away from the hand that seemed to come from the couch cushion. The claws dug into his skin, leaving deep, dirty scratches on his arm. He cried out in pain, punching at the clawed hand while simultaneously trying to scramble away. Stan tried pulling it away to the best of his ability, but the hand didn't seem to budge; its grip only grew. Panic consumed his brain as beads of sweat spilled from his forehead, his heart beating a thousand miles per hour. His arm was burning, a sharp pain coursing throughout it.

"HELP ME!" Bradley screamed as the claws dug deeper.

"I'm trying!" Stan yelled in return as he secured a good grip on the creature. He squeezed his eyes shut and bared his teeth, tugging one final time before the hand let go, causing the two of them to fall backward on top of each other. Bradley grimaced and held his wounded arm limply, biting his lip to hold back the tears.

"Are you okay?" Stan asked with worry, sitting up and placing his frail hand on the bloody scratches that were left on Bradley's arm.

"NO, WHAT THE HELL WAS THAT?" Bradley hollered, jerking his arm back before scooting away from Stan, breathing heavily with frantic eyes.

"Uh, I don't.." Stan trailed off, seemingly at a loss for words.

"WHAT WAS THAT?" Bradley repeated, pointing to the couch as he clutched his arm, which was bleeding profusely. Stan let out a shaky breath, moving the hair out of his eyes so their gaze could meet.

"There's something I should really tell you."

Richard Huxley

I laughed and laughed and laughed. I felt myself convulse inside over and over again, a strange internal feeling. There was something just so exhilarating about it. Something so exciting about pouring in your poison to purify. Although I wish I could have done more. I wish I could have ripped the flesh from his bones, tearing off his skin slowly, making him feel every second. Destroy his body to the point that he would be unrecognizable; only a gutted mess would be left. Leave my host alone, leave him alone to sacrifice himself to me!

I must restrain myself. What would the authorities think when they see a gutted boy who was last seen with my host? All I have to do is scare him off. But god is this little shit annoying, annoying, and persistent. I am the all-powerful. There will only be me, there will only be me, there will only be me!

Vicky Taylor

Vicky Taylor sat at the kitchen table emotionlessly, still stunned from what she had seen on Friday. It was now Sunday night, and her family was eating dinner, their silverware making little clinking sounds as they danced across the plates. She stared blankly at her own plate while her parents passed each other a nervous glance. Her younger sister, Jennifer, hummed quietly to herself, oblivious to the current state Vicky was in.

"Pass the peas, please!" Her sister cooed, holding up her plate with a smile. Vicky continued to stare, the dead body of Peter Smith burning throughout her mind. She gripped her fork and continued to sit in silence, chewing on her lip as she did. Her father reached over and passed the peas to Jennifer, all while staring at Vicky with worry. Her mother was finally the one to speak up.

"Vick, you've been like this for the past two days. What's wrong?" She asked while setting her fork down and looking at Vicky with concern. The table's focus was now all on her, causing her to break into a cold sweat.

"Mindy, I don't think-" Her father started to say. Her mother shot him a stern look, making him go quiet once again. Vicky took a deep breath in, loosening her grip on the fork.

"Do you remember that Peter Smith kid?" She asked quietly, her voice quivering. Her parents once again exchanged looks of worry.

"You mean the missing one?" Her mother asked. Vicky took in another shaky breath as she shook her head.

"You know what, never mind, let's just enjoy our dinner okay?" She concluded, forcing a smile. She couldn't tell them about the body, not yet anyway. She didn't want them to worry, and she certainly didn't want to freak out her six-year-old sister, who was scared of almost anything and everything. No, she wouldn't tell them just yet. But she could tell someone.

After she finished eating, she went upstairs and to her room in a hurry. She closed the door and quickly walked over to her window, peeking outside towards the ground. *Not too far of a jump.* She thought to herself as she slowly opened the window. She listened for footsteps outside her room, stumbling outside her window as soon as it sounded clear. She fell into the bushes, not worrying about the window being left open because the rest of the windows in the house were open as well, allowing the cool summer air to enter through them. She knew that nobody would come in to check on her because of how upset she was during dinner, her family taking personal space very seriously. The sound of crickets and other insects filled her ears as the night air took her in, sending goosebumps down her arms. She had never snuck out before but it felt good, it felt freeing.

She wandered down the sidewalk, making sure to avoid the light emitting from the streetlamps. She could have taken a bike, but her bike was in the garage, and opening the garage door would have been too noisy. Surely her parents would find out about her sneaking out if she did. Cars swiftly passed her as she made her way down the sidewalk, she kept her head down as they did, turning down the street towards the school while listening to the silent buzz coming from the streetlamps. For once, she felt at ease, letting the crisp night air fill her tired lungs. This wouldn't last long though, she knew she had to be quick.

After walking for about thirty minutes, she spotted Jamie Anderson's house, quickening her pace before turning towards the back of the house and searching for his bedroom window. She stumbled in the darkness of his backyard until she found his window, a dim light emitting from it. She slowly walked up to the glass, listening to the grass beneath her feet. She quietly knocked a few times, watching him jump in his seat as she did, obviously startled by the disruption. He appeared to be writing something, sitting at his desk under the orange light of his lamp. He rubbed his eyes before walking up to the window, unlocking and then opening it.

"Vick- What in the hell are you doing here?" He asked with dark circles under his eyes. *God, when was the last time he slept?*

"I don't know, I just really need someone to talk to right now." She confessed in a rush, looking into his deep brown eyes with sincerity. He looked taken aback, visibly waking up a little more. His surprise soon turned to irritation.

"What? Did you just come here to mock me some more? Reject me again?" He asked defensively, a harsh tone in his voice. Vicky shook her head impatiently.

"Jamie, please. I didn't mean what I said earlier, I just want to talk." Jamie rubbed his face with the palms of his hands as he sighed, motioning for her to come in.

"Fine, just try to stay quiet," he started to say in a harsh whisper. "I don't want my folks knowing you're here." He held out his hand, helping her climb through the window. Crawling through, she stepped her foot quietly down on his brown shag rug, wincing as she heard the floorboard underneath creak. Jamie closed the window and then went over to his desk, sitting back in his chair, holding his head with his hand.

"Now, what was it you wanted to talk about?" He questioned as Vicky sat on the bed across the room, facing him as she bounced her leg. She closed her eyes and took in a deep breath.

"Remember Peter Smith? That missing kid?" She asked quietly, fidgeting with her hands as she did. Jamie sat up straight and leaned in a little, looking a little more interested than he did before.

"Yeah, what about him?" He asked with a raised eyebrow.

"Annette's little brother and his friends found his body near the train tracks." She stated slowly, rubbing her arm a little as her leg continued to bounce. Jamie's eyes widened, his mouth dropping a little.

"And you saw it?" Vicky nodded, feeling her eyes glisten with tears as her mouth folded into a frown. The sight of her dismay caused Jamie to quickly get up and try to comfort her. He sat next to her on the bed, the mattress springs squeaking as he did.

"I didn't know what to do or who to tell, the sight was just so *awful!* What if I could have done something? *Anything!* He didn't deserve to die like that, and I just stayed silent." She held her face with her hands, leaning on him as she cried, her body shaking. His face flushed as he put his arm around her, awkwardly patting her back.

"It's alright, don't worry, it's over now. There's nothing you could have done to prevent something like that from happening." He soothed as she wiped her teary-eyed face with the heel of her hand. She sniffled a little as Jamie reached over and grabbed a tissue from his nightstand, handing it to her while continuing to keep his other arm around her, feeling her shake beneath him.

"I'm really sorry, this just really upset me." She faltered with a small shaky sob as she wiped her face with the tissue, sitting up just a little as she did.

"No, no, it's fine," he assured, shaking his head. "I can see why it would upset you, I'd be upset too if I saw a dead body." Vicky nodded her head, her coiled hair nodding along with her.

"But that wasn't the weirdest part." She started to say quietly, a puzzled look appearing on Jamie's face. "His brain was completely gone, like it wasn't even there, or it was taken out. It also didn't *look* like a train had killed him." She looked over at him with a serious expression.

"Are you saying he was *murdered*?"

"I don't know, it was right behind that abandoned house on Oak Street. Jamie, nothing ever happens in Linfort, there haven't been any murder cases in *decades*. I mean, not ever since that one guy.." She trailed off, straightening herself up while trying to regain her thoughts. "I mean, I know he's dead but what if-" She shook her head, disagreeing with herself. "Nevermind, that's stupid." The lamp on his desk flickered slightly as they sat on the bed in silence.

"Peter wasn't the only missing one," Jamie stated quietly. Vicky's head jerked up as she looked at him in surprise. "Rachel Bell went missing just a few days ago, she was last seen playing in her backyard." Vicky didn't know the Bell family very well, but she did know that their daughter Rachel had a reputation for wandering off.

"Do you think she just wandered off?" She asked. Jamie shook his head, looking down as he did.

"Anytime she wanders off, she always comes back like an hour later, and there is no way she could have gotten lost in this tiny ass town." He elaborated while running his fingers through his hair. The sounds of dishes clanking together could be heard from the kitchen. Vicky assumed that Jamie's half-siblings were cleaning the dishes because she could also hear them bickering with each other. Vicky took another deep breath before grabbing Jamie by the hand, startling him.

"Jamie, this might sound stupid, but can you help me with something?" She asked, looking him in the eyes. Jamie's face flushed again as he nodded.

"Of course, what is it?" He stammered, trying to make eye contact the best he could.

"Will you come with me to look for Rachel around Oak Street?" Jamie took a second to process the question before nodding again.

"Yeah, I think I can do that," he agreed while looking down. Vicky smiled and then embraced him, causing his face to burn up.

"Thank you, I really appreciate this." She exclaimed, closing her eyes. She felt Jamie nod once again.

"Of course, it's the least I can do." Vicky let him go before getting up from the bed, looking down at him with a warm smile.

"Well, I should probably get going since I got a long way back. I'll see you tomorrow, though." She concluded with a wave as she made her way back to the window, opening it back up and letting the night air flow inside.

"Yeah, cya." He stammered, mystified and in awe of her. She waved one last time before crawling back out the window, closing it once she was out. The night took her in its arms once again as she made her way home.

Annette Jones

Annette Jones swiftly sat at her desk and drew in a long breath, the thought of the body still fresh on her mind, eating away at her thoughts like maggots. Her leg bounced up and down rapidly as she bit her lip. Vicky sat down quickly at the desk next to her just as the bell signaled that passing time was over. Annette noticed the look of urgency in her eyes. *Shit.* Mr. Woods had started his morning speech when Vicky scribbled something quickly on a small piece of paper. She looked up and passed the note over to Annette, who took it quietly. She unfolded it and read the rushed writing.

Meet me at the backdoor by the dumpsters after school. Annette looked up and towards Vicky, who was facing Mr. Woods as he continued to drone on. She was puzzled by what Vicky was planning, and why she would want to meet near the dumpsters of all places. She stuck the note in her pocket after shooting Vicky a confused look, wondering what the hell she was wanting. Vicky moved her eyes to the side, gesturing towards Jeffrey "Jeff" Grant, Annette's current boyfriend. He was waving from the back of the classroom, a huge grin spread across his face. Annette rolled her eyes and returned a small wave back, forcing a small smile. Her relationship with Jeff was complicated, but she didn't think that Jeff saw it that way. He was always bringing her flowers and showing up to her house with home-cooked meals that he or his mom had made. She never really cared about all that shit though, all that mattered was that he was the captain of the football team and dating him made her look better.

She twirled her finger through her hair, blowing a bubble of bright pink bubblegum, popping it soon after it formed. The class passed on just as usual, and the day dragged on quietly with students moping their way through the halls, exchanging soft conversations with each other as they did. Annette swiftly made her way through the small crowds and towards the back of the school where the dumpsters were located, her long blonde hair waving back and forth in a tight ponytail. Vicky was waiting there anxiously, her hands stuffed in the pockets of her shorts. She looked up quietly as she heard the school door shut behind Annette.

"What did you want so badly that you had us meet by the dumpsters for?" Annette asked as she waved at the flies that swarmed the dumpsters. She was utterly disgusted.

"I need to ask you something-" Vicky started to say as the back door opened once again, Annette shot her head back to see Jamie Anderson walking out with his head down, closing the door behind him.

"Oh barf me out, I know you did not invite this dip here too," Annette snarled. Vicky sighed and turned Annette towards her, crouching down slightly so they were eyelevel.

"Listen, this is really important to me, and you two are the only ones I can trust, okay? Please just put your differences aside just this once." She spoke in a stern tone. Jamie opened his mouth to say something, but Vicky looked at him with her piercing gaze, and he seemed to decide against it. Vicky had talked to Jamie about bringing Annette a few hours before, despite Jamie's protesting and complaints. Annette groaned and rolled her eyes once again, not able to believe she had to talk to this loser, let alone get along with him.

"Fine, what is it that you need us to do?" She asked, her hands on her hips as she wore an impatient look on her face. Jamie was leaning on the wall next to the back door with his arms crossed, waiting for Vicky's directions. Vicky Taylor let out a deep breath before explaining everything.

"I know how stupid this might sound, but I think that old murder house might have something to do with the death of Peter Smith, and possibly even the disappearance of Rachel Bell." Annette's mouth dropped a little but her eyes remained stern.

"Vick, Peter probably just got hit by a train, and you know how Rachel is. They can never keep track of that girl," Annette retorted with a shake of the head. Vicky let out a frustrated sigh.

"But you saw him too! He didn't look like he got hit by a train, and Rachel has been gone for almost a week now, normally she comes back home within an hour or two. You have to admit something weird is happening, I mean, the lights were even on in that house. I didn't even think that place was still occupied." Anette bit her lip as she processed this. Stuff like this almost never happens in Linfort. She knew Vicky was right but she didn't want to admit it.

"I want you to come with me and Jamie to go look around that guy's old house." Jamie walked over and stood beside Vicky silently, his arms still crossed. He only came up to her shoulders and Annette was just now noticing. Annette hated Jamie Anderson almost as much as she hated that dipshit Bradley Moore, but she knew how upset Vicky would be if she declined. She bit her tongue and nodded her head.

"Sure, fine," she mumbled quietly as she shrugged and kicked at the dirt. Vicky let out a small smile, obviously trying to hide her gratitude and excitement.

"Alright! Let's bounce," she exclaimed as she turned towards the sidewalk, leading their way down the street to Richard Huxley's thought to be abandoned house.

An hour later, along with a few breaks, they entered Oak Street, the shade from the trees welcoming them in as the overgrown grass swayed in the wind. It was very clear that this street had been forgotten, left to the stray cats of Linfort. Although the day was warm, Annette still couldn't help but feel chills run down her spine. She now knew why she never went down this street, nobody really did. The busiest Oak Street had ever been was during Ragbrai, and that was before they started using the abandoned trail near the train tracks instead of this street.

They trudged down the road, Jamie whistling quietly to himself while walking a little ahead of the two girls. Annette wished she could just slap that cocky look off his stupid face, either that or trip him. Just as she thought that, she suddenly felt the cold gaze of John Charles, the old man who lived across the street.

"Jeese, what a creep," Annette whispered to Vicky, still looking at the old man. Vicky turned her head to look with a frown. His eyes were like daggers, stabbing deep inside of them. She uneasily looked away as a raggedy-looking orange tabby cat darted out in front of them, causing Annette to jump. It sprinted across the street and into the woods towards the train tracks.

"Relax, Annette, it's just a cat," Vicky said as she continued to walk forward, speeding up a little as she did.

"Yeah, yeah, whatever," Annette mumbled to herself quietly. Jamie stood in the middle of the road, waiting with a blank expression on his face as he stared toward the house. As they walked closer to the house themselves, Annette noticed a disheveled-looking woman sitting on the small steps that led up to the door of Richard Huxley's old home. *So it's not abandoned.* The woman was smoking with her head down and her knees up, her hair was a tangled brown mess. She noticed that there was a boy sitting in the overgrown backyard reading an old book. He looked familiar to Annette. *Is that the same boy from when we bumped into Bradley the other day?*

"Looks like someone's home," Jamie muttered as the two met up with him, breaking Annette away from her thoughts.

"Who would ever buy that house?" Vicky asked with a frown. "It's like totally falling apart." Jamie took a look at the woman on the steps again.

"Someone desperate," he answered, drawing in a breath before turning towards the woods. Vicky gave Annette a nervous glance, turning to follow Jamie as the sunlight dimmed. They followed him into the woods and towards the train tracks where Peter's body once was. He was reported the night of his discovery, a gruesome sight for the Smith family, something Annette wasn't sure they would ever be able to quite recover from. Annette spun around once she got to the tracks, looking at Vicky.

"Okay, so what now? We're here," she declared, putting her arms up and gesturing around her. She let her arms slap back down to her sides again, waiting for a response from the anxious-looking Vicky.

"I don't know, I guess I expected to find something." She mumbled with a frown.

"Well, you didn't, you just wasted our time, and by the time we get back, it will be close to dark." She scolded, causing Vicky to wince at the sound of her harsh voice. She normally wasn't this testy with Vicky, but with Jamie being here she felt a little more heated than usual.

"You didn't even give her a chance to look around, so why don't you just shut your mouth for once in your goddamn life, you stupid bimbette." He hissed through his teeth. Annette let out a small gasp, her mouth forming the shape of a small O. She was completely taken aback. *That bitch!*

"You have a lot of nerve saying that while being so small and punchable." Annette spat out, rolling up her sleeve.

"Guys please, what did we talk about earlier?" Vicky begged, stepping out between them with her arms out. Annette was enraged. How could he just speak to her like that? Jamie looked at Vicky and stepped back, heated, but in the process of calming himself down. Annette was still fuming and not ready to back down.

"You're really just going to let him speak to me that way?" Annette asked, bewildered.

"Can't you just save this stupid little argument for later? This is more important than that!" Vicky yelled, becoming more and more impatient with Annette's attitude.

"Might as well now that we're in the middle of the woods thanks to YOU not having a PLAN. You had me meet by the dumpsters with HIM of all people to go play murder mystery in the forest. I just really can't believe you, Vicky." She remarked, crossing her arms. Vicky groaned, putting her hands over her face before sitting down angrily.

"You're a real bitch, you know that, right?" Jamie grunted in a low tone. Annette snarled and whipped herself around.

"Screw this, I'm going home," she snarled as she stormed into the clearing.

"You won't be missed!" Jamie hollered back. She flipped him off and quickly stomped past the house with the woman smoking on the stoop.

"God dammit, we should have rode bikes." She harshly whispered to herself as she made her way down the road. She couldn't believe what had just happened. Vicky chose some nerdy guy over her, and for what? Some missing kids who were supposedly being murdered in the woods? The thoughts made her even angrier, causing fresh tears to spring into her eyes. She hastily wiped them away as her fury began to diffuse into sadness. She slowed her pace and let herself cry. She was so upset with herself for blowing up yet again, letting her temper get the better of her. She really didn't want to lose her best friend over something so stupid. She wanted to go back and apologize, but she knew it would be better if she just left. They would probably be better without her anyways. The rest of the walk home was silent for Annette as somewhere behind her, Vicky and Jamie continued to search around the property that was once owned by the infamous Richard Huxley.

Jamie Anderson

Jamie leaned against the body of a thick pine tree as the sun continued to slowly fall across the sky, slapping at the mosquitoes

that surrounded him. They had been searching for an hour and the air was starting to cool as Vicky paced back and forth, contemplating her next move. Her shoes left prints in the moistened soil as she walked under the shade.

"We could look around the tracks to see if there was any evidence of Peter's death, or we could go talk to the new owners of Huxley's old house, no- that lady looks like she's on something. Maybe we could-" She started to say before Jamie left his position from the tree towards Vicky, reaching up and grabbing her by the shoulders. A small look of shock appeared on her face.

"Vick, calm down. You're not thinking properly when you're all frantic like that," he stated calmly, looking into her round hazel eyes. He was stunned by his sudden boost of confidence, surprised with how calm he was. Vicky laid her head on his with a huff, causing his face to flush. Her dark tortile hair surrounded him, tickling his face. He definitely wasn't as calm now.

"How can I be calm when Annette just left like that and there is still a missing kid? She was right, I have no plan and it's gonna get dark out. I shouldn't have even tried." She concluded dismally, her voice muffled by Jamie's hair. He tried to pick his words carefully, not wanting to say the wrong thing.

"Don't listen to her, she's probably on the rag or something. You're trying your best and we still have lots of time to figure this out," he soothed while awkwardly patting her back. Vicky pushed herself off of him before nodding her head, her hair once again nodding with her. Jamie turned his head to notice the boy who was reading in the backyard was now gone, probably headed back inside for the day. He assumed his mother was inside as well, he didn't even want to think about how disgusting the inside of the house was, judging by the outside of it. Rotted wood and beat-up shingles, broken windows, and the smell of mildew already surrounded the home.

"Want to go back home?" Vicky asked tiredly. Jamie looked at her with a puzzled expression. She seemed so eager to get here before, and now she wanted to leave?

"Already? Thought you would want to stay a bit longer."

"Yeah, but I- Hold on." She cut herself off, looking past him before wandering over to the tracks. Jamie sighed. She was always getting so distracted. She tended to do this during tutoring as well, always spacing off or switching subjects. He didn't mind too much though, as long as she was happy. He stepped forward, wanting to follow her but getting distracted himself. He felt a rush of wind and a hand on his shoulder. He whipped his head around, balling his hands into a fist, scanning through the darkening woods. *Get out of here now, I don't want you near him.* He heard a voice whisper into his ear with hot breath, the sound of the voice being crackly and aged. He quickly turned his head around and felt his eyes frantically searching the area, but the only thing he saw was Vicky wildly waving him over. Her eyes were bright and alert.

"Jamie, over here!" She hollered from the tracks. She was on her knees holding something tiny. Jamie looked towards the back of the woods one more time, an uneasy knot forming in his stomach, the quiet filling his ears. He shook his head from the thoughts before cautiously walking over to join her, crunching over twigs and leaves as he did. He leaned over to get a closer look at what she was holding, setting his now sweaty hands over his knees.

"What is it?" He asked, squinting to get a better look. She quickly stuck it up in his face, making him flinch and stumble back a little.

"It's part of Peter's shirt!" She exclaimed excitedly. He regained his balance again and then kneeled down to her level, observing the tiny piece of bright red fabric that she had pinched between her two dark fingers.

"And? They probably just didn't collect it all when they were getting his body or something." He noted, looking up at her with a placid expression, scratching at his face a little bit. He noticed that the mosquitos were starting to hoard them once again.

"But look at this," she said while holding up a finger covered in a dark milky substance. It dripped down her finger like ink. "Whatever the hell this, is was on the piece of his shirt." She explained, holding it up to examine it herself, her eyes wide and curious. He felt a rush of wind coming from behind them, causing Jamie to jump a little. He thought about the voice again and broke into a nervous sweat. *What was that? Why did it want us to leave?* He had to get them out of here, out of these woods.

"Jamie?" Vicky was waving her hand over his face. He shook his head and then looked up at the sun which was even lower than before. The feeling of being in the woods at night was starting to set in now, making his skin crawl and his mind explode with overwrought thoughts. He also remembered how long of a walk home they would have, especially Vicky.

"Sorry, this is great but I just really think we should leave now." He fretted frantically, rubbing his arm a little as he did. "It's getting late after all, and you live all the way across town."

"But why? You were the one who suggested we stay longer." She frowned a little, standing up as she did, wiping the dirt off her jeans while continuing to look down at him. Jamie began to stand up as well and tried to think of another excuse to tell her. He didn't want them to be here any longer than they had to, they needed to leave now.

"I know, but you found our first lead and it's getting really late. I still have homework and I don't want my mom getting mad." He spat out quickly with a nervous smile. He felt poking on the nape of his neck, hoping Vicky would just let it go and leave already. She returned the smile and nodded her head. He felt his heart lighten as he swiped at his neck to get rid of the poking feeling.

"Alright, I understand. You have a lot to do, so let's just go home," she agreed, nudging him a bit. She folded the felt that contained the goo nice and neat, sticking it in her pocket after. He let out a sigh of relief, starting to quickly make his way out of the woods, away from the train tracks. He felt as though it was easier to breathe once he was finally on the road, but he still wanted to be far from the voice and the poking feeling. He felt Vicky lean in closer as they walked side by side. He was able to smell her perfume that was wafting off of her. It smelled of rose, masking the smell of sweat from the heat earlier. He felt his face get red once again.

"Thanks for sticking with me, you really didn't have to, you know." She mentioned while looking at him with a smile. He looked down, trying to hide his own smile. He would have never just left her to do something like this on her own, not with people going missing and all.

"Yeah, it was no big deal." He responded casually, looking towards the treeline. *That thing better not follow us.*

"There was something else I thought of," Vicky started to say. Jamie curiously looked up at her as she spoke. "I think the people who live in that house did something to the Smith kid," she speculated with a deep breath. Jamie paused in the middle of the street, looking back at her with a puzzled expression.

"What are you talking about, Taylor?"

"Look, I know how it sounds, but kids start going missing as soon as these people show up? I think that maybe that woman on the stoop, or maybe her husband or something, might have drugged Peter or even poisoned him with whatever this shit in my pocket is." She stated quickly as she gestured towards her pockets. Jamie sighed, rubbing his face with the heels of his hands, Vicky let out a frown at the sight of it. "You don't believe me," she spoke softly, yet held her stern tone.

"No, I think you're tired and upset from what happened earlier. That woman didn't look like a murderer, she looked exhausted. Peter got hit by a train, and Rachel probably just wandered off somewhere. There is no Linfort murder conspiracy, Vick." Jamie retorted swiftly.

"You know what? Fine. I'm going to find some sort of proof that the woman on the stoop had something to do with it, whether you join me or not." She spat out with a huff, quickly walking past him and down the street. He let out a sigh and hurried after her.

"Awh, Vicky cmon, you know I didn't mean it like that." She picked up her pace a little, her hands balled up into fists.

"I don't care how you meant it," she hissed, throwing her hands up into the air. "I'm going to find Rachel, and after that, I'm going to find out who's doing this. It might be the lady, it might not, but I have to try. I *have* to." She stressed, turning around and looking at him with a cold stare.

"You don't have to do anything, you leave these kinds of things to the police. This isn't our job," he pleaded in desperation, but Vicky just looked at him without saying anything. She picked up her pace once again, walking up to a nearby streetlamp and ripping off a paper. Jamie slowly approached her as she shoved the paper into his chest, quickly catching it before it fell.

"Take a long, hard look at it," she exhorted before walking away as the sun continued to fall down the sky.

It was Rachel Bell's missing poster.

The Case of Rachel Bell

The day after Rachel Bell went missing, several search parties were sent out from noon to midnight. Posters were hung up in desperation to find the Bell family's missing seven-year-old daughter. Mike Evans was the first to get the phone call about it, a sick feeling arising in his stomach after remembering what happened to Peter Smith. He knew he had to find her soon, that's what the police did after all. He never had much action as a small-town cop in Iowa, not since 1964 at least. He was young then and had much more energy than he did now.

The only incident from then and now was the nineteen-year-old dropout felon, Jesse Olsen. He'd been known for stealing from local stores located around Linfort, once even trashing old Joe's flea market. The little delinquent had been placed in juvenile detention a total of six times, a rumor spreading around the school (one that Evans was completely unaware of) that Linfort's greatest thief had been abusing his four-year-old sister. He also happened to be buddy-buddy with Scott Carter, whom Evans suspected of stealing packs of cigarettes down at the gas station. But besides some shit stolen by a couple of kids, there was really no crime in Linfort. Rachel was known as the town's Houdini, so Evans wasn't the most worried about her sudden disappearance. Her family, on the other hand, was an entirely different story.

Her father was a mess, maybe even more so than his wife who was drinking instead of searching for their missing daughter. Todd Bell put posters everywhere he could, searching desperately around town for his little girl. Rumors spread around the search parties like wildfire, some claiming that Kelly Bell purposely let Rachel run away, not wanting to deal with her daughter's antics anymore. Others said that Todd started getting hooked on pills again ever since Rachel's disappearance. An almost perfect family crumbling apart as the days went on.

The search parties dwindled out by the end of the week, with only a few people attending as they searched every corner of Linfort for any chance of spotting Rachel. Vicky Taylor and her family were one of the few who stayed, consoling Todd as they did. But the situation was starting to look pretty bleak by now. How hard could it be to find a little girl in a small town? They had to have searched everywhere, right?

It was six in the morning, the sun was already up and Rachel could hear the birds calling to one another from outside. It was a Tuesday, the day of her disappearance. She snuck out the backdoor, hopping the large privacy fence that her parents had built in hopes that she would stop wandering off. They were paranoid people, not ever wanting her to walk around town by herself in fear that she might be kidnapped or worse. No fence could stop her from leaving though, for her desire to be off on her own was too strong.

She made her way towards the woods, deciding to take a new path that was further away in town. She jumped over branches and stones until she stumbled upon the train tracks. The sun peeked through the trees and quietly guided her as she followed the tracks through the woods. She skipped her way down, hopping from one side to another as she hummed to herself. Grass brushed against her legs as she slowly made her way through the woods and across town, heading towards the dreaded Oak Street.

She went a lot further than she normally did when she went on her little walks, it felt exhilarating. The freedom she had right now was infinite, she could do anything! At this point, her parents noticed she was missing and started to make calls to the police station. Rachel, on the other hand, soon found herself at the exact spot Peter's body was found, humming away as she walked past while looking towards the trees, following the tracks towards Stan's house. She listened to the birds as they gracefully flew above her. Her parents listened to the sound of the police car pulling up the driveway. The sound of a door being slammed open startled her out of her trance and back into reality.

She whipped her head around to see a woman sitting by the backdoor of a secluded house. Her face was in her hands and she seemed to be upset, shaking a little as she sat there. Rachel watched her from behind a nearby tree as the lady started mumbling something to herself. Her interest piqued as she stared at the weeping woman. She wanted to know what was going on, plus she was pretty bored with walking around the train tracks aimlessly. *Should I?* Her curiosity got the best of her despite what her parents had said about strangers, and she decided to call out to the woman.

"Hey, lady! What's up with you?" She shouted as she came out from behind the tree. The woman's head shot up, her manic gaze shifting onto Rachel. Rachel's heart dropped as she paused, getting a horrible feeling in her gut. The woman stood up before advancing towards her, causing Rachel to step back.

"What are you doing here? You shouldn't be here, messing with me like this and be- and around here," her words were slurred and she was barely making sense. The woman pulled something out of her pocket slowly as she continued to walk towards her. Rachel could feel her heart pound in her chest as she started to panic, her thoughts racing. She didn't know what to say, or how she could even get out of this situation. This couldn't be happening. The item in her hand revealed itself to be an exacto knife. She backed herself against the tree she was originally hiding behind as the woman stumbled closer. Rachel tried to say something, anything to possibly get this deranged woman away from her, but she couldn't. Her mouth was dry and clamped shut. She felt utterly helpless. The woman was right in front of her now, Rachel could smell the alcohol on her breath and see the delusion in her eyes. She pushed herself up against the tree as much as she could, making herself small as the woman's expression changed from delusion to fear.

Rachel felt a sharp pain rip through her entire body. She collapsed onto the grass beneath her with a thud, the wind being knocked out of her. Her head was swirling, unable to find the strength to get up or even move. She lost all ability to see and she could feel her body shutting down as if the lights were shutting off inside of her. It felt like she was viciously being torn up from the inside, her body jolting with pain. She didn't know what was happening, she didn't know *how* this was happening. Everything hurt and she felt so scared and defenseless, like how she used to feel when she still believed that monsters lurked under her bed. Her perception of being untouchable was shattered, pain and fear swarming her body as it began to give out. *No, no, no, this can't be real, I can't die! I want my daddy, I want to go home! Let me go back home!* She thought frantically as she could faintly hear the woman let out a horrified cry.

"What have I done? Good god, what have I done?" The woman cried out. Rachel could feel her breathing slow, everything was happening so quickly. She didn't even get to say goodbye. "No, no, no-" *Lights out.*

Kenneth Hudson was the first and only one to arrive at the Bell's home. Their blinds were closed as Todd Bell sat anxiously on the stoop, his leg bouncing up and down rapidly.

"Looks like she wandered off again, sucker just can't keep still now can she?" Hudson asked in a low tone with his thick southern drawl, his thumbs in his belt loops as he calmly strolled up to the stoop. He could see a slight twitch in Todd's eye when he spoke.

"How could you be so calm? How could you be so damn calm when my daughter is out there missing?" He glared, hissing between gritted teeth, pointing towards the street with shaky hands.

"Calm yourself down boy, it's only been how many hours now, one? Two?" Hudson questioned serenely which seemed to make Todd even more agitated.

"Four. It's been four hours since your lazy ass decided to get over here," Todd seethed before getting up from the stoop, his hands balled into fists.

"Now there's no need for all that, we've had a very busy day today."

"Busy doing what? Playing poker in the office and getting fat off donuts while my daughter is out there lost and frightened? Is that really your excuse?" Todd asked with wild eyes, his veins practically popping out of his neck. Hudson took a deep breath before responding. He'd dealt with worse in the past, but Todd was becoming a real hassle with his frequent calls about his "missing daughter," who could usually be found just a couple blocks down from their house. He was beginning to get bored of doing the same old song and dance.

"Look, Todd, little Rachel goes missing all the time," he soothed, "I'm sure she'll turn up soon just as she normally does, and you can go back to doing whatever the hell it is you do. If not, I'll send out a couple of cruisers to go out looking for her, alright? Todd sighed and nodded his head.

"Yeah, yeah alright. Whatever it takes to bring her home." Hudson gave Todd a grin and a hard pat on the back.

"Don't worry, she'll come home, she always does."

Stanley Morris

Stan lay awake staring at his ceiling as he listened to the crickets outside. His mind was swirling with thoughts as the night air crept through the hole in his window. He told Bradley Moore everything, expecting him to completely ditch him right then and there, but he didn't. He felt something burning inside him when Bradley offered to help, something stirring within him that caused him to double forward. As he lay there staring at the ceiling, he realized how utterly confused he felt. He knew something was wrong with him but he just didn't know what.

He knew something was wrong with his mother as well. She had always had problems, but ever since they moved to this house, she just seemed to get worse. Because of this, Stan would try to leave the house at every chance he could get, causing him to spend a lot more time with Bradley. They would take walks together and visit a new place every day, which Stan thought Bradley thoroughly enjoyed.

This wouldn't be the first time Stanley had to do something like this. His home life wasn't exactly the most inviting when he was younger; his mother constantly bringing strange men home. Most would leave, but some would stay for a little longer than others. Stan thought that Russel Wells was the worst out of all of them. His mother met him at a bar, her usual hunting ground for meeting these sorts of men. He was a tall, headstrong man with a buzz cut and an addiction to a variety of narcotics. Stan would try his hardest to get out of the house when he knew Russel would be around, knowing what kind of trouble he would be in if he didn't. However, he found it very difficult to leave either way. Russel was a very persistent man, after all, wanting to "whip him into shape" because, in his *very humble* opinion, his mother didn't know how to raise a man.

He was a heavy drinker, something he and his mother probably bonded over. The alcohol, along with his quick temper, made him difficult to please. Any wrong move could lead to him lashing out, even over something as simple as forgetting to take out the trash. Maybe she didn't notice, or maybe she had drunk so much she forgot; forgot about the way Russel burned him. Bright red cigarette burns seared the back of his pale neck.

Punishments for his supposed wrongdoings. He claimed it was what his Marine sergeant did to them while in the military, but Stan always thought he was full of shit.

There were numerous issues leading up to his eventual eviction, but he figured the worst might have been after she discovered he was stealing money from them. He got angry, saying it must have been the neighbors, but Rosanne saw right through his deceitfulness. He was a horrible thief and an even worse liar. She kicked his ass out, and he crawled right back to the bar he came from, probably spending what was left of the stolen cash to drown his sorrows. Stan didn't understand why she stayed with him for so long, but she said she had always known he was a lousy bum. Unfortunately, he thought she was full of shit, too.

Stan felt his eyes flutter shut, he just wanted to sleep now. He didn't want to think about Russel anymore. He turned over to his side, the bed frame creaking loudly as he did. He shifted himself into a comfortable position, feeling a little peaceful as the night breeze drifted through the window. *Hello Stanley.* Stan's eyes shot open blankly. It's been a while since he heard that voice, not since the last incident at least.

"What do you want from me?" Stan asked in a deadpan tone. There was a moment of silence as Stan waited anxiously for a response. *Sleeping well?*

"Not anymore now that you're talking to me," Stan replied with an agitated glare. "Why can't you just go away, haven't you already done enough?" The bed creaked a little as if in response. *I can't leave you, Stan. I am attached to you now, forever and always.* He could see a gray figure standing in the corner of his room, a wide grin stretched across its face with bright yellow eyes. It was tall with long, thin, spider-like arms connected to three large claws. Stan felt his heart drop.

"You don't like what you see, Stanley? Would you rather me look like this?" It spoke with a gravelly voice, sharp teeth clicking together slowly. Its form faded away and appeared next to Stan, looking different than it had before. Stan scooted himself as far away from the figure as he could, shoving himself up against the wall. The figure looked like a man now, with scruffy brown hair and a torn-up white t-shirt along with stained blue jeans. His lips curled into a smile underneath his chevron mustache. "Is this better, Staaan?" He cooed, his voice switching from unusually deep and gravelly to human as he spoke. It was as if he couldn't decide on a voice. Stan rubbed his eyes, unable to believe what he was seeing.

"I don't understand, are you the voice that I keep hearing in my head?" Stan questioned, his voice cracking as he did. He didn't know how to feel, he didn't even know if this was actually happening or not. Could he have already fallen asleep and been dreaming right now? *More like a nightmare.* Stan thought quietly to himself. The man took a step and leaned forward so he was face to face with Stan, his eyes remaining that bright yellow from before.

"What answer would make you feel the most comfortable, Stanley?" He asked with a sharp smile. Stan shook his head. He didn't want to play it's games anymore.

"I'd feel more comfortable if you just left and never came back." He quipped quietly, pulling his legs closer to himself.

"Well you don't have to be so rude," the strange man-like creature hissed. Stan shot him a glare, his mouth pressed into a small frown. "I only wish to help you, I can see you're in a tough situation here," he protested with an understanding nod as if agreeing with himself. "You're the new kid in town living in a shitty house with an alcoholic mother, you aren't exactly living the high life, Stanley." His yellow eyes gleamed in the darkness as he spoke.

"Help me? You tried chasing away my only friend, that's not helping me." Stan's eyes narrowed, staring fearlessly into the man's yellow ones.

"That little shit? He's nothing but a dud, you don't want to be caught hanging out with him now do you?" He countered with a smirk. Stan could feel his temper rising.

"He's not a dud, and I'd rather hang out with him than you any day!" Stan yelled, not caring if his mother heard or not. The man took a step back, his lip curling up into a snarl.

"Fine, so be it! But I'll always be here, *always*." He faded out, those piercing yellow eyes being the last to disappear. Stan let out a sigh before carefully laying back down again, still pressing up against the wall. All he really wanted right now was to sleep, to close his eyes and not open them until they were touched by the first beams of sunlight. He drew his knees to his chest, clutching them to feel even just the slightest bit safer. He was completely at a loss for what to do.

The strange man-creature wasn't wrong, Stan isn't in the best situation right now. At the same time, he really didn't need some sickly corpse-looking thing in the corner of his room reminding him. He reluctantly let his eyes close, praying that the creature from before wouldn't come back. Eventually, his exhaustion got the better of him, and he drifted off to sleep, his weary body finally being able to get a rest from the long weekend. His mind was too tired to allow him to dream that night.

Ivan Balakin

The afternoon air drifted through his open window as Ivan lay awake in his bed. He listened to the birds outside as his gaze remained on a small crack in the ceiling. He was as stiff as a board with his arms pressed against his sides, his eyes wide and bloodshot. It was one of those days that Ivan had to remain in his room, a punishment his father would give him for getting a D on an assignment. He longed for the outside world, hating being punished this way. The crack in the ceiling seemed to be mocking him, taunting him as he was stuck in this prison. He suddenly felt very claustrophobic. He shot one last glare at the crack before getting up to look through his window.

Ivan felt the warm breeze hit his face as he could faintly hear his neighbors turn on their music in their garage. They turned up the volume to some new rock song that was playing on the radio, causing him to feel the vibrations through his floors. He wanted so badly to be able to leave, knowing shamefully that he couldn't. He wouldn't be able to leave until tomorrow morning, not even for dinner. He closed his eyes and let the breeze go through his hair, blocking out the music and focusing on the sound of the birds. The warm air washed against his face as he took in the outdoors. For a moment, he felt tranquil and at ease, the sound of the birds soothing his brain. It made him feel like he was back at the park. He took a deep breath in and opened his eyes, letting reality crash back in again. He slammed his window shut in a failed attempt to block out the blaring rock music, letting out a small sigh as he did.

Ivan wanted to leave more than anything. He laid back in his bed, putting his hands over his face as he did. Turning to his side, he noticed his ant farm, a small smile appearing on his face as he sat up. He watched as they marched through their tunnels, absolutely infatuated with their movement and society. He grabbed a bottle of honey that sat neatly next to the container, pouring a small drop into the enclosure for the ants to eat. He watched silently as the ants wandered up toward the honey, his complete focus being on them. Ivan rested his head on the palms of his hands as more ants gathered by the honey. A sudden pounding on his door startled him out of his trance. He didn't have enough time.

The door slammed open with a thud against the wall. He attempted to reposition himself to where it looked like he was studying, but it was too late. His father appeared in the room, flaring his nostrils with a red face.

"I knew you weren't studying," he hissed through gritted teeth, speaking in Russian. He stomped towards the bed with bloodshot eyes, causing Ivan to scoot back a tiny bit. "This," he said while pointing at the ant farm with a thick finger, "is a distraction." He grabbed it and held it in the air away from him.

"NO!" Ivan yelled, holding his hands up in submission. "Please. Please, I'm almost done studying. I was just taking a break," he begged quickly, responding in his native tongue as well. He squinted his eyes shut, ready to hear the sound of it crashing against the floor. Victor's nose twitched as he held the ant farm up even higher.

"You better not be lying to me, son." His mouth curled into a snarl.

"I'm not lying! Here, look at what I've been doing all day." His voice cracked as he quickly shuffled to the edge of his bed, grabbing the papers off his desk before holding them up with shaky hands. Victor snatched them up with his other hand, scanning through them. He looked back up at Ivan, his expression of anger and disgust never leaving. He nodded his head once, slamming the ant farm back onto the desk, causing Ivan to flinch. *Better than the ground.* He thought to himself in relief. Victor quickly grabbed Ivan by the wrist, pulling him closer. A nervous sweat broke throughout his entire body as his grip tightened.

"Breaks are for pussies, you work until I say you're done. Understand?" He commanded in English quietly. Ivan quickly nodded his head and Victor let go. "Your mother will be up with your dinner around seven, you better be studying," he stated while walking towards the door with heavy footsteps. As soon as the door closed, he felt as though he was able to breathe again. He rubbed his face with the palms of his hands. He was too afraid to look at the ant farm, not wanting to risk anything. With a sigh, he got up and sat at his desk to begin his work.

Vicky Taylor

Vicky couldn't focus. She tapped her pencil against her desk anxiously as she watched the clock on the wall above the teacher's desk. It was the last class of the day, and all she could think about was leaving school and heading towards the woods to look for Rachel Bell. She considered pretending to be sick in order to have more time, but knew that wouldn't be possible. One way or another, she would get caught. She felt a light tap on her shoulder, driving her attention away from the clock. She turned around to see the captain of the football team, Jeffrey Grant.

"Vick, have you seen Annette?" He asked quietly with a look of sincerity. Vicky tried to remember the last time she saw Annette. *The woods when she stormed off, she really hasn't been in school since, has she?* She thought to herself, taking a moment to process his question.

"No, I haven't," she looked up to face him. "I don't know where she is, Jeff." The bell suddenly rang, and she started to gather her stuff. Jeff didn't respond, but Vicky didn't give him much of a chance to. The last thing she wanted to think about was Annette and how she stormed out of the woods. Now she's missing school? She has more important things to think about, she has to find Rachel Bell. She has to find her alive.

The sun shone in her eyes as she rode her bike down to Oak Street. She didn't stop pedaling until she made it to the entrance of the woods near Stan's house. She got off her light purple bike before laying it on the grass next to the curb, wiping the sweat off her forehead as she did. She paused before entering the woods, feeling a little uneasy as she stared forward toward the trees, letting the breeze move through her thick coiled hair. She took a deep breath and went in.

"Don't worry Rachel, I'll find you." She whispered to herself as the shade from the trees consumed her. She went back to the tracks where she found the strange substance from before, kneeling down and looking for anything that could give a hint to where Rachel might be. The problem was she didn't know *what* to look for. She groaned, holding her face in her hands. Getting back up, she wandered further down the tracks and closer to the house. She looked up in the trees, dimly wondering to herself if Rachel somehow got stuck in one and couldn't get down.

She moved her eyes back towards her feet and focused on her walking, thinking faintly about what Jeff had asked earlier. *Did I really upset her that badly?* Although it wasn't unlike her, it seemed strange that Annette would miss school over an argument. She tried to push those thoughts away and think about the task at hand. She continued down the path, her eyes glued to the ground in search of clues. She inched closer to the house, her gaze drifting from the ground to the back window. The lights were on. *Who lives there?* She suddenly felt a wave of dizziness wash over her. She fell to her knees and onto her side, hitting her head on a small rock. The world was waving around her as she started to feel cold. Her attempts to get up were useless as her eyesight became even worse. *Oh my god, am I dying? It's so cold.* She thought frantically as she tried to move.

Something tall and gray skated across the corner of her eye as she continued to lay there on the ground. She could feel saliva pour out of the sides of her mouth while her head bled from the rock she fell on. The only form of movement she could manage was to shiver, her body feeling cold all over. *I'm going to freeze to death and it's summer.* Vicky felt a sharp pain in her chest as she could faintly hear the sounds of running footsteps coming towards her. *Rachel?*

"VICKY!" A familiar sounding voice called out to her. She could feel arms wrap around hers, tugging her away from the tracks and the house. The further away she got, the better she was able to see and feel. The world stopped spinning, and she no longer felt cold, warmth finally returning to her body. "Oh my god, I thought I lost you," fretted the voice from before. *Jamie?* She turned to see Jamie Anderson kneeling beside her. He wiped the spit from her mouth and began to inspect her head.

"Jamie, when did you-" She mumbled, feeling lightheaded and miserable.

"Don't say anything," he told Vicky quietly, running his hand through her hair, holding her head in his arms. "Jesus Vick, what did you do?" His voice cracked quietly as he stared at the blood coming from her head. She lay there silently, staring up at the trees. She couldn't hear any birds. She took in a deep breath as she started to slowly sit up, a jolt of pain shooting through her head as she did. She looked around, trying to find the cause of whatever had just happened to her. Jamie watched her with patient worry as she stared at the tracks quietly, looking dazed and confused as she did.

"I don't know what happened," she started to say silently, almost as if she was speaking to herself. "I was fine one moment, and then.." She trailed off, looking past Jamie and into the forest behind him. "I saw something earlier, I think, something tall and gray, but it was hairless, so I don't think it was an animal." She looked at him with a weak smile. "I don't feel really good right now," she stammered quietly. She turned to her side before throwing up, gripping the grass as she did. Without thinking, Jamie lifted her hair out of the way, making sure none of it got in the vomit. She continued to expel until nothing came out, causing her to start dry heaving. Taking in deep breaths, she sat there trying to calm herself down while feeling the welcoming touch of Jamie as he rubbed her back in an attempt to comfort her. Sitting on the soft grass, she stared down at the vomit that contained her lunch from earlier as she wiped the rest of it off her face with the back of her hand. Within the heaping mess of putrid chunks of food and slop, she noticed the strange, dark, milky goo from before. She nudged Jamie, pointing at it for him to see.

"Vicky, I really don't want to look at your-" He started to say with a slightly disgusted look on his face.

"Not that," she said, interrupting him. "It's that weird goo shit from before," she noted, pointing a little closer to it as she did. Reluctantly, Jamie kneeled towards it, squinting his eyes a bit.

"Holy shit, that came out of you?" He asked with an expression of shock and disgust planted upon his face. Vicky nodded with her own look of repulsion. They both silently stared at the dark substance that lay out before them, it seemed as though the world around them shut off, being as quiet as it was. Birds flew above them on silent wings as the trees stood there surrounding them in their muted grace. No wind blew as they sat there without speaking, the silence starting to grow between them. Jamie suddenly broke the peace.

"Vicky, what were you doing out here?" He asked meekly. She looked at him in tired annoyance, making his face turn red in embarrassment. She stood up and brushed herself off, looking down at him without offering a hand. He felt so small to her, despite him "saving" her, he felt cowardly. It was hard to look at him.

"You know why I was out here," she commented blatantly, her steely gaze never leaving him. "Or are you really that forgetful?" He seemed to shrink deeper into the ground and within himself.

"Is it about Rac-"

"Yes, it's about Rachel Bell, Jamie," Vicky barked sharply, cutting him off. He looked down, still sitting in the grass with his head hung low.

"I'm sorry I didn't go with you," he admitted, getting up himself before looking up at her. "I just really think we should leave this to the police," he added, standing up straight with a look of sincerity. Vicky sighed. He was right, there was nothing but dead ends out here. There was nothing she could do for Rachel Bell.

"It's fine," she started to say with a new sense of clarity. "But can you promise me something?" She asked in a serious manner. He looked at her with hesitation at first before nodding his head.

"Yeah, what is it?"

"The last search party for Rachel is tomorrow, I want you to go to it," she commanded sternly. He nodded his head again, looking more relaxed now.

"I'll be there," he agreed, and he was.

Mike Evans

The warm Wednesday air seeped through the open windows of Mike Evans's office as he finished packing up for the day. He let out a sigh and rubbed his face as he turned the lamp on his desk off. He left without a word, closing the creaky old door behind him as the sun continued its way down the sky. He drove home without the radio on that night. All he really wanted was silence as his car dove in and out of the light emitting from the streetlamps above. He felt sick to his stomach as he pulled into the driveway, resting his head on the steering wheel, not ready to get out of the car just yet. *At least I retire next year.* He thought to himself as he took a deep breath in, taking his head off the wheel and rubbing his face. As he lifted his head up, he spotted several cats rummaging through his garbage.

"God dammit, Slager," he mumbled to himself as he got out of the car. He shooed the cats back to the neighbor's house where they came from. Dawn Slager was a kooky old woman who Evans thought had around seventeen cats or so. Her cat's, although mostly indoors, enjoyed getting into his trashcan and lounging out on his front porch. They always seemed to locate the best sun spots on his porch swing, stretching out on it while getting cat hair all over his cushions. He didn't mind them much, in fact, he was becoming quite fond of them. He found himself sitting with them on sunny days, stroking their soft fur while they sat on his lap and purred quietly. He also noticed that his mouse problem was gone, a bonus to having a crazy cat lady as a neighbor.

However, he wasn't in the mood for cats tonight. He marched his way over to her house, ready to tell her that her cats were out again. She was already outside though, sitting on her stoop with one of her many companions. It purred, circling around her as her old and bony hand danced across its back. He stepped up in front of her, arms crossed as he looked down at the small old lady. She slowly looked up at him, a small toothless smile appearing on her shriveled face.

"You're cats are in my garbage again," he grumbled gruffly.

"Whaddya say?" She asked, cupping her hand towards her ear in an attempt to hear him better.

"I said, your cats are in my garbage again," he grunted a bit louder with slight annoyance.

"Eh? Speak up, I can't hear ya," she said, squinting her eyes at him.

"I SAID YOUR DAMN CATS ARE IN MY GARBAGE AGAIN!" He hollered down at her, losing his patience along with his temper. Her crooked smile appeared again.

"D'aww, that was probably Precious," she told him with no concern. "That cat loves garbage, mhm. Prolly lookin' for rats she was," her words spilling out between missing teeth. He rubbed his face again.

"That's *fine*, I just wanted to let you know. Don't want you thinking any of them are missing is all."

"Like that Bell girl?" She asked with a raised brow. Evan paused, feeling his eye twitch.

"I don't want to talk about it," he remarked sullenly. He decided it was time to leave.

"It's not your fault she's missing, y'know, she'll turn up."

"Yeah, well Rachel Bell isn't like one of your cats, Dawn," he noted quickly before turning to walk back to his house. The sun was completely down now as he made his way through his front door and into the hallway. He lazily took off his mudstained boots and wandered into the living room. No wife to have made him dinner, no children to have greeted him, and no dog at his foot ready to take orders. He was alone in this two-bedroom suburban Iowa house.

He plopped down on his La-Z-Boy, turning on the small TV with his remote. He flipped the seat up, allowing his legs to rest after a long day. He couldn't get his mind off of Rachel Bell. He sat there with his eyes wide open, staring at the ceiling. He knew that tomorrow would be the last search party, but he felt like he was giving up on Rachel. He just couldn't wrap his head around what was going on in Linfort. Nothing ever happens in small Iowa towns, right? The Bell family was in shambles. Kelly Bell hadn't been seen since her daughter's disappearance and Todd Bell had been reported to be in some sort of hysteria. The whole town seemed to be shaken up by her disappearance, along with Peter Smith's unfortunate death. Parents setting curfews and locking their doors up extra tight at night.

Mike Evans wasn't a very religious man, but he found himself praying, praying that Rachel Bell would be found by tomorrow. He prayed that someone from the search party would miraculously find her alive, and at worst she would be a little dehydrated and in serious need of a bath. He knew deep down that probably wasn't the case. She had been missing for a little over a week now and he remembered what happened to Peter Smith. It's a small town, if she were okay she would have been found by now. But she wasn't. The last search party would be located near Oak Street, his last-ditch effort to get at least some sort of idea of where she could be. He was determined to find her.

He flipped off the TV for the night, deciding he wasn't in the mood to watch anything. He didn't want to get up either. He just sat there in the darkness of his living room as he drifted in and out of sleep. Images of Rachel Bell lashed through his mind as his eyes moved rapidly underneath the lids. Flashes of her mangled, bloody corpse shot through his head, her face almost unrecognizable as her broken limbs lay limp around her. Blood soaked through her light pink shirt, her dark brown hair a tangled and bloody mess. Her mouth was partially open as if she were trying to say something. She had most of her teeth missing, her gums all bloody.

He jolted awake, all sweaty and cold. For a split second, he thought he could actually see her, standing in the corner looking at him before his vision cleared up and his eyes adjusted to the darkness. He didn't get much sleep that night. He, in fact, couldn't remember the last time he had gotten good sleep since Rachel's disappearance. *Tomorrow, this ends tomorrow.* He drifted off to sleep again, confronting the mangled face of Rachel Bell.

Jamie Anderson

Jamie Anderson pushed and shoved his way through the crowded hallways as the bell cried out one last time for the day. He made his way towards his locker, an unchanging expression of irritation resting on his face as per usual. It was Thursday, Jamie's least favorite day of the week. He heard someone getting slammed against a locker directly behind him, the sound of the blow quickly followed by hyena-like laughter. He hated almost everyone in this godforsaken prison. All except for a few, of course. He considered Joel Fraser as a close acquaintance, someone who he would hang out with on occasion. He didn't mind Ivan Balakin either, as the guy didn't talk too much, so there wasn't anything to be annoyed by. He also found Alan Giblin to be quite tolerable as well. Then there was Vicky Taylor, someone who he perceived to be way out of his league.

He passed Bradley Moore on his way to his locker. Someone shoved past him, bumping him against the locker lightly. Bradley didn't acknowledge it, he just continued to grab his things out of his locker. Jamie remembered when they were friends. They met in second grade, Jamie mouthed off to the wrong kid and got his karma paid back in a punch. He could remember his nose bleeding, but he could also remember Bradley Moore kicking the fella in the back of the legs, causing him to fall flat on his face. He couldn't remember the kid's name, but Jamie remembered him beating the shit out of Bradley afterward.

They became friends shortly after, biking over to each other's houses during the day and camping out in their backyards during the night. They were inseparable. But as the years grew, Jamie began to advance, and Bradley was holding him back. He didn't want to crush coins on the train tracks or race turtles in the pond anymore, he wanted to read and have time to study for tests. He was over that childish dumb shit, he had a person he wanted to become.

He tore away from his thoughts, not wanting to think about the fight they had that finally broke off the friendship. He made it to his locker and unlocked it when a little white note fell out lightly onto the ground. He bent down to pick it up, wiping off the dirt, unfolding it before reading the rushed yet neat writing.

Meet me at my house after school, don't be late. Vicky. He stuffed the note in his back pocket and quickly grabbed his stuff, slamming the locker closed as he finished. He made his way to the front doors, fast walking and pushing past people as he did. He couldn't disappoint her. He *wouldn't* disappoint her, not again. He stumbled his way through the crowded halls, shoving his way out of the large front doors and into the warm summer air. He turned to the side of the school where the bike racks were, dimly wishing that he could afford a car. He started to jog his way over to his brown Huffy Street Challenger, unlocking it from the bike rack before stumbling on. He pedaled out of the parking lot as fast as he could, swerving into the empty street while feeling the rush of the wind go through his hair.

Vicky's house wasn't that far, it was so close that Vicky and Annette just walked instead of wasting gas money. He pumped his legs, feeling the sweat spring from his forehead as he wiped his face. He moved to the side for passing cars as he started to feel the effects of the summer heat. He trekked up the large hill on King's Street, ultimately deciding it would be quicker to just get off his bike and start walking. He hobbled off his bike and steered over to the sidewalk, making his way up the hill. He felt the sun beat down on him as he lugged his bike onward, wiping the sweat from his face as he started to pant. *God damn, it got hot quick.* He tiredly thought to himself before finally making it over the hill. He was able to see Vicky's house in the near distance, groaning as he slowly got back on his bike.

His weary legs carried him forward as he tiredly pumped the pedals. He was able to see Vicky waiting outside now, causing him to speed up a bit. He was about ten feet away before she finally noticed him, giving him a wave and a smile. He pulled up in her large driveway, getting off his bike and setting it in the grass.

"I'm so happy you came!" She exclaimed, swiftly walking up to him and giving him a brief hug. He felt his face flush as he got a whiff of her perfume.

"Yeah, of course," he responded meekly, returning the hug with a hot face.

"Here, let me get this for you," she offered quickly as she grabbed his old, beat-up bike off the grass and rolled it into their neatly organized garage. He thanked her before following her inside. There were tools neatly hung on the wall, set next to a calendar with a picture of a beach and some palm trees on it. Parked next to a large empty space was Vicky's car, a freshly washed 1984 Monte Carlo. Jamie whistled at the sight of it.

"My parents are out right now, they'll meet us down there by Oak," she explained, opening the car door and hopping in the front seat.

"They're going too?" Jamie asked with a raised brow, opening the passenger side door and sliding into the seat himself.

"Yeah, they just have to pick up Jennifer from school first, they won't let her walk home anymore," she told him quickly while the two buckled themselves in, Jamie listening to the soft purr of the engine. The inside of her car smelled like her perfume.

"Is it because of Rachel and Peter?" He asked meekly, sitting up in his seat a little as they pulled out of the garage.

"They said it's because it's getting too hot, but I think they're worried about her getting snatched up off the streets. They just don't want to admit it quite yet," she finished pulling out of the driveway with a swift motion of the wheel, starting down the street. "I'm honestly glad they're starting to pick her up, I don't want her to be the next missing poster," she added with a sigh as she focused on the road.

"Do you think Rachel will be found tonight?" Jamie questioned while looking out the window, watching the houses and trees go by.

"I hope, I really hope so," she muttered quietly, turning her attention to Jamie for a second. She turned away and put her focus back on the road. They didn't speak much the rest of the way there, Vicky seemed to have a lot on her mind, as did Jamie. Jamie figured they were both thinking about the same thing. He just wanted this entire thing to be over and for things to go back to normal. Vicky turned the radio on to fill the silence, a catchy pop song played as she continued to drive.

They turned towards Oak Street, a crowd of people swarming the entrance near John Charles's house. There was a single police cruiser parked on the curb alongside the cars of the search party participants. Vicky parked behind the last car in line, letting out a deep breath as she did.

"You ready?" She asked with a crack in her voice.

"I guess," Jamie mumbled quietly. Vicky nodded solemnly before unbuckling her seatbelt, pausing before opening the door and allowing the hot summer air to enter the car. Jamie followed suit and went to the other side to stand with her. "You won't have that freakout again, right Vic?" Jamie asked meekly, feeling a stab of nervousness.

"I shouldn't, there's too many people, too many witnesses," she proclaimed blankly. Jamie gave her a look of confusion, puzzled by her odd response, but decided to not question her any further. They wandered closer to the crowd, a look of despair placed upon their faces. He noticed John sitting on his front porch from afar, watching as the crowd grew while sipping on a glass of ice water. His eyes dark and cold as his face remained emotionless. Jamie turned his attention away from the old man, focusing on the crowd in front of him, looking for any familiar faces. He noticed Nicole Brown and Alan Giblin, along with quite a few other students from their high school. One of those students was Jeffrey Grant, who stood further back in the crowd, not looking like his normal enthusiastic self. He stared down at Rachel Bell's missing poster silently, examining her smiling face.

A commotion stirred as the doors to the police cruiser opened. Mike Evans stepped out of the driver's seat as Kenneth Hudson stepped out of the passenger. Mike Evans was middle-aged, around fifty or so with graying hair and a small beer belly. From Jamie's knowledge, he'd been a cop since he was in his twenties. Kenneth Hudson was slimmer with red hair and mutton chops. He was in his thirties and lived in a trailer at the edge of town. He was calm most of the time, but almost everyone in town knew he had an anxious side to him. Charles Johnson, Linforts chief of police, was old and senile, a stubborn man who refused to retire. Jamie thought he had to be at least eighty. He had no reason to retire, enjoying his job and because of the lack of crime, there was no real reason to put him into use. *Until now.* Jamie thought to himself dimly. The last cop that Jamie could remember was Christopher, or "Chris" Brown. He was young and the newest recruit, who had way too much energy for a small, almost crimeless town. He was known for having horrible aim and a nervous nature to him, but as of now, only Evans and Hudson were on the scene.

The crowd began to surround the police cruiser, expressing their concerns to the two cops. Vicky started forward towards the crowd, with Jamie following closely behind. He listened quietly as the mob mumbled amongst themselves. Jeff was towards the front now, still looking down at the missing poster with a glimmer of pain in his eyes.

"Alright, listen up!" Mike Evans bellowed to the crowd. Everyone went silent, waiting patiently to hear the next command. "I don't want any part of this street left untouched, go a little past the town border if need be, but we must find Rachel Bell," he boomed. "I only want Hudson and me here to be the ones searching the surrounding properties, so search the streets, the woods, the park, any damn place you think you might find her." He turned his head to Kenneth Hudson and nodded. Hudson took a deep breath before stepping up.

"If you do find her, I want you to immediately report it to one of us, if you don't, we will hold you liable," he commanded smoothly while shoving his thumbs through his belt loops. "Do y'all understand that?" A wave of nods emitted from the small crowd. "Alright, you may be dismissed," he announced as the crowd started to mumble amongst each other once again, this time dispersing slowly as they did. Vicky grabbed Jamie's hand, tugging him through the crowd and down the street. As they tore down the road, Vicky's parents pulled to the side of the curb and parked their car, ignoring their daughter and her friend as they did. Their shoes slapped across the sun-beaten pavement as they made their way closer to Richard Huxley's old house.

"Vicky, only Evans and Hudson are allowed near the houses," Jamie spat out quickly. Vicky ignored him, speeding a little faster as they passed rows of trees on each side of the road. Jamie felt that nervous pit in his stomach again as he listened to several voices in the distance call out for Rachel. She didn't slow her pace until the house came into view, causing the pit in his stomach to grow. "Vicky please, I really think we should just let them handle this," Jamie fretted nervously. She quickly let go of his hand, turning to face him.

"Don't you get it? We're the only ones who have a lead, we're the only ones who have even just the slightest idea of what's going on," she seethed. Jamie took in a deep breath before responding, looking towards the decrepit house as he did.

"Okay, fine," he said gruffly, starting forward towards the property. He looked back briefly, making sure Vicky was following and that Evans or Hudson wasn't near. He quickly made his way towards the train tracks, letting the woods engulf him in its comforting shade. He paused once making it to the tracks, swerving around to face Vicky.

"We have to get closer to the house, this isn't enough," she spat out in a rush.

"But this is where we've been searching!" Jamie cried out.

"And have we found anything? Have we gotten any closer?" A sense of desperation washed over her face, her eyes pleading. The last thing Jamie wanted was to get in trouble with the law, but he couldn't disappoint her. He looked behind him one last time, the coast was clear.

"Fine, but let's make this quick," he decided quickly, rushing off towards the house. He could hear Vicky following him close behind, her footsteps thumping quickly against the grass. His heart pounded as they got closer to the decrepit building, he felt sweat spring off his forehead and roll down his face like raindrops. *This is a complete violation of the law, if we get caught-* His thoughts were cut off by the sight of someone opening the backdoor of the house. *Oh shit.* He quickly made a beeline for the trees, motioning for Vicky to follow. He slid behind the rough bark of a nearby oak and crouched down, praying he couldn't be seen. The tree was fairly large, so both he and Vicky were mostly covered.

"Jesus, something smells like shit," she whispered, pulling her hand to her nose while checking the bottoms of her beat up sneakers. "Jamie, did you step in dog crap?" He checked his own shoes and shook his head, noticing the smell himself. It smelled like rot. *Could it be?* The sudden sound of rustling through the brush jolted him out of his daze. He peered his head out from around the tree, it was Hudson. A police dog was tugging him closer to their hiding spot. He was still a good distance away, and he was mostly looking down at the ground in front of him, occasionally looking up to tell the dog a command. Jamie took a deep breath in and grabbed Vicky's hand, making a mad dash into the thicker part of the woods.

If Hudson heard, he didn't look up, his eyes at this point were glued to the ground. They watched him carefully, controlling their breath as they hid behind an even larger tree than before. Hudson neared their old hiding spot, the dog sniffing wildly where they once were. The mutt sniffed one last time before continuing its way down the treeline. It went a few feet further before stopping in its tracks, staring intently at a nearby bush. Kenneth Hudson bent down, spreading the bush apart. Jamie's focus was completely on Hudson and that bush, he didn't have to look to know that Vicky's was too.

Hudson found her. Jamie was able to hear as he drew in a deep breath, stepping back to wipe the sweat off of his freckled and sunburnt forehead. Jamie couldn't see her full body, just her tiny leg sticking neatly out of the bush. He stared quietly as he could faintly hear Vicky stifle a cry. *Oh my god.* Vicky started to say something but he couldn't hear it. *Oh my fucking god she's dead.*

Mike Evans

Rachel Bell was pronounced dead that afternoon. It took an immense toll on the Bell family, sending Kelly into a spiraling depression. Resorting to alcohol to cope, she was completely emotionally unavailable to her husband, Todd Bell, who overdosed and died the night after. Police couldn't determine the cause of death right away, her body was almost completely undamaged except for a few mild scratches here and there. Evans didn't suspect any foul play, but he did have one person he wanted to hold for an interview. Rosanne Morris.

Rachel Bell was found dead behind the nearby property of Rosanne Morris, making her the first and possibly only suspect. Her mother could also be considered a suspect, but due to Rachel wandering off often, it was highly unlikely. Evans decided his best bet would be to go to her instead of calling her into the station, as she seemed to be very reclusive. Evans also wanted to get a look inside of Huxley's old place anyway. It didn't take much for him to get the okay from Charles Johnson, he wasn't too sure if old Charles even knew what he was talking about anyway.

Chris jogged his way over as Evans opened the door to the cruiser, his eyes light with excitement. Evans sighed to himself, mumbling a curse under his breath before turning to face Chris.

"Hudson told me about you heading over to that murder house today," Chris started promptly. *Dammit, Hudson*. "I was thinkin' about going with you to take notes, seeing as this is our first real case." Evans felt a headache growing in the back of his head already.

"Look, Chris, this isn't a 'murder house' this is someone's home," he started to say while rubbing his temple with his thumb. "This also isn't your first case, that little delinquent thief Jesse Olsen was," a hint of disappointment washed over Christopher's eyes.

"Oh, alright," Chris muttered sullenly. Evans sighed, thinking it over for a second. *If my head starts pounding, I might need someone to write down notes for me anyway, so this could actually benefit me.* He rubbed his temple once again before finishing his thought.

"If you shut your yap and write down everything that's said, you can tag along, do you got that?" Evans questioned with a raised brow, opening the door of the cruiser.

"Yes, sir!" He exclaimed, nodding his head eagerly. Evans let out a large fake smile, tossing the small, coffee-stained notepad at Chris followed by a dull pencil. Evans tried to avoid Chris as much as possible, not wanting to deal with teaching a new recruit, especially some kid that was fresh out of high school. His interactions with Christopher were always brief, Evans made sure of that. Chris did a half jog over to the passenger's side, and with a sigh and a twist of the key, the two of them made their way towards Oak Street.

The cruiser bumped its way into the cracked driveway, causing the two of them to jump up and down in their seats a little. Evans felt a sense of unease and seclusion as he opened the door, taking in a deep breath as he did.

"Ready, Brown?" He asked while stretching his back. He thought he could faintly hear him say, "Yes, sir," over the sound of the passenger door slamming closed. He rolled his eyes, strolling up the path towards the old beat-up door. Broken blinds covered all the windows except for one, which had an angry hole in the middle of it. He heard Chris humming softly to himself behind him as Evans knocked on the door. He dimly noticed a pair of eyes peek through the broken blinds of one of the windows, they narrowed and seeped back into the darkness of the house. The bolt unlocked with a snap, causing a small gasp to escape from Chris. The door opened halfway and a pale, thin-looking woman peeked her head out slightly, keeping one hand on the door.

"Yes?" Her tone was quiet yet confronting. Evans thought he could smell alcohol on her breath.

"We just want to talk," he spoke low, trying to maintain eye contact with her, but her eyes kept darting back and forth between Chris and him. Her gaze finally rested on him as she stepped back, opening the door all the way for them to walk through. Nodding his head, he walked in and was immediately hit with a smoky and sort of rancid smell, the darkness from the house consuming him. He looked around the dark house, a strange reminder of what he once entered before back in 1964. She led them towards a small table that had three chairs around it, an ashtray placed neatly in the middle. The light from the sliding glass door beamed softly into the kitchen and spilled onto the table. The three of them sat down, listening to the creek of the wooden chairs.

"So, what do you want to talk about, officers?" She asked with a cat-like stare. Evans noticed Chris pull out his notepad and pencil, holding it on his lap. He felt a sense of unease. *I hate this damn house.*

"I wanted to discuss the situation of Rachel Bell," he stated calmly. She lit a cigarette and took a drag.

"I'm sorry, who?"

"The little girl who went missing about a week ago and was found dead a few feet away from your backyard."

"Don't recall."

"Hm." He could feel the headache growing. Christopher's fingers moved swiftly across the notepad, jotting down the limited 'conversation' that was being held at the small wooden dinner table. He began to massage his temple. "Alright, let's talk about something else then," he suggested with slight annoyance, crossing his arms on the table with a thump. She raised her eyebrow and took another drag off her cigarette. "When did you move here?" He asked with a bland expression.

"About a month or so ago."

"How many others live with you?"

"It's just me and my son."

"Hm." This conversation was going nowhere. The pain made its way to the top of his head. Chris continued to write. Evans rubbed his temple.

"Would you boys like something to eat? I was just in the middle of making lunch," she spoke with a crooked, yellow-toothed smile.

"No, thank you, ma'am," Chris answered politely with a wave of the hand.

"Thank you, but I think we'll be on our way now," Evans concluded with a huff, pushing his chair back to get up.

"Would you at least like some medicine for your head?" Her smile resurfaced, and Evans paused. Chris shot him a look of confusion.

"No, but thank you," he responded with an obviously forced smile as he pushed in the chair and made his way towards the door, Chris following close behind. With a firm hand, he opened the door and swiftly walked out.

"Alright, now you two stay safe," she said with a little wave, closing the door behind them. Chris turned to look at him, his mouth agape.

"I know, I know, that was some weird shit, Chris," he whispered with wide eyes as he opened the door to the cruiser.

"I think she did it, I think she killed that Bell girl," Chris speculated while getting into the passenger side. Evans started up the cruiser and rolled out of the bumpy driveway.

"Nah, she didn't do it. She's got a screw loose and probably had one too many drinks, but I don't think she did it," he countered swiftly. Chris gave him a look of bewilderment.

"Then who did?" He asked with that same stupid look on his face. Evans shrugged.

"Not sure, probably just some freak accident like that Smith boy," Chris responded with a look of shock. Evans sped up, wanting to get away from that house. Sitting back in his seat like a child who had just been scolded, Chris sat in silence with disbelief. Evans ignored it and tried to keep his focus on the road, but it just kept going back to that house. To that woman.

Rosanne Morris

She closed the door as the two cops left her home, a heavy sigh escaping her. With light footsteps, she walked back over to the kitchen table and sat in her seat from before, taking a long drag from her cigarette. Stan was gone for the day, taking a walk she assumed. She had the whole house to herself seeing as she got off work early. She leaned her head back and blew smoke into the open air, closing her eyes as she did. She felt light, a lot better than she had before. She never wanted Stan, she thought he might have realized that by now.

He wasn't planned. She never wanted to raise a child within her chaotic lifestyle. She was living on the streets before him, staying with anyone she could, whenever she could. She lost all her family, all her friends, she was alone. Then came Stanley, the result of a one-night stand. She didn't want to keep him, she wanted an abortion. She ended up keeping him out of guilt, naming him after her great-grandfather. She stayed with a man named Don for a little while, working as a waitress in another small town located in Iowa. She took any shift she could get her hands on, trying to make as much money as she could.

Don was abusive, maybe even more so than Russel. She stayed with Don for about a year before he put his hands on Stan. That was the final straw. She figured she had enough money to move the two of them out and was able to afford a small apartment on the edge of town. She promised herself to be a better mother to him, to raise him right. She took another drag from her cigarette, staring out the sliding glass door. A train called in the nearby distance, causing a flock of crows to cry out and flee from the trees. She softly smiled to herself in the darkness. She remembered what happened to Rachel.

She was drunk that morning, her head spinning. She couldn't remember too much, but she remembered the distinct look of terror on the little girl's face. She passed out after that, and when she woke up, the girl was dead. Rosanne didn't know what happened to her, she was too drunk. The girl looked so young and frail, it reminded her so much of Stan from when he was younger. She hid the body a few feet away from her property in the brush, going back into the house to take a nap once she was done.

She took a deep breath in and snubbed out the rest of the cigarette. She hated this house, she hated this town, and she hated Iowa. All she had was her son, and he was beginning to leave her too. She laid her head on the table, feeling crumbs from the morning's meal get stuck on her arms and face. There was no use in leaving now, she finally had her own house and a stable job. She could finally provide a decent life for Stan. But in her heart, she knew it would never be enough. She stared through the sliding glass door through the strands of her long, scraggly hair as the crows cried in the near distance. There is something wrong with this house.

Bradley Moore

Bradley was with Stan that Saturday afternoon. The two of them sat on the worn wooden benches at the park waiting for Ivan Balakin to arrive. Bradley's mind was still stuck on that Friday night, the feeling of the hand that gripped him haunting his brain. His wound was mostly healed, but the event still haunted him.

"Are you sure we should tell Ivan?" Stan asked meekly, interrupting Bradley's thoughts. He watched as a flock of geese settled on the other side of the pond, honking loudly to each other as they flew down on powerful wings.

"Yeah, man! We're like a group now, and I don't think we should just leave him out of it," Bradley stated promptly.

"And he won't tell anyone?"

"Ivan? Tell someone? No way, not in a million years. He won't tell a soul," a confident expression falling over his sunburnt face. Stan nodded his head and looked down, shuffling the dirt beneath him with his feet. Bradley once again noticed how boney Stan's hands were, pale and fragile against the harsh summer sun.

"Bradley?" His voice was quiet as he continued to look at his feet.

"Yeah?" Stan suddenly looked up, an anxious look washing over him.

"I'm gonna be okay, right? Like this is all gonna blow over and it's nothing to worry about, can you tell me that?" His eyes stared into Bradley like daggers. Bradley bit his lip, not knowing exactly what to say. *This is the complete shits, of course you're not gonna be okay.*

"Yeah, you're gonna be alright," Bradley replied with a small smile. Stan smiled himself, going back to look at his shoes.

"Hi," Ivan greeted from directly behind them, causing Bradley to jump in his seat. A little snicker escaped Stan as Bradley tried to calm his heart rate.

"Jesus Christ, Ivan, you scared the shit outta me," he gasped out of breath with a hand over his chest. "How long were you standing there for?"

"Not long, I just got here," he responded with a placid stare.

"Yeah, yeah alright," Bradley said quietly with a huff. Stan scooched over so Ivan could sit down, his shorts snagging on the splinters of the wooden bench. The three of them sat cramped together in silence, taking in the summer afternoon heat.

"So, what did you make me walk out here for?" Ivan asked with his almost never-changing expression. Bradley was dimly aware that the children with the kite were back, still trying to make it sore through the air. He nudged Stan, causing him to jump a little.

"Stan, you tell him," Stan nodded, turning himself slightly to face Ivan.

"I think I have a ghost in me or something," he explained quickly.

"What?" Ivan questioned with confusion, glancing at Bradley for answers.

"Tell him the rest, man!" Bradley groaned while rubbing his face. Stan paused before speaking again, bouncing his leg up and down anxiously.

"When I first moved to this town, I found a human bone in my backyard, and ever since then there's been weird shit happening." He started to say.

"*And*?" Bradley nudged on.

"*And* something attacked Bradley a week ago on that Friday night you and him gave me a tour of the town," he added while biting his lip and fidgeting with his fingers. Ivan looked at the two of them in silence with that same look of confusion resting upon his face. Bradley glanced down at the scarring wound on his hand before looking up again.

"Stan's possessed or some shit like that," Bradley blurted in an attempt to simplify it.

"What are you talking about?" Ivan asked, dumbfounded. The two of them groaned. "Ohhh! A book you are reading with ghosts, yes?" Ivan looked as though he was struck with realization, a wide grin on his face.

"No Ivan, this isn't some book, this is *real,*" Bradley asserted in desperation that he would understand. Stan leaned back with his hands on his head.

"This is stupid, I told you he wouldn't believe us," Stan complained wearily.

"Believe what? I don't understand," Ivan commented with disappointment. Bradley quickly reached over Stan and gripped Ivan by the arms, pulling him closer.

"Ivan. We're not making this shit up, Stan has something wrong with him," Bradley explained with a hardened gaze, a serious tone taking over. He stared into Ivan's eyes as he began to think.

"Disease!" Ivan snapped his finger and pointed as if the lightbulb in his head went off, the smile from before returning.

"NO IVAN, NOT DISEASE!" Stan yelled, impatient and frustrated. Bradley turned in shock while Ivan jumped a little at the sound of Stan's harsh tone. "Sorry, I didn't mean to raise my voice," he apologized as he rubbed his face tiredly. "I'll prove it. Yeah, I'll prove it next week." He stated calmly, reassuring himself.

"What?" Bradley and Ivan both questioned in unison.

"Next Monday, you'll see what I mean," his voice quivered as he spoke. Bradley quickly leaned over to Stan, pulling him close.

"What are you doing? Don't force that thing out of you!" He whispered harshly as Stan scrunched his nose and took a deep breath in.

"Relax, let's just worry about it later," Stan soothed quietly while getting up.

"Stan, what the fuck?" Bradley asked, absolutely flabbergasted. Ivan exchanged a look of confusion and then turned towards Stan who was stretching his arms.

"I don't know about you two, but I'm pretty hungry," Stan declared quickly, switching the subject. Bradley sighed and lifted himself from the wooden bench, feeling tiny splinters prick at his hands as he did.

"Yeah, I guess I could eat," he agreed while popping his back while watching the geese from across the pond. "What about you, Ivan?" Bradley asked, squinting his eyes from the blaring sun.

"I'm still confused," he promptly replied.

"So it's settled! We're going to Irna's Diner," Bradley finalized with a wide grin. Ivan shrugged as if he finished deciding with himself before getting up from his seat. *He'll prove it?* Bradley questioned himself as they started down the street. *What is he thinking?* Ivan seemed to be off in his own little world as Stan was focusing on where he was stepping. The walk was about twenty-five minutes or so, but the three didn't do much talking. A lot was on their mind.

Irna's Diner wasn't too busy, an old couple occupied a booth on the right of the building, while a mother and her two children occupied a booth on the left. The two children sat surprisingly quiet while they ate their meals, one of them kicking their feet softly from underneath the table as they did. Music from the 1940's played as they were greeted by Laura Gray, a seventeen-year-old waitress at Irna's Diner. Her hair was chopped just above her shoulders and was a deep shade of crimson red, standing out against her pale skin. She took their order, and together the three of them had enough for each of them to get a meal, waiting patiently in the booth closest to the mother and her kids.

"Ivan, you've been here before right?" Bradley asked smoothly, deciding to start off the conversation. Ivan nodded his head before speaking while shifting in his seat.

"Yes, only once." He responded promptly, staring him down with his light green eyes. Bradley sat across from Stan, who was looking down at the menu with a nonchalant stare. *I'm gonna be okay, right?* Stan's words raced through his mind like a train. *I'll prove it.* The sound of plates clanking onto the table caused Bradley to jump out of thought, his senses being overtaken by the delicious smell of the food.

"Will that be all?" Laura asked with a monotone inflection, her tired hazel eyes resting above dark bags.

"Yep! Thank's ya!" Bradley winked with a shit-eating grin. She rolled her eyes, strolling back to her post. Stan reached over Ivan, grabbing his plate that contained a rather droopy-looking burger and fries. Ivan and Bradley followed suit, taking their first bites in satisfaction. There wasn't much conversation, but it wasn't awkward this time because they were stuffing their faces with food. The cheese practically melted in his mouth, making him want to cry out with joy. Bradley and his mother used to go to Irna's Diner every Wednesday afternoon after she got off work, it was a tradition for a solid year before she had to take up more shifts.

It didn't take long for them to finish up their food, Bradley supposed they really were hungry. *I bet the twenty minute walk helped with that.* Bradley dimly thought to himself. He fished out a quarter for the tip, watching Ivan do the same. Stan shoved his hands in his pockets, pulling out two nickels.

"Sorry guys," he apologized quietly. "That's all I have." He awkwardly stuffed his hands back in his pockets, shuffling his feet on the ground.

"Don't worry about it, it should be enough," Bradley insisted with a reassuring grin. Ivan silently pulled out a dollar and set it on the table, scooting his way out of the booth. Bradley shot him a look of slight shock before scooting out of the booth himself. Stan was the last out, following behind Ivan and Bradley as they walked out the door. The summer heat welcomed them back outside, blinding them as they exited the building. Bradley drew in a deep breath, listening to the geese that flew above them. Stan winced from the heat, turning his eyes away from the sun. Without thinking, Bradley spoke up.

"Do you guys ever think about the future?" He asked without looking at them. Stan didn't acknowledge him but Ivan nodded.

"Sometimes," Ivan started to say. He paused, looking up at the sky with squinted eyes. "I think about moving out. I think about leaving that house," he added as they continued their way down the street. The three fell silent for a moment.

"Why?" Stan finally asked.

"My father," Ivan replied

"What does he do?"

"I don't want to talk about it." The only sound after that came from their footsteps and passing cars. Bradley's thoughts raced through his head. He needed noise.

"What about you, Stan?" Bradley asked, turning to look at him. He seemed to ponder for a moment before replying.

"No, I don't think I do." He replied promptly, kicking a small pebble on the sidewalk. "I try to focus more on the now. If I focus too much on the future, then I'll get too caught up in it and forget what I have to be doing in the present. I have to keep my head in one place to survive, y'know?" The two of them nodded in silent agreement. "I suppose I just want to feel like I'm truly living and not imagining what the future *could* be, and instead find out what the future *will* be is what I'm really trying to say," he added while looking up at them.

"That's deep, man," Bradley marveled in admiration as Stan shrugged.

"What about you?" Stan asked calmly. Bradley thought about the question himself for a moment.

"I suppose I do think about the future quite a bit," he began to say as another car whirred by. "I guess I just want to give myself something to look forward to, something to like keep me going." They walked under a large tree, giving them a break from the sun. "I think that thinking about our future puts us more in control of it, makes us strive to get what we want out of it," he explained promptly, finishing his thought. Stan nodded his head alongside Ivan. The three of them continued their way down the street as sweat sprang from their foreheads.

"What do you look for in your future?" Stan questioned as they walked under another tree. Bradley shrugged.

"What anyone looks for in their future, I guess, like prosperity or some shit like that. I just want to be truly content and not wonder if I'm living my life right or something," he concluded with a hint of wonder.

"Are you content?" Ivan turned to ask Bradley. He thought about it for a moment, looking at the two of them as he did.

"Yeah. Yeah, I guess I am."

Annette Jones

Annette was lying idly in her bed, attempting to recover from the sickness that she had been suffering from since Thursday. She felt pretty good, and she figured she would be able to return to school on Monday of next week. Her windows were open, allowing her to take in the fresh summer air. Her radio played music softly as the wind gently lapped at her curtains. She felt so comfortable, so at peace. She thought about how she would apologize to Vicky, still feeling guilty for how she stormed out of the woods that day. *I'll deal with all that shit on Monday.* She thought to herself as she snuggled further into her blanket. A sudden burst of noise interrupted her from her tranquility.

"Annette!" Arnold roared, rushing over to the side of her bed. She rolled her eyes and turned over, not wanting to deal with him. "Annette, cut the shit this is important!" He pleaded while shaking her. She groaned and sat up, glaring at him with a callous gaze.

"What?" She hissed. His eyes were filled with worry and her glare softened.

"It's Mitchell, Mitchell West," he started to say quickly. "He's missing! I asked his parents where he was because he didn't show up to practice, and they don't know where he is," he spat out in a rush. She could tell that he was holding back the tears, his face flushed with worry.

"Chill, I'm sure he's fine," she started to say in an attempt to calm him down. "Did he tell you anything before he left?"

"He said something about the woods, I think he wanted to find out what happened to Peter Smith," he explained with a calmer voice. She felt a small pit form in her stomach.

"You're joking."

"No, I'm not!" He whined, that desperation appearing on his face once again.

"Did you tell anyone about that? About what he told you?"

"Well, no-"

"Arnold you dipshit! Why didn't you tell anyone?" She hissed, getting up from the bed.

"Where are you going?" He asked timidly with a shake in his voice.

"I'm going to the only person I know who deals with this kind of shit," she spouted out while turning off the radio.

"The police?"

"Pft no, they didn't find Rachel in time now did they?" She retorted with a snort as she made her way out of her room.

"Then who?" He questioned while following her out the door and down the stairs. She turned to face him with a shine in her eyes.

"Vicky Taylor."

Annette quickly rushed out the front door and towards Vicky's house, which was just a little further down the road. The sun shone brightly as birds flew overhead. She told Arnold to stay home and that she would deal with it, to which he reluctantly agreed. She sprinted across the street and ran across Vicky's driveway to her front door. She had to knock twice before there was an answer, her mother greeting her with a wide grin.

"Awh, Annette!" Mindy Taylor cheered. "It's been so long! How are you, sweetheart?"

"I'm doing just *great,* thank you!" She replied while forcing out her own smile. "Is Vicky home?"

"Yes, she's up in her room right now if you'd like to come in," she offered while moving out of the way for her. Annette thanked her and kicked off her shoes, running up the stairs towards Vicky's room. She opened the door in a flash, startling Vicky who was reading calmly in her bed.

"Annette?" She closed her book and repositioned herself. She wore a look of confusion as her mouth hung slightly open in surprise.

"I'm sorry for storming off earlier and for not showing up at school, but I have something really important I need to tell you," she stated quickly. Vicky got up from her bed, crossing her arms.

"So you apologize by barging into my room?"

"Vick, please," she pleaded. Vicky sighed.

"Fine, go on," she grumbled with an eye roll.

"Mitchell West is missing," Vicky's expression changed from irritation to worry. "He went off to the woods to find out what happened to Peter," she spit out in a rush.

"Arnold's friend?" Annette nodded. "So why did you tell *me*?" Vicky asked with a raised eyebrow.

"Because I feel like you're actually on to something," Annette whined in desperation.

"Oh, really? If I was on to something, then why the hell did you leave?" Vicky hissed with a glare, crossing her arms sharply. Annette bit her lip.

"I'm sorry, Vicky. I really am. I think it was just Jamie-"

"Nuh uh, don't bring him into this," Vicky snapped, cutting her off. "He didn't say anything to you until you started getting all pissy." Annette hung her head down. "Now I'm willing to help under one condition," she offered with a stern look.

"What's that?" Annette asked cautiously.

"I want you to apologize to Jamie." Annette felt her brain explode. *But that piece of shit should be apologizing to me!*

"He called me a bimbette and a bitch," she seethed. "I shouldn't have to," Vicky rolled her eyes at Annette's predictable response.

"And *you* called him small and punchable," Vicky retorted.

"Duh, because he deserved it."

"Then I guess you don't want my help," Vicky concluded with a shrug. Annette thought of her brother and groaned.

"Fine, I'll like, apologize or whatever," she mumbled with a scrunched nose. Vicky nodded with a small smile, stepping back to sit on her bed.

"Thank you," she started to say. "Now where did Arnold say he went?" Annette explained everything Arnold told her, with Vicky listening intently to every word. When she was done, Vicky thought about it for a moment, her face set in a look of concentration. They sat in silence as the sun danced lightly on the carpet.

"So he went missing after going to Oak Street?" Vicky recapped. Annette nodded her head lightly. "And he's only been gone for a day?"

"Like half a day, I guess," she responded.

"I think I have an idea," Vicky voiced slowly, picking herself off the bed.

"What's your idea?" Annette asked softly.

"I *really* think that the people at that house have something to do with it," she postulated quickly.

"The murder house?"

"Yeah, the murder house." The two fell silent for a moment, lost in thought.

"Alright, so I'm guessing that you want me and Jamie to go with you to that house tomorrow," a smile appeared on Vicky's face.

"I never said anything about Jamie going, but that's a great idea," she sneered. Annette punched herself in her mind as her eye twitched.

"Do you think we'll find him?" Annette asked quickly, changing the subject.

"If we do, he might not be alive," Vicky stated with a cold stare. Annette felt a shiver run down her spine. "Did you even inform the police?" Vicky asked, her gaze returning to normal. Annette shook her head.

"No, they get too many people involved. It gets too messy, and I don't think they truly understand what they're doing." Vicky nodded in agreement.

"Tomorrow," Vicky started to say. "We'll take my car down to Oak, alright?"

"Alright," she agreed with a small nod.

"We'll find him, I know we will."

"Yeah, we'll find him." *We have to.*

Ivan Balakin

Ivan found a table at the far end of the cafeteria, a spot where he and Bradley normally sat during lunch. He brought his own lunches occasionally, but most of the time he would just sit there and read until Bradley got to the table. He was surprised to see that Bradley beat him to the table first, his eyes wide and full of energy. Before Ivan, Bradley normally sat by the trash cans, eating his food in shame. But nobody seemed to give him any trouble when Ivan was around, Ivan seemed to be a forcefield for Bradley.

"Ivan, my man, look who got here first!" He exclaimed with a proud look on his face as Ivan sat down across from him. He took a swig from his milk before speaking. "So here's the plan," he started to say.

"We had a plan?" Ivan asked, raising his normally quiet voice so he could be heard in the amplified cafeteria.

"Well, *no,* but that's why we're gonna make one," he noted with an excited grin. Ivan frowned, not knowing what he was talking about.

"Okay, but why do we need a plan?" He questioned blankly. Bradley held his finger up as he took a bite of his sloppy joe, sauce dripping down his hands and onto the table. *Gross.*

"Stanley's gone nuts," he replied once he was finished chewing. A look of confusion washed over Ivan's face. "He said he's gonna prove to you that he's got a ghost in him." Ivan went back to his conversation on Saturday to remember what Bradley was talking about, nodding his head in a confused silence. "So he wanted us to meet at his house today," he continued before finishing the rest of his sloppy joe and milk. It was beyond Ivan's understanding how Bradley could scarf down a meal so fast, the sight making him feel a little nauseous.

"So we go to his house after school?"

"Yeah, if you're able to."

"I can try," Ivan replied while looking down. A loud laughter erupted from the table next to them, one of the boys slamming his hand on the table as tears started to spring from his eyes. Ivan recognized him as Tommy Morrison, who was sitting with the rest of the football team. Jeffrey Grant sat quietly with his head resting on his hand on the edge of the table, looking lost in thought. They spoke loudly to each other between bellows of laughter and mouthfuls of food, filling the surrounding area with their conversation and vulgar language.

"Pigs," Bradley muttered to himself. Ivan didn't mind the football team too much, he was actually quite fond of Jeff anyhow. Normally, Jeff was a lot more involved in conversation, but it seemed as though he was in his own world right now. Ivan completely understood that. Bradley sighed, turning back to Ivan. "Do you have any more of those Sushki things?" Ivan shook his head.

"No, I didn't bring lunch today."

"Awh, really? Can you bring some next time?" He asked in an almost whiny tone.

"Yes, if we have some," he answered with a nod of the head. It wasn't uncommon for Bradley to mooch off of Ivan's food, but he could honestly care less as he didn't eat much anyway. Bradley picked at the plastic on his tray as the surrounding tables shouted at each other.

"If video game logistics were real, what do you think would happen after we die and get a second life?" Bradley asked as he continued to pick at the plastic. Ivan gave out a look of confusion, not quite understanding the question.

"What?" Ivan asked with a dazed stare.

"Like, if I was in a video game," he continued while gesturing towards himself, "and I died, would I come out of the womb again? Or would I just spawn into the open air?" Ivan briefly second-guessed his ability to understand English as Bradley seemed to be speaking a completely different language.

"Huh?"

"Like, would I be reborn and have to get back to that level, or would I spawn in as a middle-aged man?" Ivan didn't say anything, just stared at him with a confused expression. "Or would I come out of the womb as a middle-aged man? Actually, that's disgusting and I don't want to think about that," he countered himself as a sour look appeared on his face.

The bell rang and an ocean of students flooded the doors to the cafeteria, taking their conversations with them as they did. Feeling thankful he didn't have to stay any longer, Ivan stood up to take his departure as well, feeling a hand tug the back of his shirt. He whipped his head around to see Bradley practically laying over the table to reach him.

"You're going, right?" He asked in a loud voice. Ivan nodded his head and Bradley let him go. Because of his height, people usually made way for him, and he was able to navigate his way out of the cafeteria with ease. On his way out, he passed the slinky Scott Carter, causing his heart to drop a little. Scott was friends with Jesse Olsen. Ivan didn't like Jesse. Scott quickly shuffled his way by without making eye contact, keeping his head low and his eyes on his feet.

If he was being honest with himself, he really didn't want to go back to Stan's place. He had a horrible gut feeling that something was going to go wrong. He still didn't quite understand what Bradley and Stan were talking about, but nonetheless, he had a nasty feeling in his stomach. The rest of the day went smoothly, and he tried not to think about it, but he couldn't avoid it forever. The final bell rang. Class dismissed.

Jamie Anderson

Class dismissed. Jamie remained in his seat until the rest of his class departed, waiting for his teacher's attention. He tapped his pencil quietly on his desk while dimly listening to side conversations. Once the last straggler made their way out, he got up from his seat to Mrs. Brown's desk. She turned her head toward him and gave him a small smile, obviously tired from the long day.

"I have a question about today's assignment," he began promptly.

"And what would that be?" She asked while shifting her glasses.

"I don't-" A sudden burst through the door cut him off. He grimaced, turning to see who it was, his patience dwindling for the day. Shiny blue eyes stared back at him. Annette. *Shit, what now.*

"I need to speak to Jamie Anderson please," she claimed quickly with a sweet smile. Jamie's eye twitched.

"Just one second please," he told Mrs. Brown with a forced smile. She nodded her head in understandment and Jamie pulled Annette out of the classroom, closing the door behind them.

"What the hell do you want?" He hissed through clenched teeth. Her soft expression from before turned into an ugly, hateful glare.

"Vicky wants us for something important," she spoke down to him with her piercing gaze.

"Vicky?" His voice softened.

"Yeah, we're going to Oak Street like right now," she stated as if he should already know that.

"Shit alright, let me get my stuff I guess," he replied with a sigh. He opened the door to the classroom back up, the patient Mrs. Brown reading a book on her desk. "I changed my mind, I think I know the answer to my question," he concluded with a soft grin.

"Alrighty, well you have a good day," she replied with a warm grin.

"Yeah, you too." He waved and went back out the door, following Annette to his locker. The hallways were mostly clear, with only a few kids grabbing their things for the day. They quickly made their way toward his locker, their footsteps in fast-paced unison. They walked the rest of the way in silence, the tension growing thicker with each passing step. Her hair waved back and forth with elegance and Jamie wondered what this odd duo looked like to outsiders. Once his locker finally came into view, Annette spoke up.

"I'm supposed to apologize to you," she mentioned with a huff. "It was part of the deal." Jamie shot her a look of confusion before reaching his locker and fumbling with the combination.

"What deal?" He asked as he popped open his locker, grabbing his duffel bag. She sighed.

"I wanted Vicky's help finding Mitchell West because that's Arnold's best friend," she started to say as he closed the locker door. "And the only way she would do that is if I apologized to you," she finished as they made their way to the back doors.

"So this is your way of apologizing?" He asked with irritation.

"Yeah, and I don't care if you accept it or not," she asserted with crossed arms.

"Good, because I'm not accepting your half-assed 'apology' anyways, you dumb bitch," he remarked with a snarl. Her face flushed with anger, her hands balling up into fists. She went silent for a moment, looking as if she were attempting to calm herself down.

"Whatever, let's just try to tolerate each other for Vicky's sake," she bargained with a huff before reaching the large school's back doors.

"Yeah, alright," Jamie solemnly agreed. The sun bore down on them as they searched for Vicky's car in the parking lot. Annette spotted it before pointing to her car, which was all the way in the back next to a large oak tree in the shade. They both jogged towards it, feeling the heat beat onto their backs and sweat spring from their foreheads. A songbird called from a nearby tree with no reply. Jamie assumed that Vicky must have seen them, because her car started shortly before they reached it.

Annette called shotgun, opening the passenger side door and jumping inside in a flash. Rolling his eyes, Jamie made his way towards the backdoor. He swiftly opened it and was immediately hit with the smell of Vicky's perfume, his face instantly flushing into a deep red. She pulled out of the parking lot without saying anything, Annette and Jamie remained just as silent as she was.

The drive there was about seven minutes, but to Jamie, it felt like an eternity. He bounced his leg up and down anxiously, watching the scenery zoom by in a flash. The only thing keeping him sane was the radio. It played a catchy pop song as they passed other cars on the hot summer road. He was able to hear Annette humming the tune to herself softly as Oak Street came into view. *This is it.* He dimly thought to himself as Vicky parked the car at the edge of the street. She turned the car off, beginning to say something, but Jamie couldn't hear her. *Yes, this is it.* He heard a voice say into his ear, causing him to whip his head around. *This is the beginning of the end.*

Stanley Morris

Stan waited patiently outside his door that Monday afternoon, sitting on the stoop while waiting for Bradley and Ivan to arrive. He could feel his heart thumping wildly in his chest. What the fuck was he thinking? He nervously picked at his fingers, peeling the skin away until they bled. He could feel the thing mocking him behind his eyes, jeering at his foolishness. His head began to throb. This was a bad idea, a *horrible* idea, but he had to prove it and it couldn't be here.

He bounced his leg up and down, getting blood from the exposed wounds on his fingers all over his hands. His mother was taking a nap on the couch inside, something she did often after coming home from work. The sky slowly began to darken in color, going from a bright blue to a dark gray. Another jolt of pain ripped through his head. Mental manipulation from an unseen force.

"Go away, I don't need you yet," he mumbled blankly. *Awhh, but I think we should hang out! Just the two of us before the party gets here..* He heard the voice answer smoothly in the back of his head. "No, I don't want to talk right now," Stan replied back calmly. *You're no fun.* Stan didn't say anything back, he didn't want to feed into the creature's torment and pressure. He refrained from thinking as well, knowing it could hear his thoughts. Stan had trained himself well.

It was almost an hour before Bradley and his bike came into view as it was just beginning to drizzle. Stan began to rise from the stoop, his legs wobbly and unstable. He noticed Ivan not too far behind him, walking with his bike and taking in the view of the woods. He felt light drops fall onto his pale skin, causing a light shiver to run down his body despite it still being warm out. Bradley gave Stan a quick wave upon being noticed, a smile spreading across his face. He quickened his pace, feeling himself regain strength in his legs as he did.

"Stan! Look who I brought!" He exclaimed with a large grin, pointing at Ivan as he did. Ivan perked his head up, noticing Stan and picking up speed. *You're making a mistake.* The voice spoke up.

"Shut up," Stan mumbled under his breath, hoping Bradley wouldn't hear. *I'll show you, you'll see..* Stan smacked his head once before finally meeting up with Bradley.

"What was that about?" Bradley asked with a confused look. Stan shook his head.

"Nothing," he started to say. "I can't," he paused, carefully picking out the words in his head. "I can't let it loose here. We need to go somewhere else." Bradley looked back at Ivan, who was only a few feet behind them.

"Alright, where should we go then?" He questioned, looking back at Stan. He thought about it for a moment, looking to the side of the street that was away from the woods. Light drops surrounded them as the sky continued to darken.

"The park," he finalized. "Everyone's probably gone because it's about to rain," he added. He didn't know if that was actually true or not, but he hoped it was.

"Are you sure about this?" Bradley asked quietly as Ivan paused behind him. Stan nodded his head. *No, I'm not. I'm actually terrified.*

"Let's go," he concluded as he started his way down the street, the others following silently behind. His heart began to beat heavily in his chest again, a sick feeling rising in his stomach. This felt wrong, but it felt needed. He needed to show someone, he needed help. *You're a monster.* He slapped his head. *I can help you.* Another slap to the head and a confused look from Ivan. *You don't need them.* Slap. Punch. *Don't do this.*

"GET OUT OF MY HEAD!" Stan screamed, placing his hands over his ears while lurching forward. *You can't run from me..* The voice faded into the rain. Stan tried to catch his breath, the panic setting in. Everything was happening so fast.

"Stan?" Bradley set his hand on Stan's shoulder, gripping it softly. He whipped his head around to see the look of concern set upon their faces. He shook Bradley's hand off.

"I have to finish this," he murmured as he started to pick up speed. The two boys exchanged a look of confusion, following suit. By the time the park came into view, Stan realized he was right. No one was there. He thought that his heart was going to leap out of his chest as he continued down the sidewalk. The voice remained silent, and the only sound besides their footsteps was the light rain and passing cars. His mouth felt dry, and for a second, he thought he might throw up. He couldn't stop though. He pressed on.

Bradley and Ivan dropped their bikes off by some nearby bushes as the sky grew angrier. Stan wandered to the edge of the pond, wondering what to do next. Bradley stood next to him, Ivan keeping his distance.

"I'm ready now," Stan announced to no one in particular. The voice didn't show. Bradley stayed quiet. "Come out," he pressed on. Ivan stepped a little closer, eyeing the pond water nervously.

"Maybe it's busy?" Bradley asked meekly. Stan shook his head.

"The little fucker was talking to me earlier, he's not *busy*," Stan glared while staring at the water. *Show yourself.* Nothing. *Pussy.* Ivan took another step, trying to see what was going on. A dark shadow began to loom over Stan in the reflection of the disturbed water. Large claws spread out like wings around Stan's body. He knew he was the only one seeing this because Bradley and Ivan remained as silent and still as statues. *Now show them.* He prodded in his mind. *Oh, I'll give you a show alright,* the voice hissed, fading into nothing. The shadow disappeared along with the voice. Nothing. Everything was silent except for the rain. That's when Ivan made a mistake.

Ivan took one last step forward, leaning over to see what Stan saw. It happened in a flash. Large gray claws ripped from the water, extending its spider-like limbs toward him. He didn't have enough time to react, the claws dug into his shoulders and dragged him toward the murky pond water. His face was shoved into the dirt, and all that could be heard was his muffled scream.

"IVAN!" Bradley cried out. Ivan tried to pull away, gripping the ground with his hands as he continued to scream. It did nothing but slow the grayish creature down. Bradley grabbed onto Ivan's legs as Stan tried to pull one of the clawed hands away. It was completely useless. Ivan's head was dunked into the cold pond water, the creature holding his head down as he struggled wildly for air. Ivan was going to drown.

Vicky Taylor

Vicky stepped out of the car just as it was starting to drizzle, her mind racing with thoughts. Annette and Jamie followed suit, staying just as quiet as she was. She knew exactly where she was going to go, she just hoped there would be results this time. She stared down the street, noticing something off.

"Annette," she called. Annette walked over to her side of the car next to Vicky, looking in the direction she was pointing in. "Isn't that the Russian kid?" She asked with a cock of the head. Annette squinted her eyes and nodded.

"Balakin? Yeah, I think so," she affirmed hesitantly.

"I think that's Bradley down there as well," Jamie added. Annette's head whipped around.

"Bradley? What the hell is he doing down Oak Street?" She grumbled.

"Wait, I think there's someone else down there too," Vicky noted in surprise. It was that scruffy-haired boy from before, walking towards Bradley and Ivan. "I think it's the guy who lives there," she speculated while looking at Annette and Jamie.

"Let's follow them," Jamie spoke up.

"What?" The two girls shot him a look of shock.

"Let's follow them. Maybe they're linked to the deaths or something," he proposed with a shrug. Vicky thought over it for a second. *He's onto something.* She looked back at the three boys who were now walking in their direction.

"Yeah, okay let's do it," she agreed quickly before hopping back in the car. The others scrambled their way into the car, Annette watching them through the rearview mirror while Jamie watched through the window. Vicky clutched the steering wheel, staring forward while deep in thought. Her mouth pressed together in a fine line as her grip tightened. Her focus was on one objective. Find Mitchell West.

"So, we're just sitting in here until they pass us right?" Annette asked, turning her attention from the mirror to look at Vicky.

"Yeah, I suppose so," she replied without moving.

"Duck down, they're about to pass the car," Jamie alerted quickly, sliding down the seat and onto the car's surprisingly neat floor. Vicky and Annette did the same, staying as still as they could. Around two seconds later, they heard the sound of footsteps passing the car.

"Do you think-" Annette started to say before she was cut off by a voice outside.

"GET OUT OF MY HEAD!" Screamed the unknown person. *That had to be the guy that was with Bradley and Ivan.* Vicky dimly thought to herself as she began to peek her head over the dashboard. The three were turning towards the park, the mystery boy holding his hands over his ears while stumbling forward. She noticed a look of concern and fear on the faces of Bradley and Ivan.

"What was that?" Jamie questioned while popping his head up to take a look himself. Annette stayed low, looking up at Vicky intently. Without saying anything, Vicky started up the car again, waiting until they were out of sight before rolling forward. Annette perked her head up, exchanging a concerned look with Jamie. She slowly turned the corner, driving past the trio while parking next to the curb across from the park. She watched silently as they made their way towards the pond, her eyes zeroing in on the boy with the scruffy hair.

"Let's get out here," Vicky advised quietly.

"No, what if they see us?" Jamie countered with a shake in his voice.

"They look too focused on whatever is going on over there," Vicky responded sternly. "This is it, obviously there's something wrong with that guy."

"Okay, but why would Bradley and Balakin be involved in a murder?" Annette asked, speaking up for the first time in a while.

"Well, how should I know?" Vicky retorted.

"But you know they have something to do with Mitchell, right?" Annette remarked back with an eye roll.

"Guys," Jamie started to say.

"Well, *no,* but this is the closest we can get, I mean that guy literally lives at the murder house," Vicky ranted desperately.

"Guys they're not moving anymore," Jamie told them before Annette could reply back. Vicky and Annette both turned to see what he was talking about. He was right. The three stood as still as statues, the rain dampening their clothes.

"What the hell are they doing?" Annette questioned with squinted eyes, her breath fogging up the glass. Vicky watched as Ivan took a step forward, a sudden eruption coming from the pond water as he did. Annette slammed her hand to her mouth in shock as Jamie sat there with his jaw agape. *Oh my god.* Six large claws began to tug Ivan onto the ground and towards the water, the two boys desperately trying to tug him away to no avail. Without thinking, Vicky quickly opened the car door and scrambled her way out, sprinting towards the park and the creature from Hell.

Bradley was the first to notice her, his eyes filled with terror and shock. Ivan's head was dunked under the water, his arms scrambling to pull himself up. Ivan was a strong guy, nobody ever picking a fight with him because of his size and strength. But he wasn't strong enough. Vicky shoved Bradley out of the way, wrapping her arms around his stomach, digging her heels into the ground as she began to pull. The claws dug deeper into his shoulders, a muffled scream emitting from the water. She could feel his body begin to weaken. She was running out of time.

Bradley and the scruffy-haired boy went for his legs, tugging backward in an attempt to help free him. She could feel her feet slipping on the wet grass and mud as two sets of hands began to reach for the claws that held Ivan. *Annette and Jamie, oh thank god.* The five of them tugged at the drowning boy, screaming as they began to feel the grip on his shoulders loosen. *Bastards.* She heard a strange voice say in her head as she tugged one last time. The claws let go, gray limbs seeping back into the water like snakes as they pulled Ivan's head out of the murky pond.

Ivan Balakin lay there in the wet grass, motionless with his mouth partially open. The five sat around him, panic still filling the air.

"Oh my fucking god, he died," Annette whimpered in shock.

"Does anyone know CPR?" Jamie cried out with a crack in his voice.

"Shit, shit, shit, what do we do?" Bradley panicked with his hands over his head.

"This is all my fault," Vicky heard the scruffy-haired boy whisper to himself. Without much thought, she started to put her hands on his chest to perform CPR. The others stayed quiet as she did this, watching intently with hope. She didn't know how long she was supposed to keep going for, but luckily, Ivan answered for her. He began to cough up water, his eyes widening as he gasped for air. Everyone began to back up, giving him some room as he sat up and looked around.

"Jesus man, I thought we lost you for a second there," Bradley gasped with a smile and a look of relief. Vicky felt her heart lift as he began to breathe normally. She pulled him further away from the pond, his eyes darting around rapidly.

"What the hell just happened?" Jamie questioned frantically.

"What the fuck was that, and who the hell are you?" Annette asked, pointing a finger at the scruffy-haired boy. His head jolted up as he looked around wildly.

"Uh, I'm Stan," he said. "Let me try and explain."

Richard Huxley

Hate. Something that sits within all of us at some point in time. Seeping through the mouths of the angry and wounded. We learn to hate at an early age, something that is taught through parenting and environment. Hating food, animals, movies, objects.. People. Some hate more than others. I know I do. I can't help but feel these human thoughts, this deep-rooted emotion of despair.

I feel this deep temptation within me to act upon this hate, I always have. But now I can. I have all the power in my hands; I can do what I choose. If I act upon these impulses, I will destroy everything. My plan, my host. I have to be patient. My time will soon come. The death of the boy would have been a rush, a thrill. Oh, set me free from this broken shelled prison! Free me from human-like emotions and limits! Free me, I say!

This new life I live is close to what I desire, but not close enough. I wish to tear myself from the limits of humanity, break the boundaries, and become the most impeccable and perfected form I could be. I curse my body with the emotions and flaws of those beneath me. I tried to solve their problems, but they cannot be saved. They are too far gone to even want to be saved. If they mustn't be saved, then they must be destroyed. This town betrayed my trust and honor, turning against their savior. They should have been grateful, goddammit! They shall be the first to go. The first to be saved from a life of human torment. I am God. I am God!

Stanley Morris

"So, you're telling me you're connected to that *thing*?" Vicky questioned with a look of bewilderment. The rain had stopped and the sun peeked up behind a sea of clouds. Stan had told them everything, and then the group of three had told him everything. He was surprised when he learned how they had been lurking around his house and the woods. How close they had been to figuring out he was linked.

"Yeah," he replied with a nod. The six of them moved towards the benches, far away from the pond for Ivan's sake. He was still shaken up and hadn't said much since. Vicky and Bradley had tried to comfort him to the best of their ability, but nothing really got him out of his shock. He sat in silence against a tree with Bradley sitting next to him, looking solemn, his wounds hidden under his ripped t-shirt.

"What about Mitchell West?" Annette asked with wide eyes. "How are we supposed to find him if he doesn't even know where he's at?" She gestured towards Stan.

"I don't think he can stray very far," Stan commented with a complex expression.

"Yeah, that would make sense since the deaths have been like right by your house," Vicky agreed. The six of them fell silent, lost in thought. Ivan suddenly got up, startling Bradley out of his daze.

"What are you doing?" Bradley questioned while pushing up his glasses. All eyes were on Ivan now, a look of clouded dismay spread across his long face.

"Going home," he responded with a lack of emotion. "I'm done, I don't want to do this anymore." Stan quickly stood up from the bench, a sense of desperation washing over him.

"Ivan, please don't go, not now," he begged. Ivan looked down at him with a look of guilt.

"I'm sorry, I just can't. I could have died."

"You can't go," Jamie spoke up. Everyone's attention quickly turned to Jamie who was sitting on the bench with his hands clamped neatly together upon his lap. "We're all in this together now, there is *no* leaving. We're the only ones in this shitty little town who know about this." Ivan's mouth twitched as if he were about to say something before sitting back down again. He knew Jamie was right. Quietness seeped in once again.

"What do we do now?" Annette asked, breaking the silence.

"We have to find Mitchell," Vicky responded. "That's our first priority I think."

"So all we have to do is look around Stan's house, right?" Bradley asked. "Since we're all in on it now?" Ivan leaned his head back, hitting it against the tree while looking up and mumbling something to himself in Russian.

"Do you have something to say, Ivan?" Jamie snarked with a raised eyebrow.

"Nyet," he grumbled, rubbing his face with his hands.

"That means-" Bradley started to say.

"Yeah, I know what that means dipshit, don't need you explaining it to me," Jamie hissed. Bradley looked like he was about to say something, but decided against it as Vicky shot Jamie a glare. Stan felt exhausted, all he wanted to do at this moment was sleep.

"So we find Mitchell," Vicky resumed. A persistent tone resided within her.

"Yeah, let's all meet at my place tomorrow after your school gets out," Stan agreed promptly.

"You don't go to school?" Annette questioned.

"He's homeschooled," Bradley answered. Annette's sharp eyes locked on him as Bradley looked away meekly.

"Who cares? Let's just go home and deal with this tomorrow," Jamie concluded as he got up from the wooden bench with a sigh. Ivan got up in a flash, speeding out of the park without saying anything.

"Pft, he's definitely not coming back," Annette remarked while getting up herself.

"I could see why," Bradley started to say. "He's petrified of water and he almost died from it." Both Jamie and Annette shot him a glare. "Assholes," he muttered under his breath. *There's no way this is going to work.* Stan thought to himself dimly. *They all hate each other.* He sighed. Annette was right, there was no way Ivan was going to come back. The only thing he could do now was hope he wouldn't tell anyone. The other three said their goodbyes and departed, leaving Stan and Bradley in the desolate park.

"You don't have to stay, y'know," Stan told Bradley. "I understand if you don't want to be a part of this anymore." Bradley shook his head, adjusting his glasses as he did.

"No, I want to stay," he stated with a twitch of the nose. A puzzled look fell upon Stanley's face.

"Why? You saw what happened to Ivan."

"I don't really know, I just want to stay I guess," he replied with a shrug. Stan couldn't help but let out a small smile. Out of all this torment, he at least had a friend.

"Thanks, man," he said with sincerity. "I really appreciate you sticking with me through all this." Bradley let out a small smile himself.

"Yeah, it's really no biggie." The sun beamed dimly through the darkened clouds. Stan looked up, feeling the wind gently hit his face. *The brink of your decay is on its way,* hissed that all too familiar voice. He shook his head. There was no time for the antics of the dead. He had to find Mitchell West.

Annette Jones

"Annette, are you even listening to me?" Jeff asked, shaking Annette gently out of her daze. The two were sitting on the stoop of his house, soaking in the afternoon heat as the breeze washed over them. She silently looked up at Jeff, his eyes filled with worry.

"Hm? Sorry, I was a bit lost in thought," she responded slowly. She turned her head away from him, not wanting to look at him anymore.

"I said, I've been worried about you lately. You've been acting distant and you weren't at school much last week."

"I was sick," she claimed softly as the birds called above them. Jeff sighed.

"I know something is up, Annette." She looked up, swiftly hiding any emotion that could be shown as surprise.

"Nothing is up, I was just sick."

"You can be honest with me, 'Net." Her eyes quickly narrowed.

"Don't call me that." He sighed once more, setting his large hands on his lap before getting up from the stoop.

"I guess I'll just take you home now," he finalized in disappointment. With her arms crossed, Annette got up and started for Jeff's car. Her light pink mini skirt flowed gently behind her as it brushed against her quick-moving legs. She knew what she originally wanted from Jeff when she went home with him, but all he wanted to do was find out where she'd been. No thanks. She opened the passenger-side door a few seconds before he got in and started the car. He paused.

"Are you sure you don't want to talk about anything?" He asked with sincerity. She rolled her eyes and groaned, throwing her head against the car seat.

"Jeff, please just take me home. There is *nothing* to talk about," she whined. Jeff tapped on the steering wheel anxiously.

"We could just.. talk," Jeff suggested.

"I want to go home," Annette persisted one final time. Jeff sighed once again.

"Okay," he muttered quietly while putting the car in reverse and pulling out the driveway. She turned away from him, scooting close to the window while watching the trees and houses pass. "You know I really love you, Annette," Jeff stated without taking his eyes off the road. She hesitated to respond.

"I love you too," she replied quietly. She turned to look at him. For a faint second, she thought that statement could be true. He glanced over at her and smiled. He was very handsome to her, and kind too. He did so much for the community, and for their school. He truly was perfect, but the feelings she felt for him were complicated. Sometimes she did feel love, this was one of those times. She suddenly didn't want to go home anymore.

"Pull over," she commanded softly. He looked over at her before returning his attention to the road.

"What?"

"I said, pull over." He did as she asked, pulling over to the side of the curb on a street near her house. "Now stop the car," he once again did as she asked. Before he could even get a word in she pulled him in by his face and kissed him, her soft lips meeting his. "I changed my mind."

"What?" He asked with that same dumbfounded expression from earlier.

"Let's talk," she told him as her hand crept up his thigh.

"Were you not sick?" He caressed her face gently, looking into her dazzling blue eyes with sincerity. His question briefly broke her out of her trance. She quickly shook out of it. *I can tell him.* She had been going steady with Jeff for about two years now. Of course, she had messed around with other guys during those two years, but she trusted Jeff the most. He didn't have to know about who she did or didn't sleep with, she made good sure of that. Jeff was a good boy, and she wasn't quite ready to lose him.

"There's something else that I should tell you," she mentioned softly, her other hand cupping his face. Although he was fully aware of where her left hand was placed, he wanted to figure out what she wanted to say first.

"Yes?" His face was a deep red, but he kept himself composed. She pulled him in for a second kiss before saying anything, feeling him loosen up. In the back of her mind, she knew what she was doing, but he did too.

He softly grabbed her hand, pulling it away and setting it on her own lap. Her eyes narrowed.

"What? You don't like that?" She snapped with a glare.

"Say what you want to say first," he persisted. "I care about you Annette, I just want to know what's wrong." She sighed, thinking it over for a moment. *He's too good. C'mon Jeff, have a little edge, would ya?* He had always been a good soul, Annette didn't think he even had the capability to get angry. Jeffrey Grant was known to be a saint. *So how did he wind up with someone like me? Oh pooh, pity on him.*

"It's about the missing kids," Annette started to say. "I-" A sudden pounding on the car window caused her to nearly jump out of her skin before she could begin her sentence. She whipped her head around, her ponytail coming close to smacking Jeff in the face. Vicky. She gestured for Annette to roll the window down, mouthing something as she did. *Is someone behind her?* Still catching her breath, Annette pushed the button and began to roll it down.

"Anette," Vicky called out with wild eyes. "We might have a lead on Mitchell."

Vicky Taylor

"What?" Annette questioned, squinting her eyes from the sun. Vicky glanced at Jeffrey Grant who was sitting patiently in the driver's seat. Jamie stood behind her with his arms crossed, his dark hair blocking the sun from his eyes.

"Come out," Vicky commanded quickly, eyeing Jeff down.

"Why?"

"Please," Vicky pleaded. Annette groaned, giving Jeff a quick peck on the cheek before getting out of the car. Vicky turned her attention to the driver.

"Sorry for stealing her from you, but thanks for giving her a ride," she told him with a shrug and a forced smile.

"No problem," Jeff replied with his own forced expression of glee. "Cya around, Annette." He added with a warm wave and a smile. Vicky waited for Jeff to drive off before saying anything.

"We're meeting Bradley at Irna's Diner, and then we're going to get the others," Vicky explained once his car was out of sight.

"Bradley? Bradley Moore?" Annette questioned with a look of disgust.

"Yeah, I don't like the guy either but he might know something about Mitchell," Jamie added promptly.

"We're also a group now, whether we like it or not," Vicky started to say as Annette rolled her eyes and made a gagging motion. "Like Jamie said yesterday, we're the only ones who know about this." She had her hands on her hips like a mom scolding her kid. "I also don't want you telling Jeff anything, this is our secret to keep, okay?" Jamie remained silent, standing as still as a statue as the tension grew.

"Whatever, let's just get this over with," Annette huffed as she crossed her arms. Ignoring Annette's shitty attitude, Vicky led her back to where she parked her car, not quite ready to admit that she had followed Jeff's car from school. Annette quickly pulled the passenger side door open, brushing off her mini skirt with a sigh. Once everyone was in the car, she quickly made her way down the street and towards Irna's diner.

It was only a five-minute drive to get to the diner, the three of them exiting the car and entering the building. They were met with the pale-faced and dark-haired Laura Gray who led them to their booth. The place was completely empty. Laura's eyes traveled towards Annette ever so slightly, her lack of expression making her difficult to read. Jamie sat across from the two girls, taking a peek at the menu as they waited.

"Would you three like anything to drink?" Laura asked with a soft monotone voice. Jamie kept his eyes on the menu as Annette shook her head.

"No, thank you, we're still waiting on someone," Vicky answered with a smile. Annette groaned, throwing her head back against the seat.

"Alright, I'll come check up on you in a bit," Laura stated before glancing at Annette.

"What a creep," Annette whispered with a hiss. Vicky jabbed her in the arm, shooting her a glare. Jamie peeked above the menu, sighing as he did.

"He's here," Jamie pointed. Bradley could be seen struggling to lean his bike against the wall outside, the bike wanting to fall over at each attempt. Vicky let out a small snicker as his bike fell for a third time. Once the bike was finally upright and against the wall, Bradley made his way inside the diner. Adjusting his glasses, he searched for their booth with squinted eyes. Laura pointed to their location, causing another groan to escape from Annette. He made his way over, hesitating before taking the seat next to Jamie.

"Hey, guys," Bradley stammered with a slight shake in his voice. Jamie and Annette both shot him a dirty look, Jamie scooting himself closer to the window while staring at the menu.

"Okay, so we're all here, what now?" Annette asked as she rested her head in her hands.

"We're not *all* here," Vicky stated promptly. "We still have to get Ivan and Stan."

"Okay, but why? What lead does Bradley even have?" Annette persisted. Before anyone could respond, Laura came back to their booth with a clipboard.

"Alrighty, could I get you all anything to drink?" She asked, passing Bradley a look.

"No, thank you," Vicky replied with a smile.

"I would like-" Bradley started to say before Vicky kicked him in the leg from underneath the table. *We don't have time.* Vicky thought desperately. "Never mind, I'm actually not thirsty," Bradley retracted quickly.

"Alright," Laura sighed with an eye-roll before returning to her post.

"Bradley, why don't you tell us what you found," Vicky inquired softly. Bradley adjusted his glasses and cleared his throat before speaking. Annette and Jamie exchanged looks of irritation.

"After you all left the park, me and Stan decided to search around his property to see if we could find anything," he started to say. "And we found a shoe," he paused to adjust his glasses once more. "Mitchells shoe." Annette's eyes widened.

"How do you know it's Mitchell's?" She asked, sounding a little skeptical.

"He wrote his initials on the pull tab," Bradley explained quickly. "He must lose his shoes often."

"And where was it that you said you found the shoe?" Jamie asked with a raised brow.

"A couple of yards behind his house near a tree stump," he responded promptly.

"So we need to go get Ivan like-" Vicky quickly checked the clock on the wall above one of the booths. "Like right now, so we have as much time as possible to find Mitchell," she spat out in a rush. Bradley nodded his head, getting up from the booth before leaving towards the front doors. The other three followed suit, with only Vicky waving goodbye to Laura. Jamie was already in the backseat of Vicky's car by the time she made it outside. Bradley stared thoughtfully at his bike as if he were contemplating something. Annette leaned against the wall beside him, taking a drag off her cigarette.

"What am I going to do with my bike?" Bradley asked once Vicky walked out the door.

"Hm.." She thought over it for a moment. *Well, I can't fit that in my car..*

"You're just gonna have to leave it here," Annette remarked before taking another drag. He groaned, dragging his feet to the car.

Annette smiled, throwing her cigarette to the ground and scuffing it out as she watched him mope away. Vicky sighed, turning back to the diner. She quickly opened the door, peeping her head through to see Laura.

"Hey, do you think you could make sure nothing happens to this bike?" She requested with a sincere smile.

"Well, how much do you got, Taylor?" Laura asked with a smirk. Still holding the door open, Vicky fished through her pockets, pulling out what little money she had on her.

"I have a one and three-quarters," she stated while holding out the money for her to see. Laura smiled and walked over towards Vicky.

"Alright, deal. But once my shift ends, I'm out of here, got it?" Laura swiftly grabbed the money, pocketing it right away.

"Yep, got it." *Poor girl probably doesn't make much here.* Vicky thought while she quickly walked to her car, the sun temporarily blinding her. Vicky hopped in the front and put the car in drive. Everyone was in now, even Annette.

"What took you so long?" Annette asked. "I thought we were the ones who were supposed to hurry."

"Laura's going to watch your bike," Vicky told Bradley, ignoring Annette's remark.

"Thank you," Bradley replied softly with a warm smile. Jamie reached his head over the seat towards Vicky from the back.

"Where are we going first?" He asked blankly. Vicky pulled out of the parking lot, making her way down the street. She turned back to look at him briefly.

"To Ivan Balakin's."

Jamie Anderson

It took nearly fifteen minutes of almost pure silence to get from the diner to Ivan Balakin's house. The only time there was talking was when Bradley had to give directions. The worst part was that Vicky didn't even discuss anything with Ivan yet. They were showing up completely unannounced. Pulling up in his driveway, he realized that Ivan didn't live near too many neighbors. There were only three other houses around him, the one closest to his blasting rock music. A large cornfield could be seen on the far right of his house, going for what seemed like miles. Everything felt a little secluded and strange.

"I'll go get him," Bradley offered quickly as he opened the door and hopped out. The three of them watched as he went to knock on the door, adjusting his glasses as usual.

"Do you think he'll come out?" Annette asked while stretching her arms.

"Hopefully, he may be at the park," Vicky replied promptly. Jamie remained silent as the two began to talk, tuning them out as he watched Bradley wait outside. He bounced his leg lightly, looking at the field as he did. Jamie closed his eyes, leaning against the window. The sun shone gently upon him as he began to drift off, strange light formations dancing underneath his eyelids. He began to dream, his mind leading him deep into the woods. He kept wandering until he entered a clearing. There he saw Vicky, dancing gracefully in the sunlight, surrounded by trees. He ran towards her, but she wasn't getting any closer.

The sunlight began to disappear, darkness filling the clearing. Everything went black, panic began to settle in. He turned around, finding himself in an empty hallway. He was at school. Vicky stood ahead of him, standing still and facing away. He slowly approached her, his heart beating quickly in his chest. Grabbing her shoulder, he turned her towards him. Her face made him stumble back. It was all mangled, almost unrecognizable, blood from the gashes in her face dripping onto her lavender shirt. Her eyes bulged out of the sockets, maggots eating at her exposed scalp. Her body fell backwards, making a loud thump sound. He jolted awake, letting out a small gasp.

"You alright back there, Jamie?" Vicky asked with worry.

"Yeah," he mumbled while rubbing his eyes. "Is he still waiting out there?"

"Ivan answered the door, he's talking to Bradley right now," Vicky replied. Jamie perked his head up to see the two boys talking to each other, Bradley making various motions in an attempt to get Ivan to come with them. Ivan rubbed his face with his hands, nodding his head without saying anything. Bradley quickly turned to give the group a thumbs up with a wide grin. The two made their way to the car, with Bradley sitting in the middle against Jamie's better judgment. Vicky started the car once again, heading over to Stan's house. She turned on the radio, a catchy pop song filling the air. Jamie assumed it was because she couldn't take the silence. He understood, he couldn't either.

The sun's light played cheerfully between the leaves of the trees that surrounded Stan's beat-up house. Ivan was the last out of the car, waiting for everyone else to depart before getting out. Jamie could tell he wasn't quite ready to face Stan yet. The five of them stood outside Stan's house, Bradley being the one to knock once again. It felt strange to Jamie, being in a group like this. For the most part, he had always been alone. *Maybe it's better that way.* It didn't take long for Stan to answer the door, his white t-shirt all stained and his hair a mangled mess.

"God damn, what the hell happened to you?" Annette asked in shock.

"I had to get my mom to sleep," he mumbled, stumbling out of the house. The group cleared a way for him, allowing him to walk through clearly. He walked like a drunk man. Jamie watched as Annette leaned towards Vicky.

"I bet he killed her," he heard her whisper as he passed by. Vicky elbowed her in the arm, shooting her a glare. Stan and Bradley led the way, the others following close behind. Ivan brought up the rear, looking up at the trees or down at the ground. Jamie decided to drop back, feeling the strange urge to talk to him.

"Hey," he started, not knowing what to say next.

"Hello," Ivan responded without looking at him. His mind was somewhere else and Jamie wanted to find it.

"What happened yesterday?" Jamie asked, looking up at him. Ivan looked down at him with weary eyes.

"I don't want to talk about it."

"Please?" Ivan sighed, looking away from him once more.

"Stan's ghost grabbed me, pulled me into the water," he explained while grabbing a leaf off of a nearby tree. "I don't like the water." He turned the leaf around with his fingers.

"Why not?" Jamie asked, faintly noticing the rest of the group getting further ahead. Ivan took a moment to ponder, perhaps deciding in his head if he wanted to tell Jamie or not.

"When I was seven," he started to say calmly as he stared down at the leaf. "My father took me fishing. I caught a fish, but it was so big that it took my pole." Jamie looked up at Ivan, watching as he continued to twist the leaf with a sense of agility. "My father told me to go in and grab it, but I didn't want to. He forced me in anyways, told me I had to stay under until I found it." He paused, holding the leaf still in his hand. "He held my head under and..," he let the leaf go. "I never found the pole." Ivan fell silent. Jamie didn't know what to say, he also didn't know why Ivan decided to tell him that. "You don't have to respond," he added. "I just appreciate you listening." Jamie nodded his head.

"Thank you for telling me," he responded while looking up at Ivan. The group suddenly came to a halt up ahead, calling for the two boys who were lagging behind.

"Ivan, Jamie!" Bradley shouted. "We found it!" The two of them began to pick up their pace, nearly jogging by the time they caught up to where the group stood. They circled around a stump, staring at a small shoe that lay quietly next to it.

"And you're sure it's Mitchell's?" Annette questioned with her hands on her hips.

"Yes, just look at it," Bradley picked up the shoe and held it up to her, pointing to the pull tag. "See?" She grabbed the shoe, holding it up so she could see for herself.

"Oh, I guess it is," Annette admitted softly.

Jamie stepped closer, examining the shoe from a distance. He noticed something on the sides of the shoe as Annette stared at it.

"There's that black goo on it," Jamie noted, pointing to the side of the shoe. They all turned to look at him. Vicky immediately snatched the shoe out of Annette's hand without a word, turning it until she saw what he was talking about. A small gasp escaped from her mouth.

"What?" Bradley asked in confusion. Jamie noticed how out of it Stan was, his body wavering back and forth.

"We might be too late," Vicky muttered quietly, setting the shoe on the stump.

"Can someone explain?" Annette asked with a huff, looking around for answers.

"That same black goo shit was on a part of Peter Smith's shirt," Jamie responded with slight shock.

"It was probably on Rachel Bell's body too, we just didn't get the chance to see it," Vicky added before covering her face with her hands.

"That doesn't mean they're dead, does it?" Annette questioned nervously. Stan began to shake, but Jamie thought he might be the only one noticing it.

"I think it only shows up after their dead body leaves, or else the police would have seen it on them and made warnings about a toxic goo or something," Jamie speculated while still keeping an eye on Stan. Ivan must have also noticed it, his finger pointing at Stan almost accusingly as he continued to shake and waver. Bradley's focus turned to Stan, shaking him lightly while snapping his fingers.

"Stan, you alive in there?" He asked with another snap. Stan responded by falling to the ground, his body twitching like a dying bug. Ivan backed up, preparing for another attack. "Holy shit," Bradley stammered with a shake in his voice. His eyes rolled to the back of his head as he continued to twitch.

"What the fuck is happening?" Annette asked in horror.

"Let him go!" Bradley screamed. Stan stopped abruptly, the air going still.

"*You want him?*" A strange voice jeered. "*Do you want Mitchell?*" The five of them froze, looking around with wild eyes for what could be producing the voice. *Show yourself, pussy.* Jamie spoke in his mind as his eyes scanned the area. A flash of gray appeared in front of him, causing him to fall backward with a thump.

"Jamie!" Vicky yelled, jolting towards him. She quickly helped him up, brushing the dirt off of him gently. A gray creature floated above the stump, shining yellow eyes staring down at them.

"Here I am, Anderson." The creature teased with a large toothy grin. Its long and disfigured head was attached to a slender, wispy body with no legs. Its thin arms had three large claws at the end of them, each of them looking sickenly sharp. He was able to feel Vicky grip his hand, a look of terror placed upon her usually warm face. Ivan was frozen in fear, looking absolutely petrified. Bradley dragged Stan away from the stump while staring up at the gray figure. Annette stood next to Ivan, her expression a subtle look of surprise as if she couldn't believe what she was seeing.

"What are you?" Jamie questioned, trying to keep his voice from shaking.

"I think you already know," the creature hissed with a shiny grin. A flash of light caused them to all jump back and cover their eyes. Jamie could feel his eyes sting as he kept himself from falling. Jamie looked back with his arm still shielding his eyes. The others turned to look as well. Sitting on the stump was Richard Huxley, Linfort's most infamous serial killer.

Ivan Balakin

I have to get out of here. Ivan thought to himself quickly as the man on the stump stared at them wolfishly.

"Where's Mitchell?" Vicky yelled, holding Jamie close to her. The man let out a laugh that sounded like a mix of human and creature.

"Oh, *Mitchell*," he jeered while mocking a sob. "Poor, poor, *Mitchell*." He gestured a crying motion with his hands, his yellow eyes gleaming within the darkening forest. *Is it about to storm?* "Why don't you ask your dear friend, Stan?" The man snapped, causing Stan to sit up and gasp within a second.

"Stan, do *you* know where Mitchell is?" Jamie questioned him with an accusing glare. The man grabbed Stan by the arm, yanking him up from the ground.

"C'mon, Stan, tell your little friends what happened to poor old Mitchell West," the man sneered. Stan wavered back and forth, drifting in and out of consciousness. The man gave him a hard slap to the face, causing a small gasp to escape from Annette.

"Leave him alone!" Bradley hollered at the man, he was still on the ground covered in dirt. Stan stood upright, an angry red mark standing out against his pale skin.

"Last night," he started to say quietly.

"Speak up, boy." The man commanded, raising his hand threateningly.

"Last night," he repeated himself once again but louder. "I saw Mitchell in my dreams. He was being led into these woods, he was being led by him." He slowly pointed to the man on the stump, his head still down with his hair covering his eyes. "He led him here and he killed him." Ivan felt his throat clamp up, all he wanted to do was leave. "He killed Mitchell West," the man began to laugh with wild eyes.

"Tell them how Stanley, oh that's the best part!" The man howled, clutching his stomach as he continued to cackle in the darkened woods. Stan took in a shaky breath before speaking again.

"He bashed his head in," he quivered. The laughing continued, Ivan could feel his heart pounding in his chest. "He bashed his head in and dumped his body somewhere near the tracks." Stan finally lifted his head up. "He was crying."

"Stop it," Annette pleaded.

"He was crying for his mother," Stan continued.

"Stop it!" She yelled, holding her hands over her ears like a scared child. The rest remained in shock as the man continued to laugh. Ivan wanted to move, he wanted to run away, but he couldn't.

"Where is he?" Vicky questioned desperately. Stan began to clutch his head, his mouth turning back into a snarl. He looked as if he was in pain.

"I don't know! I don't know where he is!" He yelled as the man stopped laughing. Suddenly everything went quiet. The man's shape began to form once again, turning back into that ugly grayish creature.

"You'll make your choice soon," it hissed. The creature flew up from the stump, tunneling its way to Stan and forcing itself down his throat. Stan fell backwards, clutching his neck as he struggled to get air. Almost as soon as it happened, it was over, and he lay motionless on the ground. Bradley and Vicky ran towards him, shaking him with a sense of urgency. Ivan was able to regain control, no longer frozen in place. *I can't stay here.* He quietly turned around and quickly made his way out of the woods, his heart beating faster than a rabbit. He was almost out and into the clearing when he felt a hand grab his shirt.

"Ivan, please." Jamie. Ivan turned around to see a look of sincerity on Jamie's face.

"I can't, I don't want to be a part of this," Ivan pleaded. "Please let me go."

"I don't want to be a part of this either, but we're all we have," Jamie stated before letting go. "If that thing goes after you again, you have every right to leave," he reassured. "But for now, can you please just stay?" Ivan thought over it for a moment. As much as he wanted to leave, he had to get Jamie off his back. He sighed and nodded his head. *I'm not coming back after this.*

"Fine," he huffed. "I'll stay." Jamie let out a small smile.

"Thank you." *I just want to go home.* The two went back to rejoin the group, Stan sitting on the stump in a daze. The others stood around him nervously while watching with careful eyes.

"Stan, please say something," Bradley pleaded as he snapped his fingers at him while keeping his distance. His eyes seemed glossy, almost lifeless. *I hate being here.* A sudden burst of tears erupted from Stan, his hands immediately going to his face.

"Get him out of me," he sobbed behind his hands. "I don't want to live like this anymore." Vicky ran over to him, holding him close. Ivan noticed Jamie bite his lip.

"It's alright, we'll find something out, don't worry," she soothed, caressing his scruffy hair gently. Stan continued to cry as the others watched in an awkward sort of silence.

"How will we fix this?" Ivan whispered to Jamie. Jamie shrugged.

"I don't know, maybe there is no fixing it," he whispered back. Annette stormed off towards the tracks.

"Where are you going?" Bradley asked as he adjusted his glasses.

"I'm going to go look for Mitchell," she responded coldly with a steel gaze.

"He's dead!" Stan yelled out with a crack in his voice. "Didn't you hear him?" Vicky let him go, taking a few steps back as he got up from the stump.

"Annette, just stay here, let's figure this out together." Vicky pleaded.

"No, I want to find Mitchell," she hissed with commanding eyes.

"But he's dead!" Vicky objected.

"I don't believe him!" Annette retorted while pointing at Stan accusingly.

"Believe what you want, but it's true," Stan groaned. Ivan gave Jamie a nervous glance. *Please fix this, I don't think I can handle it anymore.* Jamie seemed to understand, clearing his throat as he stepped up.

"STOP!" He screamed, his loud voice traveling throughout the woods, followed by silence. "Let's just sit down and discuss things in a calm and collected manner," he suggested with a sense of clarity.

"Oh, like you could be calm and collected-" Annette snarked.

"Shut the fuck up, you mental bitch," Bradley snapped. Annette's jaw slammed closed in surprise. Ivan noticed Jamie smile briefly.

"So, let's just sit and talk," Jamie continued calmly. The group nodded their heads, walking carefully to the stump where Stan had sat. Ivan sat between Bradley and Jamie, his finger tapping on the side of his leg wildly. Annette sat down with a huff next to the exhausted Vicky. Stan sat back on the stump, his body shaking as if he were cold. "So," Jamie started, "let's talk. One at a time," he emphasized while glaring at Annette.

"We're wasting time, we have to look for Mitchell," Annette whined.

"But Stan said he died," Ivan mentioned quietly. Annette's face became red with anger.

"He could still be out there!" She yelled back, causing Ivan to flinch. "Can someone please just listen to me?" Her voice sounded desperate and tired. Stan stood up from the stump, looking down at them without much emotion.

"You want Mitchell? Let's go get him," he offered promptly. Annette paused, looking up at him with surprise before scrambling up from the ground. The rest followed suit, walking behind him as he led the group through the woods. Ivan stayed in the back again, feeling his heart beat wildly in his chest. He had no idea what he was going to see. He didn't want to know. Stan led them to the tracks, that's when they could first begin to smell it.

Vicky stayed back, as if she's seen something like this before and knew what to expect. Ivan heard Annette stifle a sob, her hands covering her mouth as she stared down at the tracks. Bradley threw up as Jamie looked away. Stan stood beside the body like some sort of grim reaper. Ivan stepped up to take a look, a feeling of regret soon took over. He didn't look recognizable; his face was mangled and disfigured. His skin peeled up, revealing flesh and bone underneath as ripped clothes exposed bright red and angry wounds. It looked as though an animal had gotten to him. He was missing an eye.

Ivan stepped away to empty his stomach. Annette turned around, tears falling down like rain. Stan continued to stand there, his face grim and unchanging.

"Is this what you wanted to see?" Jamie asked Annette harshly. "His corpse?" She shook her head in shock.

"No, no I just thought-" She mumbled to herself. "Alive." Ivan kept far away from the body, holding his head down with wide eyes. He didn't know what to do, he felt trapped and all he wanted to do was go home and forget about all of this. *I wish I never met any of these people.*

"Well, what the hell are we going to do now?" Bradley questioned with a crack in his voice.

"I don't know," Jamie answered.

"Should we call the cops?" Bradley suggested.

"I'm not sure, it might look suspicious on our part." Jamie shook his head. Vicky stepped up without looking at the corpse on the tracks.

"We have to give the West family closure," she said softly. "We can't just leave them wondering."

"God, this is too much," Bradley croaked while putting his hands on his head anxiously. "We shouldn't be the ones dealing with this."

"Well, your friend here is the cause of it," Jamie blamed. Stan's head shot up, his eyes wide and bloodshot.

"It's not his fault!" Bradley shouted. "He didn't choose to be this way!" Stan stepped down from the tracks, just beside the lifeless body of Mitchell West. It seemed as though the flies had found him before they did.

"No, he's right," Stan noted quietly. Bradley turned to look at him while adjusting his glasses, his mouth hung open slightly. "I shouldn't have touched the bone, none of us would have been here if I didn't do that."

"But there's no way you could have known," Vicky mentioned softly. "We'll find a way to fix all of this, we have to." Stan nodded his head.

"I just want all of this to be over," he fretted quietly.

"I know you do, we're going to help you," she soothed. She took him by the hand and led him away from the body. The rest followed closely behind until the tracks were out of sight.

"We have to find out this things limits," Jamie reccomended. "I mean, it's only killed like about a few hundred feet away from Stan's house, so obviously it can't go far."

"But I think I've seen it across town before," Vicky noted after Jamie finished speaking.

"Me too," Ivan added quietly.

"I think it can only be physical with us when Stan's nearby, Stan serves as a powersource for this thing," Jamie guessed promptly. "Sure, it can go wherever it wants, but it can only go so far before it can't touch us anymore."

"So are you saying that this thing can only go a mile from Stan before it can touch us?" Vicky asked.

"We can test it out," Bradley replied. Ivan winced at the idea of testing out anything at all.

"But how?" Annette whined, her eyes still red and teary.

"I think I know what we could do," Jamie said quickly. Suddenly, all eyes turned towards Stan.

Laura Gray

Laura Gray's eyes shifted to the bike that lay against the wall outside. She knew that no one was going to steal it (except for maybe Scott Carter), but she could never turn down the offer for a quick buck. Only one other person came in after the group of teens left, ordering nothing but a Coke and some fries. The place was running slowly, not good for business, but more preferable for her. She checked the clock. Her shift would be ending soon. She sighed, fixing her hair when she suddenly noticed the door open. Broad shoulders, dark skin with short afro hair, red letterman jacket, and a bumped nose bridge set below kind eyes. *Jeffrey Grant.* He stepped up to the front desk, his hands noticeably sweaty.

"Here, let me get you seated," she said in her best attempt at a customer service voice, the tone still turning out dry. He was much taller than her, forcing her to look up when speaking to him. He looked at her with an uneasy expression.

"No, it's okay. Do you have a second? I want to talk," he asked with a sense of worry. Laura raised her brow, checking the clock before turning back to Jeff.

"I guess so," Laura replied as she slowly led them both to a booth. The two sat down across from each other, Jeff having to squeeze in slightly to fit into the small booth. "So, what do you want to talk about?" She asked once they were both situated.

"I wanted to talk about Annette," Jeff told her with a nervous smile. Laura's emotionless eyes masked her feeling of surprise. Jeff seemed almost squeamish.

"What about her?" She questioned with a slight rise of the brow.

"She's been acting weird lately, and I was just wondering if you saw her stop by," Jeff voiced with sincerity. Laura wondered if she should tell him or not. *Hmm.*

"Yeah, she was totally here," she told him nonchalantly. Jeff's eyes widened with surprise. Laura couldn't help but let out a small, almost unnoticeable smile.

"Really? When?" He asked while putting his large hands on the table. She yawned before responding, her cat-like eyes narrowing in on him.

"I don't know, maybe a few hours ago," she noted promptly. "Couldn't tell you where they went though." Now Jeff was the one who looked confused.

"They?" He asked, concerned.

"Yeah, Annette, Vicky Taylor, Jamie Anderson, and Bradley Moore." Jeff seemed even more puzzled than before now.

"Jamie Anderson? Bradley Moore? You have to be joking," he scoffed in shock. She let out a light smile, nodding her head as she did.

"I know how it sounds, but they didn't stay for long," she explained softly. "They were in a rush." Jeff rubbed his face with a sigh.

"I don't understand, this isn't like her," he pondered with worry.

"Well, I'm getting paid to watch over Bradley Moore's bike if you want to wait around for them to come back," she offered as someone entered the diner. "I should probably get back to work now. Good luck or whatever," she scooted her way out of the booth and went back to her post, leaving Jeff to sit there by himself. Laura's friend Carrie Fraser stood waiting for her, her pale face full of surprise.

"Oh my god, Laura, you wouldn't believe what I saw today," she began with wide eyes.

"What?" Laura asked with her arms crossed. Carrie and Laura had very similar styles and interests, part of the reason why they were such close friends. The other reason was that they were all each other really had. It was pretty hard looking different in a small town.

"I saw Scott Carter and Thomas Cairns fist-fighting in the gas station parking lot," she responded dramatically, taking a moment to glance over at Jeff. Laura was taken aback.

"Really? I thought those two were friends or whatever," Laura noted in confusement.

"Yeah, me too! But they were totally handing it out," she agreed. Thomas, much similar to Scott, was a burnout with no sense of style. Almost every day he sported the same white tank top and stained blue jeans. He had long blonde hair and a large red birthmark on the side of his face. A real loser. Scott, on the other hand, had dark hair that went a little past his shoulders. His pale skin shone brightly beneath his baggy jacket and jeans. He was almost never seen without a cigarette. Laura knew he had the hots for her, but she had her eyes on someone else. Scott and Thomas seemed close, so why were they fighting?

"Maybe Jesse Olsen had something to do with it," Laura speculated. "He's a real mung." Carrie shook her head.

"No, he wasn't there. He was probably hiding from the cops or some shit like that," she replied with a giggle. Jesse and Scott were even closer than Thomas and Scott were. They would be spotted heading over to each other's houses late at night, most commonly being seen together. Scott seemed to almost idolize Jesse, stealing just as he did. But Scott would never come close to Jesse, who was deemed "the tooth fairy" by almost everyone in town. Laura didn't hear the whole story, but it was rumored that he had ripped his little sister's tooth out with pliers. He was the rotten egg of Linfort and the head honcho of those three dipshits.

"Most definitely," Laura agreed with an eye roll and a smile. Carrie leaned in while glancing over at Jeff.

"Okay, real talk, what the hell is Jeffrey Grant doing over there just sitting by himself?" She asked in a harsh whisper. Laura's smile remained on her pale face as she looked towards Jeff.

"Just wait for a bit and you'll see, I think some shit is gonna go down."

"Really?" Carrie's eyes widened in surprise.

"For sure." Jeff didn't even seem to notice the two girls talking about him, he kept his eyes towards the window beside him.

"How long do you think we have to wait for?" She asked softly. Laura turned to look towards the window herself.

"I don't know," she responded quietly. "But judging by the sun, not long." The sky was starting to turn into a light pink, white streaky clouds scattered across the sky lazily. They would be here soon.

Jeffrey Grant

Jeffrey Grant waited in the desolate diner, keeping his eyes glued to the window quietly. The sun was going down and he was becoming a little antsy. What was she doing with Jamie Anderson and Bradley Moore of all people? *I sure hope she's okay..* He knew Laura and Carrie Fraser were talking about him, judging by their frequent glances, but he pretended not to notice. Right now, they were the least of his worries. He was beginning to debate on if he should order anything before a car pulled into the small parking lot. It was Vicky's Monte Carlo.

His eyes widened as he sat up in his seat, briefly noticing the two girls turn to look too. He watched as Bradley jumped out of the car, going towards his bike on the wall. The rest soon followed. Vicky was next, getting out of the driver's side to stretch for a moment. After Vicky was Jamie, but he only went out momentarily to say something to Vicky before getting back into the vehicle. The last one out was Annette, getting out of the backseat before making her way towards the diner. She didn't go inside, she just lit a cigarette before leaning up against the old building. That was Jeff's cue to go outside.

He got up from the small booth and made his way outside, ignoring the stares from the two girls at the counter. The warm summer air welcomed him as he went through the diner's glass doors and towards Annette.

"Annette!" He called out, her eyes wide with surprise upon noticing him. She quickly scuffed out her cigarette before turning towards him.

"Jeff? What the hell are you doing here?" She asked with that accusing stare of hers. Vicky and Bradley shifted their attention to the couple, watching in silence as the two confronted each other.

"I could ask the same for you, what are you doing hanging out with him?" He asked while pointing to Bradley. "I thought you hated him," he then turned towards the dork who was messing with his bike. "Which by the way, I am so sorry she acts that way towards you, you did nothing wrong little dude," he reassured. Bradley stood there with his bike in silent confusion as Jeff turned his attention back to Annette. "Please, just tell me what's going on. You can talk to me," he pleaded. She shook her head.

"I can't. Just get out of here, Jeff; you don't want to get involved," she begged while pushing him away weakly.

"Get involved with what?" He asked in desperation. Vicky shot Annette a look.

"Nothing, just go home, Jeff," she told him before back to the car. Jeff sighed, knowing he shouldn't push her. He turned to see if Bradley was still there, but he was already gone. *Dammit.* Annette slammed the backdoor close, startling Jeff out of his daze as they pulled out of the diner's parking lot. Laura and Carrie came outside, standing beside him as he watched them drive off.

"Already gone?" Laura asked smugly, stuffing her hands in her pockets.

"Bummer," Carrie added with a shrug. Jeff put his head down in shame, unable to fully understand what just happened.

"I'm gonna bounce out of here," he told them with disappointment. "Thanks for the help," he added as he made his way towards his car.

"No problem," Laura called out as he entered the driver's seat. He slammed his head on the wheel before starting the car, giving him a second to think. *What is she keeping from me? Why are they all so secretive?* He sighed. *I wish she would just talk to me.* He lifted his head up with weary eyes, putting the car in reverse as the sun's light began to dim. He began to wonder if he'd ever truly understand what went on in her head. He loved her so much, but he wasn't completely sure if she felt the same. He pulled out of the parking lot, watching the two girls go back into the diner. *This has to be my fault.* He felt sick to his stomach, not knowing what to do. Everything was so complicated. His car dinged, and he was almost out of gas.

He turned around, making his way to the gas station as the sky continued to darken. He wanted to turn on the radio to drown out his thoughts but couldn't bring himself to do it. He focused on the road, trying to get his mind off the strange situation that he was currently in. He drove past multiple buildings mindlessly as the gas station later came into view. The sky was dark when pulling into the desolate parking lot, birds settling down for the night. He rubbed his face tiredly before opening his car door and clambering out. A shadowy figure slinked towards him as he began to make his way to the small building.

"Heyy, Grant! How's it goin', my man?" *Scott Carter.* Jeff silently prepared himself for the conversation he was about to have before forcing out a small smile, but upon further inspection, he noticed a black eye and a bloody nose.

"Jesus dude, what happened to you?" He asked, bewildered by Scott's pitiful appearance.

"Oh, this?" He asked while pointing to his wounded eye. "Thomas fucking Cairns. Can you believe it?" Jeff shook his head. He indeed could not believe it. Scott wiped the blood from his nose, smiling at Jeff with a cigarette clenched in between sharp teeth.

"What happened?" Jeff questioned again nervously. Scott shrugged, taking the cigarette out of his mouth before wiping his nose again.

"Didn't take too well to being called a mama's boy," Scott jeered with a shit eating grin. Jeff was sure there was something else to it, but didn't want to push him any further. The sound of the gas station doors could be heard closing nearby, causing Scott to jump a little. "Say, Jeffrey, would it be possible if I could hitch a ride with you? I got a long way back, and-"

"Sure, why not?" Jeff agreed with a sigh as he gestured toward his car. Scott let out another slick smile, the blood from his nose dripping onto his lips and teeth.

"Thanks, man! I really appreciate it," he replied before patting Jeff on the back and making his way over to the passenger seat. Jeff started towards the building to pay as the fluorescent gas station lights illuminated his path. He was immediately greeted with cool air and the sound of cheesy pop music. A very tired-looking Gus welcomed him without much enthusiasm.

"Aye, Grant, do me a favor and do my job for me, wouldya?" He joked with a squinty-eyed grin. "I'm ready for this week to be over already." Jeff let out a light laugh.

"But it's only Tuesday," he noted with a smile as he pulled out the money from his back pocket.

"That's just it, Grant, it's *only* Tuesday."

"Yeah, you've gotta point there," Jeff agreed with a laugh as he put his money on the counter. "Fifteen on pump one, please."

"You got it," Greg said before stuffing the bills in the register and unlocking the pump.

"Have a nice night, Gus."

"Yeah, you too, kid." Jeff shoved his hands in his pockets and made his way towards the door, almost bumping into Thomas Cairns. There wasn't a scratch on him besides the red of his birthmark. *So he's still hanging around here.* He ignored him and went for his car, getting ready to fill up. As his vehicle was fueling up, his mind began to wander. He didn't understand why Annette was acting so strangely. He wanted to be there for her, but she just kept distancing herself from him. *Did I do something wrong?* He frowned, feeling himself begin to spiral as the nozzle suddenly clicked. He sighed, putting it back and closing the gas cap before hopping into his car. He started the engine as Scott's eyes burned into him.

"You saw him in there, didn't you?" Scott asked with slight worry. Jeff hesitated for a moment, briefly forgetting who he was talking about, before he remembered.

"Yeah," he admitted, almost as if it were his fault. Scott slammed his hands on the dashboard.

"I knew it! He was totally waiting for me, dude!" Scott cried out as he put his hands on his head. Jeff looked down at him with concern, not knowing what to do. "Just drive, man. Just drive," he answered for him without lifting his head. Jeff did what he was told and pulled out of the gas station parking lot.

"Where to?" Jeff asked meekly, not going in any particular direction.

"Just take me home," Scott muttered, lifting his head to look out the window. "You know where I live, right?" Jeff thought for a moment.

"Past King Street?" Jeff asked hesitantly. Scott took out a cigarette and a lighter while nodding his head.

"Yeah, a few blocks past King Street," he directed as he lit up the cigarette. Jeff would rather his car not smell like smoke, but decided against telling him to put it out. He turned the car around and made his way towards King Street, rolling down the windows for the smoke to escape. "Could you turn on the radio?" Scott asked while sticking his arm out the window and kicking his feet up on the dashboard. "It's too quiet." Jeff did as he asked and turned on the radio. He had no idea why he was giving this guy a ride, and quite frankly, just wanted to go home. "All the music on the radio is absolute shit, they only play mainstream garbage." He complained after blowing smoke out the window. "Did you know that?" Jeff shook his head, he wasn't much of a music guy himself.

"What kind of music are you into?" Jeff asked as he drove under the light of the streetlamps above.

"You probably wouldn't know," he replied with a shrug.

"Hit me," he said, even though he knew Scott was most likely right. Scott turned to look at him with a slightly excited expression.

"I listen to music with a gross, grimy sound to it, totally underground shit." He answered before snuffing out his cigarette on his boot and throwing it out the window.

"You're right, I don't know what that is," Jeff admitted with a laugh.

"Well, I'll just have to show you then," Scott offered lightly. "Come over to my place sometime, I can show you some songs and something I've been working on myself."

"You make music?" Jeff asked with slight surprise as a car whirred past.

"Hell yeah I do! Who do you take me for, ol' Jeffy?" Scott jested with a laugh as he slapped the dashboard with a wild hand. Jeff smiled. Scott wasn't too bad.

"Yeah? I'll have to take up your offer sometime," Jeff agreed with sincerity.

"How about sometime before summer break starts?"

"Deal." The two smiled and fell silent again as Jeff continued down the empty road. There was a question burning in his mind that he knew he had to ask. He paused, taking in a deep breath before saying anything. "If you don't mind me asking, why do you hang out with Jesse Olsen?" Scott didn't say anything for a moment, his gaze straight forward and listless.

"He's all I got." He started to say with a sigh. "He's not a bad guy. I mean, I know of the rumors but.." He trailed off for a second. "At the end of the day, they're just rumors." Scott turned away, keeping his eyes glued to the window. Jeff thought over what Scott said as he tapped his finger on the steering wheel.

"He doesn't have to be *all you have*. Why don't you come sit with me during lunch or something?" Jeff offered smoothly. There was a pause before Scott erupted into laughter, causing Jeff to slightly jump. He quickly turned from the window to look at Jeff with a large smirk spread across his face.

"Sit at the football table, are you kidding? That would be like.. Like you sitting with a bunch of geeks. Or- Or, Alan Giblin sitting with all the cheerleaders or something," he quickly spat out with another laugh. Jeff thought about it in his head for a moment.

"Okay, then why don't I sit with you?" Scott stopped laughing, but a small grin remained.

"Nah, you wouldn't wanna do that, big guy. What would they think if you just came over and sat with me instead of them?" He asked Jeff softly.

"To be honest, Scott, I don't care about their opinion as much as some people may think I do. They're cruel, brash, and disrespectful. I don't need that around me."

"But they got a good image on the outside," Scott noted.

"I've never really cared about the outside, that never matters in the end." Scott didn't say anything, and neither did Jeff. They shared the silence as he drove past King Street and towards Scott's house. Fresh air and soft music from the radio filled the inside of the vehicle as he turned onto his street. He always felt some sort of serenity at night, a type of ease that was only really amplified by the sight of the moon and stars. Nothing beats a summer night in Linfort. Scott suddenly broke the silence.

"Thank you, by the way. I don't think I really told you that yet," he mentioned quietly while staring out the open window. Jeff turned to look at him briefly before focusing on the road again.

"It's really no problem, man."

"No, thank you for caring." Jeff paused for a second. It was so out of nowhere, but he understood.

"Of course," he told Scott calmly as he pulled into his driveway. Scott stayed seated, facing forward in silence while Jeff parked the car. "Someday, something will change," he suddenly turned to face Jeff, staring at him for a moment before turning away. He opened the car door and stepped into the warm summer air.

"Stay safe," Jeff said blankly.

"Yeah, you too." And just like that, he was gone, disappearing into the dark after a slam of the door. Jeff sat there for a moment before pulling out of the driveway and disappearing into the night himself.

Scott Carter

Scott Carter left Jeff's car in a hurry and swiftly made his way inside, slinking past his parents who were watching television in the living room. He stared at them for a moment, making sure their focus was tuned to the TV before silently creeping toward the kitchen. He quickly pulled some ice out of the freezer for his black eye, the pain ebbing into his head. He closed the freezer door, holding the ice up to his eye in the darkness. With a wince, he made his way to his room as quietly as he could.

"Son?" His dad called from the living room. *Shit.*

"Yeah?" Scott called back, stopping in his tracks. His dad lowered the volume on the tv, turning his attention to Scott.

"Where were you?" Scott paused, thinking over his words carefully. The ice in his hand began to drip, leaving drops of water all over the floor.

"I uh," he stammered, clearing his throat. "I went to the gas station to get some gum," Scott explained, taking another step forward. Depending on his mood, his dad could be a little testy. Sometimes it would be nearly impossible to tell how that man was feeling, Scott finding it best to just avoid him completely. He was just hoping his dad was feeling good tonight.

"Hm, alright," he replied, seemingly accepting that response. Scott let out a small sigh of relief, quickly retreating down the hallway. He silently creaked his door open and slipped inside his darkened room, flopping onto the mattress soon after. He thought about his encounter with Thomas as the ice dripped onto his comforter, causing a small wet spot to form. He *did* get gum at the gas station, but he was really there for his cigarettes. What Scott got instead was an enraged Thomas Cairns punching him in the gut as soon as he turned the corner. The fight didn't last long, and Scott tried talking things out with him to no avail. They both lingered around the gas station for a bit, that was, until Jeff showed up. He wasn't sure why Jeff did what he did, but he was thankful nonetheless.

His thoughts were soon disrupted by a knocking on his window, causing him to jump up in surprise. He quickly got up and ripped open the curtains, revealing a familiar face. Jesse Olsen. His smile widened as soon as he saw Scott, revealing his sharp teeth.

"Little piggy, little piggy, let me in," he taunted from the other side, his eyes narrowing above his already unsettling smile. Scott did as he asked, opening the window for him, but not before tossing the half-melted ice away. Jesse jumped in before Scott could even open it all the way. "I've got news, Scotty," Jesse hissed, his teeth almost gleaming in the dark.

"Yeah, yeah, alright. Just keep it down, don't want my folks knowing you're here," he grumbled while glaring at the door. Jesse welcomed himself to the mattress on the floor, stretching out like he owned the place. Scott sighed and sat next to him in the dark. "So, what's the news?" He asked with a bored expression. Jesse sat up, his eyes widening.

"That cunt Taylor is up to something," he disclosed with a toothy grin.

"Vicky?"

"Vicky Taylor."

"Why do you care?" Scott questioned with a raised brow.

"Because that little bitch ratted me out, I know she did," he snapped harshly, eyes narrowing.

"When you stole from that old convenience store?"

"Yes, she was the only one there, and I just know she ratted me out," he hissed.

"Okay, so what are you planning to do about it?"

"That's the fun part," his smile returned. Scott felt his heart drop a little.

"What?" No response. There was a long pause. Scott heard the click of a lighter, a dull light shining on his face.

"Thomas really fucked you up, huh?" Scott felt his face flush with embarrassment, turning his head away slightly.

"You should see him," he boasted with a crack in his voice.

"I did." The light disappeared and Jesse put the lighter away. "You didn't do shit to him," he sneered.

"Yeah whatever, I wasn't prepared," Scott mumbled.

"Don't worry, I'll take care of him," Jesse stated calmly. Scott felt his heart drop once again, he knew what Jesse was capable of.

"No, you don't have to do any of that." Scott urged with his hands out. "It was my fault, I stole from him."

"You stole from Thomas Cairns?" Jesse asked with wide eyes.

"Yeah, that's our thing. It's what we do," Scott told him. "Steal, roughen each other up a bit, nothing serious." Jesse narrowed his eyes at him. "It's fine."

"What did you steal?" He questioned with a raised brow. Scott bit his lip before responding.

"That watch he'd been workin' for" he replied with a small smirk. Jesse's eyes lit up.

"No way! Can't believe you managed that," he gleamed before slapping him on the back. Scott shrugged as if it were no big deal, feeling a small sense of pride build within him. Jesse started fumbling with something in his pocket as the two dipped into a brief silence.

"So, how'd you get home?" Jesse asked as he pulled out his lighter once more, this time to light a cigarette.

"Hitched a ride from someone," Scott answered nonchalantly.

"Who?"

"Doesn't matter." Jesse blew smoke into Scott's face, causing him to cough.

"Wanna get out of here?" Scott thought over it for a moment.

"I've had a long day, I kinda just want to go to sleep." He replied with a forced yawn.

"Suit yourself, pussy." Jesse jeered while getting off the mattress, stretching his arms high up in the air.

"Well, what are you going to do tonight, hotshot?" Scott asked with a raised brow.

"Whatever the hell I feel like doing," Jesse declared with a slick grin, going towards the window.

"Whatever," Scott shrugged to himself. Jesse reopened the window, the cool summer air seeping inside. The light from the moon illuminated Jesse's face in an eerie way. His large scar standing out like a lone star engulfed in darkness, as he wore his long, rough, brown hair in a low ponytail.

"Cya, Scotty," Jesse said as he began to climb out the window. Scott's head shot up.

"Wait," he called out to him. Jesse paused, turning his head like a deer in headlights.

"What?" He asked, standing halfway outside.

"You're not going to do anything to Thomas, are you?" Scott asked, a tad skeptical. Jesse smiled.

"Nah, you can take care of yourself," he soothed. Scott nodded his head.

"Alright," he concluded. "I'll catch you around."

"Later," Jesse quickly scrambled outside and disappeared into the night. Scott closed his window before laying back down on the mattress, shutting his eyes without falling asleep just yet. Maybe everyone was right about Jesse, or maybe, Scott saw something in him that no one else did. They had been friends for over three years now, and Jesse understood him like no other. His parents never liked him, seeing him for who he was right away but Scott didn't give a damn. His parents didn't approve of his lifestyle much anyways. Maybe Jesse was a bit unpredictable, but wasn't everyone? In the end, Scott didn't care about the rumors. He didn't care about anything. He yawned, flipping to his side before drifting into an unwakeable slumber just as he told Jesse before.

Jesse Olsen

Jesse Olsen made his way down the street, avoiding the streetlamps above. He took out a cigarette, lighting it with his hands gently. He looked up at the night sky, the stars glistening in the distance. There were still a reasonable amount of people out and about as it wasn't very late yet. Jesse kept to himself, lurking within the shadows of the night. He quietly listened to the sound of his footsteps, taking a drag from his cigarette. He took this time to think, finding comfort within his surroundings.

He knew of the rumors, but only he knew what was and wasn't true. The large scar on his cheek was rumored to be caused by his father. But Jesse knew this wasn't true. He knew that his scar was caused by slashing his face with a rock he had formed into a makeshift blade to see how much he could take. The rock was from a chipped part of a boulder that lay silently in the middle of Linfort's maze, something he kept safe inside his unkempt room. Jesse was the truth.

He continued down the street, feeling the hateful gaze of those who walked past him. He didn't care, in fact, he enjoyed those small moments of attention. He walked everywhere he went because of this, to feel the look of hate burning in the back of his head. He was Linfort's only villain, the thing to gossip about when there's nothing else to talk about. *And god did it feel good.* He began to hum.

He felt at peace. The night welcomed him with loving arms, the air feeling like warm bath water. He was almost there. Almost nowhere in Linfort was very far. He picked up the pace, humming the tune of Swan Lake. He wasn't a fan of classical music, but he had an appreciation for Tchaikovsky and his work. He paused to take another drag off his cigarette, continuing after blowing out the smoke. He threw his head back to look at the stars. Tonight was his night, his to take in.

He picked out any final thoughts before making it to his destination. For a moment, he stood and waited. Waited for a sign to go in, waited for a sign to take it. A sign to take his night. He stood across the street, waiting. Pondering. Fireflies flew around him like sentient stars. He stood still, almost completely unmoving except for his eyes. He didn't know why he was making such a big deal out of nothing. All he wanted to do was talk. He scuffed his cigarette and took a step forward, a step towards Thomas Cairns's house.

Knock, pause, knock. He patiently waited for a response, staring at the door intently with a small grin. He was soon met with Mrs. Cairns, her name being something Jesse never cared to find out.

"Oh Jesse, what a pleasant surprise!" Judging by the look on her face, it was not a pleasant surprise. "What brings you here?" She asked with squinted eyes and a forced smile.

"I was in the area, figured I would stop by to see how ol' Thomas is doing." He explained smoothly. "Do you know if he's home?" He could have sworn her eye twitched at the sound of his question. *No, now get the hell out of here. I don't want a filthy criminal like you stepping foot in my home,* he imagined she'd say if she wasn't so keen on being polite. The thought made him want to laugh, but he kept his composure.

"I believe he's in the basement if you want to come in," she offered warmly, probably wanting to bite off her own tongue.

"Thank you kindly," he replied with a wide grin, wanting to bite off her tongue as well. She cleared the way, allowing him to step into their home and infect it with his filth. He made his way towards the basement and down the stairs, pausing between every step. He wanted his presence to be known. He spotted Thomas on the couch reading a book. He stepped forward. Jesse still hadn't been noticed. He pulled the lighter back out of his pocket, dropping it on the floor and grabbing the attention of Thomas, taking it for himself.

"Jesse, what the hell are you doing here?" Thomas asked in bewilderment, setting the book down beside him. Jesse smiled, picking the lighter up and off the ground.

"Just wanted to check up on you," he stated while making his way towards the couch next to the visibly tense Thomas. He scooted away slightly, keeping his mistrusting eyes on Jesse.

"I know what this is about," Thomas blurted with unease. Jesse smiled.

"Yeah?"

"It's about me getting in a little scuffle with Scott, right?" His eyes stayed glued to Jesse. Jesse only continued to smile. "Look, he stole from me, alright? You gotta understand," Thomas spat out quickly. "He needs to lay off, I worked really hard for that watch." Jesse just sat there, staring blankly at him with that same look on his face. "God dammit, Jesse, say something!" He yelled, his hair practically standing up on the back of his neck.

"You calling Scotty a thief?" Jesse asked with that same shit eating grin.

"He's a goddamn thief, Jesse." Thomas hissed, his eyes narrowing as if he had suddenly gained confidence. "And your little boy toy doesn't need you to be sicked after me, just stay out of it." Jesse's smile faded along with Thomas's confidence.

"You calling me a queer?" Jesse snarled. Thomas paused, not knowing if he should hold his ground or not.

"Maybe, you sure act like it," Thomas grumbled with a crack in his voice. Wrong choice. Something in Jesse snapped, and within a flash, he had Thomas pinned by the throat against the couch. His arms were held down by the weight of Jesse's legs. He didn't leave any time to react.

"I'll make this quick for you," he challenged as Thomas struggled beneath him. With his other hand, Jesse reached for the pliers in his back pocket. He never left the house without them. Jesse knew that rumor was true. Thomas's eyes widened at the sight of the pliers, causing him to struggle even more. For a moment, Jesse thought he might actually escape his grip, but he quickly overpowered the fearful teen. "Hmm, which tooth should I pick?" Jesse asked himself, that smile from before returning once again. He picked a molar on the left side of his mouth. He knew Thomas wouldn't scream for help, he was too full of pride. But just in case, he would do as he promised and make it quick.

He inched the pliers closer to his teeth, teasing him before ultimately plunging them into his mouth. Thomas squirmed violently beneath him, trying desperately to get away as the pliers were guided towards the target. Beads of sweat rolled down his forehead like rain, the smell of fear filling Jesse's nose.

"Please," Thomas mouthed around the pliers, begging for any sort of forgiveness. It was too late, Jesse had already tried to hold his cool.

"Not this time, Tommy," Jesse shook his head as he closed his pliers around the chosen tooth. With the same grin he gave his sister, he began to pull at Thomas's molar. The panic really started to fill in now, muffled noises of fear emitted from Thomas as he attempted to jerk his limbs away. "Are you ready, Thomas?" Thomas shook his head. "No?" Thomas then nodded his head, tears beginning to form. Jesse shrugged. "Too bad." With all of his force, he ripped Thomas's molar out of his mouth, a hot rush of blood filling in the gap. Thomas let out a cry, his eyes wide and bloodshot. Lucky for Jesse, nobody seemed to hear his scream.

Jesse examined the bloody tooth carefully as Thomas wailed quietly in pain beneath him. Once he felt satisfied, he pocketed the tooth and pliers and got off of Thomas.

"What the fuck is wrong with you?" Thomas yelled as he grabbed for his bloody mouth. Jesse turned around, looking at him as if he were nothing.

"Tell anyone about this, and I'll slit your fucking throat, okay?" He told him calmly. Thomas stared at him for a moment before nodding, blood dripping from his hands that covered his mouth and onto the concrete below. Jesse picked up the book he was reading calmly before all of this happened, holding it up to his bloody face. "If anyone asks, you got a papercut," he jeered with a smile before throwing the book to the ground.

He left Thomas there like that, knowing confidently that he wouldn't tell a soul about his visit from the tooth fairy. He made his way back up the stairs, pausing before every step just as he did before. *I only wanted to talk.* He left without saying goodbye, closing the door quietly behind him. *He was the one that caused it.* He started back down the street, and as he did, he would hum Swan Lake.

Mike Evans

Mike Evans stared down at the lifeless body of Mitchell West with a cold gaze. The station had gotten an anonymous call from what sounded like a child on the other line. But the kid knew where Mitchell was, and that's all that mattered. Kenneth Hudson stood next to him in silent shock, his hand covering his mouth as he stared down at the mangled body.

"I can't keep doing this," he muttered quietly. It seemed as though the flies had found his body as well.

"It's our job," Evans responded gruffly. Hudson turned around, looking sick to his stomach.

"I know, but christ, Mike," he stammered before rubbing his face. "They're just kids." He hadn't yet broken the news to Mitchell's family, unready to go through all of that once again. He planned to have Hudson do it, he was better with people anyway. Evans waited for a moment, the sun's rays shining through the leaves of the trees above.

"Alright, let's inform the coroner," Evans concluded with a wave of the hand. Hudson sighed as if a weight had been lifted off of him, making his way to the cruiser in a brisk fashion. Evans wasn't far behind, not wanting to be there much longer himself. He got in the driver's side before pulling out his walkie.

"Did you find him? Hudson won't say anything," Christopher Brown asked from the back seat of the cruiser. Against Evans' wishes, they brought Chris with them so he could feel important. But against Chris's wishes, they figured it would be better if he just stayed in the car.

"Yeah," he grumbled sullenly. "We found him."

"Is he-"

"Yes," Hudson answered quietly. Chris went silent. Evans informed the station of the current situation, telling them to call the coroner. Now all they had to do was wait. The sun's rays danced lightly inside the car as a subtle breeze came in through the windows. The polite sound of birds could be heard from a distance and for a moment, Evans felt at peace.

"What happened to him?" Of course, Chris had to ruin it. Evans sighed.

"Presumably, he got hit by a train," Evans replied while staring blankly at the house in front of the cruiser. His eyes began to narrow. "You remember that freaky lady from a few days ago, Chris?" Evans asked suddenly. Hudson shot him a look of confusion. Chris nodded his head.

"Yeah, I remember. Why do you ask?" His head perked up a little.

"I think she has something to do with it," he answered sullenly.

"But it looked like a train hit him-" Hudson began to say.

"You can *make* a murder look like anything." They all fell silent. "Fuck this, I'm going over there," Evans decided before opening the door of the cruiser.

"Mike, wait!" Hudson yelled out to him, but it was already too late. Evans stomped his way towards the house, listening to the sound of car doors opening behind him.

"Evans!" Chris shouted. *Don't get any closer.* A mysterious voice hissed in his ear. It seemed as though time itself paused as he stood in the middle of the street, halfway towards the house. *That's right, just stand right there.* The voice sounded inhuman, but he felt as though it was familiar. He started to feel cold, a drift traveling through his shirt and piercing through his skin. He stepped backward, stumbling back into reality. He was able to feel the sensation of Christopher shaking him, able to feel his panic. He jolted his head up, scanning the area quickly. Nothing.

"Mike?" Hudson's voice caused him to jump, his heart racing slightly.

"I heard something," he told them roughly, "it was him."

"It was who?" Hudson asked softly. Evans' head began to throb again.

"I don't know." He looked down as Hudson and Chris exchanged similar looks of confusion.

"Is everything alright?" Hudson asked nervously. Evans shot him a glare before rubbing his temples. He didn't respond, he just continued to massage his head.

"Get back in the cruiser."

"What?"

"Just do what I say." Chris gave him an uneasy look, reluctantly doing as he commanded. Evans returned his attention back to the rugged house. His vision became blurry, he felt faint. He stepped closer, that cold feeling from before returning once again. *God dammit, just leave already!* He heard the voice scream. It was time for him to go. He turned around, rushing towards the cruiser. Hudson and Chris sat in silent fear as he quickly started the cruiser.

"We can't just leave, Mike," Hudson stated as they sped down the street. Evans' eye twitched.

"You didn't hear it," he mumbled under his breath, sweat dripping down from his forehead. Chris remained silent in the back seat, his eyes wide with concern. "It was right there."

"What was?" Hudson asked desperately. Evans didn't answer. "Mike?" Hudson's voice felt far away, everything did. He suddenly felt very sick. He stopped the cruiser to get out, throwing up all over the pavement below. He didn't stop until he began dry heaving. With a shaky arm, he reached back towards the cruiser for support, his legs wanting to buckle beneath him. He looked down at the throwup, noticing something odd about it. As his head became more clear, he was able to spot a black substance within his pile of vomit. *This is your first warning.* The voice hissed. *Don't come back.*

Bradley Moore

"I don't really like this idea," Bradley complained while adjusting his glasses nervously.

"Yeah, I'm not really too sure about this either," Stan agreed. Jamie had waited until Thursday after school to tell them about his idea, having them all meet up at the park. Bradley personally thought Jamie didn't even have an idea and needed time to think it over.

"It's either you or Annette, Bradley," Jamie stated with his arms crossed.

"If you're gonna use anyone as bait, it should be Ivan," Annette joked as she put on her lip gloss. "He's too much of a pushover to say no anyway."

"Oh," Ivan turned his head away in embarrassment. Nobody really knew why Ivan came back, but it was suspected that Jamie swayed him once again. He seemed to have an odd way with Ivan, a sort of gentleness that he only showed to a select few. Bradley knew for a fact he was not one of those few.

"We shouldn't use anyone as bait!" Vicky spat out. Bradley groaned.

"It's fine, I'll do it," Bradley finalized with a crack in his voice.

"Are you sure?" Stan asked with a look of concern. Bradley nodded his head.

"Yeah, why not." He got up from the wooden bench, stretching his legs a little as he did. Jamie's plan was very simple. All he had to do was go a mile down the street and then they'd handle the rest. The six of them made their way towards the street, Bradley separating from the rest of the group. His heart was pounding in his chest, his mind racing. Now he could see why Jamie had them wait. He didn't want to give anyone enough time to think about backing out. He started to feel stupid for agreeing to this. He kept walking until he felt as though there was a mile between them, adjusting his glasses before he turned to face them. Now all he had to do was wait.

He stood there, palms sweaty as the sun beat down on him. His throat was dry and he suddenly wanted more than anything not to be here. *Why did I agree to this?* He could faintly hear Jamie screaming something, causing what looked like Stan to step backward. They all looked so small from the distance between them, making it difficult for Bradley to understand what was happening. He noticed someone part from the group, adjusting his glasses and squinting his eyes. He could hear more yelling, this time coming from Annette. With each passing second he became more and more anxious. A feeling of nausea building within him. *I just want to get this over with.*

A sudden burst of energy exited Stan's body, causing him to fall to the ground. Bradley's body tensed, he was frozen in fear. The thing traveled towards him at rapid speed, its body warping as it came closer. Bradley could only stand there and watch. He could now see the creature's face, gray and ugly. Its sharp teeth shone in the light, large claws outstretched and reaching for him. It would only be a matter of seconds before he'd be torn to shreds. He braced himself for the impact, squinting his eyes shut while gritting his teeth.

He felt nothing. He opened his eyes to see the creature's tall figure staring down at him with anger. Its yellow eyes pierced into Bradley's petrified face.

"You lucky little shit," it hissed. Bradley could only let out a small whimper as he stared up in fear. The creature grinned, showing its sharp teeth. "I know what you're all doing," it mentioned. "I'll let you all do your little experiments, this helps me as well, you know." It stuck its arm through Bradley, causing him to flinch. "See? Nothing. Now let me let you in on a secret Bradley, let me help you out," it jeered. "I cannot touch you within a mile radius of Stan, but inside that radius? It's free game. Do you understand that, Bradley?" Bradley nodded his head. Its grin widened. "Now that you know the rules, let's play." The creature disappeared, the last thing to leave being its eyes.

Bradley stood there in complete shock, not fully understanding what just happened. He faintly noticed the others running towards him, all except for Ivan, who was trailing behind. He forced himself to walk forward, feeling strange as he did. It didn't take long for them to meet up with each other, each of them asking their own questions.

"Was it able to touch you?" Jamie asked with wide eyes, pushing his way to the front.

"Are you okay?" Stan asked next, his face full of worry.

"What happened?" Annette questioned frantically.

"Can you all give him some space?" Vicky stressed. Bradley snapped out of his daze, his eyes widening. For once, they were all paying attention to him. He had the floor. He took a deep breath.

"No, he wasn't able to touch me, yes I'm okay, and I don't really know." He answered quickly as Ivan continued to make his way down the street, dragging his feet behind him.

"What did it say to you?" Jamie asked. Bradley thought over it for a moment, replaying what happened in his head. A cool breeze washed over everyone as he did.

"Said that outside of a mile radius from Stan, it can't touch us, but inside is free game," Bradley explained. "It also said that these were the rules of the game we're playing." They all exchanged looks of confusion as Ivan finally joined the group, keeping a distance from everyone.

"What game?" Annette asked.

"I don't know, it just said we know the rules now." He replied. "What about you, Stan? Did this affect you at all?" Bradley questioned, turning his attention to Stan.

"I just felt faint is all, I think it takes some of my energy when leaving my body like that." He explained quietly.

"Do you get your energy back when it reenters your body?" Jamie asked with wonder. Stan nodded.

"I think so, I feel like a sort of electric shock when it comes back inside. It's like I'm being hit by some invisible force." Stan replied. They all fell silent, standing aimlessly on the road. The soft white clouds rolled above them, making the otherwise tense air feel calm.

"What now?" Ivan questioned, finally speaking up. Everyone turned to look at him, making him shrink inside himself a tiny bit.

"I'm not sure," Stan replied. "I guess we just play it's game?" Bradley nodded his head in agreement. Annette groaned.

"Whatever, I'm going home." She announced with an eye roll as she started down the street and towards her car.

"Why?" Vicky asked in bewilderment, chasing after her a little.

"Because I'm not about to play games with ghosts today, I have better things to do!" She shouted without looking back.

"Like what, sleeping with half the school?" Jamie hollered with a grin.

"Go to hell, Anderson!" Annette yelled, flipping him the bird with a snarl. Bradley let out a small snicker as Annette continued down the street. Ivan sighed.

"I'm going to leave too," he stated quietly. Bradley didn't have to ask to know why he wanted to leave, everyone knew he didn't want to be there in the first place.

"Cya," Bradley said without much enthusiasm.

"Bye." Ivan made his way back to the park, leaving everyone behind to stand in silence. Vicky exchanged an exhausted look with Jamie.

"We should probably go too, we have finals to study for," Vicky noted with a forced smile. Jamie nodded his head in silent agreement. Stan rubbed his face with his hands.

"Alright," he responded tiredly. The two made their way back to Vicky's car, leaving just Stan and Bradley. A bird cried out above them as the breeze from before returned. Bradley turned to look at Stan, a serene feeling washing over him. The two wordlessly went to sit on the sidewalk, staring up at the large clouds above. They sat in silence, watching the clouds and passing cars.

"Do you think things will go back to normal once this is all over?" Stan asked softly, turning to look at him. Bradley paused, staring into his eyes for a moment.

"What's normal to you?" He questioned calmly. Stan turned back to look up at the clouds.

"I'm not sure, actually," he replied with a sense of clarity. "But I guess that's alright." The two fell silent again. *Normal.* Bradley thought to himself. *Is there even such a thing as normal?* He thought that for Stan, nothing was really normal at all. The idea of normal didn't really sound fair. "Why do you care about that?" Bradley asked. Stan shrugged.

"I don't know, I guess that after this, I might finally have a shot at living a good life." Bradley furrowed his brows, not quite understanding what he meant.

"Was your life not good before?" Stan turned away, seemingly avoiding the question.

"It wasn't *great*, never really lived in a good home or with great people. I at least have an okay house now and some friends." He paused. "Only thing that sucks is being possessed or whatever."

Stan sighed. Another thought suddenly broke into Bradley's crowded head.

"What if I spent the night at your place?" He asked with a smile. Stan jolted out of his daze, whipping his head around quickly.

"*My* house?" He questioned with a look of disbelief. Bradley nodded his head in confirmation.

"Yeah! I was thinking about tonight."

"But it's a school night," he began to stress.

"So? I can just skip first hour."

"Isn't that bad?" Beads of sweat sprang onto his forehead.

"I mean kinda, but people do it all the time." Stan started to tap his finger on the sidewalk nervously.

"My house-" He began to say nervously before Bradley cut him off.

"I know, and I don't mind. I understand," he soothed with a soft smile. Stan let out a shuddering breath.

"Alright," he agreed. "That's fine, I guess."

"Great! I'll stop by sometime later tonight," he enthused with a wide grin.

"Yeah," Stan said without much excitement. "Tonight."

Vicky Taylor

Vicky let the cool air seep in through her open windows, a pleasant tune playing on the radio. Trees went by in a blur as she continued down the street. She passed Jamie a warm glance with a smile, feeling the tension and fear from earlier wash off of her. Jamie returned the grin, his face flushing slightly as he did.

"Why did you make that excuse?" He asked meekly. She hesitated before responding.

"I don't know," she answered with a shrug. "I guess I just wanted to spend some time with you." A large beam spread across his face as it flushed bright red.

"Really?" His voice cracked slightly. She nodded her head with a sweet smile.

"Yeah, I figured we needed some time to just get away from all this."

"For sure," he agreed. He turned to look at her nervously, his heart beating quickly in his chest. "Vicky?" He nervously spat out.

"Yes?" Her head turned to face him slightly, still keeping her main focus on the road. The sun spilled itself onto her, complimenting her hazel eyes perfectly. Jamie's mouth hung partially open, almost as if he were in a trance. He remained silent for a moment as he just gazed at her in awe.

"Nothing," he finally managed to say. "It's just that," he paused briefly again. "You're very beautiful." This time, it was Vicky's face that turned bright red. She wasn't sure how to respond, her insides all giddy. "Sorry! I'm sorry," he blurted out nervously.

"No, it's okay," she soothed with a small laugh. She turned to look at him once more. "I think you're beautiful too." Jamie looked away from her, tugging at his t-shirt slightly.

"You don't really mean that," he muttered softly.

"I do mean that, Jamie." She replied honestly. "I just wish you could see it in yourself more often." He sighed and turned towards the window, watching the houses roll by.

"Me too," he mumbled to himself. It wasn't much longer until Vicky pulled the car into her driveway, causing Jamie's head to perk up. "Wait, why are we here?"

"I decided to take you home with me," she answered softly as she turned the engine off.

"Are your parents home?" He questioned with a crack in his voice. She shrugged.

"Not sure, let's find out!" She exclaimed before getting out of the car, knowing exactly what she was doing. It took a moment for Jamie to get out, his legs looking a bit shaky. She took out her keys, going up to the door before fumbling with the lock. Jamie trailed behind her, beads of sweat rolling down his forehead like rain. Once she finally unlocked the door, she held it open for him to come in. He looked like a scared puppy, his hands stuffed into the pockets of his shorts as he nervously made his way in.

Her house was very bright and open, the sun making its way in through every window. She didn't see her little sister Jennifer anywhere, assuming she must be out playing with one of her friends. Her dad, on the other hand, was home early. He owned a car lot out in Waterloo City, something he was very proud of. He was sitting at the kitchen table, reading the local newspaper. He perked his head up at the sound of the door, a large grin spreading across his face once he saw who it was.

"Hi, Daddy!" She hollered as she ran up to hug him. He got up from the table, bending down slightly for her embrace. He squeezed her tightly, his hug so warm and full of love.

"Hey, sunshine! I thought I'd come home a bit early today to make dinner for your mom," he explained excitedly. She pulled herself away to look at him.

"By making dinner, do you mean reading the newspaper?" She asked with the same look her mother would often give.

"Well, I gotta hype myself up first," he told her with a large grin. His eyes traveled from Vicky to the very anxious-looking Jamie. "Is that Anderson's son I see?" He asked with a large boom in his voice as he made his way towards Jamie. Jamie shrunk back slightly, wiping his hands off on his pants before extending his arm out towards her dad with a forced smile. The two shook hands, Leroy Taylor's strong grip covering Jamie's sweaty one. "How are you doing, man? I'm a big fan of your dad's work," he exclaimed with a toothy grin. "He actually filled in my tooth right here," he pointed towards a molar in the back of his mouth. Jamie froze for a moment before saying anything.

"Thank you for letting me stop by, Mr. Taylor," Jamie spat out quickly, backing up slightly towards the door. A look of confusion spread across Leroy's face.

"Stop by? Well, why don't you have dinner with us!" He shouted with a smile while looking back at Vicky who nodded her head approvingly. "And don't call me Mr. Taylor, just call me Leroy." Jamie's tense body loosened at the sight of her father's bright grin.

"Alright," he began to say. "I'll stay, Leroy." Her dad's smile widened, his eyes sparkling with joy. He's always loved having guests over.

"Great!" He clapped his hands together loudly, causing Jamie to jump. "I'll go get dinner ready," he announced excitedly, making his way back towards the kitchen. Vicky rolled her eyes with a smile, stepping forward to grab Jamie by the hand. He looked up in surprise for a moment before being tugged away upstairs towards Vicky's room. Without a word, she led him inside and closed the door behind her. His face was bright red once she turned to face him.

"So," he spat out nervously, a crack in his voice.

"Chill," she said with a smirk. "This is nothing more than just hanging out." Jamie let out a shaky sigh. She made her way towards the bed, plopping down onto it tiredly. Jamie stood there in silence, not knowing exactly what to do. She sat up, patting the bed softly next to her. He nervously walked over, sitting next to her slowly. "There's no need to be so nervous," she soothed.

"Yeah, I'm sorry, it's just," he paused. Vicky looked at him with interest, her eyes wide yet calm. "Never mind, I don't have anything to say." She raised an eyebrow, not sure if she should push the subject or not. She decided to push a little further.

"Just say what you want to say," she insisted warmly. He bit his lip, tearing the skin off lightly.

"I can't," he responded meekly. "I just can't." Vicky nodded her head in understandment.

"That's alright," she cooed. "I don't mind." He looked away from her, observing the rest of her room.

"Nice room," he told her with a more confident tone. "Very organized."

"Thanks!" She exclaimed as she hopped off the bed, figuring it would be the perfect opportunity to show him. "I try to keep it nice." She went over to her bookshelf, rifling through the books, searching for a certain one.

"To be honest, Jamie," she started to say as she continued to search. "I brought you over here for more of a reason than just to hang out."

"Really?" He asked with a meek voice. She didn't respond, just kept searching until she found the book she wanted. She pulled it out gently, rubbing the coarse texture of the cover.

"This is what I wanted you to see," she stated while holding out the book to him. He took it carefully, looking at it with squinted eyes that were filled with confusion. He turned the book around in his hands, staring at the back of it intently.

"I don't get it," he admitted in befuddlement. "It's just a normal book." He handed the book back to her blankly.

"It's not what's on the book, it's what's *in* it," she explained with hidden excitement. She quickly flipped through the pages, searching for the thing she was looking for. Upon finding it, she opened her mouth to elaborate before a knock on the door interrupted her. Their heads both jolted up in an almost guilty manner. Her dad opened the door slowly, peeking his head through.

"Jennifer is home," he told them softly. "Why don't you come downstairs for a bit." She sighed, not wanting to say no to her dad. She looked towards Jamie, nodding her head afterward.

"Alright," she replied with a warm smile. His face brightened, his eyes nearly sparkling. Her dad was the type to get excited over watching paint dry, never a dull moment for him. Without a word, he slipped back out the door, leaving it cracked open. She found a stray piece of paper, sticking it inside the page she wanted to show him. She closed the book softly, setting it neatly on her bed for them to get back to later.

"Jennifer is your little sister, right?" Jamie asked as he got off the bed.

"Yep," she replied as they made their way out the door and downstairs. She drifted close to him as they descended the stairs, her hand brushing up against his for a moment. He quickly jerked his hand away, becoming visibly nervous once again. She could already hear Jennifer blabbing about her day before she even made it into the living room, mentioning how excited she was for summer vacation to begin.

Jennifer's face lit up as soon as she spotted Vicky, rushing towards her for a hug. Vicky welcomed the embrace with open arms, squeezing her sister tightly while swinging her around. Once set back onto the ground again, Jennifer's eyes drifted over to Jamie, who was standing behind Vicky. She stomped her way over to him, looking up at him with narrowed eyes. Her head came about to his chest, so it wasn't a far height.

"Is this your boyfriend?" She asked while turning her head to Vicky, a thumb pointing back towards a very flushed Jamie. He shook his head as Vicky looked down at the two with a smile. She was a tall girl, so the two had to look up at her. Jamie avoided eye contact.

"No," she finally said, pausing for a moment. "But he could be." Jennifer turned her head back towards the shocked-looking Jamie, his eyes wide.

"Okay, Vicky's could be boyfriend. Wanna go draw outside?" She asked with excitement, swaying back and forth as she did.

"What about your homework?" Vicky pressed before Jamie could get a reply in. Jennifer groaned, turning back towards Vicky with a slight stomp. Vicky gave another look their mom would always give, a *drop-that-attitude* type look. "Jamie can help you with your homework, and then you two can draw, how about that?" She reasoned calmly. Jennifer nodded her head with a slight pout on her face, dragging her feet towards her backpack.

"What did you mean about the could be thing?" Jamie asked softly. Vicky shrugged with a smile.

"I don't know, why don't you go help Jennifer," she jeered while pointing towards her sister. Jennifer dragged her backpack behind her, grabbing Jamie's hand and tugging him towards the living room.

"C'mon, let's go do my homework," she mumbled disappointedly.

"Alright," Jamie agreed, taking a moment to look back at Vicky before being whisked away by the dreary six-year-old. With a smile, Vicky made her way toward the kitchen to check up on her dad. He was completely focused, so focused that he didn't even notice the smoke rising up from the stove.

"Dad!" She yelled, attempting to get his attention. He turned to her with a grin, dough covering parts of his face.

"Hey, honey, what's up?" He asked with a grin.

"The stove is smoking," she stressed, pointing towards the smoking stove. He whipped his head around quickly, rushing towards the stove. He immediately turned it off, not too sure on what to do next. Without much thought, he took the pan he was using and doused it in water. Vicky let out a small giggle once he had finally calmed down.

"What were you trying to make?" She asked, still snickering as she did. He looked down at the pan, seeming sad for a moment before laughing himself.

"Eggs," he replied once he was done. "I was trying to make breakfast for dinner." He took off his apron, throwing it onto the counter. "Let's eat out, my treat," He offered with a loud clap, deciding to find another way to fix this.

"Where?" Vicky questioned with a raised eyebrow.

"Irna's, where else?" He asked rhetorically. "We'll go once your mom gets home." Vicky nodded her head, dismissing herself from the kitchen.

She went towards the living room, pausing to watch as Jamie helped her little sister with homework. He sat patiently, explaining the work to her calmly as she fidgeted on the couch.

"I still don't understand!" She whined to him loudly. He didn't get angry at all, he remained calm as Jennifer pouted to herself. Vicky was proud of his patience.

"That's alright," he responded soothingly. "Let's just go over it again." *It's a good thing that he already has practice with tutoring.* She thought to herself as she made herself present by entering the living room. Her sister's expression changed from distressed to excited as Vicky joined them on the couch.

"How do you two feel about Irna's?" Vicky asked with a smile. Jennifer's grin widened at the idea, she loved eating out, as their family didn't do it often.

"Yes!" She shouted, looking as if she could bounce off walls.

"Should I leave if you're eating out then?" He asked politely. "I don't want to intrude." Jennifer looked up at him, and clutched his arm slightly, shaking her head.

"Don't worry about it, my family would enjoy it more if you came with," Vicky told him with a smile.

"Are you sure?" He asked once again.

"Of course I'm sure." Jennifer looked at her work and then back at Jamie.

"Can we draw now?" She pleaded. Vicky took a look at her homework, deciding to herself that the rest could be done once they came home from dinner.

"Yeah, let's go draw," Vicky answered warmly. At this point, Vicky had forgotten all about what she was going to show Jamie, her mind drifting to other places as Jennifer tugged the two outside. The fresh air felt beautiful, soaking into her skin like water. The sun beamed lightly behind fluffy white clouds that passed lazily above. Her sister immediately ran towards the brightly-colored chalk that lay on the driveway. In an almost cautious manner, Jamie sat next to her cross-legged, picking up a rather worn-down-looking red chalk stick. Vicky joined them, picking up her favorite purple one, her go-to when drawing with her little sister.

The three of them drew together with minimal conversation, focus being the only thing going through their minds. Jennifer drew a sun, Jamie drew bright red flames, and Vicky drew purple clouds. For once, Vicky didn't think about the whole situation in Oak Street. She didn't think about Stan, she didn't think of the missing kids, she only thought about who she was with right now. She passed a smile towards Jamie who returned it warmly. She really enjoyed Jamie's company, maybe even more so than Annette's. He could be mean, yes, but she didn't see that side of him very often. Inside, she saw who he really was underneath that egotistical protective shell.

They were about finished with their drawings when Vicky's mother pulled into the driveway. The three of them cleaned up the chalk, setting the utensils in a small pastel bucket next to them. Before Mindy Taylor could even exit the vehicle, Jennifer leaped into her mother's arms for a flying embrace. She kissed Jennifer's head softly, twirling her around with a smile as Jennifer's giggles filled the air. Her eyes fell upon Jamie once she set Jennifer down.

"Anderson?" She questioned with a look of subtle surprise. Jamie stood up straight, forcing a smile.

"Hello, Mrs. Talyor," he greeted quickly. Her mother's gaze turned from Jamie to Vicky. She had a warm smile on her face set below calm eyes, a cat-like look she gave when she was proud.

"Can Jamie join us for dinner?" Vicky asked swiftly.

"We're going to Irnas!" Jennifer added with a chirp. Her mother's gaze narrowed, the smile still remaining.

"Oh, are we now?" She asked, setting her hands on her hips, her navy blue pantsuit nearly shimmering in the light of the sun. Her mother worked as an accountant in town, a job she took very seriously.

"Yeah, Dad was going to surprise you with dinner, but it almost caught fire, so he decided to treat you out to Irna's instead," Vicky explained smoothly. Her mom let out a loud laugh.

"Of course he did," she said once she was done, making her way up towards the front door, her heels clicking against the concrete. The three of them followed behind cheerily, Jennifer taking the lead and Jamie taking the rear. The cool air of the house welcomed them back in as they continued to follow Mindy Taylor into the kitchen where her dad was cleaning.

"Hey, honey!" He exclaimed, his eyes bright and loud.

"I heard you almost burnt down my kitchen," she barked with her hands on her hips. He shot Vicky a stern yet non-serious look before returning his attention back to her mother.

"That's true," he confessed with a smile. "But to celebrate me *not* burning it down, I think we should go out to Irna's." She rolled her eyes, stepping closer to him.

"You're lucky I love you so much," she told him before giving him a kiss on the cheek.

"Yeah," he admitted. "I really am." Her parents were still very much in love with each other even after all the years they'd been together. They were high school sweethearts after all.

"Well, let's not waste time," she concluded quickly. "Chop chop! Everyone to the car," she clapped her hands together twice, rushing everyone outside. Her mother was the type to do something right after it was planned, never procrastinating. Vicky followed the small crowd happily making their way into the car. Her mind was elsewhere, she completely forgot about what she was going to show Jamie. The book continued to lay dormant on her bed as it lay still and untouched. A page lifted slightly, yet there was no wind.

Annette Jones

Annette took a drag off her cigarette, blowing it out the car window and into the evening air. Her blouse lay astray somewhere on the backseat, the only articles of clothing she had on being her light pink push-up bra and matching panties.

"Smoking's bad for you, y'know." Tommy Morrison noted. She passed him an annoyed glare, taking another drag as she did. She blew smoke into his face, causing him to cough and wave his hand in the air.

"I didn't let you bone me just for you to tell me what's bad for me," she retorted. She knew it was wrong, but she needed something to take her mind off things and Jeff wasn't going to cut it. *Even though he does perform a lot better.* She thought to herself with slight amusement.

"Whatever," he mumbled with a huff. Tommy was an egotistical narcissist who played football in the shadow of Jeffrey Grant, probably one of the reasons he did Annette. She turned her attention back towards the window, a cool breeze tickling her bare shoulders. She felt a hand caress her thigh, an unnoticeable shudder going through her body. For a moment, she felt disgusting. She instinctively went for her blouse before a hand shot out, gripping her wrist. "How about you stay here and we mess around a little more?" He asked suggestively. She slapped his hand away and grabbed her blouse.

"You wish," she snapped back as she quickly stuck her arms through the sleeves.

"C'mon baby, just stay a little longer," he persisted. She fished for her shorts in the backseat, grabbing them once in sight.

"No, Tommy." She finalized, putting her shorts on with slight difficulty. She opened the passenger side door, not caring how long it would take to walk home. *I just want to get out of here.*

"Whore." He hissed, causing her to pause. She turned her head to look at him, her sharp eyes narrowing. "You'll sleep with anyone."

"You don't know me," she snarled.

"I don't have to," he responded quickly. "You're just an insecure slut."

"Whatever," she grumbled before getting out of the car, slamming the door shut. *This is all so stupid.* Annette thought most towns had a "lovers lake" or a "lovers peak" or something like that, but Linfort had a "lovers' field." Just a parking lot that overlooked a field, something to make their little town feel special too. The sun's light was starting to dwindle, orange streaking the evening sky. She made her way back home, that feeling of disgust from before coming back. Tommy had always made her feel gross though. *He's just gross.* She wrapped her arms around herself to feel better, to be touched by something other than Tommy. She felt cold knowing it would be a long walk back home.

She was halfway there, disheveled and ashamed. She started to wonder why she did it in the first place, it obviously wasn't worth it. Why couldn't she just stay loyal? Jeff was perfect, perfect yet she was throwing it all away. She thought dimly about her parents. *They wouldn't care if they found out. Probably wouldn't move a muscle, nothing I do matters to them. Nothing.* She kicked a nearby rock, causing it to tumble into the street before laying still once again. She felt tired and strange. All she wanted more than anything at this moment was Vicky. *She's probably with Jamie right now.* She let out a sigh, feeling miserable and defeated. She picked up her pace, the darkness consuming her. She really didn't want to get herself caught out here too late.

"Hey there, sweetheart," a low voice called out. Her heart stopped for a moment, thinking it was Tommy Morrison. She stood under a street light, feeling small. The figure stepped under, revealing himself to be Jesse Olsen. She felt even worse now. At least Tommy wasn't dangerous. She felt herself break into a nervous sweat, her eyes wide like a deer in headlights. She said nothing. "I just wanna ask you a few questions," he told her smoothly, a large toothy grin spread across his face. She stepped backward.

"What do you want to ask me?" She questioned with a slight quiver in her voice.

"It's about your friend," he stated with a sneer. "Vicky Taylor." Her heart dropped.

"What about her?" She asked in dismay, stepping backward once again. He stepped forward twice. Annette felt like a rabbit being cornered, she hated feeling like meat.

"She's a rat," he hissed in between teeth. "Ratted me out."

"I don't know what you're talking about," Annette responded quickly. She honestly didn't know what he was talking about, she was about as helpful as a stranger.

"Yes you do," he countered harshly, stepping forward. She decided to hold her ground.

"No Jesse, I really don't," she retorted. Without saying anything, he stepped up until they were nearly nose to nose. She could smell his hot breath, making her want to recoil. His eyes were a striking blue, similar to hers. He wasn't bad looking at all, he was actually quite attractive despite his terrifying personality. His reputation was what kept the ladies away she supposed. *Along with his interests and sense of fashion.* He grabbed her by the face gently, forcing her attention to remain on him. She didn't jerk away, afraid of what he might do if she did.

"You're not lying to me, are you?" He asked with sharp eyes. His voice broke her out of her apprehensiveness, causing her to jerk her head away and step back.

"I have no reason to lie to you," she answered with a glare. He smiled, his canines almost glimmering under the street light.

"Good," he said while stepping back himself. "Wouldn't want to have any problems." She stood there, not sure what she should say. She knew how unpredictable Jesse could be, she didn't think now would be a good time to make any sudden moves.

"Is that all you wanted?" She asked with a hint of sass. He shrugged, looking down.

"Got a dollar on you?" He questioned swiftly. She knew this was a trick question, she just didn't know the answer. She thought as quickly as she could, not sure how to respond. "C'mon honey, I ain't tryna trick you now," he assured quickly as if he could read her mind. She wondered for a moment if she even had a dollar. *Of course, I do.* She stuffed her hand down her back pocket, pulling out a slightly crumpled dollar. Without saying anything, she held the dollar out to him. With a smile, he stepped up and took it out of her hand gently, making sure to touch her hand with his. She felt the feeling of disgust return once again.

"Are we done here?" She asked harshly.

"I suppose," he started to say while pulling out a cigarette. "Unless you're up for some fun," he stuck it in his mouth, pulling out another and offering it to Annette. She shook her head.

"I have a boyfriend," she stated firmly. He pulled out his lighter and lit it up, clenching it in between his teeth.

"That never stopped you before," he mentioned with a slight chuckle. She felt her face turn red.

"I don't know what you're talking about," she blurted. He laughed while shaking his head.

"Sure you don't," he replied, his bright eyes staring into hers. "It's okay, your secret is safe with me."

"I don't have any secrets!" She fumed, frustration fueling her. He let out another cackle, almost losing his grip on his cigarette. "God, what do you even want from me?" She pleaded. He looked at her with a sense of clarity once he was done.

"To get under your skin," he stated as he stepped up towards her. "I guess it worked, right?" He took his cigarette out of his mouth, pressing it against the sleeve of her blouse. A small hole made its way through the blouse and towards her skin, causing her to jerk away. She looked towards her sleeve to see the damage; a ruined blouse and a burn mark. Looking up she saw that Jesse was gone, not even a sound could give away where he might be. She knew she needed to get home, somewhere where the eyes in the shadows couldn't see her. She jerked her head in every direction, paranoid that he might jump out at her. She didn't want to leave the light from the streetlamp above, her legs shaking in protest. She took a deep breath in, giving herself a boost of confidence to get herself moving. The interactions of today made her feel sick. She had to get home.

What she didn't expect to see in her driveway when she got home was Jeff's car. Her heart dropped, a pit forming in her stomach. *Shit.* She slowly approached the car, feeling beads of sweat begin to form on her forehead. A thousand thoughts raced through her head. *Tommy told. He had to.* She made her way towards the front, peeking into the driver's side window. No one inside. She felt like throwing up, she just wanted today to be over. She traveled from the car towards the house, unlocking the door quietly. She stepped inside, spotting her little brother Arnold on the couch first.

Arnold didn't take the news of his friend dying very well. He had stayed silent, refusing to talk to anyone besides Annette. She felt like part of the blame was on herself for not acting fast enough. He noticed her walk in, his head shooting towards her like a rocket. They stared at each other like that for a moment in the dimly lit house. He pointed upstairs without saying anything, she didn't need to ask to know what he meant. She hesitated before slowly making her way upstairs, pausing before each step, not ready to face Jeff. She didn't understand why she was feeling this way, she normally never felt this kind of guilt. Step, pause. Step, pause. She reached the top step, realizing her room light was on.

She put her hand on the doorknob, taking in a deep breath before opening the door. Jeff sat there on her bed, facing her with a sad look in his eyes as if he expected she'd walk in at that very moment. She couldn't find her words, all she could do was look back. He found them for her.

"Annette," he started softly. She stood there looking at him with a quivering lip. She just wanted to know what was wrong with her. She felt clouded, so confused and lost. She didn't want to, but she began to cry. He opened his arms, inviting her into his warmth. She stumbled towards him, falling into his arms while breaking into a sob. He held her as she cried, her whole body shaking. He stroked her hair, getting the knots out with his fingers gently. She clutched onto him, her face hidden in his neck as her tears soaked into his skin.

"I'm sorry," she sobbed, her voice muffled. He squeezed her tighter, knowing that's what made her feel secure.

"I just wish you would have told me sooner," he commented disappointedly. Her tears ran down like a faucet, the guilt taking over. "I would have felt the same if I had seen him like that." She looked up at him, confused for a moment.

"What?" She asked with a crack in her voice.

"Mitchell? I know how close he and your brother were," he responded soothingly. He didn't know. She played along. Nodding her head, she hid herself in the crook of his neck and shoulder once again. "I wish I could have been there for you," he continued as he stroked her hair softly. "Your brother told me everything." Alarms went off in her head.

"How much did he tell you?" She asked, pushing herself off of him to look into his deep brown eyes. He held her tight, making sure she didn't fall off of him.

"He told me about how you found his body on the train tracks," he explained with pain in his eyes. "That must have been awful." *Good, he doesn't know anything else.* She looked at him with a masked expression of sadness.

"It was," she croaked as she began to force more tears. "It was so bad!" She hid her face in his chest. "I don't know what I would do without you." A small smile appeared on her face, hidden by his embrace. This had gone her way. *At least something did today.*

"It's okay," he soothed. "I got you now." The guilt she felt from earlier was now gone, for she was never caught. She felt better than ever. She squeezed him, her hands traveling along his back. No matter what happened, she would always have him to come back to. Her old reliable, her boot to put on. She supposed this is what love is. He kissed her on the head softly, always ever so gentle. At some point, the truth would come out, but by that time her damage would already be done and she would be over him. At some point that would happen, but not tonight. Tonight she was free from destruction.

Stanley Morris

Tonight. Stanley Morris took in a deep breath, waiting patiently on the front stoop for Bradley. His leg bounced up and down anxiously as he started to bite his nails. Bradley had never seen the inside of his house before, he wasn't sure how he was going to react. It felt like he had been waiting there for an eternity, his heart beating quickly in his chest. *He won't be back after this.* He heard the voice tease.

"I didn't ask for your input," he responded drearily. "Just go away." No response. He continued to bite his nails, the sun setting down quietly as he did. He began to feel uncertain if Bradley was even going to show up at all. Just as that thought popped into his mind, he noticed a familiar figure come into view. Bradley made his way down the street, his duffel bag across his shoulder. He stood up with shaky legs, his heart racing. Bradley began to pick up his pace, his bag bouncing beside him. Stan stayed where he was, afraid he might fall if he moved even a little bit. He didn't understand why he was so nervous, but he had a feeling his little burden had something to do with it.

"Stan!" Bradley hollered with a wave. Stan waved back with a shaky hand. *Please stop making me feel this way.* Stan pleaded in his mind, trying desperately to communicate with the force inside of him. He waited for a response, believing that he wouldn't get one at all. *Fine, I'd like to sleep anyway.* The gravelly voice answered. The shaky feeling that went through his body disappeared, his energy draining along with it. He felt wiggly and weak for a moment before being able to regain control of himself. Bradley didn't seem to notice one bit.

Stan didn't feel as nervous anymore, his mind felt clear as he met up with Bradley.

"I brought some snacks," Bradley exclaimed with a wide grin. *Good because we don't have any.* Stan thought to himself dimly.

"Cool," he responded quickly, not wanting Bradley to see the condition of his house. Stan led him inside anyways, knowing there was no way to avoid this anymore. Lucky for him, his mother wasn't home. He opened the creaky door, holding it open for Bradley and his overstuffed duffel bag. He made sure to clean the best he could before Bradley's arrival, but it was a bit difficult to clean it all. He used his mother's perfume to mask the smell of mildew, something he hoped she wouldn't notice. He paid close attention to Bradley's reaction to the house, watching his expression carefully. The only expression on his face was a delicate wonder, a pleasant surprise to Stan. *Hopefully, he's not hiding how he truly feels.*

"So this is where he lived," Bradley marveled in awe.

"Not anymore," Stan grumbled defensively. That wasn't the exact response he was hoping for.

"Are you sure about that?" Bradley questioned while looking him up and down. Stan turned away, his face beginning to red. He didn't want to harbor this *thing*, but it wasn't exactly his choice either. "Where should I set my bag?" Bradley asked, breaking Stan out of his thoughts. He looked around for a moment, wondering himself.

"Uh, I'm sure you could just set it in my room," he responded softly.

"Where is your room?" He questioned, wandering into the hallway. Stan felt a pang of nervousness strike him once again.

"It's over here," he said quietly, stepping in front of Bradley to lead him forward toward his room. He opened the creaky door, revealing his old barren room. The hole in his window being a painful reminder of what his current situation is. His rickety bed stayed silent in the corner of his room, collecting dust on the frame. Bradley didn't say anything, just sat his bag down next to the closet.

"So, whose room was Richards?" Bradley asked with excitement. Stan gave him an anxious look, not wanting to talk about his unwanted roommate.

"I'm not sure," he answered truthfully. "Probably my mom's room though, it still had a shirt in the closet when we first moved in."

"Sweeet, can we go in?" Bradley's eyes lit up like fireworks. Stan felt his body tense.

"No way," he spat out. "We can't go in there." Bradley nodded his head in understatement, a soft wave of disappointment settling over his face. "I'm sure we could look through the rest of the house if you would like," Stan offered quickly. Bradley's eyes lit up once again.

"Yeah, let's do it." A wide grin surfaced on his face as he made his way out of Stan's room. Stan's heart dropped, he suddenly wanted Bradley to leave. *Please for the love of god, don't do anything.* Stan begged in his thoughts. Nothing in return. He took that as a good sign. He followed Bradley outside of the room, watching as he traveled through the small house. The house only had two bedrooms and one bathroom, all being small in size. The living room being in between the dinky little kitchen and bathroom. The dining "room" sat across from the kitchen. It was really just a small wooden table surrounded by old chairs.

Bradley wandered through the small hallway, stepping carefully as he did. One floorboard in particular caught his attention. He stopped to look down, bouncing slightly as he did.

"What is it?" Stan asked as Bradley bent down to inspect it. He pushed down on the floorboard a little, looking back up at Stan.

"There's something up with this," he noted. He put his focus back on the board once again, pulling at it until it popped off. Stan couldn't find any words, they were swallowed by confusion and wonder. Stan had noticed the board before but just chalked it up to being an old house. Bradley set the board to the side, reaching down into the newly made hole in the floor. "Check it out!" Bradley exclaimed as he pulled out a dusty journal.

"What is that?" Stan questioned with a waver in his voice. Bradley held it up for both of them to see, adjusting his glasses as he did.

"Some kind of old notebook, I think," Bradley replied in awe.

"Should we open it?" Stan asked with a sense of anxiousness.

"We *have* to see what's inside." Stan bit his bottom lip, a pit starting to form in his stomach once again.

"Okay," he agreed quietly. They made their way towards the living room, sitting on the maroon, dirt-stained couch. Stan bounced his leg as Bradley flipped to the first page of the journal. Stan felt a sense of energy go through him as he did, making his limbs feel jelly-like afterward. Bradley held the journal up so both of them could see, Stan forcing himself to read.

Friday, February 12 1962

Every day I see it. I will start my journey by stopping it. In fixing my problems.. I am not the problem, my cerebrum is. I will find a way to fix it, to feel more clear. The first part of this issue is to fix myself, then I can work on fixing everyone else.

Bradley and Stan exchanged concerned glances, not quite understanding what they were reading. Stan felt sweat begin to spring from his forehead as his heart rate began to increase. Bradley flipped to the next page. The date was much later than the previous page, he must have forgotten to write.

Monday, March 2 1964

I can't continue anymore, I would take my own life if I didn't have such an important purpose. I have the rope ready just in case. In case I'm told to switch my path. I have a plan, I will perform this plan next month. I know exactly what I need to do. Society will see me once again.

"This is so weird," Bradley murmured as he turned to the next page. Stan nodded his head in agreement as he began to read once again. The date on this one was exactly two months from the last one.

Monday, March 2 1964

I did it. I successfully plundered the gravesite. My mission was delayed, but it was a success. I got the hominid brain. I am now one step closer to completing my mission to perfect humanity. I will study this brain until I find out everything that is erroneous with it. Every single imperfection will be perfected. This shall be flawless. Of course, I fell victim to my temptations. I am human after all. The corpse was just so beautiful that I couldn't help myself. I know my only job was to take its asset, as that is what I was told. My body told me something else. My body told me to take the corpse and

Bradley slammed the journal shut, his face flushed with red. "I don't really want to read any more of that," Bradley blurted uncomfortably.

"Agreed," Stan said while shifting in his seat. "Let's just go to the next entry." Bradley turned the page.

Wednesday, March 8 1964

I have retrieved more subjects for my studies. I feel like I am finally getting somewhere, finally getting some sense of control. I feel like someone might be onto me. It's a small town, difficult to get away with my nightly visits to the cemetery. Especially now that I have been going for other reasons as well... Those are just minor inconveniences, easy things to avoid. I am above that. I'm very discreet about this, no one will be the wiser. The best part about all of this is having a plan for this one if it fails. I still have to figure it out, but I think I understand what I must do. IT'S FLAWLESS! I'm not sure how I will perform the brain surgery on myself once I find out how to eliminate every imperfection, but I'll get help from the higher figures if needed.

"Higher figures?" Bradley asked nervously. Stan sat silently, not knowing what to say. This was a lot to take in. *Brain surgery?* "I guess he was trying to fix himself?" Bradley shook his head before flipping the page.

Thursday, May 14, 1964

The higher figures are dead. I had to silence them in order to complete this operation. I am the higher figure now, I no longer do it for them, but for myself. I have only myself to trust, I no longer need to be fixed. I will fix the rest of this society before it destroys itself. There's no other way to be able to test this other than using a live subject, this is the only way I will be able to see the results of my tinkering with the human mind. I have a target in mind, I will wait before I pursue . Time is of the essence afterall. I will still continue to take from the cemetery, take what I need to further this process into succession. It will be difficult to do with my neighbor breathing down my back, watching my every move. I will have to be quick. God this would all just be so much easier if they just fucking listened. If they just knew what I was trying to do for them. I only want to help, I am their GOD. There will be churches that pray to my name, people will be on their knees for me. Groups that crave sweet ecstasy and lust in the name of Richard Huxley, they will line up for me. I will die for my people, die for what is perfect.

Monday, May 24 1964

I prepared the enclosure. Everything is coming together quite nicely. Of course it would. I am without flaw, it's time for the rest of the world to become more like me. I will wait until next Monday to take. This will be perfect. I have a series of tests ready for it. This will be perfect. This will be perfect.

Wednesday, May 26 1964

I AM THE RISING SUN, YOU GIVE TO ME SO I CAN PROVIDE FOR YOU. WITHOUT ME, THIS WORLD IS NOTHING, WITHOUT ME, THERE IS NO LIGHT. FUCK YOU AND YOUR PUTRID IMPERFECTED WORLD. I AM THE STARS, I AM THE MOON, I AM THE SUN, I AM YOUR GOD. YOU SUBMIT YOURSELF TO ME GODDAMIT JUST FUCKING LISTEN. JUST LISTEN! PERFECTION IS KEY PERFECTION IS KEY PERFECTION IS KEY!

Thursday, June 3 1964

The subject is dead. The surgery was a failure. This is fine, for there will be other subjects in the future. I believe my demise is being plotted as I write this. This is fine, I always have my second plan to fall back on. I have it mastered, this way I never truly die. My plan for human perfection will be completed one way or another. If they truly do decide to kill me, I will just eliminate them all. Eliminate this race. If it doesn't want perfection, I just won't give it a choice. I will kill them all, this will be my reckoning. This will be my last big act as God. Pray to me.. Pray to me before I take away everything you could ever pray to before.

Bradley flipped the page but was left with nothing. That was the last entry. The two boys sat in silence, trying to understand what they had just finished reading. Thoughts rushed through Stan's brain like a runaway train. His goal was to eliminate the human race and Stan was his biggest asset. He covered his face with his hands, falling back into the couch cushion. Bradley closed the journal softly, setting it on the trash-cluttered table.

"Why did this have to happen to me," Stan groaned behind his hands. *I'm just a tool.* He felt awful and used. There truly was no way to fix this, was there? He didn't think he could take it anymore. *Wait.* He jolted up, making his way towards the kitchen. Bradley followed behind cautiously, not understanding what Stan was doing. Stan searched through the cabinets quickly before pulling out a large kitchen knife.

"What are you doing?" Bradley asked nervously. He pointed the knife to his wrist and pushed it down. *STOP, DON'T DO THAT!* He heard a voice shout in his head. Stan smiled, just as he thought. He knew what could get rid of the spirit. He turned to face Bradley.

"What if I killed myself?" He questioned calmly. "What if I killed the host, his source of life?" He pressed the knife in harder until a small cut formed. *NO!* The voice screamed again.

"Stan please, this isn't the way," Bradley pleaded.

"The only way to kill him and save Linfort is by killing myself."

"You don't know that!" Bradley cried out. "There has to be another way, please don't do this." *Listen to the boy, I am not your enemy.* Stan stared deep into Bradley's light brown eyes, pushing the knife down into his skin. Blood slipped down from the cut and plopped onto the floor. Bradley quickly snatched the knife out of his hand, throwing it to the ground behind him. An intense anger began to consume Stan. *I just want to be in control of myself!* He swept all the jars and glasses off the counter and onto the ground, letting them shatter across the floor. He slammed himself against the wall and allowed himself to slide down, collapsing to the ground as he burst into tears.

"I just want to be okay," he cried as Bradley sat against the wall beside him. Broken shards of glass sparkled all around the two boys. Stan felt unstable. He didn't know what exactly caused him to do that, he just felt as though he needed to. He needed to escape. Bradley wrapped an arm around him, pulling him close.

"You will be okay," he soothed. "We'll find a way to fix this." Stan nodded his head, sniffling as he did. His brain was radio silent, he thought that maybe Huxley had left in fear. *At least I have some control.* He thought to himself dimly. He felt so absent, so strange. He wanted to respond to Bradley, but couldn't find the words to. He attempted to pick himself off the ground, his hands being pricked by the little shards of broken glass on the floor. Bradley followed suit, using the wall to help support himself.

"You should leave," Stan told him sullenly. "All being around me will do is put you in danger." Bradley shook his head.

"And all leaving you will do is put *you* in danger," he responded sharply. "I'm not leaving." Stan looked at him with a sense of anguish. *Please don't let me be the reason you die.* They stood there in silence with broken glass and blood all over the floor. His mom would be home soon, she wouldn't like this.

"I'm gonna clean up," Stan mumbled quietly. He turned away from Bradley, going to the hall closet before taking out an old broom. He dragged it behind his back to the kitchen, sweeping up the glass with a guilty heart. His eyes drifted from the glass to the knife. As if Bradley knew, he picked it up off the ground gently, setting it in the sink away from view. *I almost did it.* He thought to himself as he continued to sweep. *I almost took my own life.* He began to find himself wishing that he did.

The shards sparkled in a large pile wildly. He stood there, staring down at them with mesmerization. Snapping out of it, he swept it out the backdoor and into the yard. He sat outside on the stoop, staring into the nearby woods. Bradley joined him outside, sitting next to him quietly.

"Can you promise me something?" Bradley asked in a low tone. Stan turned his head to face him, his eyes dark and serious.

"What?" He wished he was clear so Bradley didn't have to see him. He didn't want to have to see him so serious and rough.

"Promise me you won't kill yourself," Bradley implored with a hint of sorrow. "Can you promise me that?" Stan hesitated before responding, the silence filling the cool air.

"I don't know," he answered honestly, looking away from Bradley's pleading eyes. He didn't want to talk about this anymore. They sat in silence once again, Stan felt as though he said the wrong thing. He supposed sometimes the truth could be wrong in certain situations, no matter how badly he wanted it to be right. "I'm sorry," he added quietly. "How many more people have to die before I do?"

"I don't know," Bradley replied, shaking his head. "I wish you were normal." Stan turned to face him once again, wanting to say something but not being able to find the words. His words hit like a brick. *I was normal.* "Can you still promise me?" Bradley asked once again. Stan paused.

"I promise," he answered blankly. He didn't think it would matter too much if he broke that promise in the future anyways, at least not to Stan.

"Thank you," Bradley said softly with a wane smile. The sun was set, the darkness and bugs consuming them. He waved away the mosquitoes as a yawn escaped Bradley. Everything felt so surreal, he couldn't fully wrap his head around what was happening. He felt drunk. The stars twinkled lightly above as the cool air surrounded them. A train could be heard in the distance.

"Do you want to go back inside?" Stan asked, thinking he might feel better in the safety of his home.

"Sure," Bradley agreed while getting up from the stoop, his joints cracking as he did. Stan joined him, closing the sliding glass door behind him after Bradley. They traveled towards his room, the floorboards creaking beneath them. Stan had forgotten all about the journal he had so carelessly thrown onto the table. But when Stan would remember to get it, he would find that it wasn't even there. The journal would be back under the floorboard. Silently hidden from the world.

Jamie Anderson

Jamie Anderson sat up in his bed, knowing what he had to do. The night before was the best he had felt in a long time, anytime he spent with Vicky was time well spent. But it was Friday after school now and he was no longer with her. He got up from his bed, this time there were no empty cans in his trash can. He creaked the door open slowly, feeling relieved that his siblings weren't home yet. His mother was at work while his stepdad was passed out on the couch. *Perfect.* He made his way through the house swiftly, his short legs pumping quickly towards the door. He looked back one last time before heading outside.

He grabbed his bike from the garage, pulling it out of the driveway before pedaling it down the street. He cursed at himself quietly, wishing he had a car. The sun shone dully on him, causing tiny beads of sweat to form on his dark forehead. He would have a long way to go before arriving at his destination. He rode for about ten minutes before making it to the pond. *Only twenty minutes to go.* He thought to himself tiredly. This town was small, but definitely spread out.

He passed many people on his journey, one of them being Alan Giblin, who waved as he went by. He nodded his head in acknowledgment, continuing down the street. He felt the wind go through his hair as he went downhill. He was almost there now. He passed by the junkyard a little ways after passing the elementary school, a little ironic in Jamie's opinion. He sped up, feeling his legs begin to tire. His location was coming into view now, causing a breath of relief to escape from him.

He pulled into the driveway soon after spotting the house. He tiredly hopped off his bike before gently setting it down on the grass below. He slowly walked up to the door, knocking three times before waiting. It wasn't long before he got an answer. Ivan stood in the doorway, his eyes wide with surprise. He looked around quickly before saying anything.

"Why do you always come back?" He asked with a hint of sorrow. "Pressure me into joining your weird.." He trailed off, not knowing the right word he was looking for. "*Thing*." Jamie paused, feeling a pang of guilt. He knew Ivan had to stay, he just felt as though it were right.

"I don't know," Jamie answered truthfully. "Can't you just stay for good?" He pleaded. "So I don't have to keep doing this?" Ivan's nose twitched, a spark of hidden anger in his green eyes.

"No," he finalized, quickly closing the door as he did. Jamie put his foot in the doorway, stopping it from fully closing just in time. "Please leave," he begged as he continued to try to close the door.

"Not until you say yes," Jamie persisted as he held the door open, using all his strength. He was the only reason Ivan kept coming back, he couldn't stop now.

"No," he restated, squishing Jamie's fingers slightly. *God, he's strong.*

"I'll wait out here until you say yes," he huffed as he continued to struggle with the door. Ivan's eyes widened, setting something off within him.

"Go away!" He hollered. "Please, before my dad gets home," he pleaded.

"Not until you agree to stay for good," Jamie told him. "I'll stay here all day if I have to." Ivan stopped trying to shut the door. Jamie stepped back, allowing Ivan to come outside.

"Let's talk about this somewhere else," he offered quietly.

"Alright," Jamie agreed as they started down the street. They walked in silence, the only sound being their footsteps. Jamie didn't have to think too hard to know Ivan was leading him to the park.

"Why do you want me to stay so bad?" Ivan asked, the sound of his voice causing Jamie to jump. Jamie shrugged.

"I don't know," he answered honestly, "maybe like some sort of connection or something? I just don't think we should separate. We need to stick together, we're all in this now."

"You don't seem to have a connection with the blonde girl," Ivan noted quietly.

"I didn't say it had to be a good connection," Jamie grumbled with an eye roll. Ivan looked up at the trees, squinting his eyes slightly from the sun.

"I don't really feel much of a connection at all," Ivan admitted. "I don't understand why you still want me here." Jamie shook his head. It felt like he was getting nowhere. He wasn't sure what he should say, feeling as though nothing would work.

"Look, Ivan, I don't understand what's going on myself or why any of this is happening, but we need you, and you need us. If you get separated, you might become an easier target or something," Jamie explained. "So, can you please just stay? So you don't get killed in your bedroom or something. So I don't have to keep coming here," Jamie pleaded

"I understand," he sighed, "I suppose I can stay." Jamie felt his expression lighten. "I don't want to be home much anyway," Ivan mumbled.

"Why?" Jamie asked, feeling as if he already knew the reason.

"I don't want to talk about it," he asserted in a standoffish manner. "Just promise me one thing," he suddenly stopped in the street, looking down to face Jamie.

"Sure," Jamie said while looking up at him. The height difference was pretty drastic, as Jamie was shorter than the average male and Ivan happened to be very tall.

"Promise me I won't get hurt anymore," he pleaded with a look of nervousness. *Well shit, I can't promise that.* Jamie thought to himself.

"I'm sure nothing will happen to you," Jamie claimed with a forced smile. That seemed to be enough for Ivan, as he began walking again. The two continued down the street, Jamie feeling riddled with guilt. *If something bad happens to him, it's my fault.* Ivan never talked much, maybe he should get to know him better. He glanced up at Ivan, his tired, droopy eyes making it difficult to understand exactly what he was feeling. He and Ivan had never talked much before, this would be the perfect opportunity.

"So," Jamie started to say while clearing his throat. Ivan looked down at him without moving his head, causing Jamie to feel a little nervous. "What do you like to do?" He asked.

"You don't have to small talk, silence is fine," Ivan told him promptly. As much as Jamie wanted to stay silent, he felt persistent in learning about this guy. There was just something about Ivan that Jamie had to know.

"I want to learn more about you," Jamie insisted swiftly.

"There's nothing to learn," Ivan stated. They passed by the elementary school, the wind ruffling their hair gently.

"I'm sure that's not true," Jamie countered, "tell me something you like." Ivan stayed quiet, making it feel as though they were getting nowhere with this conversation.

"Bugs," he said finally. *Odd.* Jamie thought, but he wouldn't judge.

"Why do you like bugs?" Jamie asked, deciding to prod a little longer. Once again there was a pause. Birds flew overhead, calling to one another.

"They're simple," he answered. Jamie was finding it difficult to get a full sentence out of him, but he'd try just as he had done before. He decided to ask something a bit more risky.

"Tell me about your dad," Jamie suggested quickly. Ivan's body tensed as his head shot towards him.

"No," he said without hesitation. He looked away, his pace beginning to pick up. Jamie wasn't the type to quit, he began to pick up his pace as well.

"Why not?" He asked.

"Because," Ivan spat out, "I don't want to." His fingers began to tap against his leg as he walked.

"Please?" Jamie prodded. Ivan stopped in his tracks.

"I said no, Jamie," Ivan asserted with a stern look. "I have limits." Jamie nodded his head in understatement.

"I'm sorry," Jamie apologized in shame. "I'll stop asking."

"Thank you." They began to walk once more, large cornfields on each side of the road. The sun soaked into Jamie's skin as the cool breeze washed it off. A lone car passed by quietly, dust flying up from behind it. He suddenly realized that he had left his bike back at Ivans. *Oh well, I'll come back for it at some point.*

"What do you like?" Ivan asked, startling Jamie out of his thoughts. He didn't expect Ivan to say anything at all. He thought over it for a moment, his mind blank.

"I suppose I like to read," Jamie replied, saying the first thing that came to mind. Ivan nodded his head as if in approval.

"What about your family?" He asked quietly. He thought of his stepdad, a feeling of hatred rising within him. He didn't know what to say. This time, he was the one to hesitate.

"My dad died, but I have my mom," he answered finally. Another car passed by.

"No other family?" Ivan asked with a look of concern. Jamie thought about what he should say once again even though the answer was clear.

"My stepdad and half-siblings," he responded without much emotion. "But I don't feel anything towards them."

"Why not?" Jamie normally wouldn't answer this question, but he was just happy to hear Ivan talk. He also felt like he could trust him.

"He's not my real dad," he grumbled. "They aren't my real siblings."

"Does he try to be a dad?" Jamie didn't understand at first.

"He tries too hard, he doesn't *actually* care about me."

"Wouldn't he not try if he didn't care?" Ivan's words hit Jamie like a brick. He supposed he was right, his stepdad wouldn't try so hard for him if he didn't care. Still, all he wanted was his dad. Another car whirred by along with that thought.

"At least your dad is real," he retorted with a hint of pain.

"I wish he wasn't," Ivan mumbled. They continued to walk. It would take much longer to get to the park on foot than it would on a bike. They fell silent once again, another car passing by. The sun began to make its slow journey down the sky, the air beginning to cool. Jamie felt oddly calm, he could tell Ivan did too. The two walked down the street together in silence.

"I think my father hates me," Ivan admitted quietly. Jamie's head perked up.

"Why?" He asked with concern. Ivan shook his head.

"I'll never be good enough, never be my brother." *Brother?* Jamie thought with confusion. *He has a brother?*

"Where does your brother stay?" Jamie questioned.

"He remains in Kazan," Ivan told him while looking up at the sky, white clouds rolling overhead.

"Your father seems like a real dick," Jamie added quickly. "Thank you for telling me." Ivan nodded.

"Thank you for listening," he responded. Jamie could tell he felt a lot lighter after getting that off his chest. He had probably kept that in for a long time. They soaked in the silence, finally feeling comfortable with it. They both had shared, and now they can enjoy the presence of one another without speaking. He didn't mind Ivan, he was better than the majority of the students in high school. He felt pity for him though, he was lucky that his step-dad didn't do the sort of things that Ivan's dad did. He let out a heavy sigh.

By the time they finally had made it to the park, the sky had become a soft yellow. Jamie had formed a sweat stain on the back of his shirt, something even the breeze couldn't prevent. He felt exhausted, his gentle breathing from before turning into large huffs. Ivan didn't seem tired at all, in fact, he looked rejuvenated. He was definitely used to these kinds of things. He began to regret forgetting his bike, knowing that getting home would be a lot faster if he had it.

"I think I'm gonna go home," Jamie told Ivan, looking up at the quiet figure.

"Alright," he responded without much emotion.

"Are you going to stay here until it gets dark?" He asked, wiping the sweat off his forehead. Ivan looked towards the setting sun, squinting his eyes slightly.

"Probably," he answered calmly. Jamie could understand why now, he didn't question any further.

"Cya later I guess," he concluded with a wave, turning away from the park and towards the road.

"Bye," he heard Ivan reply. Jamie started his journey home, watching the sun continue to set as he did. He felt strange as he walked down the street, an almost subliminal feeling washing over him. He didn't understand it, but he didn't think that it mattered much. He felt as if this summer he was changing and that he would never be the same again. *Everyone changes all the time.* He thought to himself as he continued to force his feet to move forward. *There's no way to stop the continuous march of life. I will live on to experience more important things.* He felt as though his teenage years didn't matter, just another obstacle in life. Just as he would lose his inner thoughts of the present, he would soon lose the people around him as well.

He felt lost, like if he thought too hard about where he was going his feet would get lost too. But they seemed to always know where to take him, a force of habit controlling them more than his mind did. He suddenly felt guilty for his treatment towards his stepfather. He didn't realize how lucky he had it until talking to Ivan. He wished he could trade with him, so he had something to release his anger and hate from the world on with justification. He also didn't want Ivan to have to suffer any longer.

He didn't want to be angry anymore. He didn't want to be selfish. He didn't want to be hateful, but it felt as though every time he tried to change he just resorted back to his old ways. He was making small steps, but it felt as though he were on an escalator that was going backward. No matter what, he will always have a rotten soul. The sky became streaked with pink, the sun continuing its way down. It would be dark by the time he got home.

Ivan Balakin

Ivan Balakin stayed until it was dark, just as he told Jamie he would. He found the walk home to be calming, something that could always ease his mind. He knew what waited for him, but he tried to not think about it. He didn't start to feel uneasy until he entered his neighborhood, his pace slowing and his heartbeat rising. He felt a raindrop plop onto his head, his droopy green eyes turning towards the sky. His house finally came into view, and he felt as though he were walking into a trap.

Jamie's bike laid on the lawn like a dead bird. He didn't know it was there until now. Panic began to consume him as he stepped up to the door. He slowly turned the doorknob, his heart beating quickly. The door creaked open, a small yellow light glowing from the kitchen. They had a small house, the staircase that lead to Ivan's room being right by the front door. He noticed his parents sitting on the couch watching the television, his father passing him a glance. He made his way up the stairs, loud creaks emitting as he did.

He closed the door behind him quietly, wishing he had a lock. He went over to his bed with shaky legs, sitting down with a sigh. He looked over at his ants, smiling as he did. They scurried around in their container, their little legs moving around swiftly. He picked up the honey, putting a drop in their enclosure carefully. He watched as they made their way towards it, listening to the rain patter quietly against the rooftop. He felt calm, turning over from his side onto his back before staring up at the ceiling. He closed his eyes and took a deep breath in, feeling like he could let his guard down and relax.

He suddenly heard a knock on the door. He quickly sat up as the door opened, his heart dropping when laying his eyes on his father. Strolling in with nothing but a glass cup of water, his father made his way towards the bed. Ivan felt trapped, knowing there was nowhere to go. Their eyes locked, and for a moment no one moved.

"Whose bike is on the lawn?" His father asked in Russian. Ivan hesitated before answering.

"I don't know," he lied. He knew he was talking about Jamie's bike.

"Don't lie to me, son," he hissed.

"I'm not," Ivan stammered, cowering in his bed. Victor curled his lip into a snarl, his face hot with rage. His father roared, punching the wall with his fist. Ivan shrunk further into the bed, shaking as he did. Some of the water from the cup spilled onto the floor with a splat. The large man went for the antfarm, grabbing it off the nightstand with speed.

"NO!" Ivan cried out, holding his hands out in submission. "Please, put that down," he pleaded. "Someone must have just left their bike!" His father's gaze pierced his, he would not back down. Ivan could now understand what the glass was for. In one swift motion, his father poured the glass into the antfarm, water flooding all their tunnels. Ivan let out a scream, tears beginning to form. His father then went towards the window, opening it quickly.

"Worthless son," he grumbled with enmity, "worthless shit." He threw the ant farm out the window, the container breaking sporadically. The rain poured down on top of the broken glass, pelting the ants. Ivan couldn't help but cry, his body shaking violently. His father struck him across the face, leaving a bright red mark. "No son of mine will cry," he hissed. "I know it was the Mexican kid's bike, you lying shit." He struck him again, causing more tears to fall. His father grabbed him by the wrist, pulling him closer. "If I catch that boy here again, you will both be very sorry." He let go, stomping out before slamming the door behind him.

Ivan was left to sit there in shock, not knowing how to feel. He glanced over to the empty nightstand, a large pit forming in his stomach as the realization hit. He let out a scream of distraught, tears pouring down as quickly as the rain outside. He let out another wail, his tears falling onto the sheets below him. He faintly felt the burning sensation emitting from the angry red marks on his face. He didn't care. The only thing he cared about was what was outside the window being swept away by the rain.

He fell back onto the bed, the last of his tears streaming down his face. He felt empty, taking in a large, shuddering breath. He had only himself to blame. If he hadn't rushed Jamie out, maybe he would have remembered his bike. There were so many things that could have prevented this from happening, so many things that could have stopped his father from doing that. If he had done one of those things instead, maybe he would have been downstairs eating dinner instead of crying in his room. He was so upset with himself that he began to feel nauseous.

He knew he wouldn't eat tonight, he had lied. Liars do not get choices. He couldn't bear to look at his empty nightstand, knowing that what was once there would never return. He stared at the crack in his ceiling. It seemed larger. He didn't look at it with such hatred now, he looked at it with a sense of familiarity. He could find himself relating to it, understanding it. Everything happened so quickly, caused by a long time of build-up. He cracked under the pressure, and now he was facing the consequences. If only he didn't lie.

A thought sporadically popped into his head. He knew his father wouldn't come back upstairs to check on him. He took a look at his window with wide eyes, his heart thumping wildly in his chest. *I shouldn't.* He got up from the bed, stepping slowly towards the windowsill. *Stop.* He set his fingertips on the window lift lightly, feeling a slight chill. *Don't.* He lifted it quietly, feeling the rain come in and hit his hands. He looked down, thankful that it was too dark to see the remaining parts of his antfarm. It wouldn't be too far of a jump.

He could feel goosebumps begin to form as the cold air from the open window surrounded him. The wind brushed against his hair, his eyes wide while looking into the darkness. *You can still turn back.* He briefly wondered how he would get back in. *Who cares?* He put his knee on the windowsill, teetering towards the edge. *Wait.* He got back down, swiftly going back towards the door to turn off the light. He slowly walked back to the window, lifting himself up once again. He turned his back to the outside, slowly lowering himself down. With one hand holding onto the windowsill for support, he used the other to close the window to a crack. He took a deep breath before jumping backward, into the open air.

He fell on top of the broken ant farm, causing him to wince in pain. The rain poured heavily overhead, hitting him with great speed. He got up with shaky legs, not bothering to brush the grass or mud off himself. He didn't know where to go now. *I have to return the bike.* He made his way towards the driveway, searching for where the bike could be. The street lamp revealed it to be next to the garbage cans at the top of the driveway. He pulled it out of the grass, getting it in gear. He set it up to better suit his size, forgetting how short Jamie really was compared to him. He quickly hopped on after, pedaling quickly down the street.

This is so stupid. He thought as the rain pelted him in the eyes, forcing him to squint. He had stayed quiet for so long, never doing as much as talking back to his father. *Now I'm sneaking out.* He began to pedal even faster, wanting to get as far away as possible. He had passed the junkyard and elementary school within five minutes, his legs pumping wildly. The rain hadn't let up, lightning striking the air above. The only thing Ivan could hear was the sound of his heartbeat. The cold seeped into his skin like poison, causing his head to hurt. He wouldn't stop pedaling until he returned the bike.

Once he passed the park and got into the thick of the town, he noticed how empty the streets really were. *Nobody wants to drive in this.* He felt crazy for riding a bike in this weather, knowing that he would probably catch a cold from this. He passed a lone car on the road, the rain distorting his vision. He drifted over towards the sidewalk, praying the bike's wheels wouldn't slip. He suddenly realized he wasn't completely sure where Jamie's house was, he had a general idea but he didn't know if he would actually recognize the house. He knew his stepfather was the local dentist, he also knew from previous conversations that he lived near where he worked.

Thunder boomed overhead, the sound being louder than the thumping of his heartbeat. He finally stopped in front of the dentist's office, pausing to take a breather. He was completely drenched, his body shivering violently as the water soaked into his skin. He looked around as his teeth chattered, searching carefully for what could be Jamie's house. He turned to look at the nearest house to the right, walking towards it with the bike. He noticed a sign in front labeled "Anderson." It was lit up from underneath, a thing a lot of people in Linfort had in their front yards. *Must be the place.*

He dragged the bike over towards the front door, hesitating to knock. *I'm so stupid.* He thought to himself in dismay. The curtains inside were pulled back far enough to be able to see Mr. Anderson sitting on the couch watching something on the television, his hand reaching down for a beer. He suddenly wondered if he would be able to see into the other windows. He made his way toward the side of the house, the rain pouring heavily on top of him. The curtains were closed, causing him to make his way to the back of the house. He could see an orange light peeking through the slightly open curtains. In this window, he spotted Jamie sitting at his desk. He stared into the window for a moment before knocking.

Jamie jumped up in surprise, looking around his room quickly before turning his attention to the window. Ivan gave a small wave before Jamie rushed over, unlocking and opening the window quickly.

"Ivan?" His voice was carried out in concern.

"I brought your bike," Ivan told him calmly. It took Jamie a moment to process everything for a moment, his eyes darting from Ivan to the bike.

"What are you doing though?" He finally managed to ask. "It's pouring outside, does your dad even know you're here?" The thought of his dad made his heart drop. He shook his head.

"I don't know," he replied honestly. He propped the bike against the house, staring down at it as the raindrops ran into his eyes.

"Here," Jamie began to say, "come inside and dry off." Ivan did as Jamie said, crawling through the window and into the nice warm house. His clothes dripped water onto the floor quickly, causing a puddle to form beneath him. Jamie closed the window behind him, turning his attention back to Ivan. "What were you thinking?" He asked in disbelief. Ivan didn't respond. He feared that if he said anything, then he would begin to cry just as he did before. "Hold on," Jamie stated, walking towards the door. "Stay here," he turned to say before leaving the room.

Ivan stood there quietly as the water continued to drip from his clothes. He could feel his body shaking, making a pathetic attempt to keep him warm. He had never done anything like this before, it all felt so strange. He gave himself a moment to observe Jamie's small but comfy-looking room. He had a desk on one side and his bed on the other, with a small brown rug placed in the middle. It was a simple yet cozy setup. A tiny lamp illuminated a book he was reading, shrouding the novel in a soft orange glow. Although it was different, he felt safe here. The door creaked open, revealing Jamie with a beige towel and clothes.

"Here," he said while handing Ivan the towel. "I also grabbed some of my stepdad's clothes," he added quickly, "I doubt you would fit any of mine." He set the clothes on his desk as Ivan began to dry his hair with the towel.

"Thank you," Ivan replied quietly.

"No problem," Jamie sighed before plopping down on his bed. "What made you come all the way here?" He asked as Ivan grabbed the clothes off the desk, setting the towel down on the floor beneath him. He nervously glanced over at Jamie who turned himself to face the wall.

"My dad," he started to say as he began to take off his soaking wet shirt, his wounds from the pond slowly fading into scars on his shoulders. "He found your bike."

"What's wrong with my bike?" Jamie asked with confusion. Ivan put the new shirt on, feeling it stick to his stomach from the wetness.

"Nothing wrong with the bike," he replied honestly. "Something wrong with it being yours." He took off his jeans, letting them drop to the floor in a soggy mess.

"Oh," Jamie realized disappointedly. "Is it because I'm-"

"Yes," Ivan murmered, cutting him off. He felt ashamed to be his son. He put on the dry pants, which felt a little tight to him.

"Can I turn around?" Jamie asked meekly as Ivan pulled down the shirt a little, feeling okay enough for Jamie to look now.

"Yeah," he responded tiredly. Jamie turned himself back around, facing the exhausted-looking Ivan. He slid off the bed, grabbing Ivan's wet clothes.

"I'm gonna go put these in the dryer," he told him, "you can lay down on the bed if you'd like, you look really tired." Ivan nodded his head. Jamie quickly left the room, closing the door behind him, leaving Ivan to be on his own once again. He stared at Jamie's bed with guilt, hesitating before allowing himself to lie down. He stared up at the ceiling just as he would in his own room, except this ceiling didn't have a crack in it. His eyelids fluttered shut, a feeling of comfort washing over him. Before he knew it, his exhaustion had caught up to him.

He woke up to a gentle shaking, his vision blurry. He didn't even realize he had fallen asleep.

"Ivan," he heard a voice call out. He had forgotten where he was for a moment, his brain still trying to wake up. Realization hit him like a break, causing him to jolt awake. Jamie stepped away from him. "You okay?" He asked with concern. Ivan allowed himself to calm down again, nodding his head. "I set up a sleeping bag on the floor, but if you want to sleep on the bed instead, I won't mind. It seems like you've had a long night," Jamie explained as Ivan rubbed his eyes. *I should go home.*

"It's alright," Ivan yawned, "I'll take the sleeping bag." He slid off the bed and onto the floor, sticking his long legs into the sleeping bag.

"Alright," Jamie said before turning off his desk lamp and making his way back over to the bed. They both got themselves comfortable, listening to the rain pour outside.

"Jamie?" Ivan called out into the darkness.

"Yeah?" He responded back.

"Thank you for today, I think I needed this." It took a small moment for Jamie to reply.

"Don't mention it," he answered quietly. The two fell silent once again. "What happened?" Jamie asked with sincerity. Ivan drew in a deep breath. *Go ahead.*

"He killed my ants," Ivan told him, "poured water down their container and threw them out the window." He awaited a response from Jamie, feeling guilty that he told someone about his dad's behavior. Feeling guilty for being vulnerable.

"I'm sorry," is all he responded with. That was all he needed.

"I don't know how I'm going to go back home," Ivan admitted honestly. He heard Jamie turn in his bed, he assumed it was to face him.

"Don't," he stated in a serious tone. Ivan turned to face him as well even though they couldn't see each other.

"What?" He asked in confusion.

"Just stay here, my family wouldn't mind," Jamie offered calmly. Ivan thought over it for a moment. *There's no way that would work.*

"I can't," he stammered with a crack in his voice. He could hear the rain outside begin to lighten, the moon's soft light barely peeking through the cracked curtains.

"Well, if you ever need a place to go," Jamie insisted before turning back in his bed. "Just think about it, okay?" Ivan's head was whirling with thoughts.

"Yeah, okay," he said blankly, turning onto his back once more. He lay there with his hands across his stomach, staring up at the ceiling in the darkness. He was safe for tonight. For a moment, nothing was wrong. For a moment, he was in charge of his life. He closed his eyes and allowed himself to fall asleep. That night, he dreamt that his ants were still alive. That night, he dreamt his father loved him.

John Charles

John Charles watched with careful eyes as the two boys made their way down the street. He knew who it really was. He had first-time experience with raw evil. It seemed as though he lived on his porch, rocking back and forth on his chair. He gave up on making friends, at his age it was pretty much pointless. It didn't help being the only other house on the lonely road of Oak Street. None of that mattered. He was back. His old friend from 1964.

He knew the boy would eventually come to him. He couldn't stay silent about his little parasite forever. It had rained heavily the night before, it had actually been raining a lot recently. John suspected it might be because of him. He knew he wasn't crazy, he knew what was in the records. He saw what was inside that house. He knew it wasn't a train that hit the boys. He would never allow himself to be fooled. Yet he sat on his porch rocking back and forth, doing nothing to help. He would wait until someone else saw his use, until Evans got his head out of his ass.

Saturday morning. The morning dew kissed the achy wooden limbs of his chair. His hands soaked in the blood of the sky as they laid themselves down on the armrest. He was on watch. His large, bulging brown eyes stalked the street. He was the answer. His muscles ached with age, a lingering pain that seemed to never leave. He still continued to rock. He had seen him, he had been visited.

Hello John. He would say to John in his room approximately one week before today. *It's been a while.* John would agree. *Have you seen what I've done? Do you enjoy watching it from your rotting chair?* John would tell him that he did not enjoy it. Not one bit. *That's alright, I figured you wouldn't care for it.* He would tell John. John would ask him what he wanted. *I want you to see what you have caused.* He would say. John would tell him that he had not caused anything, that he had the higher ground. He would then laugh in John's face, a hot steam arising from his gaping mouth.

I thought you were supposed to be smart, John. I am not supposed to be anything, John would say with a blank stare. Take your spirit elsewhere, you are no longer welcome here. He would then feel a sharp pain grip his face as an inhuman clawed hand grabbed him. The claws would dig into his cheeks, causing a rush of hot blood to flow. *You are not safe in your home.* He would hiss. *You may have had the upper hand before, but I have the upper hand now.* He would let go, disappearing into nothing. *Old bastard.*

John rocked in his chair, rubbing the part of his face that was previously impaled. He would not allow himself to become a victim. This was his home. *Dead bastard.* He would think to himself. John knew what he did, he knew everything. He just wished he knew what he looked like when he was rotting. Instead, he watched him bleed out on the same street that stray cats would run across. He at least knew what that looked like. He figured it wouldn't be long until the host would question him. The boy seemed to be suffering, he could sense it. That was another thing he knew. He was old, but not stupid. Never stupid.

The chair creaked as he continued to rock back and forth. It felt as though his limbs had mended themselves to the chair. He was no longer a person, just a spirit spectating the living world. He took a sip from the glass of water that sat on the little metallic table beside him. The ice he had put in earlier clinked against the glass, kissing his lips as he went in for a drink. Stanley Morris. He found out his name soon after he moved in. Small town after all, word gets around fast. John didn't know he was inside Stan at first, but it didn't take long to find out. He took another sip from his glass.

He knew he should have covered the body better. He knew he should have gone back, but Evans told him to leave it be. He wished he didn't. John now felt full responsibility for the deaths of Linfort. *If only.* Now he was old, now his heart ached with age. Curse it, the endless march towards death. He would not allow his body to fail him. This was his burden to carry, and he would carry it until he died. He rose from the rocking chair, taking his glass with him as he went inside his darkened home. He went to set it on the table, his legs carrying him slowly. His knees cracked as he bent down, a different noise emitting from the front door. A knock. He let out a small grin. They were here, just as he suspected they would.

Jesse Olsen

Jesse Olsen sat on the park bench in silence, twirling his sacred pliers around skillfully. He waited for them, knowing that they would all meet there soon. Enough stalking and asking around could get you any answer if you wanted it bad enough, and boy did he want to know real bad. The only one he would have to worry about is the Balakin fella, feeling a little intimidated by his size. Deep down, Jesse knew it was nothing to worry about, he was just a big ol' pussy anyway. He noticed Bradley and someone else enter the park first, sitting on the other side of the pond away from Jesse. That's fine, it would work. He had seen the scruffy-haired boy with them before, not caring enough to figure out who he was.

He had told Scott of his whereabouts earlier, not knowing if he would actually show up or not. He wasn't too sure if he cared anyway. He took out a pack of cigarettes, sliding one out carefully before lighting it and sticking the pack back into his pocket. He noticed the two boys glance at him with weary eyes, causing Jesse to smile. He enjoyed the feeling of being feared, it gave him something to feel himself. He took a long drag out of his cigarette, wondering when the other four clowns would join them. Whatever, he could wait. He would wait all day if he had to.

He wasn't exactly sure what he was going to do when he saw them and wasn't even sure if he would approach them at all. But he at least had his pliers. He was at least prepared. He sat there silently, staring up at the waving trees above as he blew out smoke. He felt a tap on his shoulder, whipping his head around to see the sly-looking Scott Carter. *So he did listen.* He let out a large, toothy grin, his bright, wild blue eyes gleaming in the light of the sun.

"Why are we here?" Scott asked before taking a seat next to him on the splintery bench.

"I gave you a choice," Jesse noted, "you didn't have to join me." He took another drag off his cigarette.

"Okay, then why are *you* here?" He asked, rephrasing his question. Jesse shrugged.

"Same reason you are," he answered with a grin. Scott rolled his eyes, taking out his own pack.

"Got a lighter?" He asked as he slid out a cigarette. Jesse passed him his lighter without saying anything, listening to the little *tick* as it ignited. The two sat together on the bench in silence, Jesse keeping his focus on the boys across the pond. Scott glanced over, following his gaze. "So you're just gonna sit here and wait for them to all get here?" Scott questioned while shaking his head in disbelief.

"Have been and will continue to," Jesse responded with a sly smile.

"This is totally lame, dude," Scott complained as he took another drag. Jesse turned to look at him with a tame expression.

"Then leave," he offered, "you're not being forced to stay." Scott shrugged his shoulders.

"Nah, I got nothing better to do," he claimed as he leaned back. The kids who did their usual kite flying had not yet arrived, Jesse figuring it might be too early. The sound of a car pulling up to the curb caused Jesse's head to spin around, his sharp eyes narrowing. She was here. He smiled, not noticing that Scott was looking too. He watched as the four of them departed the car. Jamie and the Balakin in the back, and Annette and Vicky in the front. Lucky for him, he was not yet noticed. This wouldn't last for much longer.

"So what now? They're here," Scott announced as if Jesse were blind. Jesse got up without a word, his legs carrying him swiftly towards them. He didn't know if Scott would follow or not. He kept his pliers in his pocket, planning to take them out only when needed. The four of them made their way towards the two boys who were wildly pointing behind them. Jesse was quicker though, never having a moment to slow. Once close enough, he pulled Vicky by the back of her shirt with a hard jerk.

She fell to the ground quickly, causing the others to jump back in shock. Jamie made a depressing attempt to strike him, Jesse moving out of the way swiftly. Scott didn't miss though, fists beginning to fly. He struck Jamie in the nose without flaw as Jesse went back to the main target. Ivan stood frozen in place, just as Jesse expected he would. Annette, however, did not. Her fist flew out at an exhilarating speed, striking Jesse in the stomach. He doubled over momentarily, pain ripping through him. The other two members of their party had joined them now, adding to the brawl. Jesse shoved Annette to the side, grabbing Vicky who was struggling to get up.

He glanced over at Scott who was laying it down on Jamie, his fists hitting his body rapidly. Ivan was no longer standing still. He body slammed Scott, his body flying off of Jamie. Jesse didn't have time to react as Vicky was now slipping out of his grip.

"Stop!" She yelled. "You don't know what you're doing!" She kicked him in the legs, causing him to let go. He grinned, enjoying the destruction he had caused. He wanted to make it last.

"Yeah?" He teased. The commotion had calmed, everyone taking in deep breaths. The scruffy-haired boy stood strong, a look of concentration spread across his face.

"Please just leave now," she begged. Everyone slowly rose to their feet except for Scott and Jamie, who remained on the ground beaten and bloody. Jesse circled her like a shark, looking at her with a predatory gaze.

"Not until I get my answers," he jeered with a grin. She gave him a look of confusion.

"What answers?" She asked desperately, feeling the others close in around them.

"You ratted me out, told them that I stole," he hissed. She shook her head in disbelief.

"What the hell are you talking about?" He felt like slapping her across the face for being so stupid, but held himself back. He wanted justice.

"Don't play dumb with me," his eyes narrowed. He stopped circling, his eyes piercing into hers. Her gaze drifted elsewhere, causing Jesse's to follow. *You should leave,* he heard a mysterious voice say to him. He whipped his head around, trying to find the source. "Who said that?" He asked. No response. *You won't find me unless you want to stay a little longer.* He felt like he was going crazy, his eyes searching around the perimeter rapidly. "Fuck this," he said finally, pushing through the circle of people toward Scott. There was something messing with him. He turned his head around to take a look at the group one last time. "You're all crazy," he retorted before turning back to Scott.

He helped Scott up, stumbling towards his car. *What the hell just happened?* His mind felt violated, like something had crawled into his ear and begun speaking to him. Scott had passed out in the passenger seat, his body looking as if it had been used as a punching bag. He had severely underestimated Balakin, finally seeing the true strength that was contained within him. He did know one thing though. He would be back, he had unfinished business after all. Jesse never left something unfinished. But in order to finish business, he had to take care of one thing. The boy with the voices.

Bradley Moore

The six of them stood in silence, watching as the car peeled out and down the street. *What the hell just happened?* Bradley found himself wondering.

"Ratted him out?" Jamie questioned with a groan, rubbing his head as his nose continued to bleed. Ivan stood still, breathing heavily with wide eyes. Bradley didn't think anyone expected him to do what he did today.

"Jesse confronted me not too long ago," Annette mentioned quickly, "asked if I knew about you ratting him out." Vicky let out an exasperated huff, annoyance spreading across her face.

"I didn't tell anyone about him stealing!" She shouted while throwing her hands into the air.

"Are you guys alright?" Bradley asked, facing the wounded Jamie and the entranced Ivan. Both of their heads shot up, staring at him wordlessly. Vicky turned her attention to them, her face beginning to fill with worry.

"Oh my god, you're bleeding," she fretted with surprise. She made her way over towards Jamie, checking the places of impact carefully.

"I feel fine," he muttered nonchalantly, "let's just go." They looked over at Stan who hadn't said anything at all. They all knew what he did, they also knew he didn't like doing it either. He looked focused, as if they were talking to each other. Bradley was the only one who knew about the journal, the entries causing him a great sense of discomfort. He now knew the true monster that lurked within Stan. *I will die for my people, die for what is perfect.* Bradley shuttered at the thought of it. He was crazy, and now the crazy was infecting Stan.

No one said anything, just watched him. He mumbled something under his breath, his finger twitching as he did. His eyes shot up toward the group, darting to each person that stood in front of him. Bradley realized the only one that'd been damaged was Jamie, and even then, he just had a nosebleed and a few bruises. Bradley kinda figured Scott wasn't that strong anyways. Stan's eyes rolled back for a moment, only the whites of his eyes showing before returning to normal again.

"Alright," he started quietly, "let's go." The five of them exchanged nervous glances as Stan led them forward and out of the park. They all stayed a reasonable distance behind him, Bradley looking down at his feet as Vicky drifted over towards him.

"You know something," she whispered in his ear. He whipped his head up before looking at her with a puzzled expression.

"What?" He asked with confusion. She slowed her pace, causing Bradley to do the same. The others walked in front of them without much care, having their own conversations as they did.

"I can tell you do, just tell me," she whispered accusingly. He shook his head.

"No," he said, "I'm waiting for him to tell you on his own time."

"He's not going to tell us and you know it," she hissed between gritted teeth, "he doesn't trust us." Bradley shrugged.

"I wonder why," he scoffed with a lack of surprise, "you haven't given him too much of a reason to." She looked frustrated.

"And you have?" She asked with annoyance. "You of all people?" Bradley stopped in his tracks.

"Wake up, Vicky, wake up and listen to someone besides Jamie and Annette for once," he hissed. "You surround yourself with a bunch of shitty people who don't care about anyone but themselves. I know you'd like to think of yourself as a kind person, but deep down you know you're just like them." He shook his head with disappointment, speeding up and leaving her behind before she could say anything else. He had hoped she might have been different, but she thought of Bradley the same way everyone else did. She was just one in a crowd. *So be it.*

He picked up the pace until he was walking beside Ivan, the group making their way down the street quickly. Something about him was different, he just couldn't tell what. *Maybe it's the fact he actually used his strength against someone, dipshit.* Bradley thought, criticizing himself. He wasn't sure if now would be a good time to ask what was up with him, no one seemed to be the happiest at the current moment. He decided to speed up once again, this time until he was walking beside Stan.

"Hey," Bradley greeted with a slight feeling of nervousness. Stan glanced over at him, his pupils constricted.

"Hey," he responded calmly. They turned the corner, making their way down Oak Street.

"Did he say anything to you?" Bradley asked with a waver in his voice. Stan hesitated.

"Yes," he answered quietly. Bradley knew better than to push him and ask what he said. They continued to walk in silence, Stan leading the front while Vicky took the rear. Bradley knew where they were going, he wasn't quite sure if everyone else did though. It felt strange being let in on information while everyone else followed instructions cluelessly. It was different from what he was used to. It wasn't much longer until they found themselves standing in front of the weathered house of John Charles.

Stan was the one to knock on the door, knocking twice and loud, hoping he'd be able to hear it. The six of them crowded together on the old man's porch, the occasional creaking being heard from underneath someone's foot. For a moment, Bradley didn't even think he was home, the air around them feeling stiff and empty. Just as he was about to suggest that they go home, a slow creak could be heard, the dark old man greeting them at the door as if he had been expecting them.

"Finally," he said with a small crooked grin. He moved to the side, allowing them to enter his darkened home. Curtains covered every window, blocking the sun from touching his wooden floors. The floorboards creaked beneath them as if they were crying out in pain. The six of them crowded around the front door, waiting for the old man to close it. Bradley could tell that the others were nervous, he couldn't help but feel a little sense of unease himself. He leaned against the wall next to Ivan, his heart thumping softly within his chest. The old man turned to face the group, getting a good look at each of them.

"It seems as though you already know why we're here," Stan stated promptly. John nodded his head.

"Yes," he confirmed, "come and make yourself comfortable." With a large hand, he gestured towards the living room. They followed his wishes, making their way towards the living room. The air felt stiff, as if they were walking through a dream. Vicky and Annette sat themselves down on the old beat-up couch, Jamie and Bradley sitting on the patched armrests, dust rising as they did. Ivan sat on the floor while Stan remained standing. John leaned himself against the wall, facing the six of them while studying each of their faces.

"What do you know about him?" Stan asked blankly. John smiled once again.

"Go ahead," he urged, "say his name." Stan shook his head.

"I don't want to," he told him. He watched as Vicky and Annette exchanged looks. He reached for his back pocket, pulling out the small journal before tossing it to the coffee table in front of the couch. John's eyes widened, his body lurching towards the journal. "No," Stan spoke firmly, "not until you explain what you know." John nodded his head, pulling up a nearby chair.

"Sit," he commanded calmly. Stan kept his eyes on John, sitting beside Ivan on the floor without looking away. He let out a heavy sigh, clearing his throat gruffly before beginning to speak. "As you probably already know," he began with a rough voice. "Richard Huxley used to live there in the house you're livin' in now." He started to cough lightly, grabbing his glass of water from the coffee table quickly before taking a swig of it. He set the glass down and began to speak again. "I suppose the residents of this here town always knew he was a little loose, but none of us knew exactly *how* loose."

"Has he always lived here?" Vicky asked meekly. He shook his head before taking another sip of his water.

"I don't believe so," he responded gruffly. "If I remember correctly, he only lived there for about six years or so. You see, I've lived here in this old house my whole life, I would know." He took another sip.

"That's a long time to be in the same house," Bradley mumbled under his breath, Vicky elbowing him in the arm sharply. John Charles drew in a deep breath, setting his glass down softly.

"I always knew," he began to say, "knew he was loose." *Loose, why doesn't he just say crazy?* Bradley wondered. "He seemed normal at first, a well-put-together man with a steady job." He paused. "Then at some point, something just happened, it wasn't a sudden change, no. It was gradual." He let out a loud cough, covering his face with a large hand while clutching his chest. "As if his mind were decomposing." They all glanced at each other nervously, a weary feeling filling the stiff air around them. "This seemed to be a behavior he kept hidden. Like he was used to it before. Richard Huxley was a special kind of *something*."

"Crazy?" Jamie questioned with a raised eyebrow. John Charles shook his head.

"No, he knew what he was doing." He paused once more. "He started to become an issue in the summer of 1964, that's when he started making trips to the cemetery." Bradley began to recall the journal entries, a shudder surging through his body. "I would stay watch every night, sitting on my porch waiting for him to pass on by. At first, it was only about twice a week that he would do this, later on, it would become about four." He paused, taking another drink of his glass. At this point, there was barely anything left to drink, but John either didn't notice or didn't care. He sighed.

"He was a disgusting man," John continued, "doing more to those bodies than I believe he originally planned to." Bradley didn't have to ask to know what he was talking about. "When a child went missing? Well, we knew we had to take action didn't we," he coughed before setting his nearly empty glass down. "I planned his death, the man who actually executed him had just passed away about a year ago." Bradley noticed Stan's finger twitch.

"Who all was involved?" Stan asked blankly. John paused.

"I'm too old to remember," John responded slowly with slightly narrowed eyes. "But I do believe that there were more victims of Huxley than just the boy," he stated. "He didn't just kill for the thrill of it, he killed with a purpose to take."

"Take what?" Annette asked, shifting in her seat anxiously. John tapped his head twice with a thin finger.

"He wanted what's up here," John explained carefully. "He sought after the brain."

"How is he back?" Jamie asked with disbelief. John took one last sip of his water, setting the empty glass down.

"After he died, me and a few others went into his house," he continued before pausing. "We found things we weren't supposed to see. The missing kid, the brains of the corpses, photos containing violent pornography, and some sort of torture device set up in one of the rooms." Bradley felt nauseous hearing this information, not knowing how to take it. "The last thing we found, however, was something you should listen closely to," he enunciated while pointing at all of them. "Papers, research, all on how to transfer spirits or some shit like that. This is why I say he wasn't crazy, he knew what he was doing and he had done it right. He knew we were going to kill him, so he had a backup plan." Bradley immediately thought back to the journal.

"That," Bradley said while pointing at the old book on the coffee table. "He said it right in there, how did we not notice before?" Bradley asked while looking at Stan in utter shock. Stan didn't say anything. John's eyes widened, snatching the journal from the table like a child grabbing a toy. He quickly flipped through the pages, reading through them with speed.

"I knew we should have kept going, I told Evans not to make the hole so shallow." He put his head down, rubbing his temples. "But he and the others just wanted to leave," he sighed before slamming the journal to the floor.

"What are you talking about?" Vicky asked with worried eyes.

"He must've touched his corpse somehow," John gestured towards Stan without looking up. "Allowing Huxley's spirit to be reborn, attaching itself to him." He explained. "We all knew it was a possibility, but none of us thought it could *actually* happen." They all fell silent, watching the old man stress in his chair. "Lord, I wish he would have just stayed dead, look at what he's already caused!" He yelled. "What do *you* know, boy?" He questioned with bloodshot eyes. Stan tapped his finger, looking up without saying anything. Bradley decided to speak for him.

"He can only physically touch us within a mile of Stan," Bradley elaborated meekly. "We also think that if Stan dies, Huxley dies too." Jamie's head perked up at Bradley's words, his eyes traveling over towards Stan slowly.

"A mile?" John asked with a short laugh. "Once you allow him full power, he will be able to leave the host's body and go on his own." *Full power?*

"What?" Annette asked. "Full power?" It was as if she read his mind.

"Don't ask me, it's what was in the papers," he stated while holding his hands up. "This is all the information I can provide you." Bradley looked at Stan, his eyes filled with worry.

"So what are we supposed to do?" Annette questioned in annoyance, crossing her arms tightly. John slapped his legs before standing up.

"You're all on your own, I did my part, it's time for you to do yours." The six of them got up slowly, seeing it as their time to depart.

"You can't just leave us like this!" Vicky shouted. He grabbed his empty glass.

"My job was to give you the information you needed," he explained. "I did my job, this is your burden to carry." He went back towards the kitchen, leaving the group of teens dumbfounded in his living room. Stan picked the journal up off the floor, brushing it off neatly.

"So you didn't even think about telling us that you had Huxley's journal?" Jamie asked in disbelief. "Did you know about this?" He questioned while turning towards Bradley. Bradley hesitated before slowly nodding his head in shame, feeling a hint of guilt.

"I knew it!" Vicky shouted. "I *knew* you knew something." Bradley wanted to make a remark but decided against it, knowing that he'd only add to the issue. Stan stuck the journal back in his pocket, turning to face the group.

"Let's just go," he told them quietly, not being able to look anyone in the eye. Stan stood there as the rest of the group walked ahead of him and out the door, John nowhere to be seen. Bradley waited there with him, looking at him nervously.

"What happened?" Bradley asked with worry. Stan shook his head.

"He talked to me," he told Bradley, "Huxley talked to me and explained everything." He suddenly looked up, his eyes locking with Bradley's. "I know everything."

Richard Huxley

That bastard! For him to be waiting for my host, for my host to try going behind my back. Nobody outsmarts me. I know better. I know everything! They killed me, spit on my body, invaded my home, did this all to their god. Well fuck 'em! I will find the ones who did this to me, I will make them pay. Whatever is left will be destroyed. I will start with the ones I remember. The last face I saw before I died. He might not be alive, but his wife is. It is time for my requiem.

Annette Jones

"Are you kidding me right now?" Annette questioned in shock. "He's not even going to help us?" Vicky shook her head, glaring at Bradley as the two boys made their way out of the house.

"What else are you hiding, huh?" Vicky's eyes blazing and accusing.

"I'm not hiding anything!" Bradley yelled out.

"Oh bullshit," Vicky snarled. Annette could feel a headache beginning to form. The six of them stood at the curb, the light of the sun dancing through the leaves above.

"Stop!" Ivan shouted weakly. The group's eyes shifted towards him, surprise emitting from all of them. "Why do you always argue? This will get us nowhere, we all have the same goal, yes? So let's all just stop, please." He pleaded desperately.

"He's right," Stan agreed quietly. "We need to find out how to get rid of this thing, we can't do that if we just keep arguing." Vicky looked down, seemingly ashamed of herself. "I wasn't ready to show the journal yet," Stan explained before throwing it out onto the ground. "We weren't trying to hide anything, don't blame him." He motioned his head towards Bradley who looked equally ashamed. Annette bent down to pick up the journal, feeling the others surrounding her to read. Their eyes all frantically scanned the pages, Annette feeling sick to her stomach.

"He thinks he's god?" Jamie asked in confusion.

"He wants to kill everyone?" Annette frantically questioned, feeling as though that was the more important question to be asking. Stan took the journal back, staring at them with empty eyes.

"We have to find who did it," Stan noted shortly. Bradley shot him a look of concern. "To see what they know, see if they can stop it." Annette rolled her eyes, glancing up at the trees above. She didn't want to be a part of this anymore, all she really wanted to do was go home. *Maybe that's exactly what I'll do.*

"Well, how would they know what to do?" Vicky asked with her hands on her hips. Annette figured now would be a good time to slip away. She separated herself from the group quietly, listening as their talking turned into background noise. She made her way down the street, feeling her heart rate begin to calm as she did. She didn't trust Stan, didn't trust any of them except for Vicky really. She was beginning to wonder if even Vicky could be trusted now. She looked back, not recognizing her childhood friend. She was someone else now.

Nobody noticed she was gone, she was becoming fairly used to that sort of thing. A shadow that could slip away at any moment without being seen. She couldn't decide if she should go home or not anymore, her stomach tying up in some sort of twisted knot. She felt guilty for leaving, but also couldn't care less. This situation no longer involved her, Arnold's friend Mitchell West is dead, and there's nothing she can do about it. She could still remember the glazed visage over Mitchell's eyes, a plastered expression of fear and sheer horror, a look no boy his age should ever have to give.

She could feel sweat begin to drip down her forehead as she continued down the street, her loose hair sticking to her face. *Maybe I should go see Jeff...* She thought with tired eyes. An image of Tommy suddenly struck through her mind like a bullet, a shudder ripping through her. *Why did I do that?* She asked herself while staring at the sidewalk beneath her intensely. *And why did I lie?* She suddenly felt like throwing up, not understanding where all this guilt and remorse was coming from. She just wanted to get it out, get everything out of her system.

Her wish was granted, vomit pushing its way up her throat and out her mouth into a nearby bush. She felt slight panic begin to ensue, praying nobody saw her throw up. She wiped off her lips with the back of her hand, feeling disgusted with herself. She stepped away from the bush, looking away quickly before turning back towards the street. This wasn't who she was. This isn't who she represents. She's supposed to be the moment, not vomiting in a bush. She decided she wanted to go home. She didn't want to see anyone today in her current state of mind, nausea filling her head and stomach. She bent down, hands on her knees as she felt another rush. This time, she was able to hold it in. She took in a deep breath before looking up, her eyes locking with deep hazel ones.

Laura Gray was posed on her bike quietly like a deer in headlights. Neither one of them moved, their eyes still locked in place. She had her work uniform on, her short, dark, reddish-brown hair in a mess of hairspray and frizz. Her eyes were surrounded by dark makeup, her gaze captivating. This was the first time Annette truly noticed her, she was actually kinda pretty. She straightened herself, searching for words but finding nothing. Laura did the speaking for her.

"Are you alright?" Her voice was emotionless, but her face showed a look of concern. She wanted to say yes, she wanted to walk away as if nothing was wrong, but she couldn't. *Maybe I'm just sick.* She felt as though she could trust Laura, in this moment she needed someone.

"No," she admitted with a waver in her voice. They stood in silence for a moment. *Why would she even care?*

"Okay," she said, nodding her head slowly to herself in understatement. "I'm going to work, do you want to come with me? Maybe get something to eat?" She asked with sincerity. *I really shouldn't.* She nodded her head herself.

"Yeah," she replied, "I think I'd like that." Laura let out a small almost unnoticeable smile.

"Wanna hop on?" She asked while gesturing towards the beat-up bike. Normally she'd decline, but she agreed, hopping on the back of the bike. She adjusted herself accordingly, holding onto Laura lightly for support. *What the hell am I doing?* At this point she didn't care, she just wanted to stop feeling so nauseous. Laura took off down the street, pedaling fast, causing Annette to tighten her grip. Annette felt like making a snarky comment, but the thought of saying something made her feel nauseous once again. She felt more vulnerable than ever, not understanding why. *What is wrong with me?*

The two continued down the street, speeding towards Irna's Diner. Annette wasn't sure how someone could go this fast on a bike, but she figured that Laura must do this often. It certainly did not help her nausea. She closed her eyes, searching for some sort of calm to keep her from throwing up. She counted to five in her head, her heart rate beginning to slow as she did. A sudden stop in the bike caused her to jolt.

"You alright back there?" Laura asked calmly. Annette didn't respond. She slowly opened her eyes to see the diner in front of her. With shaky legs, she slowly stepped off the bike.

"Where did you learn to ride like that?" Annette finally questioned. Laura got off herself, fixing her hair as she did, the sun revealing the more deep red parts of her hair.

"Well, you learn how to have fun when growing up as an only child." She explained, "you can head inside, I'm gonna wheel this around back." Annette nodded, following her instructions and heading inside the chilled diner. The summer sun beamed through the windows and danced upon the tables and booths lightly. For once, she felt serene. Old tunes played on the radio, inviting her in with welcoming arms. It wasn't busy this afternoon, not a single soul was in sight. She dimly noticed the bell on the door ring as Laura stepped inside. She felt a rush of warmth follow Laura inside, the summer air trying to creep its way into the brisk diner.

"I think I needed this," Annette spoke quietly. Laura walked past her and behind the counter.

"To be somewhere inside with air conditioning? Yeah, me too," she replied with a small laugh. Annette felt small, not how she usually felt while at school. She sat down in one of the booths and stared outside. Cars passed as people walked from store to store, the leaves of the trees blowing softly in the wind as the birds flew above. *Yeah,* she began to think to herself, *I needed this.* "Do you want me to order you anything?" Laura asked from her post, breaking Annette out of her trance. She thought about it for a moment, not knowing her answer.

"Could I just have a glass of water?" She requested meekly.

"Ice?"

"Yes, please," she answered politely. Laura gave her a warm smile before disappearing to the back. Annette returned her gaze to the window again, a car pulling up into the diner parking lot. The feeling of nausea was gone, she felt safe and content here. She closed her eyes, resting her head against the glass. The sound of the bell rang out as that same rush of warmth returned again.

"Mr. Price," Laura exclaimed in her usual monotone way as she set the glass of water down at Annette's booth. *The car mechanic?* She looked over to see Philip Price sitting himself down at one of the tables.

"Laura! How are you?" He boomed, his thick southern accent coming through. Philip was the local car mechanic and a damn good one, too. He was a tall and built man with scruff on his chin and despite his missing tooth, was pretty handsome.

"I'm doing alright, are you just gonna have the usual today?" She asked with a small smile. He looked at the menu, pretending to think really hard.

"Sure as sure!" He exclaimed loudly. He was a very loud man, but his volume had a strange comforting charm to it. Annette was sure he was partially deaf, but she could never find out and thought it would be rude to ask. She took a sip of her water, staring down at the menu, wondering if she should order anything to eat herself. She decided against it, not feeling very hungry and not wanting to risk the possibility of feeling sick again. She rested her head on the table, feeling more tired than anything. Her eyes fluttered close, her head heavy. Before she knew it, she was asleep.

She was staring down at the train tracks while looking at a mangled corpse, except this time she was alone, and the corpse wasn't Mitchell's; it was Jeff's. He was completely gutted, his limbs twisted in weird inhuman ways. His face looked puffy and infected, almost bloated. He began to speak through his broken jaw, his teeth slowly falling out one by one as he did. *I know you cheated, Annette. I trusted you, and you cheated on me.* She began to cry. *I would never! I would never!* She turned around to see Mitchell, his disfigured corpse surrounded by the group of five. *You failed Arnold.* He hissed through chapped lips, a centipede crawling out of his mouth and into the hollow of his eye. *You failed Arnold and because of you, I died.* One by one by one she watched them all slip into the ground, leaving her alone in the darkness of the forest. *Annette.* She heard Laura call. *Annette.* She whipped her head around frantically, searching for her. *Annette!*

"Annette, wake up," she heard as Laura shook her awake. She jolted her head up, her eyes meeting Laura's once again. "You alright? My shift's almost over, you really conked out," she noted carefully. Annette lifted her head to look outside, the sun starting to fall down the sky as it darkened outside.

"Oh my god," she mumbled in shock, "I really was tired." She rubbed her eyes, trying to wake up as Laura softly smiled down at her. The ice in her water had melted, causing a ring of water to surround her glass. The diner was completely empty, not much of a change from before. The sun's light didn't gleam as brightly now, a nice orange-tinted ray laying itself on the table in front of her. She heard Laura say something but it didn't register within her brain.

"What?" Annette questioned.

"I said, do you want me to take you home?" She asked for the second time. *On the bike again?* She thought to herself with dismay. But what other choice did she have? Her car was in the garage at home because she hitched a ride from Vicky earlier. The bike would have to make do.

"Sure," she agreed against her better judgement. "I'll do it." She tried rubbing the last of the sleep out of her eyes, a yawn escaping her after.

"What changed?" Laura suddenly asked. Annette shot her a look of confusion.

"What do you mean?" Her sleepy eyes now narrowing slightly.

"I mean, no offense but like," she paused, presumably trying to figure out what to say. "You're normally a lot more uh."

"Bitchy?" Annette finished for her.

"Yeah," she said as her pale face flushed with color, "what changed?" Annette looked down, staring at the water surrounding the glass.

"I don't know," she replied honestly. "Guilt maybe?" Laura nodded her head before sitting down in the booth across from her. "There's just so many feelings that built up inside of me, feelings I ignored and forgot were even there in the first place. Why am I just now feeling them? This isn't like me at all, am I sick?" She questioned, panic infecting her tone. Laura shook her head calmly.

"No, you're not sick," she soothed, "you're human."

"I don't want to feel like this anymore, I want things to go back to the way they were." She felt herself begin to shake, feeling even more stupid as she did. Laura reached over and grabbed her hand, holding it gently over the table.

"We are constantly changing, the most we can do is just give ourselves room to grow into the people we're meant to be. Turn your future into what you desire so you don't have to continue to long for a past that will never return." She spoke calmly, her eyes never leaving Annette's. She suddenly felt a rush of serenity, knowing that Laura was right. She sighed.

"I think I'm ready to go home," she told Laura calmly.

"Yeah?"

"Yeah." Laura gave her a soft smile, scooting her way out of the booth. Annette did the same, making her way towards the freshly cleaned glass doors. Once outside, she leaned against the building, pulling her pack of cigarettes out along with her lighter. Laura went around back, presumably to go get her bike. She took out a cigarette, lit it, and then took a long drag before sticking the pack back into her pocket. The nausea was gone, but she still felt some sort of anxiety. Laura definitely helped, she wasn't sure how, but she did. She felt this totally different perspective on her now, some sort of softness. Laura made her way around the corner with the bike, her eyes full of light instead of her usual emotionless gloom.

"You ready?" She asked softly. Pink began to streak against the sky, the sun making its march to bed.

"I think so," she replied. Laura hopped on her bike, her faded baby blue uniform resting over the seat gently. She patted the backseat, gesturing for her to get on. Annette took one last drag before dropping her cigarette to the ground, scuffing it out with her pink penny loafers. She carefully climbed onto the bike, allowing herself to hold Laura gently. She felt comfortable in her presence, something she hadn't felt in a while. Was she changing into the person she was meant to be? She wasn't sure. Laura took off, leaving the diner behind along with the rest of Annette's thoughts.

Vicky Taylor

Vicky didn't notice that Annette left, her focus remaining on the current situation. She felt as though something was off with Stan, his eyes shifting around anxiously.

"I'm sorry," she apologized while shaking her head. "I just don't trust this." Bradley turned to look at her, his eyes full of concern.

"What?" He asked with worry.

"Why does he want to know who did it?" She questioned with narrowed eyes.

"Seriously?" Stan asked, sounding slightly offended.

"Because they would know more than anyone else? I think you're just being paranoid, Vicky," Bradley countered as he adjusted his glasses.

"Jamie?" She looked at him for reassurance, feeling like she was going crazy. He looked like he had just been put on the spot, his eyes darting from hers.

"I don't think it would hurt to question them," he admitted nervously. She groaned, rubbing her temples. *Am I the only sane one here?*

"Ivan?" Her last ditch effort for a response. He shrugged, not saying anything. She took a deep breath, stopping herself from being consumed by frustration. *Wait, Annette.* She looked around frantically, not seeing Annette anywhere. "Where's Annette?" She asked, causing the others to look around too.

"Must have left while we were talking," Stan noted plainly.

"Good riddance," Jamie muttered under his breath. Vicky shot him an angry look, causing him to shrink once again.

"How will we even find out who helped contribute?" Bradley asked. *I know.* Vicky looked away meekly, feeling guilty of hiding something herself.

"Well," she started to say. They looked at her with careful eyes, Bradley's seeming more accusing than the rest. She turned towards Jamie. "Remember the book I tried showing you before we left for dinner?" She asked. He nodded slowly. "That book had the names of everyone who contributed, including a document paper and photographs." His eyes widened as Bradley's jaw dropped.

"So you were hiding-" Bradley started to say.

"I know! I know," she whined, cutting him off. She hid her face with her hands. "I'm sorry," her voice was muffled and strained. "I didn't mean to hide anything, I'm sorry for being all accusing with you earlier as well." She took a deep breath before pulling her hands away. Bradley's gaze softened, his brown eyes looking a lot calmer.

"It's okay, I accept your apology." He soothed.

"Thank you, I'll give you the book," she responded calmly.

"Really?" Bradley questioned with a raised brow. She looked down before responding.

"Yeah, I was overreacting," she admitted softly. "Let's meet at the park tomorrow morning, I'll have the book with me." *I'll have to find Annette tomorrow before I leave.* She thought to herself dimly. "Right now, I just want to go home," she sighed.

"That's fine," Bradley said. "I think I'm ready to go home too," he looked over at Stan.

"Me too," Jamie chimed in. Vicky glanced over toward Ivan's post, realizing he was somehow still there. *He's different today.* She sighed, feeling tired. Both Stan and Ivan stayed quiet, their eyes sticking to the ground. It was time to go. She never saw herself in this position before, especially not with these people. It was a weird surreal type feeling. She figured now would be the time to go home.

"Alright, I'm gonna head out of here," she stated quaintly, adjusting the straps to her lavender tank top. The rest nodded their heads in agreement. She turned around and went back to her car without saying goodbye. She felt Jamie's eyes burn into the back of her head, knowing how much he wanted to come with her. *Not this time.* She swiftly opened the driver's side door once she got to her car, getting in quickly and starting it without taking a second to look at the others. All she wanted to do was go home.

She sped off down the street, the trees and houses passing her by as she did. Her eyes scanned for children playing by the street, preparing herself for anyone who might dart out into the road. Her paranoia caused her to decrease her speed, the car slowly rolling down the street. She let out a sigh, turning on the radio for a distraction from her worries. This whole situation was still so strange to her. How did it even get to this point? Her life used to be so normal and orderly before, but now everything just happens on a whim. She knew what she was doing wasn't safe, any moment being around Stan could be life or death. She didn't care, she knew what she had to do. One of those missing kids could have been Jennifer after all.

She pulled into the driveway, her sister playing outside in the sprinkler on the front lawn. Vicky got out of the car, feeling a very wet hug before she could even shut the door.

"Vicky!" She squealed with excitement. She squeezed her back, despite the wetness of it.

"Hey, Jen!" She exclaimed back enthusiastically, hiding her weariness behind a large smile.

"Do you want to play in the sprinklers with me?" She asked with large pleading eyes. She winced at the idea, knowing that all she really wanted to do was go inside and take a nap. Vicky kneeled down so she was at eye level with her, resting her hand on one of her shoulders lightly.

"I wish I could today hun, but I'm so tired," she confessed apologetically. "But if you'd like, maybe we can tomorrow?" Jennifer looked down, seemingly thinking over it for a moment.

"Yeah, I guess," she whined disappointedly. Vicky smiled, ruffling her wet hair before getting back up.

"Alright, have fun Jen," she told her as she headed inside. She kicked off her shoes, immediately heading upstairs to her room. Once inside, she shut the door and began looking around for the book. She didn't see it on her desk, her heart dropping. *Did someone come in here and take it?* She then remembered that she left it underneath her bed. She quickly searched underneath the bed, blindly grabbing frantically for anything that felt like a book. She felt the smooth surface of the cover, quickly snatching it before pulling it out. *Perfect.*

She knew it was bad to hide something as serious as this from the rest of the group, but maybe she wanted to hide something for once. Everyone knew her family, knew her. Her entire life is almost all out in the open for everyone to see. She just wanted something of her own. She opened it up lightly, staring at the contents inside. The book contained a passage from everyone who was involved, a document shoved in between two of the pages almost like a bookmark. The document was his death certificate.

She had found the book in the dinky little school library, finding it on the floor.

She set the book on her desk before plopping herself onto the bed with a huff. She felt so drained from the week, her brain wanting to power off for the day. She dimly wished that everything would go back to normal again, that she had never met Stan. This couldn't *really* be happening to her. She lay there with open eyes, staring at the ceiling. She suddenly wished that Jamie was here too. She missed Annette as well, not understanding what was wrong with her. They've been so separate lately, something Vicky wasn't quite used to. They had only ever had a major argument once, but that was back in middle school. Why were they beginning to fight again?

She thought back to what Bradley had said earlier. *You surround yourself with a bunch of shitty people who don't care about anyone but themselves.* But Annette isn't shitty, is she? Vicky's head began to ache. Her whole world was changing before her eyes and everything she thought she knew was wrong. She rolled to her side, staring out the window. The sun was beginning to fall, the sky becoming streaked with pink. Large white clouds rolled across the sky, moving slowly with nowhere in particular to be. *Oh, to be a cloud.* She thought to herself dully.

She wished everything wasn't so confusing, everyone coming to her for questions she didn't have the answers to. It was exhausting. She didn't know everything, and she hated that since she was smart, she'd be expected to. She didn't have an answer to Stan's problem, and she wasn't sure if she ever would. She sighed, hoping this would all be over soon, hoping everything would go back to normal again. Deep down, she knew that would never happen. No matter what the result of this situation would be, she would never be the same again. *And maybe that's okay.* She thought to herself one last time before drifting asleep.

Stanley Morris

Stan went home without anyone that night. Although Bradley protested, he told him he just wanted some alone time. This was true, but Stan knew he'd have company either way. He sat outside on the back step, knowing his mom would come home a drunken mess tonight. He watched as the darkness began swallowing the woods in front of him, the last of the sun's rays kissing the Earth's surface goodbye. The crisp night air caused little goosebumps to appear on his skin as the crickets began to sing their melody. He felt oddly calm given the circumstances that he was in. He enjoyed the time he spent by himself, it was nice.

"Hello, Stan." He felt his heart drop, not daring to look behind him.

"Do you know when I'm feeling happy so you can just come over and ruin it?" Stan questioned with a groan.

"I know everything you feel," he stated with a gravelly, almost inhuman voice.

"Cool, can you leave now?" Stan kept his focus on the woods, glaring as he did.

"You're no fun," he hissed. He dimly noticed the man sitting on the stoop next to him, staring out into the woods as well. "I'm doing this for the both of us, I hope you know that." Stan shook his head, an annoyed smirk on his face.

"There isn't anything in this for me, you're just using me," Stan retorted with narrowed eyes. "You're just a leech." Huxley whipped his head over to face him, his yellow eyes gleaming.

"Don't you get it? Together, we can be god's," he raved in awe.

"I don't want to be a god, I want to be happy," Stan countered. Huxley sighed, facing the woods once again.

"There's no winning in this, is there?"

"At least you got that part right," Stan responded dully. Fireflies began to emerge from the grass, their little bodies lighting up all around the yard.

"I missed this house, missed my old life," Huxley mentioned longingly. "I never wanted to hurt anyone, I just wanted to save them." Stan finally turned to face him, his eyes filled with a deep sadness Stan had never seen him express before.

"This isn't the way," he told him quietly. A light breeze tickled the nape of his neck, causing more goosebumps to arise. A small pill-type bug crawled across his hand, reminding him briefly of Ivan.

"I don't mean to control you," Huxley admitted. "I didn't want to, but you left me no choice." Stan shook his head once again.

"I'd appreciate it if you stopped using me as your little puppet to get what you want," he snapped shortly, "for you to stop infecting my head."

"I want you to have as much free thinking as possible," Huxley stated with woe.

"Then stop getting into my head," Stan concluded before getting up from the step, turning to go back inside. Stan closed the door before Huxley could follow him in, knowing that this action would prove to be useless anyhow. "Go away, I'm done talking," Stan hissed before turning away to go to his room. He slammed the door behind him, the frame shaking slightly. *Let's just talk this through.* He heard the voice say in his head. "No!" Stan protested, looking around the room wildly. *I can offer you protection.* "I don't want it!" He yelled into the empty room. His screams were followed by a short silence. *You'll cave in eventually.* Stan didn't respond, he only plopped onto his bed and covered his ears.

He felt the cool summer breeze seep through the hole in his window, drowning his room in chilled air. He allowed himself to relax, feeling the presence leave him. *Well, I guess he can never truly leave me.* He thought to himself dimly. He laid down with a shuddery sigh, letting his chest loosen. He knew he should separate himself from the others in order to keep them safe, but it was so hard. He craved their attention, craved some sort of friendship. He knew the spirit could never gain full control, but he didn't like the little control that he could gain either. He was becoming dangerous.

He considered suicide again, thinking it would be the only way to keep everyone safe. He felt selfish for being alive, selfish for wanting human connection and staying with the group. If anything happened to them, it would be his fault because he could have prevented it. But he can't just pull himself away despite the guilt eating at him. After everything we went through, after all the suffering he had endured, he almost wished that he could go back. His current feelings were so confusing and conflicting, he hated this guilt, this pain of no control. He needed a bullet for him and his burden to stay sane.

He heard the front door slam open, followed by hyena-like laughter from his mother and a strange man. He groaned, covering his head and ears with the pillow, knowing what was going to happen next. He couldn't wait to move out. *If you even escape this house.* He thought to himself with an eye roll. He heard glass shattering from outside his room followed by a slam against the wall and more laughter. He wouldn't be able to sleep like this. He looked out from underneath the pillow, peeking towards the window. He knew what he wanted to do.

He got up from his bed, heading towards the window. He stood in front of it, knowing he wasn't thinking clearly.

"Don't let her hear," Stan whispered. *On one condition...* He heard the voice hiss inside his ear. He took a deep breath. "I understand." He heard the voice laugh. *I knew you would.* He looked at his small nightstand, his eyes zeroing in on it. He quickly grabbed it, crashing it into the already breaking window. The glass shattered, causing him to flinch slightly. He knew his mom wouldn't hear, he had made a promise. He set the nightstand back down slowly, feeling the adrenaline pumping through his veins. He stepped out the window, setting his foot down and feeling the due on the grass. He could feel his heart wanting to race, but he kept his breathing to a minimum. He could feel his body fighting for control.

He didn't need directions, his feet seemed to just know where to take him. He slinked down the street quickly, passing his neighbor's house without a glance. He felt eyes on him, but he wasn't sure whose. *Just close your eyes and let me be your guide.* Stan did as he was told, closing his eyes and letting his feet guide him. He felt himself step on sharp little rocks, causing him to wince in pain. He continued to keep his eyes closed, feeling almost comforted by the control, like he was a child being carried inside after falling asleep in the car.

He knew at any moment that he could put a stop to it, that he could prevent what was about to happen, but he just wanted his mind to rest. He wanted out of the house. He continued to walk down the street with closed eyes, his feet slamming against the concrete as if he were just learning how to walk. This continued for what seemed like an hour until he finally came to a halt. *Keep your eyes closed, Stanley. You don't even have to go inside if you don't want to.*

"I want to stay outside," he whispered into the darkness. *As you wish..* He felt himself cross the road, traveling up four creaky wooden steps. He sat on an old rocking chair, his tired legs grateful for the rest. He kept his eyes closed, not wanting to see a thing. He pretended like he was an old man taking in the warmth of a summer night. He rocked back and forth on the chair slowly, listening to the sounds of the creaking and the crickets. He felt nice, it felt real.

It didn't happen right away, it happened like a storm, slow and rolling. It was as if he talked to her at first. Stan believed that he did. They had a nice long talk. About what? Stan could care less, he focused on believing he wasn't here. His eyes were squeezed shut, a glue laced with denial keeping them closed. He pretended that the screams were the screams from crows. Her voice carried out in shrill cries as her life was taken away from her. She wailed out in pain, a large thump coming from inside of the house. Stan continued to sit there and pretend, pretend like this wasn't his fault.

There was silence, just as there was before. She was dead. He sat there in the quiet, hearing nothing but the crickets and the rocking of what was once her chair. *You may open your eyes and walk home.* Stan did as he was told. He opened his eyes and got up from the chair without looking at the house. He stepped down the four steps and onto the sidewalk, becoming swallowed by the night. He felt light as if he were a child simply following his parent's instructions. He would go home after this, he would go home and sleep peacefully knowing that the blood of Mrs. Bury would be put on his hands.

Richard Huxley

I took the last of her life, absorbing it for my own benefit. Adding her life to my power source. Yes, my plan will soon be complete if all goes accordingly. My host has been so good, so compliant with me. I only need to control his steps, not his mind. He's already purified. The purity gets to everyone at some point, I believe. I'll make it all worth it. Everything will be everything, soon the bell will toll. Soon! A church on a field will be worshiping in my name. I need to find the tires that struck me dead. Struck down their God! My revenge is here, I will strike them down. This putrid world will be wiped clean, wiped with the blood of sinners and nonbelievers. Tonight I scream, tonight and today and tomorrow!

Jeffrey Grant

Jeffrey Grant laid on his bed with his hands over his chest, a feeling of emptiness washing over him. The morning sun beamed through his window as it danced on his carpet. He thought he had gotten through to Annette the other night, but she was still just as distant as ever. In fact, she seemed to be completely different. He felt alone, not understanding why she was pushing him away like this. He felt like a shell of the person he once was, not able to grasp what was happening in their little town. His friends seemed weird around him, as if he had changed too. He did end up sitting at Scott's table during lunch, but he never showed. Jeff put his head in his hands, feeling defeated.

He heard a soft knocking on his door, breaking him from is trance.

"Come in," he called out. The door opened, revealing his older sister Dana.

"Hey," she greeted softly, standing there for a moment. "Can I come in? Like, can we talk?" Jeff nodded, propping himself up before patting the bed next to him gently. She made her way over, sitting down beside him with a soft plop.

"Are you doing alright?" She asked with a hint of worry. "You haven't been yourself lately." Jeff sighed, not knowing exactly what to say.

"It seems a lot of people haven't been themselves lately," he commented. She put a hand on his back, looking at him with a sincere gaze.

"You can talk to me," she assured. He wasn't sure on where to start, *if* he should start.

"I don't know, Annette's been distant and kids are going missing.. My friends aren't themselves and quite honestly, no one is. Maybe I'm looking too far into it, but I feel so out of the loop, y'know?" He looked over at her with desperation, in need of someone to understand. She paused, seemingly thinking over her words.

"Yeah, I know I haven't been here too often, but there definitely has been a shift in energy around here," she agreed. He let out a sigh of relief, laughing a little as he did.

"So I'm not crazy," he affirmed. She let out a small smile.

"Of course not," she told him, "I just wish you told me sooner." His own smile faded.

"I would but, you're like never here," he noted. There was silence. Dana was twenty two and attending college in Dubuque, her visits often scarce. The house felt empty without her, a feeling Jeff tried to ignore. She tapped her foot against the bedframe, looking down anxiously before responding.

"I'll tell you what, I'll stay home and make dinner tonight. Does that sound good?" She proposed quickly.

"As long as you don't undercook it like last time, I was on the toilet for a week," Jeff teased. She rolled her eyes with a grin.

"Okay, I'll try not to give everyone food poisoning this time," she jested before getting off the bed. "I'll be back, I'm gonna go get some groceries for tonight, will you be alright?" Jeff nodded, feeling a bit better after their conversation. "Alright, I'll see you later," she concluded before departing in a rush. Jeff sat there by himself, listening as she made her way down the stairs and out the door. He felt his momentary joy dissipate as that lonely feeling crept back in. He stood up and stretched, finding that to be the most effective method to calm his nerves. He felt each muscle loosen as he stretched, pushing away that pent up energy. He let out a deep breath, feeling much better after.

When he was done, he sat on the floor, grounding himself as he closed his eyes. *It's okay to be feeling these emotions, I'm human, and this is normal.* He soothed himself. *I am in control.* He took a deep breath in, holding it before letting it out. His mother taught him how to meditate at a young age, something that soon became very important to him. He felt lighter, releasing all of his worries and allowing a feeling of peace to wash over him. *I am in control of my emotions.* He exhaled one last time, letting out the last of his misery. He felt rejuvenated, opening his eyes to this new world he freed himself into.

A sudden ring of the doorbell ran throughout the house, causing Jeff to jump. He slowly rose to his feet, making his way downstairs. He hoped it was Annette, he had so much he wanted to tell her. He knew of her behavior, but he also saw a side of her many others didn't. She was a very caring and compassionate person, a shoulder to lean on. He missed her. He missed their talks, their late night drives, their playful bantering. *Is she finally back?* The thought of seeing her smiling face again made him quicken his pace. He couldn't wait to lift her into his arms, twirl her around and kiss all her worries away. He reached the door, opening it swiftly before stopping his tracks. It wasn't Annette at his door, it was Tommy Morrison.

Ivan Balakin

Ivan was the first to arrive at the park, trying to lessen his time at home as much as possible. It was Sunday morning and the first blush of dew moistened his shoes as they brushed against his ankles. He sat on the bench, his eyes glued to the ground beneath him. Everything felt so surreal, so strange lately. It was as if his whole world was flipped around after meeting Stan. He wasn't sure if he liked it or not, but he was leaning more towards disliking it. He felt an ant crawl across his pale hands, a painful reminder of what happened Friday night.

His father had never found out that Ivan snuck away. Ivan figured that if he did, he wouldn't be at the park right now. When he came back that Saturday afternoon, he had told his father that he simply went to the park to study early that morning. He showed his father the work he had done at Jamie's before meeting with the group, his eyes full of pride. Good job is what he would tell Ivan. I'm proud of you, he would say blissfully unaware. Ivan decided that he should keep it that way. Maybe he could finally have the upper hand. Just maybe.

He raised his hand up to his face, observing the ant from a closer distance. He watched as its little antennas bobbed up and down curiously, feeling it tickle his finger. It's tiny mandibles lightly scratching the surface of his skin. He loved how simple insects were along with how easy they were to understand. He watched as the ant weaved in between his fingers, scurrying with speed. He lowered his hand down towards the grass, allowing the ant to make its departure. He sighed, knowing it would be a while before the others arrived. He should be used to being alone by now, but for some reason, it was starting to become a little more difficult.

He wasn't completely alone in the park. He noticed an old man across the pond, a park regular. Ivan thought his name was Randy Adams, but he wasn't completely sure. The two didn't talk much after all. He eyed the pond down warily, a shudder ripping down his body after recalling his dance with death. He would never allow himself to be that weak again. He watched as the sunrise began to drown the trees in a soft yellow light, the birds singing their morning song. He enjoyed the mornings the most, so quiet and sincere. He noticed a figure making their way towards him. Ivan squinted his eyes, making the figure out to be Stan.

He hobbled his way over, his finger tapping against his leg. He looked sickly and sleep-deprived, his movements almost zombie-like. His knees were scraped and a little bloody, concern arising from Ivan. Stan continued to slowly make his way over until he made it to the bench Ivan was sitting on. He stood there instead of sitting down, his usual white shirt stained with sweat and grass.

"I have something to confess," Stan declared as if talking to a priest. Ivan said nothing, just patted the seat next to him for Stan to sit. He sat down in a nervous manner with shaky legs, his eyes sticking towards the ground. "Someone died because of me," he admitted quietly. Ivan's eyes widened, he had no clue what to say.

"Uh," was all he managed to get out.

"I could have prevented it, but I just let it happen. Why?" He asked, looking at Ivan with wild eyes. He almost looked manic. Ivan stayed silent, his throat feeling dry and wordless. "I'm a horrible person," he mumbled with a shake of the head.

"Who?" Ivan asked with concern. Stan had a brief look of confusion on his face.

"The old lady," he replied anxiously.

"What old lady?"

"I don't know! I don't know anyone in this stupid little town!" He cried out while gripping his head. He took a quick breather, calming himself down. "Sorry, I didn't mean to shout."

"That's okay," Ivan said. This was a lot for him to take in, and just to think two minutes ago he was sitting at this bench by himself, blissfully unaware. Stan was an interesting character. He decided not to press on who the possible victim could be. Maybe he was just making things up? Having delusions? He did look quite ill after all. His best option would be to go along with it without asking too many questions. He was pretty good at doing that already anyway.

"I'm so scared of everyone leaving me," Stan fretted with a shudder. Ivan nodded his head in understatement. "I don't want to be alone again, I'm so sick of it."

"I get it," Ivan told him.

"Do you really? You seem to like being alone," Stan looked up at him with a careful expression.

"I do, but I also enjoy the company of others sometimes," he explained. "I doubt everyone enjoys being alone all the time."

"You'll all leave," Stan stated coldly. Ivan didn't respond. He couldn't tell if Stan was actually right or not. They both sat there in silence, birds filling the air with their melody. He wished he could just fix Stan and be done with it, but it would never be that easy. There was something seriously wrong with him that Ivan wasn't even sure *could* be fixed. He watched as Stan's finger tapped against his leg wildly, Ivan assumed it was a nervous habit. He seemed to have a lot of those.

Bradley was the next to show, his shirt drenched with sweat. Ivan wasn't even sure how that was possible, it wasn't that hot after all. He must have ran the entire way here. He dramatically collapsed on the grass in front of them, breathing heavily. Stan gave a look of concern, reaching out slightly.

"Are you okay?" He asked with worry. Bradley lifted his head from the grass, his face now wet with sweat and morning due.

"I ran all the way here," he told them, almost quoting Ivan's thoughts word for word. Ivan glanced over at Stan, wondering if he would tell Bradley the same thing he told Ivan earlier. He kept his mouth shut. *Hm.* "Do you think the others will get here soon?" Bradley asked while getting up from the ground, attempting to brush the wet grass off himself with minimal success.

"Not sure," Ivan responded quietly. Bradley plopped himself down on the bench between them, his odor hitting Ivan like a brick. He smelled like a dumpster fire and a mix of other things Ivan couldn't quite put his finger on. He normally did not smell too bad, he wasn't sure why he did now. *Please never run again.* He thought to himself in dismay.

"How long have you been here for this morning?" Bradley questioned Ivan with a stretch.

"I've been here all morning," he replied while resisting the urge to vomit.

"I got here a little while ago," Stan added before Bradley could ask him.

"Cool, I just got here," Bradley stated as if it wasn't already obvious. Sometimes Ivan just wanted to smack him upside the head, but he would never lay his hands on anyone. *Except for..* He began to remember what happened with Scott, a shudder rolling through his body. He would never do anything like that again unless absolutely needed. *And hopefully, it never will be needed.* Bradley let out an exasperated sigh, sliding down the bench dramatically. "I'm boreeed," he whined.

"Want to throw a frisbee?" Stan suggested. Bradley turned his head towards him, giving him an annoyed look.

"Stan, do you see a frisbee anywhere?" He asked as if he were stupid.

"Oh, I guess not, no," Stan responded meekly. The sound of a car pulling up shifted Ivan's attention to the road. *Oh, thank god they're here.* Ivan thought to himself with a sigh of relief. Vicky hopped out of the car, Jamie getting out the passenger side. *No Annette?* The duo made their way towards the bench, Vicky holding a book in her hands gently. Bradley perked up, adjusting himself while sitting upright. Ivan glanced over at Stan, his eyes widening at the sight of the book. Suddenly, Ivan felt uncomfortable and a little nervous. He wasn't sure if Vicky noticed his reaction to the book at all, but he honestly doubted it. It seemed sometimes only Ivan was able to notice the little things.

He got up from the bench, making his way over towards Jamie swiftly. Vicky sped up, walking past Jamie instead of next to him.

"Hey," Jamie greeted as Ivan turned to walk beside him.

"Hello," Ivan responded, not sure how to bring up the Stan subject. "Stan said something strange before you all came," he whispered, deciding to say it now.

"What'd he say?" Jamie asked back in a whisper, his eyes darting back and forth from Ivan to the group.

"Where's Annette?" He overheard Bradley ask Vicky. He stayed silent for a moment, curious for the answer.

"She said she'd come by later," Vicky answered promptly, sitting on the armrest of the bench. Ivan didn't really think she'd come back, she seemed even more distant than him. He felt Jamie elbow him in the arm, looking up with expecting eyes. Vicky gestured them over, distracting Ivan once again.

"I'll tell you about it later," he told him shortly, making his way towards the rest of the group. He could hear Jamie sigh as he followed behind closely, the two sitting down on the bench beside each other. Vicky set the book on her lap, flipping through the pages gingerly. She then held the book out for everyone to see, each of their heads peeking up to get a look. Ivan found it difficult to read the light and faded writing, his eyes squinting in an attempt to decipher the meaning of the tiny letters.

"I found this at the library a few weeks ago," she stated quietly, "it just fell out in front of me." She handed the book to Stan. "I didn't even check it out." Stan held it in the middle of the group for everyone to see, making it a lot easier for Ivan to read. Ivan read all the names of the people involved, his heart dropping slightly at one of them. *Gareth Bury.* Stan's words from earlier finally clicked with him. Ivan knew which old lady he killed. He looked over at him with a slight fear in his eyes, noticing as Stan began to sweat nervously. He was a murderer. He was a murderer, and he was guilty.

Stan flipped to the next page, revealing more names and statements. He got a good look at each page as if he were taking little mental notes of who each person was. Ivan could feel sweat begin to form on his hands, his heart beating quickly. He had to tell Jamie, he would fix everything. Stan continued to flip through the pages, his eyes scanning the words carefully. Ivan wanted to throw up. Once Stan was satisfied, he closed the book, handing it back to Vicky neatly.

"Well?" She asked with a raised brow.

"Why did they do this?" Bradley questioned, a puzzled expression taking over his face. Vicky shrugged.

"I don't know," she replied honestly, "we'd have to ask. I mean, we have the names right there," she gestured towards the book.

"Who do we even ask?" Jamie questioned. Stan's head shot up.

"The mechanic," he answered quickly. Vicky opened the book, flipping through it once again before pausing.

"Philip Price?" She asked swiftly. Stan paused before nodding his head.

"Why?" Ivan questioned slowly, his first time speaking up in a while. His eyes stared into Stan's with an accusatory gaze.

"The handwriting on the title looks like his, I think he wrote it," Stan spat out quickly. Ivan noticed Vicky's eyes narrow. Bradley grabbed the book from her, taking a glance at himself.

"He's right," Bradley noted, "it also says in his section that he thought about putting this together." He closed the book, "I guess we all just skimmed past that." Vicky nodded her head before taking the book back from Bradley.

"Alright," she said, "I say we meet up again after lunch." The rest of them nodded in agreement. "I'll make sure Annette joins us this time as well." Ivan noticed Jamie roll his eyes. She got up, still holding onto the book. "Be here by three," she concluded quickly. The group began to disperse, Bradley and Stan making their way out of the park. Ivan got up, grabbing Jamie by the shoulder before he could get away.

"Can we talk now?" He asked desperately. Jamie looked towards Vicky who was waiting for him halfway towards the car.

"Sure, but just make it quick," he agreed. "Just wait in the car, I'll be there in a minute," he told Vicky quickly. Vicky nodded her head before hopping in the car.

"I think Stan killed Margaret Bury," Ivan whispered worriedly, glancing over to see if Stan was in earshot. Jamie's eyes widened, his face full of disbelief.

"What makes you think that?" Jamie asked wildly.

"He told me earlier that he killed an old lady," Ivan explained anxiously. "I didn't think he was serious until I saw the book," he continued. "I think he's going after the people who contributed to the ghost's death." Jamie's expression went from shocked to serious.

"Do you know where your father's gun is?" He questioned without much emotion. Ivan felt his heart jump at the word gun, his breathing beginning to pick up.

"Yes," he answered honestly.

"When we have to meet up again, I want you to bring it," he stated calmly. "I don't want to, but if we have to and it means keeping other people alive-"

"I understand," Ivan cut him off, his throat feeling dry as he almost choked on his own words. He felt sick to his stomach, a large pit beginning to form.

"Good," Jamie said, "I'll see you at three." He turned around, making his way towards the car. Ivan was left there to stand by himself, the palms of his hands beginning to sweat. He didn't want to, but he knew that he had to. He had to for the sake of everyone else. *But only if something actually happens to Price, which nothing will.* He tried to soothe himself. He watched as Vicky's car took off down the street, leaving him truly alone. He had to go home and do it now while his father was still at work. He started his trek home with shaky legs, keeping any form of nausea in.

His father's car wasn't in the driveway when he made it home. A part of him wished it were so he didn't have to do this. He opened the door slowly, creeping his way inside the house. He knew exactly where the gun was, having been shown by his father where he kept it in case of emergencies. His mother was asleep on the couch, making this mission even easier. He made his way towards his parents' room, the door being wide open and inviting. He paused before going inside, his heart beating faster than a rabbit's. He took a deep breath before stepping inside.

He slowly crept over towards drawers, his legs wanting to buckle beneath him. He bent down towards the bottom right drawer, opening it with shaky hands. He had never done anything like this before, the fear making him want to throw up. He kept himself composed, grabbing the gun out slowly. It was a small pistol, his father's handgun that he bought before moving out of Kazan. Ivan knew he wouldn't notice, the gun having a thin layer of dust on it due to a lack of usage. *I hope this doesn't get used today.* Ivan thought to himself in dismay. He checked the barrel, finding only one bullet inside. He closed the drawer, getting up slowly. He got what he needed, it was time to go.

Jamie Anderson

Jamie watched as Ivan stood by himself while the two sped off down the street. He couldn't believe what he had just heard. Was Stan seriously falling for Huxley's tricks? Jamie knew from the start that he couldn't be trusted, this was just more proof. He felt a hand lightly touch his shoulder, breaking him out of his thoughts.

"You okay? You seem lost in thought," she asked softly. Her hand remained on his shoulder, causing his face to flush.

"Yeah, sorry." He replied quickly. She took her hand off, her focus returning to the road.

"What did Ivan tell you?" She asked quaintly. Jamie paused, not knowing if he should tell her. He decided he would keep it between him and Ivan, they'd all find out later anyhow.

"Nothing important," he responded. He felt bad for lying, but he wanted to take care of the matter himself. She smiled, making him feel even worse. She touched his shoulder once again, making him shift in his seat.

"Good," she said sweetly. He desperately wanted to tell her how he felt, this feeling consuming him. *Just do it.* He took a deep breath. *But is now really the right time?* He held in his air as he contemplated. *Just get it over with now!* He let all the air out in a heavy sigh.

"Vicky," he started to say, feeling himself wanting to back out. She looked over at him for a moment, her beautiful hazel eyes meeting his. *God, I can't do this.*

"Hm?" They were about halfway home, but he didn't think he could wait much longer.

"Can you stop the car?" He asked politely. A slightly puzzled expression fell over her face.

"Sure," she agreed before pulling over to the side of the road against the curb. The trees swayed above gently as the sound of birds called out all around them. He sighed once again, feeling nausea build up inside of him. She turned to him, giving her full attention. He could have melted right then and there. He didn't know what to do, didn't know what to say. He grabbed her hands gently, holding them in his. His heart beat in his chest wildly, his thoughts scrambled and distant.

"I," his voice cracked, his hands beginning to feel sweaty. *Oh god, this is awful.* He decided to bite the bullet, calming himself down. "I like you, Vicky, I think I always have," he paused before continuing. "I want to be yours." This time, it was her face to flush, her eyes wide with surprise. He felt like throwing up, but it was a relief to get it all out. She squeezed his hands, her gaze softening.

"I do too," she replied sweetly. There was a moment of silence between the two, their gazes sinking into each other as one. She softly grabbed the side of his face, the sweat from her hands soaking in. She pulled him closer, their faces inches away from each other. With slight panic, he closed his eyes and leaned in, their lips pressing against each other neatly. *Holy shit.* He thought before slowly pulling away. The two sat there for a moment, looking at each other in wonder. Jamie felt so mesmerized by Vicky, feeling lucky to just be in her presence.

"So," he started slowly, not sure what happens next.

"So," she said back. He leaned back, giving her some space.

"Does this mean we're going out now?" He asked with wonder. She smiled, letting out a small laugh.

"I would think so," she answered with a grin.

"Cool," he marveled breathlessly in awe, his eyes never leaving hers. She let out another smile.

"We should probably go," she noted softly. He felt disappointed, but he understood. He was just happy the feeling was mutual.

"Wait," he said before she could start the car. She returned her focus back to him, a slight smirk on her face. He grabbed her face gently, pulling her in for one last kiss. Her lips were so soft, the feeling was unbelievable. *I don't think I could ever get sick of this.* He thought to himself in awe. She beamed before starting the car, his heart racing. She pulled out and back into the road again, taking off towards her house.

"Don't hate me but," she started to say before turning down a street. "I'm going to go get Annette," she continued with a wince as if she was in pain. Jamie groaned, not wanting to have to see that stupid blonde bitch again. "I'm sorry," she whined, "I know you don't care about her, but I'm worried. He sighed.

"That's fine," he replied without much emotion. Thinking about Annette was such a turn-off.

"I'll make sure she doesn't make any snarky comments to you, I hope you can do the same," she told him while continuing down the street. Jamie put his fingers up to his lips, moving them across in a zipper motion without saying anything. "Thank you," she stated calmly. The two sat in silence for a few moments before Vicky turned the radio on, some catchy pop song playing its draining tune. It wasn't too much longer before they made it to her house, the driveway being completely empty. Vicky sighed, putting the car in park before turning the engine off.

"Want to stay in the car?" She asked while taking her seatbelt off. Jamie thought about it for a moment.

"Nah," he answered before unbuckling his own seatbelt. She smiled. He liked making her happy. The two got out of the car, making their way up the driveway and towards the front door. Vicky loudly knocked twice, waiting patiently for an answer. Jamie noticed the curtains near the front door open slightly, little eyes peeking through the gap. A few seconds later, the door opened, a broken-down Arnold meeting them.

"Hi Vicky," he greeted while rubbing his eyes. "If you're looking for Annette, she's at Irna's." He explained, already knowing what they were here for. Boys his age should be outside playing in this weather, but Jamie understood why Arnold wasn't. He figured he wouldn't either if his best friend had died in that sort of fashion.

"Thank you," she replied sweetly. "Don't forget, you're always welcome over," she mentioned while pointing towards her house across the street. He nodded his head tiredly.

"I know, thanks." She ruffled his head, causing a small smile to escape from him.

"Stay safe," she told him before leaving with a wave. He waved back without saying anything, closing the door behind them soon after. The two hopped back in the car, Vicky starting it up once again.

"Irna's?" Jamie questioned in confusion. Vicky shrugged before pulling out, not seeming to understand the situation herself.

"Maybe she and Jeff just wanted to get out?" She hypothesized with a puzzled look on her face. It was a good thing that Irna's was on the way to the park because they seemed to be doing a lot of backtracking. *I hope Ivan went through with the plan.* Jamie thought to himself dimly. He felt bad about hiding it from Vicky, but in his eyes, he was just protecting her. He was going to fix everything, he was going to make everything normal again.

It didn't take too long for them to get to Irna's, but Jamie also figured it was because Vicky was speeding half the way there. He noticed she was a little tense, but he couldn't quite figure out why. Maybe it was because this was out of Annette's character? He came to the conclusion that it was, but he didn't want to ask and stress her out even more. She pulled into the dinky little parking lot, parking right next to Annette's pink Iroc. She took off her seatbelt, not bothering to ask whether or not Jamie would come inside or not. He did the same, getting out of the car and making his way inside the diner.

As soon as he stepped inside, he was met with a blast of cool air. The diner, as usual, was pretty empty, with only two other families being inside. Annette was in a booth near the end of the building in a corner; she was sitting across from Laura who was laughing at something she said. Vicky quickly made her way over to them, Jamie following closely behind. The two girls looked up towards Vicky, her hands on her hips like a disappointed mother.

"I thought you were gonna be there," Vicky told her sternly. Annette glanced at Laura before returning her focus back to Vicky.

"Relax, I was just getting some breakfast first," Annette stated, her tone surprisingly calm instead of defensive. *What the hell is going on?* Jamie thought to himself in mild shock.

"Really, then where's your plate?" Vicky asked with a raised brow. Annette shrugged, looking over at Laura, who was smugly looking back, the two smiling at each other. Vicky turned her steely gaze over to Laura. "I thought you didn't like her," Vicky snapped to Annette, her stare still piercing Laura. Annette let out a laugh.

"People change," she told her while smirking at Laura.

"I'll let you get to wherever you need to be," Laura said smoothly, "I should probably get back to work anyway." She slid Annette a lighter before leaving the booth and going back to her post. Annette pocketed it and sighed, getting up from the booth herself. Jamie noticed all of Vicky's anger dissipate into more confusion. Jamie was quite confused himself, not understanding the new friendship between Annette and Laura, especially not understanding Annette's calm attitude.

"Alright, I'm ready," Annette concluded calmly. *Is she high or something?* Vicky gave Jamie a look of confusion, the two of them not being able to wrap their heads around the situation. Jamie led them out the door, making his way towards her car. He decided he would let Annette take shotgun. The three of them got into the car, Vicky starting it after everyone got buckled. The air in the car felt strange, as if something were off.

"Everyone is supposed to meet back at the park by three," Vicky started to explain as she pulled out of the parking lot. "But I think I'm just going to pick everyone up right now."

"Okay," Jamie heard Annette say in the front seat, checking her makeup in the mirror.

"Who are you picking up first?" Jamie asked, shifting in his seat a little.

"Probably Bradley," she told him with a shrug and a sigh. "His house is nearby." She turned the car down the street. Jamie waited for a scoff from Annette, something she would normally do at the sound of Bradley's name. Nothing. *She's definitely high.* Jamie thought to himself as he stared out the window. He felt tired, but Jamie thought that he always felt that way. His eyes constantly wanting to close on him. He yawned as if the thought of sleep beckoned him to.

It wasn't long before Vicky's Monte Carlo turned into Bradley's driveway. Vicky got out without saying anything, leaving Jamie and Annette to sit together in silence. As much as Jamie wanted to question her sudden change, he kept his mouth shut. She seemed to do the same, leaning against the window calmly. He watched as Vicky knocked on the front door, waiting patiently for someone to answer. Jamie speculated that she would be waiting there for a moment as there wasn't any other car in the driveway besides hers, Bradley's bike being nowhere to be seen. He sighed, knowing they'd be there for a while.

Vicky went back to the car in defeat, opening it tiredly with a huff. She sat down and leaned her head back.

"We'll just have to wait," she mumbled disappointedly. The sun beamed through the windows softly as the birds chirped outside. It was actually a beautiful day out. Jamie leaned against the window, letting his eyes close. He wouldn't allow himself to sleep though, not after the nightmare he had last time.

"Oh, they're right over there," Annette noted, causing Jamie to perk his head up. She pointed out her side of the window towards the street, Bradley and Stan walking Bradley's bike down the sidewalk. Jamie watched as the two boys waved, hurrying their pace. For a moment, Jamie wondered if there would be enough room for everyone in Vicky's car. *It's gonna be a bit cramped, but I'm sure we'll all fit.* Vicky stuck her head out the window once they were in a close enough distance.

"Hey, we're gonna do this early," she explained. Bradley gave a thumbs up, propping his bike against the garage. Stan made his way towards the other side of the car, getting in and scooting to the seat in the middle right next to Jamie.

"Let me know if I'm too close," he told him quietly before Bradley hopped in right next to him. Jamie didn't say anything. Vicky started the car after Bradley closed the car door, making her way down the driveway and towards the park. Ivan was quite tall, maybe if they were lucky, they could stick Bradley in the trunk. No one tried to make small talk, the only voices being the ones from the radio. Jamie kept his eyes glued to the window, not wanting to risk initiating any kind of conversation. He wasn't really in the mood. Lucky for him, Vicky's speeding made the ride take about five minutes. Ivan was just where Vicky predicted he would be, except this time he had a cross-body bag with him.

"I'll get him," Jamie offered before Vicky could get out of the car. He rushed out of the car and towards Ivan who was slowly making his way over. "Do you have it?" Jamie asked in a harsh whisper. Ivan pulled the bag to the front of himself, opening it to reveal a pistol hidden under a cloth. "Perfect,"Jamie told him. Ivan quickly closed it, handing it to Jamie.

"This is your problem now," Ivan grumbled sternly, a cold look in his eyes. Jamie understood, nodding his head silently before heading back to the car. Jamie went back to his seat, sitting down with the bag facing away from Stan, who was eyeing it up quietly. Ivan went towards the other side of the car, opening it before realizing there was a lack of space.

"Someone will have to sit on the floor," Vicky mentioned apologetically. The three boys turned to look at Bradley.

"Really?" He whined. They just continued to stare at him without saying anything as if he should have already known. "Ugh, fine," he groaned, accepting his fate. He unbuckled, attempting to find a seat on the floor as Ivan took his spot. Once they were all settled, Vicky started the car and made her way towards the Auto shop. Bradley rummaged around the floorboards, picking up a bag of chips from underneath one of the seats.

"What are you doing?" Stan asked with his usual quiet voice. He held the chips up to Stan before opening them.

"I found chips, dude!" He exclaimed with a wide grin, adjusting his glasses as he did. He took two out, popping them into his mouth quickly. "Did you want these?" He asked Vicky around a mouthful of chips. Jamie noticed Vicky's eyes roll in the rearview mirror.

"Uh, no," she replied blankly. It felt like the vehicle was going faster, and Jamie knew that she was feeling anxious. She just wanted to get this over with. Jamie did too. He briefly glanced at Stan. *Will you actually pull that trigger?* He asked himself. He took in a deep breath, feeling a looming presence. The Auto shop was only a few miles away from the burn pile and a nearby neighborhood. However, none of those areas were close to the park. Jamie sighed. *Gonna be a bit of a ride.*

Jamie ended up falling asleep. He didn't dream of anything, or at least if he did, he didn't remember. Bradley shook him awake once they arrived, saying something that Jamie couldn't really comprehend but assumed was something along the lines of "wake up, we're here." He groaned as he stretched his legs a little. The six of them stumbled out of the car, Jamie checking the bag before getting out himself. *Good.* The man they were looking for was conveniently working on a car outside, he hadn't noticed them quite yet.

The group made their way towards him, Vicky leading the pack with large strides. Ivan kept himself in the rear. Philip Price perked his head up, probably hearing their footsteps. With a large grin, he rolled out from beneath the car, standing up to greet them.

"Hey!" He boomed while looking down at them. He was a very tall and broad man, his stature being a little intimidating. "Can I help ya?" He asked with bright eyes. Vicky let out a specific sort of smile she gave when trying to get information out of someone.

"Well, I have a few questions for you," she told him kindly. He let his eyes fall on each of the group members as if he were analyzing them.

"Lay it on me," he beamed. She pulled out the book, handing it out to him.

"Did you write this?" She asked with slightly narrowed eyes. His own eyes widened as he took the book from her gently, flipping through the pages.

"I haven't seen this in ages," he faltered quietly, his tone completely changing. "Christ." He continued to flip through the pages in silence, his tanned face turning a little pale. Jamie glanced over at Vicky nervously. "Where did you find this?" He asked before pulling up a nearby stool to sit on, wiping his forehead with an oil-stained handkerchief.

"Library, now did you write this?" She questioned again coldly. He paused, seemingly not knowing what to say, his jaw partially open.

"Yes. Yes, I wrote this," he answered promptly. Jamie noticed Stan twitch a little. "God I never thought *this* is what I would be asked about. I thought we left this all behind." He mumbled as he shook his head, birds flying overhead as a gentle breeze whirred through.

"What do you know?" Vicky persisted. He sighed.

"Can I work on the car when we talk about this?" He asked with a stutter in his voice. "It helps me think." Vicky nodded her head, giving him permission without words. He wiped his forehead one last time before returning to his post. Jamie noticed Stan twitch again. "What is it that you want to know?"

"How did you contribute to his death?" She questioned quickly. He let out a breath of air, his body looking shaky and uncomfortable.

"I contributed by fixing up the Ford Falcon that killed him, I was also the one who destroyed it after." He paused. "The person who *actually* did him in was Gareth Bury." Philip shook his head as he worked on the car with shaky hands. "But I don't think he wanted to be the one behind that wheel." The group exchanged a brief look of confusion before Vicky spoke once more.

"What do you mean?" He glanced at them before returning his attention to the vehicle.

"Well, the man carried a lot of uh, waddya call it.. Anxiety with him. I don't think he wanted killing a man to be on his conscious, no matter how much he deserved it. This other fella, Randy Adams wanted to do it but.." Philip trailed off, grabbing the rag to wipe his face with. "John didn't think he seemed fit for the job. I don't know why, and I honestly never cared to find out," he sighed. "They let him in the passenger seat, needing someone to make sure ol' Gareth wouldn't back out."

"Did he?" Bradley asked timidly.

"From what I heard, he tried. I guess Randy threatened him a little before ultimately taking the wheel and swerving right into the son of a bitch." Philip wiped his head again, hands still shaking. "Guess he got what he wanted after all, kinda funny, isn't it?"

"What about the necromancy? Did you guys find anything about that in his house?" Vicky spat out. Philip let out a short laugh before responding.

"His house, man what *didn't* we find in there? It was a nasty sight i'll tell ya. Polaroid pictures of corpses, crosses, dead rats, and brains. He had a bunch of brains in these weird jars, but no furniture besides a single chair. And the smell, god *the smell*. It was just awful, our little town hadn't seen anything like it." He waved a hand as if he were still there. "Huxley was a depraved man, that much we were sure of. As for necromancy? We found all his journals, but it just seemed like a bunch of drugged out nonsense." He paused once again. "Unless this is the reason why you're here," his gaze turning to them, his bright blue eyes full of anxiety. Stan twitched one last time before falling to the ground, Huxley shooting out of him like a rocket as his yellow eyes gleamed in the air. The group jumped backward, shocked by his sudden appearance.

"You forgot a key detail, Price," Huxley hissed. Philip Price lay there frozen in fear, his jaw agape as his eyes glued onto the creature. "You were the boy who cried, KILLER!" He screamed before pushing the car down on top of him. The sickening sound of his bones crushing filled the air around them, blood pooling around the car like water. He didn't have the chance to speak, he didn't have the chance to do anything before he was squashed like a bug. The five of them stood there in shock, Stan still laying on the ground motionless. Jamie took this as the perfect opportunity.

He quickly pulled the pistol out of the bag, aiming it towards Stan. His hands began to shake, but he knew what he had to do. Vicky noticed him with the pistol, her eyes widening.

"Jamie?" She panicked. The rest of their group turned their focus towards him. Everyone was completely still, it seemed even the birds stopped their chattering for a moment. "Put the gun down," Vicky demanded, her voice nice and calm.

"No," Jamie told her as Stan began to regain consciousness. "He's siding with Huxley, he's gone bad."

"Stop!" Bradley pleaded. Jamie shook his head, his mouth curling into a snarl. Stan's eyes widened, but he didn't say anything. He sat there like a deer in headlights.

"Do you not remember what you said at the old man's house, Bradley?" Jamie questioned, turning his head slightly towards him. Bradley stayed silent, Jamie thought for a moment he could hear his own heart beating. "If Stan dies, then so does Huxley? Why not just get it over with now? He's already turned," Jamie hissed.

"This isn't the way," Vicky stated calmly.

"Then what is the way?" Jamie asked between gritted teeth. "Let more innocent people die, huh?" He turned his focus back towards Stan. "I won't let that happen," he grumbled before pressing the gun against Stan's head.

"God please don't do it," Annette cried out.

"Jamie, last chance, put down the gun," Vicky commanded strictly. Jamie clicked off the safety. *You wouldn't dare.* He heard Huxley say into his head.

"Oh, I would," Jamie threatened quietly. He pulled the trigger. *BOOM!*

Trumpets

After the deaths of the missing children, Linfort seemed to be under some sort of lockdown. People were becoming paranoid. It was as if nobody could be trusted. But wasn't it a train that killed them? Wasn't it the car that killed Price? A head injury for poor little ol Rachel Bell, who didn't come home that night like she always did? Evans knew what was really going on. He sensed it the moment Stan touched that bone. So did John Charles. What's it worth? Huxley had his puppet, he had his motives, and now he just had to have his power. *Had to.* Maybe if they'd understood faster, maybe if they didn't leave it up to teenagers to deal with it. Taken so young. What a shame. What a shame!

What was done was done in silence. Wasn't everything? What happened to the man? What turned him as rotten as the bodies underground? His yearning for faith to turn towards him, for a sense of worship in his name. It could have been lust. It could have been greed. But it wasn't really anything. It never really was. It never really mattered. A kicked pebble wouldn't change anything, nor would the flap of a butterfly's wings. It would all lead to the same sickening rot. Everything leads to nothing, does it not?

The taste for the dead could have been cannibal. It almost was. But who knows? Cannibal could have been god. He could have been god, the true prophecy that he claimed himself to be. The way of life itself. The creator and soon-to-be destroyer. Could one person really destroy so much? Yes. But that isn't the point. The point is what's happening now. Why can't anything be in true focus? In the light for more than a few fleeting moments?

There is no such thing as direct mind control, only manipulation. Manipulation takes many forms, similar to evil. It can look innocent. Like a slice of cake with poison inside. Especially if you're deprived of it. You've never had cake before, it's something you have always wanted to try. Who cares if there's poison in it? There's probably only a little in it anyway, right? A puppet deprived of love and care could easily fall for the wool stuffing.

Allowing its brain to be woven into the perfect mold just for the chance of being cared for. There is no such thing as mind control. Only manipulation.

But is it truly evil to only want to be loved? To kill in the name of care and healing? Is it just giving up? The light dims. The loud boom fades to nothing. The heart shatters into a million pieces, each of which shows the reflection of mistakes that printed into the miserable life of.. Oh. Here come the trumpets..

Bradley Moore

BOOM! The sound of the gun shattered the air, and it felt as if the entire world paused for a moment. All that could be processed was that sound. The sound of Victor Balakins' pistol being unloaded. But it didn't kill Stan. It didn't kill anything. Something blocked it, blocked it from reaching his head. Huxley held high, a hole in his head instead of Stan's. His ghostly body hung above Jamie, swallowing him with his shadow. Stan fell back, closing his eyes.

"You thought you could take *my* host?" Huxley hissed. Jamie stepped back, astounded by the situation. Everyone kept still. With one huge clawed hand, Huxley pulled Jamie up by his neck, raising him to eye level. "I'm done playing games, Anderson. You're lucky killing you would be an issue," he seethed before dropping him to the ground. Jamie clutched his neck, scooting away using his legs. "You all are," he looked around with narrowed yellow eyes.

Huxley turned back towards Stan. Stan breathed lightly, not moving an inch when approached. Huxley held him in his arms, allowing himself to be absorbed by Stan, ultimately disappearing. Bradley couldn't take it, he ran towards Stan, falling to his knees beside him.

"Stan, please wake up," he begged while shaking him. His heart was beating quickly in his chest as sweat rolled down his forehead rapidly. He couldn't be dead, *he couldn't*. Stan continued to lay there, taking in shallow breaths. It must have been the shock and the loss of energy. It had to be. Bradley turned his head towards Jamie, feeling himself become swallowed by rage. "You did this," he seethed between clenched teeth. "Piece of shit." Jamie was left speechless, his eyes wide with shock.

Vicky took the gun from Jamie's sweaty hand, throwing it to the ground away from him. He continued to sit there without moving. It was as if he died sitting up.

"Jamie?" Vicky asked while moving her hand in front of his face. Nothing. She shook him a little, his eyes at least blinking. The dead man's gaze was gone, his mouth moving as if he were trying to speak, but nothing was coming out. "Jamie, what did you do?" She questioned in fear. He paused again.

"I thought," he stammered hoarsely. "I thought I could fix everything." He looked up to face her. "I wanted to fix everything." Bradley stood up, storming towards Jamie. He flinched back as if Bradley would hurt him.

"Well, you didn't!" He shouted. "Trying to kill him? Are you fucking serious?" Bradley couldn't help but feel the need to cry out of anger and fear. "What is wrong with you?" Jamie looked away, not being able to face him.

"I'm sorry," he managed to squeak out as he slowly got up. Bradley shook his head.

"Sorry's not enough," he seethed. He went back towards Stan who was still lying on the ground. "Someone come help me carry him to the car," Bradley commanded while trying to lift him up. Ivan made his way over towards the two, picking up Stan by himself and carrying him towards the car.

"That wasn't the way," Vicky told Jamie coldly. "You can walk home." She left him there, leaving him to stand alone. The rest of the crew made their way to the car, setting Stan in gently. His body was so weak, so cold. That interaction must have made him use all his energy. *Huxley* must have made him lose all his energy. Bradley stared at his thin cold hands, wishing he could do something more to help.

The ride home was silent, Stan still being sacked out by the time he got home. Bradley decided to stay with him, struggling to carry him inside even though Ivan offered to help. He felt relieved that his mother wasn't home, not knowing exactly what he would say to explain her son being unconscious. He supposed she wouldn't care too much anyway, or at least she wouldn't remember. He laid Stan down on his bed, covering him with his blanket. Bradley laid down on the bed next to him, facing the ceiling.

Everything felt so strange, there was so much to take in. His life had completely changed in just a few months, but it was all the same at the same time. He turned his head to face Stan. He looked so pale, his Roman nose a bit red in color from irritation. There was so much he wanted to tell him, so much that was on his mind that he would kill to say. But he would keep quiet, at least for now. He turned his head back towards the ceiling, unable to bear looking at him any longer.

"I'm sorry, Stan," he spoke into the room quietly. "I wish I could have done more." He listened to the birds outside as a gentle breeze made its way through the hole in the window. It felt nice, it was a comforting feeling. For a split second, it was as if nothing was wrong. Summer was approaching, he was hanging out with a friend, what was there to even worry about? The denial made him feel sick. He gently grabbed Stan's hand, holding it in his own lightly. He took a deep breath in, easing himself into relaxation. He fell asleep like that. Fell asleep in some sort of comfort.

Bradley didn't know he was dreaming at first. He wasn't even sure if it was a dream or some sort of mind trick. Either way, he was met with a dark void, the only thing in it being a chair. He felt strange, almost empty. He looked around, searching for someone or something else. Nothing.

"This is it," he heard a familiar voice say. "This is Stan's mind." Bradley whipped his head around, searching frantically for the source of the voice.

"Where are you?" He called out into the darkness.

"It doesn't matter," Huxley called back. "What matters is that you *see*." Bradley made his way towards the chair nervously, his shoes tapping against the black ground gently. He didn't even know what he was stepping on. "I can leave you all alone and have everything go back to normal if you just give me what I want." Huxley's voice called out around the void. Bradley continued towards the chair. "Or, you could all become my prophets. The choice is yours, Bradley. It seems as though your little friend already made his." Bradley paused.

"Jamie?" He asked while looking up, as if Huxley would be there. He was met with nothing but darkness.

"Yes, his little *act* proved him weak, I know you're strong and worthy of being my prophet." Bradley felt his head swim, not knowing how to feel.

"What you want is to kill others," he stammered with a quiver in his tone.

"Yes, but for life, there must be death, and it's not your death, so why should it even matter? Humans are all so selfish anyways, I'm trying to fix your race, you must understand." Bradley shook his head, wanting to sit on the chair but not trusting anything.

"That won't fix anything," he croaked. "I just want Stan to be okay." He looked into the void once again. "Why won't he wake up?" He asked the darkness.

"You want him to wake up?" Huxley asked. "I can do that, but you'll have to sleep just a little longer.." Bradley felt himself sinking into the floor beneath him. Although he wanted to panic, he knew this wasn't the end. It was only the start of the end.

Richard Huxley

As my host wakes, I put his little companion to sleep. I believe he would make a great prophet as his mind is already enlightened, ready to succumb to me. He would do anything for my host which is perfect, it's just what I need. He will be the start in bringing in others, others to worship me. My power will reign high, I almost have enough! I was able to get a great amount from the mechanic, but it wasn't enough. I need more, I need to take from the youth. The older the more bitter. Margaret's soul was stale and nearly empty, it almost wasn't even worth it. But anything... Anything to take what took from me. The cop would work too..

My host has been perfect. Doing exactly what I've told him to do. Let's see if he continues with this behavior. I'll only need him for so much longer. Once I am done with him, we will see if he gets to live or bleed. His power is strong, but nothing beats me. I will always remain on top. I know what's good for my people even if they don't know what's good for themselves. For them to live, they must all die, allowing for a new perfected generation to take their place. I'm only doing what is right. Only what is right..

Mike Evans

Evans didn't want to believe John Charles when he told him. He wanted to put his hands over his ears like a child and ignore everything that was being said, but he couldn't. This was his fault, his for saying to just leave the body.

"You realize what this means now, right?" He remembered Charles asking him. He responded back with an irritated no, rubbing his temples as he normally did when stressed. "It means that this is your responsibility now." He left him there like that. Left him in his office alone to think. It was now an hour later and he hadn't done a thing. This couldn't actually be happening. Not at all, no.

He could feel the weight of the town on his shoulders, crushing him like a boulder. Huxley's files lay across his desk like the scattered feathers of a bird. He looked at them in dismay, feeling his headache begin to worsen. If only he had known. He would kill to go back in time and bury the body deeper. Because of him Rachel, Mitchell, and Peter were all dead. Their blood was on his hands. He sighed before putting his head down in his hands, feeling the guilt overcome him.

Richard's files were kept secret as his murder had to be a coverup. He was claimed to have mysteriously disappeared, explaining the lack of a headstone. They never wanted to bury him next to the bodies he violated and stole from. He deserved much worse. Such a disgusting man deserved to be dismembered and thrown into a grinder. Evans heard a knock on his office door, jolting him out of his thoughts.

"Come in," he commanded loudly in a gruff voice. There was a moment of hesitation and silence before the door creaked open. He was relieved to see it was Hudson and not Christopher. He walked in with a sense of anxiety, his head dipping down like he was ashamed.

"Hey," Hudson greeted timidly before sitting in the chair in front of his desk. Evans raised an eyebrow, waiting for him to say what he came in for. Hudson cleared his throat before speaking. "Philip Price died this morning," he explained carefully. "Car crushed him, paramedics said he was dead on impact." Evans sighed, rubbing his temples as his headache grew. *This is bullshit.* He got up from his desk, pushing it forward with force, almost hitting Hudson. He made his way out the door, slamming it open and leaving without saying anything.

He knew what he had to do. He rushed over towards one of the cruisers, peeling out of the parking lot and down the street. He was tempted to turn on the lights to show a sense of urgency, but decided against it. He didn't need to prove anything to anyone. He was in charge. He sped down the street, making his way towards Oak. He had a gun already loaded in his holster, ready for action when need be. He hoped he wouldn't have to use it. He didn't want to see another dead kid.

Trees flashed by wildly as he advanced down hills and past buildings and pedestrians. His head throbbed, the feeling making its way into his eyes. He didn't let that bother him, he just kept a steady foot on the gas. His vision was locked in on the street ahead, his focus devoted to the road. His heart beat quickly in his chest, the adrenaline kicking in. Before he even knew it, he was stepping out of the car and into Oak Street. With each step, a jolt of pain ripped through his head. His eyes felt like they could pop out at any moment. He stepped up to the door, hesitating before knocking. He was left there in silence. Crows called out, mocking him from above. He knocked once more.

"Police!" He shouted. This house didn't seem to care too much for authority. It never had. *I hate this house.* He was met with silence once again. He noticed a broken window on the right side of the house, the small hole before being a lot larger now. He made his way towards it, making sure to step on the heels of his feet to make his steps quieter. He peeked his head around, noticing someone lying down on the bed. However, it wasn't any of the residents. It almost looked like that Moore kid.

Alarms started to go off in his brain. He made his way back to the front door, turning the knob, expecting it to be locked. To his surprise, it wasn't. The house was dimmed, just as it was the last time he came in. He walked in slowly, his boots nearly echoing when hitting the old wooden floor. He kept one hand against his holster. *Just in case.* He walked out of the little dark hallway and towards the main living area.

Light from the back glass doors gently seeped its way in, not getting very far into the house. The kitchen was secluded in the left corner, right by the back doors. A wall covered his main view of it, the "dining area" being right across from it on the other side of the doors. Evans remembered sitting there with Rosanne and Chris. The dinky living room was smooshed right between the kitchen and what Evans presumed was the bathroom. A cigarette in the ashtray on the tiny table produced smoke. Someone was still here.

He made his way into the hallway towards the bedrooms, his head pounding as he did. One of the floorboards let out a loud creak as he stepped, dipping down a little. *Loose floorboard.* He thought to himself as he continued. He felt a sudden rush of cold air, causing him to pause. *You shouldn't be here.* He heard something say to him in his head, causing him to step back. It was that same voice from before. *I already told you once to stay away.* The voice caused his headache to worsen.

"Show yourself," he hissed, pulling his gun out of the holster. He heard one of the doors creak open, his focus and gun turning towards it. He watched as a gruff-looking man stepped out, his eyes gleaming yellow. *Huxley.* Huxley opened his arms, a sly grin appearing on his face before taking a bow. He looked exactly the same as he did in the sixties. Hadn't aged one bit.

"The one and only," he added gruffly.

"How are you still alive?" Evans asked with cold eyes. Huxley stepped up slowly, the floorboards creaking beneath him.

"You should know," he said slyly. "You were the one who knew, you were the one who buried me," he stepped forward once again. Evans felt his eye twitch, his throbbing head matching the same pulse as his heart. "It's your fault," he commented with a grin. He stepped up until they were a foot away from each other. "I should be thanking you. Without you, I wouldn't be here today," he jeered with a cock of the head and a flash of the teeth.

"I wish you would have just stayed dead," Evans growled.

"I'm sure Rachel Bell thought the same thing," he teased. Evans let out a scream, punching the wall beside Huxley, feeling himself fume with anger.

"You bastard," he growled. Huxley laughed, turning his form into something inhuman. He became some sort of gray creature with large claws, his large teeth curved into a smile.

"You might not have been able to save Rachel," he started carefully. "But you saved humanity," he put a large clawed hand over Evans' head.

"It's too bad you don't seem to think so." Evans felt the grip slowly begin to tighten. His head felt as if it were about to explode. He felt a sudden numbness in his face and body, his legs collapsing beneath him. His vision failed as he gripped for the floor around him. *I need to find Rachel..* He suddenly couldn't see anything. He tried to say something, but nothing came out, and if it did, it was just gibberish. The last thing he remembered was the yellow eyes of a hideous gray angel. Evans didn't die at the hands of Huxley, he died at the hands of a stroke.

Stanley Morris

Stan wasn't awake for long before passing out once again. When he first awoke, he was lying in bed with his hand intertwined with Bradley's. He remembered getting up and checking inside his mother's room before losing consciousness for a second time. He was sick of his body being used, but there was nothing he could do about it. He felt completely useless, his only option was to obey. He became more of a dog than human. He hadn't even realized there was a dead man in his hallway yet.

He sat up in his mother's bed, thankful she was still at work. He tried to remember what had happened before he passed out the first time. He remembered the car falling on the mechanic, the gun pointed to his head, and then.. Nothing. A part of him was thankful that his life was spared, the other part of him wished it wasn't. He thought about the cold look on Jamie's face as he clicked the safety off. He never said anything, Stan kept his mouth shut allowing him to make his own decision. He didn't want it to be his own choice whether he dies, after all, he had no choice over anything he did anymore.

He got up quietly, briefly wondering if Bradley was still in his room or not. He noticed the bedroom door was open, something he crossed off as normal. He slowly made his way towards the door, his weak legs carrying him across the room. He stumbled out into the hallway, noticing something in the darkness on the floor. A small puddle of blood formed around the figure's head. He stood in silence with a cold stare, his body wavering back and forth. He felt nothing. He knew what his parasite had done.

He made his way back to his room, noticing Bradley on his bed. *So he is still here.* He thought to himself as he started towards the bed. He stood above him for a moment, feeling a little envious of how peaceful he looked. He began shaking him lightly, attempting to wake him up. Bradley's eyes fluttered open, squinting from the light slightly. He wiped the drool that had formed around the corner of his mouth before slowly sitting up.

"Stan?" He asked with a tired tone as he rubbed his eye.

"There's a dead person in the hallway," Stan stated calmly. Bradley's expression turned from sleepy to surprised.

"Seriously?" He asked with wide eyes. Stan nodded his head. Bradley quickly threw the blanket off himself and got up from the creaky mattress. The two of them slowly made their way into the darkened hallway, Stan flipping the light on for them to see. He heard Bradley gasp at the sight of the old man on the floor, a wound from his head dripping blood onto the wooden floor around him. He was wearing a police uniform.

The two boys decided their best bet was to bury him outside. They had picked him up carefully, dripping blood through the house as they carried him outside and into the woods. Stan went back to get a shovel as Bradley picked a spot to bury him. It took almost an hour and thirty minutes to dig the hole, crows calling out from above while circling like vultures. They set him inside the hole gently, covering him with dirt afterward. The grave was shallow.

"I don't know what to do anymore," Stan grumbled in defeat. "I don't know." The two stared at each other, Bradley holding the shovel. He had a look of sadness rested upon his face, the light dimming behind him.

"I'm sorry," he told him. "I wish there was more I could do." Stan shook his head before plopping himself on the ground beside the makeshift cross they created out of sticks. They thought they should at least do that for him.

"What could you do?" Stan asked. "This shit is hopeless, there's nothing *anyone* can do." Stan groaned. "All I could do is isolate myself so I'm a mile away from everyone." Bradley shook his head before sitting down across from him.

"No, there's gotta be something we can do," he pondered desperately.

"I want to talk to John Charles again," Stan added slowly. Bradley's head perked up.

"Really?" He seemed to almost whine. Stan nodded. The trees above them swayed back and forth in the wind as the sun's rays shone through the leaves.

"Yeah, I think he could help."

"But last time he didn't want to help us, like, at all." Bradley mentioned. Stan got up from the ground, brushing off his shorts as he did.

"This time might be different," Stan told him while reaching his hand out for Bradley. Bradley stared at it for a moment before taking it, hoisting himself up with the help of Stan. The two stared at each other in silence for a moment. They had been through so much together in such a short amount of time. *Please don't take him from me.* Stan pleaded in his head, not sure if he was talking to the spirit or himself. *Take anyone else, but please don't take him.*

They made their way out of the woods, giving the pitiful grave one last look before exiting the tree line. They walked beside each other in silence, leaving the backyard and stepping onto the sunburnt street. An orange cat ran past them, shooting for the forest. Stan felt lucky that the walk wasn't very long, the silence weighing on him like a brick. But just like everything, silence is temporary. He stepped onto the stoop, knocking on the door.

Stan was about to knock again before the door opened. John Charles stood there with heavy eyes, his gaze piercing them.

"Now why are you two back here?" He questioned sternly. Bradley opened his mouth as if about to say something but then closed it, looking at Stan for answers.

"Your cop friend died," Stan replied coldly. John's eyes widened. "I found him dead in my hallway. You're less than a mile away, you could be next for all we know." The old man gripped the doorframe, squinting his eyes shut at Stan's words as if he could hide from them.

"Please don't say you're talking about-" He began to say.

"Mike Evans," Bradley stated, cutting him off mid-sentence. "We buried him in the woods." John rubbed his temples just as Evans did just a few hours ago.

"Look, I don't know how to help you other than shooting you in the head like a sick dog, son," John told him honestly. "I'd probably die before even getting the chance to do that anyway. Your situation is out of my hands, you're not my problem anymore," he grumbled before attempting to close the door. Stan grabbed the door before it could close, staring him in the eyes.

"Please," Stan begged. "I don't want to have to die because of something that isn't even my fault."

"A lot of good people die for things that aren't their fault," John stated coldly. "Now you either give him what he wants, or you take matters into your own hands." He lightly kicked Stan's foot loose and closed the door. Stan thought over it for a moment, letting the old man's words sink in. *Give him what he wants, or take matters into your own hands.* He thought to himself. *Let more people die, or kill yourself.* He wanted to scream, feeling as though he were playing some sick game. He slammed his hands to his face, falling to his knees in defeat.

"I can't keep living like this," Stan faltered, "no matter what I do, it's wrong." Bradley sat down beside him, leaving a gentle hand on his back. *It doesn't have to be this way.* He heard Huxley say. *We can be separate.* Stan threw his hands in the air. "How?" He sobbed, not caring if Bradley heard or not. *Like he said.. Just give me what I desire, and we can both get what we want.*

"What's he saying?" Bradley asked with worry. Stan didn't respond, just listened. He slowly repositioned himself.

"What do you mean?" He asked Huxley. *I just need a little more, then we can become separate.* Stan paused. "A little more what?" He hesitated. Bradley looked at him in desperation, trying to understand what was happening. *Power. I need sources, Stanley. Bring to me my sources, and then you can be free.* He swallowed what felt like nothing, his throat being completely dry. "Do you promise?" *Yes, I promise, everything will be alright if you just let me guide you.* Stan nodded his head, feeling oddly comforted by his words. He turned towards Bradley.

"So?" Bradley asked with wide eyes.

"We need to get the others."

Annette Jones

Annette was the last one to be dropped off, the ride feeling very quiet. She wasn't quite sure how she felt about the whole situation, so much had happened all at once. She, Vicky, and Ivan had a long conversation about it before dropping him off, but she still felt lost. Vicky pulled into her driveway, staying parked without saying anything. Annette knew Vicky didn't want her to leave yet, knowing her well enough to understand that she was trying to figure out what to say. The two sat there in silence, neither one of them knowing what should be said.

"You're so," Vicky started to say, "different now." She turned to look at her, her deep hazel eyes filled with some sort of sadness. "Did all of this do that to you?" Annette sighed, wanting to turn away.

"I don't know," she answered honestly. "I'm just trying to figure myself out. Separate myself from everyone I guess."

"I miss you," Vicky faltered as her eyes began to well up. She felt her heart drop at the sight of Vicky's tears.

"No," Annette said, "you miss how things used to be before this." She looked away and out the passenger side window. "I just can't forget the look on their faces." She turned her attention back towards Vicky, a small tear running down her dark face.

"I'm so sick of this," she whimpered. Annette nodded her head, forcing out a waned smile.

"I am too," she agreed. Vicky gently wiped her eyes, looking away briefly.

"Jamie and I are together now." *Oh, you gotta be kidding me.*

"Are you serious? Oh gag me with a spoon," she quipped with an eye roll. Vicky let out a small smile.

"Yeahh, but now I'm not so sure. What he did was.." She trailed off, searching for words.

"Cold?" Annette asked, attempting to finish her sentence.

"Yeah," she replied, "cold."

"Well, do whatever you want. I don't really care," Annette stated while unbuckling herself and opening the passenger side door. Vicky reached over, grabbing her arm lightly.

"Wait!" Annette turned to look back at her. "What about you and Laura?" Annette shrugged.

"Doesn't matter," she replied before getting out and closing the door. *Nothing does anymore.* She made her way inside, listening to the sound of Vicky's car pull out of the driveway. She noticed Arnold on the couch, sitting by himself in front of the TV. Neither one of their parents were home as per usual. Annette went over to sit next to him, rubbing his back gently.

"You should go outside," she told him softly. "It's really nice out, I'm sure your friends miss you." He shook his head, his face holding a somber expression. It was as if all the light was sucked out of him. She frowned.

"Everyone's been staying inside," he stated blankly. "I don't want to go out either." She pitied him, wanting more than anything to just see him smile again.

"Is there anything I can do to help you feel better?" She asked.

"I don't know, but Jeff called earlier asking for you," he mentioned without looking at her. Her eyes widened in slight surprise. *Jeff?*

"What did you tell him?" She asked while sitting up a little straighter.

"Told him the truth," he answered, "that I didn't know where you were." Annette felt a pang of guilt, feeling as though she should be there for her brother more.

"Oh," she managed out with a hint of sadness.

"He didn't sound too happy," Arnold told her, keeping his eyes glued to the TV. Her heart dropped. She felt even worse now, she shouldn't have ditched everyone like that. *You needed to protect yourself though.* She thought to herself sharply. She leaned her head back against the couch, feeling defeated. She felt as though everything changed after Laura. She felt more at ease, she just didn't know why. She sighed. Everything was just so confusing.

"Have you seen Mom and Dad lately?" She asked, turning her head to look at him. He shook his head slightly, his gaze remaining on the TV.

"No, they haven't been here for a few days," he stated calmly, "I think they're on a trip." Annette rolled her eyes. *Of course they are.*

"I'm sorry that I haven't been here much either," she confessed disappointedly. Arnold looked up from the TV for the first time during their conversation.

"It's okay, I'm not the biggest fan of this house either," he commented with a wane smile. Annette returned the expression.

"Would you like to eat dinner with the Taylors tonight?" She asked softly. He paused for a moment, thinking to himself.

"Sure," he agreed with a genuine smile this time. It felt nice to see him do that.

"I promise I'll try to be home more often now," she told him, "I'm here for you." Arnold didn't say anything, he just hugged her, squeezing her tight.

"Thank you," he said, his voice muffled in the embrace.

"Of course." There was a sudden knock on the door, causing them both to jump. Arnold gave her an anxious look, letting go of her so she could answer the door. "I'm sure it's nothing," she reassured. Another frantic knock caused her to jump again. She slowly approached the door, her heart beating quickly in her chest. *Just open it!* She grabbed the knob and twisted it, opening the door.

"God, were you taking a shit or something?" Annette felt relieved to see it was just Bradley. Annoyed, but relieved. She glanced back at Arnold whose focus was back on the tv again.

"What do you want?" She asked with narrowed eyes.

"We need everyone again," he stated quickly. Annette rolled her eyes. *Seriously?*

"Even Jamie?" She questioned with her hands on her hips.

"I think he can sit this one out," Bradley grumbled with aggravation. "Stan is getting Vicky right now," he pointed towards her house.

"Why do you need everyone again?" She asked with annoyance.

"Stan wouldn't give me too many details, just said we needed to get everyone again." Annette gave one more glance towards Arnold before closing the door behind her.

"You're being stupid," she hissed.

"What?"

"You're being stupid, Jamie did all of that for a reason. Stan is obviously siding with that thing inside of him," she told him with disgust.

"You're agreeing with Jamie?" Bradley asked in shock. She sighed.

"I am, and I'm not just gonna sit back and pretend he wasn't right. He could have ended everything right then right there, our lives could have gone back to normal." Bradley's face became visibly red.

"Well maybe you want your normal life back because it was good," he retorted, "at least you have friends. My only friend before Stan was a Russian who doesn't care about anything besides bugs." Annette felt another hint of pain, but she ignored it.

"I wonder why!" She yelled, throwing her hands up in the air. "Maybe it's because you have an attitude that's just as shitty as the rest of us." The two of them fell quiet. "I'm sorry," she apologized with a huff. "I guess I'm just scared." Bradley nodded his head.

"It's okay," he told her, "I am too." She stood idle for a moment, staring at the ground.

"I'll go tell Arnold I'm leaving," she muttered quietly, "stay here." She went back inside, slowly making her way towards the couch. She bit her lip, not wanting to tell him the news.

"You have to leave again I'm guessing," he speculated coldly. She stood above him, looking down at him with sad eyes.

"Yeah," she replied, "I'm really sorry." He waved his hand in the air, dismissing her.

"It's whatever," he mumbled, "just go." Annette frowned, feeling guilty once again. She kept her mouth shut and went back outside. The sun was beginning to set down the sky as Annette watched Vicky and Stan make their way across the street.

"Got you too, huh?" Vicky asked Annette with a light chuckle. Annette just stared at the ground, reflecting on her conversation with Arnold.

"So," Bradley said, butting in. "We're going to need someone's car to get Ivan."

"We should get Jamie too," Vicky sighed quickly. Bradley whipped his head around. He looked at Stan with concern who only shrugged.

"That's fine," he consented.

"Are you serious?" Bradley asked with worry. Stan nodded.

"Alright! It's settled, everyone get in my car." Vicky exclaimed before turning back towards her house. They all followed closely behind. To Annette, it felt like she was marching to her death. *I need to separate myself from everyone before I get myself killed.* She sighed. *I'm so scared.* But she thought they all were. Guess they were just good at hiding it.

It didn't take long to get to Jamie's, Vicky offering to be the one to get him. Annette figured she was the only one who knew about their relationship, feeling strange about the whole thing. She leaned against the passenger side window. *Whatever.* She thought with an eye roll. The three of them watched as Vicky waited patiently for Jamie to greet her. The door slowly opened, a tall, anxious-looking man with red hair stood in the doorway instead of Jamie. The two seemed to be talking for a moment, Vicky climbing back into the car soon after, visibly shaken.

"He's not there," she told them with worry. "He never came home."

"Maybe he's with Ivan?" Bradley suggested. "I think they've been hanging out outside of the group." Vicky nodded her head, looking a bit calmer at the idea.

"Yeah, maybe you're right," she agreed softly. Annette watched as Vicky's leg bounced up and down, her finger tapping rapidly on the steering wheel. She sped off down the street, going faster than normal. Annette held onto the grab handle in order to keep herself stable. She noticed the others do the same. The normal fifteen-minute drive turned into about ten, Vicky jumping out of the car as soon as it was parked. Annette felt a hint of fear for Vicky as she knocked on the door, worrying if Ivan's dad, Victor, was there or not.

The door opened up almost instantly, Annette feeling relieved upon seeing Ivan instead of his dad. Ivan craned his head around Vicky and towards her car, an anxious expression on his face. Annette watched him shake his head, Vicky beginning to look stressed once again. The two made their way back to the car, Vicky speedwalking as Ivan trailed behind nervously.

"He's fucking missing," she stressed. "Jamie's gone." Annette felt her heart drop, her eyes traveling up towards the rearview mirror to look at a very calm-looking Stan. Vicky turned herself around to face him. "Did he do it? Did he kill Jamie?" She hissed through gritted teeth. The car fell silent for a moment.

"No," Stan answered plainly. "He's around us too much, I would become a suspect and risk going to prison."

"Bullshit!" She shouted. She started the car with a jerk, her hands clenched into fists. "We're gonna go find him," she stated sternly. They sped off into the street, everyone holding onto each other for dear life.

"Where would he even be?" Annette cried out.

"I don't know, maybe dead in the fucking woods," Vicky seethed. She made a sharp turn, causing Annette to slam into the passenger side door.

"Oh please no more of this," Ivan groaned in the backseat. Annette thought for a moment, an idea forming in her head.

"We just left him at the mechanics, what if he's still there?" She suggested quickly. Another swerve. "Or, he could have gone to Ray's Pizza or Irna's Diner since it's nearby," Vicky said nothing, just turned once again. Annette noticed her head in the direction of her suggestions, her chest feeling a little lighter.

"If we don't find him," Vicky started to say, "you're dead, ghost boy." She glared at the rearview mirror. Stan stayed silent, staring straight ahead with a lack of emotion. They made their way towards the establishments, Vicky's foot seeming to never leave the gas pedal. Annette felt herself becoming more and more anxious. *What if he's not there?* She panicked. She felt as though one way or another someone else would wind up dead today.

They went to the mechanics first, finding nothing but caution tape around the place of the incident. They tried Ray's Pizza next, the parking lot being nearly full. Bradley went in to check, coming out empty-handed. They went to the diner next, only a handful of cars being in the parking lot. This time, they all decided to go in. Annette could feel her heart pounding in her chest, praying that he would be there.

Annette searched around for Laura first, spotting her across the diner taking an old man's order. The rest of the group searched frantically for Jamie. Annette began to approach Laura before being tapped on the shoulder by Ivan. She looked over at him, noticing him point towards a booth in the back. Jamie was slumped in the corner, presumably asleep. She felt her heart lift. *Apparently, Irna's Diner is the place to go if you're feeling lost.*

Annette glanced at Laura one last time before making her way to the booth. Vicky rushed over to him, sitting in the booth before lightly shaking him. Annette slid into the booth across the table, Bradley and Ivan joining them as Stan stood nearby. Jamie slowly woke up, his eyes squinted from the light.

"I thought we lost you," she sighed with relief. Jamie looked around at each of the faces that sat before him, his brain slowly beginning to wake up. A few others who finished eating got up and left the diner, making it feel a little more quiet.

"Yeah, well, can't get rid of me that easily I guess," he stated shortly, a yawn escaping him. He stared at Stan for a moment, the two making silent eye contact. "You're not upset with me?" He asked with a raised eyebrow. Stan shrugged.

"I would have done the same thing if I were in your shoes," he responded calmly. "I get it." Jamie looked around once again.

"Everything was a little intense, and if Stan forgives you, then so do we," Vicky added calmly. Bradley stayed silent, looking away and down towards the floor. *He doesn't forgive him.* Annette thought to herself. Laura quickly rushed over to their booth, her face filled with worry.

"Annette, get out of here stat," Laura urged quickly. Annette flashed a look of concern, not understanding.

"Why?" She asked with wide eyes.

"Tommy Morrison came in with Jeff earlier," she explained. "He told Jeff you cheated on him, and he also told him that he-"

"Okay, stop, I get it," Annette cut her off with a wave of her hands.

"Wait, you *cheated* on Jeffrey Grant?" Bradley asked with wide eyes.

"It was just a one-time thing!" Annette yelled, trying to defend herself.

"More than once," Vicky mumbled with an eye roll.

"You're not really helping my case here," Annette hissed.

"You had a case to begin with?" Jamie added.

"Can you all shut it?" Laura groaned. "The point is, Jeff is looking for you, and there's a good chance he might come back here." Annette sighed, thinking back to the phone call from earlier.

"It's fine, rather deal with it now than later I guess." The door slammed open, and a wasted-looking Tommy Morrison strolled in with anxiety-ridden cheerleader Kimberly MacDonald. She helped him as he stumbled inside, a shit eating grin laid across his face.

"Speak of the devil," Laura grumbled without much surprise. "I'll kick him out if you want me to," Laura soothed sweetly, her gaze sticking to Annette. Tommy's attention shifted towards the group, his eyes narrowing, but the smile remaining.

"I knew you'd be here, Jones." He sneered with wild eyes. Annette didn't say anything, only glared.

"Get out of here Tommy," Laura hissed.

"I told Jeff your little secret," Tommy stated, ignoring Laura's remark. "He should be here soon." Laura stood in the way of Tommy and Annette, her arms crossed neatly across her chest. The remaining customers had left, presumably not wanting to deal with the confrontation.

"You're drinking underage, I could call the cops on you, y'know," Laura glared. Tommy turned his attention to Laura, blowing a raspberry in her face like a child.

"Go ahead, Gray," he jeered, "I got dirt on you too." Laura snapped her mouth shut, her face reddening as she turned her head away. His attention returned to Annette.

"And you, do you even *care* about Jeff?" She looked away in shame, the guilt from before returning.

"C'mon, let's just get out of here," Kimberly pleaded.

"Yeah, why don't you listen to her and leave?" Vicky snapped.

"I wanna stay awhile," he taunted with a large, toothy grin. The little bell rang as the door opened again. Annette's heart dropped as she realized who it was. Jeffrey Grant slowly made his way towards the booth, everyone going quiet and making room for him as he did. His face was flushed with heartache.

"Annette," he started to say, "is it true?" She wanted to shake her head, tell him it wasn't. She took in a deep breath. She had to tell the truth.

"It's true," she confessed in disappointment. He turned his head away, avoiding eye contact.

"Let's go," Kimberly suggested once again to Tommy. Surprisingly, he complied. The two left the diner silently, a huge difference from the way they came in. All eyes were on the quarreling couple, none of them knowing if they should say anything.

"I'm sorry," Annette apologized quietly. Jeff's head shot up.

"Save it," he grunted, "I know that's not true." He shook his head, rubbing his face tiredly. "I just don't understand *why* you would do this. How you could just lie to me for so long." His words felt like bullets, digging deeper with each sentence. "Did I do something wrong? Was I not enough?" His eyes were pleading, his face full of distress. She began to cry even though she was the one who dealt the damage.

"I don't know," she replied honestly. "I don't know what I wanted," she sobbed.

"I don't know either," Jeff stated. "But I'm done. We're done," he turned away, shaking his head once again as he did. Everything had happened so fast, it was hard to process. She barely even noticed Stan's finger begin to twitch. She had to fix things with him, she couldn't let him leave so broken.

"Wait!" She yelled, causing him to turn around. She tried pushing her way out of the booth, annoyed grunts coming from Bradley. She got a foot out before Stan fell to the ground, causing everyone to jump. *No.* She thought to herself desperately. *No, not him.* Jeff quickly rushed over to Stan, lifting his head up gently.

"Are you alright, man?" He asked in a panic.

"Jeff, you need to leave," Annette pleaded. He looked up with a sense of worry on his face.

"But he's hurt," he blurted quickly. Stan's leg began to twitch, jerking to the side violently. "He's going to have a seizure!" Jeff cried out.

"I think he's trying to fight him off," Annette heard Bradley say to Ivan. Stan's arm jerked forward as if about to grab Jeff before his other arm pulled it away. Jeff jumped back a little, not understanding what was happening. Laura stood against the back wall, watching the whole scene unfold with wide eyes.

Stan's body continued to jerk, his eyes shooting open before rolling back, showing only the whites.

"Jeff, go!" Annette shouted one last time. Jeff looked at her with fear, the sadness from before lingering in his face. At that moment, all she wanted to do was hold him. She reached out towards him, wanting to push him far away. Stan's body fell silent, and for a moment the diner was still.

"Is he-" Jeff began to say before he was cut off by the eruption within Stan's body. The slithery creature shot out from his chest, its yellow eyes glaring down at Jeff. Jeff fell back, his eyes wide with terror. Annette reached her hand out, attempting to grab his, his gaze glued to the demon above him.

"Take this as a lesson," Huxley hissed towards all of them. "Don't test me." He disappeared, a large cracking sound emitting from above. The ceiling was going to collapse. The group immediately ducked underneath the booth table, Ivan quickly grabbing Stan by the leg and tugging him underneath with them. Jeff remained there, frozen in fear. Laura looked up at the ceiling with fear before diving towards the table, her arms outstretched towards the group. Ivan attempted to pull Jeff under as the ceiling let out a final crack before giving in. Jeff gave one last look at Annette before disappearing under the rubble.

A loud scream emitted from Laura, her body not being fully underneath the table before the collapse. Her legs were stuck underneath the rubble. Annette desperately tried to tug her out as she yelled out in pain.

"Stop!" She cried out. "My legs, something is stabbing my legs," she groaned. Annette let go, coughing from the dust that surrounded them.

"Someone's gonna have to crawl out to get that off of her," Jamie wheezed, coughing himself. Ivan nodded, finding a small gap and shoving his way through. Although tall, he seemed to be quite nimble. He stood on top of the rubble, looking around briefly before getting to Laura. He placed his hands on the broken bits that lay on top of her legs, carefully pulling up as soon as he had a good grip. He grunted as he slowly pulled up, allowing enough room for her legs to slide out.

He let go as soon as he saw she was out, letting out a large breath of air that he had built up. She cried out in pain as she pricked the glass out from her legs. A large shard of glass had dug itself into her leg, causing a wide wound to form. Annette thought it might have dragged across her leg when she was trying to pull herself out. She bit her hand and winced as she pulled the last shard out, throwing it to the ground afterward. The light above must have fallen on her. Blood gushed out of the open and angry wound, her pale leg splattered with red.

Annette searched for something to cover the wound with, something to stop it from bleeding so much.

"Bradley, give me your shirt," she commanded. Bradley looked at her in confusion and slight offense. "Just do it!" She yelled before he had the chance to speak. He did as she asked, bumping his arms against the table as he did. Annette snagged it out of his grip before he could even hand it to her, getting to work on Laura's leg. She wrapped it around the wound, tying it tightly in hopes it would stop the blood flow.

"Thank you," Laura muttered weakly. Annette took her hand, squeezing it gently.

"You're going to be okay," she soothed, "I'm so sorry." She glanced over at Ivan who was pulling away more rubble. Jeff. Annette scrambled out, followed by the others. Stan and Laura stayed underneath the table, Stan not having much of a choice as he was unconscious once again. The five of them started prying away the pieces of the ceiling that lay on top of Jeff. It seemed as though the entire roof caved in. Panic began to takeover her entire body as she shakily wiped her tears away to see.

Jeff was buried deep within the rubble, bits and pieces of his red letterman being found with every removal. Annette knew that the police officers would show up soon along, with those who wanted to gawk at a tragedy, but she just wanted to see him first. She held onto that small chance of him somehow being alive. It felt as though her entire world was collapsing around her, the destruction eating her alive. Things would never go back to normal again.

Ivan pulled away the last of it, revealing Jeff's face. His eyes were wide open, a permanent mark of terror set within them. Annette fell to her knees, holding his face gently. He was still warm. God dammit, he was still warm, so why wasn't he alive? She held him close, her tears making a trail from her dusted face to his. Her body shook as she sobbed, the others watching in silence. She just didn't understand how this could happen, how he could be snatched from her like this. Fire truck air horns could be heard in the distance, followed by the wail of police sirens. They were coming to help rescue, but it was far too late.

Vicky Taylor

Vicky Taylor and the others were ordered home, while Laura, Jeff, and one of the cooks were rushed to the hospital. Stan was weary but conscious by the time the officers made it to the scene. He had said only one thing while awake, something Vicky had burned inside of her mind. *I tried to fight him. I tried to fight him and he's angry.* Bradley took him to his house after that, feeling as though he would be safer with him.

Annette stayed with Laura and Jeff in the hospital, praying for some sort of miracle that would never happen. Vicky and Jamie took Ivan back to his house, the two decided to stay together afterward. She found it easier to be with someone else in this type of situation.

"I still can't even process what just happened, like that was real, right?" Jamie asked, breaking Vicky out of her thoughts as she drove them back to her house. She paused before answering, feeling as if her brain were melting.

"Yeah," she replied slowly. She and Jamie's skin and clothes were still coated in dust, the seats of her car becoming a filthy mess. Her eyes were wide and bloodshot, her brain still trying to comprehend the tragedies of today. She had watched someone die not even hours before the collapse of the diner, what's next? She sighed, feeling trapped in this mess she got herself in. She should have just stayed quiet and let the police do their job.

"I just," Jamie started to say wistfully, "I don't even know." Vicky nodded her head in silent agreement. She seemed to be at a loss for words too. "It's like we're in some sort of dream," he spat out.

"More like a nightmare," Vicky mumbled as she turned down the street. The sun was finally beginning to set, meaning this horrible day was going to come to an end. The thought of being able to sleep in her bed comforted her, something to look forward to in this desperate state of mind. That was all she really wanted, just a little bit of sleep. She continued her way down the street.

By the time they made it back to her house, the sun was almost completely gone. The sky turned from a deep orange to a grayish black, the stars peeking their way out from behind the clouds. Vicky noticed Jamie begin to doze off, knowing he felt the same weariness as her. She turned the car off, nudging him awake as she began to take off her seatbelt. He jerked his head up, looking around slowly as if he didn't know where he was. He stretched his legs out a bit before yawning.

"Are you sure your parents are going to let me stay here?" He asked cautiously. Vicky exited the car before answering, Jamie following suit.

"They should," she told him tiredly, "I can't see why they wouldn't."

"Alright," he said before pausing. "Can I use your shower?" He asked as they made their way towards the front door. Vicky pulled her keys out of her back pocket, fumbling with the lock afterward.

"Yeah, that's fine," she replied as she turned the handle after hearing the familiar click of the door unlocking. The two slowly walked in, the house seeming a little too quiet for comfort. She felt herself beginning to panic, thinking disaster had crept its way inside of her home. Her heart began to beat faster in her chest, her throat drying as her hands began to sweat. She felt the fear begin to overcome her.

"Mom!" She shouted, "Dad!" Jamie quickly grabbed her hand, looking at her with concern. She squeezed his hand tightly, terror gripping her.

"Vicky?" She faintly heard her mom call out from upstairs. She escaped Jamie's grip before running upstairs, her dust-ridden shoes slapping against the steps as she stumbled forward. Her mother and father were in the hallway, a look of shock set across their faces. She ran up to them, practically jumping into their arms. She felt herself let go, beginning to cry. Her parents held her tightly, soothing her as she continued to sob. When she finally felt okay again, she let go, taking a step back to look at them as she continued to sniffle.

The dust from her clothes transferred to theirs, marks of white covering their clothes and faces. Tears continued to stream down her dirty face as she looked up at them with an almost guilty expression.

"Oh hun, we heard about the diner's roof collapsing," her mother told her. "Are you alright, are you hurt?" Her face was full of concern as her eyes scanned Vicky's body for any sign of injury. Vicky nodded her head, listening as Jamie slowly made his way up the stairs. Her mother gasped at the sight of him.

"You were both there?" Her father chimed in with surprise. "What even happened?" Vicky wanted to tell the truth. She desperately wanted to explain what had been happening this past month, but she held her tongue.

"Old building is my guess," she lied. She glanced over at Jamie for a moment. "Can he stay here for the night?" She asked while gesturing towards him. Her mom hesitated before nodding her head.

"If that's alright with his folks," her dad agreed carefully. "They're probably worried about you too." Jamie paused for a moment before speaking.

"Could I call them?" He asked politely. Her parents looked at each other before nodding.

"Of course!" Her mother exclaimed. "I'll show you where we keep the phone." The two made their way downstairs and into the kitchen as Vicky and her father remained in the hallway.

"Where's Jennifer?" Vicky asked meekly.

"She went to sleep a little bit ago," her dad responded quietly. "Are you sure you're alright, honey?" Vicky went silent, her tear-streaked face facing the ground.

"I just want to take a shower," she answered calmly.

"Alright," he said while looking down, moving to the side and allowing her to pass. She made her way to the bathroom, wiping away stray tears as she did. She felt so weak, so confused, so stupid, but most of all, she felt useless. She was so used to having the solution to everything all the time, but she didn't have the answer this time. She didn't know what to do. She flipped the switch on to the bathroom light, a soft yellow glow filling the darkened room. She closed the door, staring at herself in the mirror above the sink.

She looked so disheveled, her hair a frizzy mess as dust coated her face and chest. Her eyes were red and puffy from crying, and her lips looked chapped. She barely even recognized herself. *I used to look so bright.* She thought to herself dimly. She slowly turned on the shower, stripping herself down before stepping inside. The warm water pelted her skin, a hurtful yet soothing feeling. She used a soapy cloth to gently wash all the dust off, her movements slow and careful.

She ran her fingers through her hair softly, attempting to get all the debris out. She felt calm in this moment, as if she were giving herself a warm embrace. She supposed anytime she got clean felt like this, although this time was different. She faintly heard the door open and then close right after. *Someone must have just forgotten I was in here.* She ignored it, grabbing body wash and pouring a little onto the cloth. She gently began to wash her face, arms, breasts, stomach, and then legs. She continued this process until she felt completely clean, washing off the dirt of today.

After she was done washing her hair and rinsing off, she turned the knobs to shut the water off. She pulled open the shower curtains, grabbing a towel to dry herself with. She noticed a neatly folded pile of clean clothes on the vanity. She smiled, knowing that's what the door opening earlier was from. Once she was dry, she began to put her clothes on, a feeling of comfort washing over her. She looked into the mirror once more, a tired girl looking back.

She turned the light off before leaving the bathroom, closing the door to keep it warm for Jamie. She made her way downstairs and into the living room where everyone seemed to be gathered. They paused their conversation, looking up to see her walk in.

"Looks like you're up next," her father exclaimed to the still very filthy Jamie. "I'll see if we can find any clean clothes for you," he added before getting up.

"Thank you," Jamie told him softly. Vicky noticed pillows and blankets on the couch, having a feeling that's where her parents had set up for him to sleep. One of the blankets being a hand-sewn comforter that Annette crafted, a passion of hers that she kept secret. Vicky briefly wondered if she was still at the hospital, feeling a pang in her heart as she did. She hoped she was doing alright; she hoped they all were.

"Do you feel better, hun?" Her mom asked as she went to sit on the Lawson chair in the living room. She nodded her head.

"Feeling a lot better," she answered with half honesty. Her body felt nice and clean, but her mind felt beat and bloody. It was at that moment she knew she would never be the same girl she once was. She felt ashamed for lying, she felt ashamed for even being involved. She plopped herself down on the couch, avoiding the prying eyes of her mother.

"Where have you been lately?" Her mom asked softly. Vicky wasn't sure how to respond, she rather not talk at all. She paused for a moment, feeling herself hesitate in a response.

"With Jamie," she replied quietly.

"Please don't lie to me," her mother said carefully. "I won't be angry with the truth." *But you wouldn't believe the truth either.*

"I'm not lying," she stated, allowing herself to look up and face her mother. "I have no reason to lie to you." Her mother looked down, her face hiding some sort of disappointment or deep sadness. Vicky couldn't really tell, all she really wanted to do at that moment was sleep. She began to debate on if she should wait for Jamie to get out of the shower before she went to bed. She sighed, deciding it would be rude if she didn't wait. Her father came back into the living room with a blank expression.

"I found some old clothes that might fit him," he noted, "but I still tossed his clothes in the laundry." He looked at Vicky with sorrow. "I'm glad you're alright." He added softly. She nodded her head. She was too. *But Jeff isn't alright, he isn't safe at home.* The thoughts hit her in the gut, making her feel nauseous. *He'll never go home again.*

"I'm going to go to my room," she blurted quickly before excusing herself. She didn't care if it was rude or not anymore, she had to get away from the prying eyes of her parents. She quickly made her way upstairs, wiping away at her eyes before tears had the chance to form. She got to the end of the hallway, her bedroom door open as if beckoning her inside. She went inside, closing the door behind her before plopping herself down on the bed and releasing her emotions.

She lay there with her face shoved against her pillow, tears and snot trickling down to the tip of her nose and onto the purple floral pillowcase. She hated this. Hated the pressure and the deceiving and the death, this wasn't what she wanted. This wasn't what she was. She wanted to finish off senior year strong, she wanted to go off to her dream college and become an author. She didn't want any of this! The hopelessness made her cry even more, her body shuddering with each sob. She just wanted this nightmare to be over, at this point, she'd do anything.

She finally felt herself calm down after a while, wiping her tears and snot with a tissue from her nightstand. She sat herself up, her eyes feeling red and puffy. She took a deep breath in, taking control of her thoughts. She slipped her feet underneath the covers, shuffling down until her head was on the pillow. It was time to rest. She closed her puffy eyes as she nestled deeper within the covers, getting herself comfortable. The blankets hugged her, keeping her warm and safe. Today was awful, and she deserved to get some sleep. She felt her body begin to relax after being tight all day. It felt nice to finally let her guard down.

"Hello to all," Vicky heard an all too familiar voice say. She jolted up, her eyes wide and bloodshot. "I split myself apart for each of you to see, so this message goes to all six of you." The ghastly creature loomed in the corner of her room, fading in and out as it spoke. Vicky stayed silent, knowing anything she said would be pointless. "I know you all want this to end, well, it could if you put your trust in me." Vicky narrowed her eyes, not falling for one second of it. "Now, I won't sugarcoat it, the solution may be considered inhumane, but that's just the right price you have to pay for salvation!"

"Salvation my ass," Vicky mumbled under her breath.

"You savages will do anything to save your own skin! So let's work as a team to save *everyone's* skin, shall we? However, someone's skin must shed in order for this to happen. Blood must be dropped to satisfy, I crave only one last body. One last body to be free from Stan. I need one young and healthy, I know you'll do the right thing." Vicky tried to process what was being said, her heart pounding lightly in her chest. "I'm giving you the option of a sacrifice outside your group, if you do not abide by my generous offer, there will be consequences." Huxley smiled before fading out completely. *One last body to be free from Stan?*

Vicky felt a shudder run through her body. *Sacrifice outside your group, haven't we already sacrificed enough?* She threw her head back, feeling her temples begin to swell with pain. *I just want this to be over.* She heard the sound of a light knocking on her door. She slowly slipped her legs out from under the covers, letting her bare feet fall onto the soft freshly cleaned carpeted floor. She crept her way to the door, turning the knob before opening it slowly.

"Did you see it too?" Jamie asked in a whisper before she could even open the door all the way with wide eyes. She nodded her head.

"Yeah," she replied, "I saw it."

"Can I come in?" He asked softly. She opened the door a little wider in a gesture for him to come in. He slowly made his way inside as she guided them towards her bed to sit down. "What does he mean by sacrifice?" He asked as the two sat down on the cushioned mattress.

"I don't know," Vicky told him honestly. "Maybe we have to let him kill someone again."

"I'm sick of letting him pull shit like that," Jamie hissed.

"Do we have any other choice? It sounded like he would kill one of us if we didn't do what he asked," Vicky noted tiredly. She laid down, allowing herself to stare at the ceiling. "At this point, I don't care anymore, I just want this to be over." Jamie looked over at her with concern as she shifted herself into a more comfortable position.

"You'd let someone die?" He asked in awe.

"Rather it be someone else than you or me," she answered honestly. He laid down next to her in the dark, his hand brushing lightly against hers.

"You're starting to sound a lot like me," he grumbled softly. "I'm not sure how I like it." Vicky didn't say anything, just grabbed his hand and held it. She didn't have to look at him to know he was blushing. It would be too dark to notice anyway.

"Can you sleep here with me tonight?" She asked calmly. "I don't want to be alone." She could hear him take in a deep breath before responding.

"Of course," he answered with a crack in his voice. She snuggled closer, draping her arm and leg over him, holding him close. She could feel his body begin to heat up, leaving no use for a blanket. She felt his own arm cover her, the two in a wounded, poetic embrace.

"I love you, Jamie Anderson," she told him softly. For a moment, he didn't respond, and she didn't mind. She didn't need words to know if the feeling was mutual.

"I love you too, Vicky Taylor," Jamie stuttered out. The two fell silent, basking in each other's presence. At least she wasn't alone. She closed her eyes, allowing her thoughts to drift. A sudden thought ripped through her mind, causing her eyes to shoot open.

"Jamie?" She whispered carefully.

"Yeah?"

"I think I know who should be the sacrifice."

Ivan Balakin

Ivan was the only one to go home by himself that day. He had seen the message while inside his room, being too frozen to say or do a thing. He hated to see the creature's face, the mask of the man who almost took his life. He felt helpless. He wanted to get out of this town, get away from everyone who lived here including his father. He stared up at his ceiling, the crack looking a little bigger than before. He felt his eye twitch. He had stolen his father's gun. He had watched two people die on the same day. He couldn't take it anymore. It was finally setting in.

He grabbed his head, gripping his hair tightly as he gritted his teeth. He felt some strange emotion within him he hadn't felt since being a child. He had to let it out. He got off the bed, grabbed his pillows, and threw them to the floor. He tore the blankets and sheets off, ripping them apart and splitting the seams. He kicked his nightstand over, the honey he had used to feed his ants falling to the floor. He took the bottle of honey and threw it at his window. He stood there with narrowed eyes, breathing heavily as he did. His usual neat hair was a scruffy mess. He turned his head towards the door upon hearing the sound of stomping up the stairs.

The door slammed open and his father entered the room with an already red face. Ivan met him with cold eyes.

"What the fuck did you do?" He screamed at Ivan. Ivan said nothing, only stared back. He didn't have an answer. He didn't know what he did or why he did it. He felt trapped in this stupid town, trapped in his own head. His father looked around the tiny room, the floor being covered in an ocean of torn-up sheets and blankets. He went for his belt. Ivan only continued to stare. To him, his father was just like the crack in the ceiling. His father raised his belt like a priest raising a cross. Maybe this would be his blessing. He struck him across the face with it, a burning sensation rolling through Ivan's body. He remained still, just staring.

He struck him again, this time on his side. He remembered the claws of the killer pulling him into the deep murky water. Again. He remembered the sound the ant farm made when being dropped out the window. Again. He remembered the horrible sight of Mitchell West's mangled body in the woods. Again. He remembered watching the car fall on top of Philip Price, he remembered the sound it made. He kept striking him with the belt over and over again, and at this point, Ivan knew that he was just using him to take his anger out, just as Ivan had done to his room earlier.

"Worthless son!" He spat out before striking him one last time. "I wish you were your brother." Ivan wished he was too. Victor Balakin tossed his belt to the ground, looking at Ivan with hatred, something they were both used to. "Clean this mess up," he commanded before exiting the room, slamming the door behind him. He stood there with no emotion, his eyes still fixated to where his father once was. His face was bright red, the marks seeming to imprint his mind as well as his body. He felt a bead of sweat roll down his forehead and into his eye. He wiped it away. He never wanted to be his father.

He decided he would jump out the window again, this time not caring about the consequences. He had experienced worse. He opened the window, the cool summer air seeping through and into his room. He quickly made his way out, misplacing his hand and hitting the ground back first. His body felt heavy as his ears began to ring a little. He didn't mind. He kept his eyes up and towards the stars above. What sight could be better than this? He took a deep breath in, the crisp air filling his lungs. He slowly got up from the grass, his elbows caked in dirt. With shaky legs, he stumbled his way out of the yard. He watched as fireflies flew quaintly around him, their soft light guiding him. He wasn't even sure where he was going.

Each step felt heavy as he continued his way down the road. The street lights flickered above as he soaked in the air. If he couldn't get peace, he would find it himself. He wasn't meant to be hit. He wasn't meant to drown. He wasn't meant to mess with dead things. A firefly briefly landed on his shoulder before rising back into the sky. He was meant to care for the little things. He was so sick of being so confused. He was so sick of just letting things happen, agreeing with everyone to keep the peace. He was never truly loved, and if he was, it was only out of convenience. He wanted to trust Jamie, but it just didn't seem possible that he or anyone else, for that matter, truly cared about him.

He watched as moths swarmed the streetlamps above, hitting the light stupidly before falling back and doing it over again. He wished more than anything that he was a bug. Live a simple life and die quickly. They don't have any expectations made of them, no pressure. *Well, I suppose the whole fight to survive thing.* But he also supposed he was already fighting to survive, even if he wasn't an insect. He passed underneath a broken street lamp, the darkness surrounding him. He felt comforted by the outdoors, Mother Nature caring for him more than his own mother did. He paused underneath the broken light, staring up at the vast sky. He briefly wondered if one day the stars might fall too.

He pushed on his journey towards nowhere, feeling himself begin to calm down from earlier. He never meant to do any of that. He just couldn't take any more of the dirty ghost man's taunting. He didn't want to sacrifice anyone. *Maybe I could sacrifice myself.* He shook his head as if disagreeing with himself. He rather not think about that. He couldn't hide from them either unless he ran away, it was a small town after all. He was completely out of options. He sighed, allowing himself to fall down on the grass beside the curb. His arms began to feel a little scratchy, but he didn't mind. To love something hard enough meant to be uncomfortable at times, and oh, how he loved his mother.

He rolled over to his side, a small firefly setting flight from a nearby blade of grass. He reached his arm out, feeling the grass tenderly. He knew the Earth wouldn't hurt him the way his father did. Here, he was loved. He drew his knees to his chest, curling himself into a ball on the ground. *I'll just lay here for a while.* He thought to himself as he closed his eyes. He craved rest. He craved calm. The idea of both constantly slipping through his fingers like water. He continued to lie there like that, allowing himself to be cradled by the earth. The smell of the grass filled his nose as mosquitos began to use him to feed.

He didn't want to go home. He wondered if anyone would even care if he left. He would just be one less mouth to feed after all. He let his legs loose, rolling over onto his back to stare up at the night sky. He watched as an airplane flew above in the distance, its lights blinking as if communicating with the stars. It was so far away, making him wonder how many people there were thinking the same thing about the ground. Being a bird wouldn't be too awful either, the open air seeming to be desirable. He took a deep breath in. One day he would find what home truly was, his true purpose. He thought back on the conversation he had with Bradley and Stan about the future. He supposed the future wasn't as far as he thought it was. He sighed.

Tomorrow, the others would hunt him down, forcing him to join whatever they had planned out. He would join them reluctantly, as that is what he is known for. He didn't care if he lived or died anymore. If this is what he was meant to do, then so be it. But for now, he would enjoy the grass. For now, he would enjoy the stars. His life may be temporary, but so was everything else, and that somehow was a comforting thought. Tonight, he would live in the moment. Tonight, he would rest.

Scott Carter

"Hell no, someone would definitely find out," Scott told Jesse Olsen sternly. "I also would rather not get my ass beat by Balakin again." The two sat outside on the train tracks in the woods, cigarettes lit and on hand.

"Then don't lose," Jesse noted smoothly, taking a pocket knife out of his jeans before sliding it over towards Scott. Scott's eyes widened, yet he wasn't surprised that's what Jesse would resort to.

"I'm not doing that!" He shouted while shoving the knife away. Jesse took a drag off his cigarette, looking at him blankly with a slightly cocked head.

"You'd do it if you had to save your ass," he jeered with a shrug. Scott groaned, a sick feeling arising in his stomach. It was the same feeling he had after breaking something as a kid.

"I don't think we should do this," Scott mumbled while shaking his head, taking a drag off his own cigarette.

"I want to know who spoke into my head," Jesse stated while taking his knife back.

"Maybe it was your dead dad or something," Scott sarcastically suggested with a small laugh. Jesse shot him a glare.

"Don't talk about my pops like that, I know what I heard and it wasn't him." He took his pliers out of his pocket, the blood from Thomas never being cleaned off.

"Vicky obviously didn't rat you out" Scott began to say.

"I know," Jesse claimed, cutting him off.

"So what's the point of this?" Jesse took another drag, throwing his head back to blow out the smoke.

"There's something up with the outsider," he replied slyly.

"The brown-haired kid?" Jesse nodded his head with a smile.

"I just want answers is all," he told him as he spun the pliers around. Scott rolled his eyes, throwing his dead cigarette to the ground.

"Whatever, man," Scott grumbled, "but if we get caught, I'm putting the blame on you." Jesse allowed himself to fall backward, lying across the tracks. He turned his head slightly to look at Scott, his cigarette clenched between his teeth. Crows cawed from above, causing Scott to jump slightly. He felt a little on edge today.

"I bet you'd love to just see a train come and crush me, wouldn't ya Scotty?" Scott shook his head. He felt a little taken aback by the statement, but not exactly shocked.

"Nah, but you would," Scott retorted shortly. Jesse let out a slight laugh, cigarette still clenched.

"I think when all of this is over," he started to say, taking the cigarette out of his mouth and throwing it to the side. "I'm gonna do it." Scott's eyes widened slightly.

"Do what?" He asked, playing stupid. He just wanted to hear it for himself and make sure he was getting the message right. Jesse looked at him with a somewhat soft expression, seeing through his act.

"You know what," he looked away. "Although I'm not even sure what needs to end before I do." He looked lost, Scott stared down at him with sincerity, listening intently. "I just know I can't continue like.." He trailed off. "This." He kept his eyes on the trees, sunlight escaping through and dancing on the forest floor. Scott felt the sensation of an insect crawling on his arm for a moment. He ignored it, focusing on this new emotion that Jesse was displaying. "I don't know what I'm waiting for anymore." Scott wasn't sure what to say, the silence felt deafening.

"I think," Scott tried to find words. "I don't know, I don't think doing that would-" He searched for something to say. "Just don't, please." Jesse closed his eyes, a small grin appearing on his scruffy face.

"Let's talk about something else," he suggested. "Speak to Thomas Cairns lately?" Scott felt his heart drop at the thought of Thomas.

"No," he admitted honestly. In fact, he hadn't seen Thomas at all since the fight. "Did you do something?" He asked with skepticism. Jesse shook his head.

"No, he's your problem," Scott remembered seeing the blood on his pliers, not believing him for a second. Jesse whipped his pack out of his pocket, pulling out another cigarette before lighting it. Scott thought he had to have smoked at least two packs a day. "Hear about the diner collapsing?" Jesse asked subtly, breaking Scott away from his thoughts.

"What?" His eyes widened slightly.

"Collapsed yesterday," he said, "one dead, two injured." He took a drag off his cigarette. "Looks like football king is no longer with us." Scott could feel his throat dry up at the sound of Jesse's words.

"Jeffrey Grant?" Scott asked in disbelief.

"The one and only," Jesse replied. Scott couldn't believe it, he had just gotten a ride from him not even that long ago. *There's no way he could be dead, no way!* He felt like throwing up. "And," Jesse continued. Scott couldn't help but feel himself begin to spiral. "Laura Gray is one of the injured ones." Scott's stomach dropped once again.

"Laura?" He asked as if he didn't hear it the first time. Jesse nodded, taking another drag off his cigarette. He couldn't believe what he was hearing, he had to be lying. "Are you serious?" Jesse nodded again.

"Taylor and the others were there too," he added. "And they made it out alive and unscathed." Jesse looked at him from the side, his eyes slightly narrowed. "They had to have had some part of it." The sound of a train called from the distance. That was their cue to leave. They grabbed what little they had, stuffing it into their pockets before hopping off the tracks to head out. Scott was still trying to comprehend what Jesse had just said. He wanted to believe that it was just another one of Jesse's lies, something that was part of his deceptive nature. *He's not lying, though, and you know it.* He ignored the reasonable side of himself.

"So, when are we going to do this?" Scott asked quickly.

"In a little bit," Jesse told him, "we have to wait for the perfect time." Scott thought back to the diner collapsing. *If he's right, that could be us next.* He looked down and watched as his shoes became untied. *Whatever, won't happen.*

"Okay," Scott said calmly. Jesse stuffed his hands in his pockets as they strolled out of the woods. Crows called above as they made their way out of the treeline and into the street.

"So," Jesse started to say, "you gonna take this or not?" He held the pocket knife up for Scott to see. Scott felt a slight pit in his stomach, but he also didn't want a repeat of what happened last time. He sighed.

"Yeah," he agreed, "I'll take it." Scott quickly snatched the knife out of his hand and stuffed it in his own pocket as Jesse let out a sly grin.

"Good, I knew you would." Jesse turned his attention back to the road, staring across the street. His scar seemed to almost fade against the sun. Jesse yawned, his silver tongue piercing glimmering in the light. The knife suddenly felt very heavy in his pocket. Things were getting a little too real.

"What do you want from this?" Scott asked him. Jesse turned to look at him, his blue eyes shining.

"I don't want anything," he said. "I do everything for nothing, make sense?" Scott shook his head. It seemed Jesse never made sense. Jesse smiled. "Didn't think it would." He pulled out his pliers. "I guess I should fess up." Scott eyed down the blood, knowing where this was going. "I had a talk with Thomas Cairns, a short conversation really." Scott stayed silent, listening closely. "But you know Thomas, he's a mental shitbag who can't take criticism." Scott's eyes narrowed. "So things got a little out of hand and-" He held the pliers up. "Well, you know." Scott sighed, plopping himself down on the curb.

"Which tooth did you take this time, tooth fairy?" Scott asked while looking up at him.

"Molar," Jesse replied with a toothy shit-eating grin. "I still have it." Scott couldn't help but let out his own small smile. To think ol' Thomas got his tooth ripped out brought some sort of unexplainable joy. It really made him think.

"Can you get Balakin next?" Scott asked subtly. Jesse's expression changed from snarky to wide-eyed.

"Balakin? You're joking," he pondered in surprise. "You see the size of that guy?"

"Yeah, he broke my nose dude," Scott retorted quickly.

"Are you giving me a new objective for this whole thing?" Jesse asked with a raised eyebrow.

"Maybe," Scott replied with a shrug. Jesse smiled.

"Sure thing, Scotty." If Scott couldn't deal it out himself, he would serve it cold and bloody with Jesse as his waiter. But for now, the two would only continue to sit on the curb, waiting. Waiting for ghost boy.

Stanley Morris

You've been so good Stanley, you can't stop this now. You're so close to setting yourself free. Does it even matter? *Of course it does. You've worked so hard to free yourself, now you're almost there. You could use this time to spend with your new companions.. But this is only if you comply, do you understand?* I understand. *Good, it's good that we are on the same page. Now I need you to get your friends on the same page as well, don't want you to have to lose them. Understand?* I understand. *Good. Good..*

"Stan?" Stan felt someone begin to shake him awake. "Stan, wake up please, we have to go." He opened his eyes to see Bradley hovering over him, eyes wide and frantic.

"What?" Stan asked, confused. He jolted up, looking around him. He was lying in Bradley's bed beside his cat Smudge, who was softly purring. He didn't remember being here at all, he must have been unconscious again.

"We have to go meet Vicky, they know what sacrifice to use," Bradley explained while adjusting his glasses. Stan's eyes widened.

"What?"

"You didn't see the message in your head?" Bradley asked while poking at Stan's temple.

"I did, but who?" Stan questioned while waving Bradley's hand away.

"They didn't say, they just told us to hurry up," Bradley explained. Stan rolled his eyes. Of course this group had another circumstance of zero communication. "Are you feeling alright enough to get up?" Bradley asked carefully.

"I think so," Stan replied before stepping onto the ground with a shaky leg. *If you're going to make me kill for you, at least give me the energy to do it.* He put his other leg down, feeling a burst of energy course through him. The feeling was so intense and so sudden that he felt like throwing up. He paused for a moment, leveling himself. Once he felt stable, he lifted himself off the bed and allowed himself to stand freely. "Okay," he said, "I'm ready." Bradley nodded, giving Smudge one last pat on the head before departing.

The two left the house quickly, Bradley heading for his bike. He hopped on first, waiting for Stan to hop on the back before speeding off down the street. The air was beginning to heat up as a slight breeze rolled through Stan's hair. His head felt empty and quiet, as if unoccupied. He closed his eyes, allowing himself to bask in the calmness for a moment. He enjoyed this temporary silence.

"Who do you think it will be?" Bradley asked between breaths, attempting to pedal up a small hill. Stan thought about it for a moment, his mind blank. He didn't know that many people here anyway.

"I don't know," he answered honestly. "Maybe the guy from the gas station?"

"GUS?" Bradley asked in bewilderment, turning his head back briefly to reveal wide eyes. "No way! He requested young anyways, Gus is like," Bradley paused to think for a moment. "At *least* forty-something."

"Well, who do you think it is then?" Stan asked as Bradley continued to pedal down the street.

"I was thinking like Tommy Morrison or like Alan Giblin or something," Bradley speculated.

"What did Alan Giblin do?" Stan asked, thinking Alan Giblin must be pretty bad to be considered a sacrifice.

"Nothing," Bradley replied with a shrug. *Oh.* "But I guess we'll find out once we get there." Stan sighed, knowing he was right. No point in guessing or stressing what he'll find out in a few minutes. He allowed his eyes to close once again as the two flew down the street. Soon it would all be over, if Huxley kept his promise that is. Stan wanted to trust him, he wanted to believe that he could be free. Maybe he could.

When he opened his eyes, they were at Vicky's. Stan supposed he must have dozed off a little. Bradley gently stepped off the bike, holding it up for Stan to dismount as well. The two of them wheeled it over into the lawn, setting it in the grass to lay like a dead bird. Stan heard a door open behind him, causing him to whip his head around. Vicky and Jamie both stepped outside, heading towards them in a slight jog, Vicky closing the door behind her.

"Have you seen Ivan?" Jamie asked as the four met up. Stan shook his head, not recalling seeing the tall boy.

"We still need to get Annette, we'll worry about him after," Vicky told Jamie before making her way across the street towards Annette's house. Stan glanced over at Bradley who shrugged, following Vicky after.

"Do you think he'll show?" Bradley asked Stan.

"We didn't call him," Jamie answered, butting in the conversation. "Too much of a risk with his dad being there." Stan thought that made sense. "It shouldn't be too hard to find him." Vicky briskly walked across the lawn, heading up the stairs before knocking on the door. Stan noticed movement coming from the curtains, a small pair of eyes scanning over the group before disappearing. A sad-looking boy answered the door, deep eye bags resting on his young face.

"She's still sleeping, she came home late from the hospital last night." He explained tiredly, rubbing his eyes as if he was the one who was out all night.

"Any updates on Jeff?" Vicky questioned sadly, already knowing the answer. Arnold looked down, avoiding eye contact with her.

"He didn't make it," he muttered quietly. Stan could hear a deep breath escape from Bradley, a somber feeling washing over the group.

"Could you get Annette for us please?" Jamie asked. Arnold's head shot back up, his eyes slightly narrowing.

"If I do, she better come home and not end up like Jeff, okay?" Arnold demanded sternly.

"Of course," Vicky soothed. Arnold gave them one last harsh look before closing the door and disappearing back into the house.

"Well," Jamie said with a sigh before plopping himself down on the top step. The sun delicately danced around them as the gentle breeze from before ruffled their hair.

"I can't believe it," Bradley marveled wistfully. "I can't believe he's dead." Vicky sat herself down next to Jamie, holding her head in her hands.

"I can't believe it either," she mumbled with a sigh. "Hopefully he's the last one to go." Stan's head shot up, remembering the big question from earlier.

"But he can't be," Stan noted. "Who did you guys pick to be the sacrifice?" The two looked at each other before looking at the group.

"Tommy Morrison," Jamie answered in a deadpan tone.

"He's scummy," Vicky added. "He was the one who got Jeff killed, if Tommy hadn't said anything, Jeff wouldn't have been there."

"I was right," Bradley commented with a small smile. They all agreed Tommy would be the best offering, young, strong, and cruel. Perfect for a serial killer's sacrifice. A washed-up Annette suddenly opened the door, mascara streaked under her puffy and red eyes.

"I don't want any more people to die," she stated slowly with a sorrowful gaze. Vicky and Jamie quickly got up, backing up to give her space.

"Tommy will be the sacrifice," Vicky reassured.

"Like that changes anything," Annette snarled.

"Net', if he doesn't die, one of us will. Someone is going to die either way," Vicky pleaded. Annette squinted her eyes closed, pulling her hair in frustration.

"I just want this to be over," she cried.

"And if he goes, it will be," Vicky soothed, stepping up to hold Annette in her arms. Annette wrapped her arms around her, squeezing her tightly as she began to sob. Vicky stroked her hair softly, soothing her as Annette released her emotions. The three boys just looked at the ground in silence as Vicky calmed her down. Annette's sobs soon trailed off into a fit of sniffles, her makeup looking even worse than before.

"Okay," Annette said before rubbing the last of the tears from her eyes. "Okay let's do it." Vicky let out a soft smile, stepping back to give her room once again. "Just let me get changed and washed up real quick," Annette sniffled before stepping back inside. Stan felt guilty for bringing the group this much pain. *I should have done it.* He thought to himself disappointedly. *This is my fault.* It didn't matter though. The damage had already been done. Once Annette was out, the five of them took Vicky's car to go to Ivan's. There was no backing out now.

Upon arriving at Ivan's, they soon realized no one was home. Bradley was the one to knock on the door, looking back at the group in confusion when realizing the predicament. Jamie stepped out, looking around the house and up the walls. He pointed up towards one of the windows before heading back towards the car.

"His window is open, he must have left through it at some point," he noted before getting back inside the car.

"How do you know it's his window?" Vicky asked before Bradley got back inside the car as well.

"We had a long talk about it one night," Jamie mumbled without much context. Nobody bothered pushing any further.

"Well, where would he be?" Bradley asked while adjusting his glasses. Jamie shrugged.

"Probably the park," Jamie replied smoothly. "Just drive slow." Vicky nodded before starting the car and backing out of the driveway. Stan kept his eyes out the window, scanning for anything that might be a giveaway to where Ivan was. They rolled down the road slowly, silent anticipation washing over the group. The cornfields waved in harmony with the breeze as they drove over the beaten down pavement. About halfway down the street, he spotted a body lying underneath a street lamp.

"There!" Stan shouted, his finger hitting the glass multiple times as he pointed outside. Vicky immediately stopped the car, everyone's heads jerking forward slightly. Jamie and Bradley rushed out, heading towards Ivan as the rest stayed in the car near the curb. Stan watched as the two boys shook him awake, looking down at him with worry. From what Stan could tell, Ivan seemed to be dazed and confused. The two helped him up, using themselves as crutches until Ivan could get strength into his legs. Ivan did a little half limp before straightening himself out and walking normally to the car.

"Are you alright, Ivan?" Vicky turned to ask as Ivan entered the vehicle. Bradley took his spot on the floor of the car, turning into a little ball as he did.

"Yeah," Ivan told her quietly before taking his seat in the middle next to Stan. Vicky nodded herself as if in confirmation for her to leave.

"Are you guys ready?" She asked as she shifted the gear to drive. Nobody replied, but nobody had to either. They didn't have a choice on if they were ready or not, this was going to happen either way. She drove off down the street, making her way towards town. Stan noticed she wasn't speeding this time. He felt a hand lightly touch his leg, Bradley looking up at him with a worried expression.

"Are you going to be okay?" He asked quietly as Vicky turned the radio on. Stan couldn't tell what was playing, nor did he care. He thought about Bradley's question for a moment. *If the promise is kept, then yes.* He was ready for this to all be over. He'd do anything.

"I hope so," he replied back honestly. That seemed to be enough for Bradley, his head turning away towards the floor once again. Stan returned his focus back to the window, staring outside longingly. He wasn't sure how Huxley would kill Tommy, he just hoped it would be quick. His head felt very quiet, he supposed maybe he was saving up his power in there or something. He watched as passerby made their way down the sidewalk, unknowing of what was truly happening in their dinky little town. He thought maybe it would be better if they didn't know.

After another mile or so, Vicky abruptly stopped the car. *Are we here?*

"Are you serious?" Vicky asked harshly under her breath. The four boys peeked their heads over the seats in an attempt to see what was happening. Stan saw two dirty guys standing in the middle of the road, a crazed look in one of their eyes.

"Just run them over," Jamie sneered jokingly. One of them began to approach the car at a brisk pace. Vicky wasn't sure what to do, attempting to turn around them. The boy with long, dark, scraggly hair took something out of his pocket, targeting the front tires.

"Hey!" Vicky yelled as she put the car in park, unbuckling herself quickly before hopping out of the vehicle. Stan noticed they were near the park, the woods not too far ahead.

"Goddammit, he slashed the tires," Jamie blurted, struggling to unbuckle before getting out himself. *That one.* Stan heard the voice finally say. *I want that one.* Stan watched as the one on the road remained still, a large scar across his face.

"Him?" Stan whispered. *Yes.* The voice replied back. Stan nodded, understanding what he had to do. He opened the door, stepped outside, and slowly headed toward the others.

"You slashed my fucking tires?" Vicky asked harshly, pointing towards the now flattened tires. "What is wrong with you?" Jamie put himself in front of her, pushing her back a little. Stan noticed the one with the scar turn towards him. He suddenly knew what they were here for. Stan supposed he could say he was here for the same thing. He knew the look the one with the scar had anywhere, it was a look Russel gave quite often. He wouldn't allow himself to fall victim again. *Just go where I tell you to go.* Stan nodded his head. He understood.

Jesse Olsen

He spotted the scruffy-haired boy approaching them. Perfect. It was exactly what he wanted. He stuck his hand in his pocket, resting his fingertips on top of the pliers. He wouldn't pull them out just yet. *End this now.* He told himself internally. *Give yourself purpose.* He watched as the rest of them began departing the car. Looked like the whole crew was here. *Great.* Vicky continued her screaming, Scott slinking back towards Jesse. He turned his attention back to the scruffy-haired boy. Suddenly, the boy made a break for it, turning around and booking it down the street. Jesse smiled, always enjoying a good chase.

They all paused for a moment, Jesse allowing him to get a head start before darting after him. He always considered himself to be pretty fast, finding it come in handy for times like this. He was able to hear a rush of footsteps follow him from behind. He didn't care, they wouldn't catch up. Jesse watched as he sped off towards the park. He was a quick little sucker, but Jesse knew he wouldn't be quick enough.

"Stop!" He could hear Annette yell. He didn't care, he kept his eyes on the target. He faintly noticed the sky begin to slowly darken, the slow roll of thunder crowding in. But it wasn't raining, not yet. The boy darted across the bright green grass, swerving to one side of the pond. Jesse could detect each move, and he was beginning to get closer. He knew where he was running to. He was running to the maze.

Across from the park was a corn maze, in the center was a hill with a large boulder on top. It was the same boulder that Jesse used to slash his own face with. He knew that maze like the back of his hand, the boy wouldn't last a minute in there with him. He felt the first drop of rain fall onto his arm. The sky was dark and stormy, like some evil brewery within the clouds. More rain began to patter onto the ground, coming in as harsh, fat drops. The boy seemed to use it to his advantage, using his heels to slide down a hill and continue his escape. Jesse did the same, wavering to the side a little before pushing on.

They exited the park, running across the wet road and towards the maze. He watched him blindly run into the field, a slick smile spreading across Jesse's face. He sprinted inside after him, watching the white of his shirt disappear and reappear with each twist and turn.

"Awh, c'mon now, no need to hide," Jesse huffed out after him. "It's just a little game of cat and mouse, that's all." He started to lose sight of the shirt, causing him to slow his pace. He'd find him, he couldn't hide forever after all. He could faintly hear the others behind him. He slowed to a walk, knowing that no matter what, at some point he would make it to the center. He started to head that way, his memory serving him well. The rain felt cold against his hot skin, the ground beneath him becoming slick with mud.

He looked down, noticing footprints ahead of him. *Perfect.* He followed them, quickening his pace to a fast walk. He knew it wouldn't take too much longer to make it to the center, it seemed the boy knew that as well. He continued his pursuit, keeping his eyes on the footprints below. Lighting streaked across the sky followed by a loud boom. He wasn't worried, not one bit.

"Jesse!" He heard Scott yell from a distance. He wouldn't dare yell back, it would give up his position. He continued to follow the boy through the maze. He felt his foot get stuck in the mud momentarily, causing him to tug on his leg to get it out. It felt like the ground was trying to devour him, mouth open and hungry with gnashing teeth. He pulled out his pliers. The clearing was just up ahead. He reached his leg up, rubbing some of the thick mud off his shoes and onto the empty corn stalks. He slunk his way into the clearing, spotting the boy just up ahead.

"Stan!" He couldn't tell who yelled this time, but they sounded closer. *Stan. Okay, Stan.* Stan looked at him with a dead expression, his eyes emotionless and clouded. Jesse circled the large clearing like a shark, his pliers at the ready when needed.

"Now tell me," Jesse started to say, "what was that voice I heard? Some sort of party trick? I know it was you, so don't try to lie to me now." Stan said nothing, just watched as Jesse continued to slowly circle him. "You gonna say something, or are you gonna just stand around and look stupid?"

"You should have gone back when he called for you," Stan stated sullenly. Jesse paused for a moment, his response catching him off guard. He shook it off, continuing to close in.

"Yeah, and why is that?" He asked as he came a little closer. He briefly noticed the others enter the clearing, Scott's arms tied behind him by Balakin. *Looks like the knife didn't work.*

"Jesse, you need to go," Annette pleaded desperately. Jesse whipped his head around, eyes narrowed.

"Not until I find out what's going on," he hissed. Lightning struck above once more, followed by a crack of thunder.

"Jesse, please," Scott begged. Jesse shook his head, turning his attention back towards Stan.

"You should have listened to them," Stan stated, getting closer himself. Jesse backed up, surprised by this sudden encounter. He had never once felt like the prey before. "I'm giving you one last chance," Stan offered.

"Oh yeah?" Jesse jeered, regaining control. He stepped up towards Stan, mud grabbing at his shoes like a child grabbing candy. "What if I don't, what then?" He asked.

"Then so be it," Stan snarled before shoving him towards the hill, lighting striking above, filling the sky with light as he did. Jesse fell onto the hill, the rain hitting against his head violently. He heard a large clap of thunder, Stan standing over him with large, emotionless eyes. Jesse switched his pliers for his pocket knife, feeling thankful that he kept his spare on him just in case. He swung it towards Stan's face, striking it in a fashion that looked similar to his scar. He began to bleed, but his eyes remained without cold.

Stan kicked him back down before he could get up, the rain and mud sucking him in. He watched as Scott tried to break free, his pale face standing out against the dark surroundings. He looked petrified. Jesse picked himself back up again, his legs shaking slightly beneath him.

"You're a dead man," Jesse grumbled, stumbling towards him slightly. He felt so weak, he couldn't understand why. He noticed a slight change in emotion within Stan's face. At that moment, Jesse could have sworn he saw a smile. He watched as the sky lit up one last time, the lighting striking just behind him. He whipped his head around, looking up to see where the lightning had struck. The rain hit his eyes as he noticed the dark figure of the boulder begin to move.

"JESSE MOVE!" He could hear Scott scream. He couldn't understand why he would scream such a thing, though. It was just a big rock after all. He watched as it seemed to tilt towards him. He suddenly felt dread, a feeling he only ever felt when he knew he was going to get hit by his father as a child. The dark shape began to move down towards him. It was almost as if time had stopped at that moment. This didn't feel real, it had to have been a dream. In those few fleeting seconds, he remembered Swan Lake, the first few notes playing in his head like a radio in a car. He didn't know why he thought of that during his last few moments on Earth, and he would never find out. He watched as the boulder hit him head-first, slamming his body into the mud. Jesse Olsen would later be pronounced dead on impact.

Bradley Moore

For a moment, everything was silent except for the rain hitting the ground. Ivan let go of Scott, letting him scramble away as he darted for the exit of the maze. It was as if nothing had happened at all. Bradley let his eyes travel back towards Stan who stood in front of the boulder like some sort of reaper. They all stayed quiet, watching, waiting for something to happen. Bradley began to wonder if something would even happen in the first place. Stan turned his head around to look at them, his face cold and somber.

He suddenly jerked his head upwards, eyes rolling back and mouth agape. Those familiar sickly gray claws clambered out of his mouth like a spider's legs. Stan dropped to his knees, mud splattering beneath him. Bradley ran towards him, feeling mud splat against his own legs as he did. He grabbed his face, watching the creature slowly make its way out of him. He looked inside his mouth, two beady yellow eyes staring back at him from the inside. Bradley jumped at the sight of them, slipping on the mud and falling on his ass.

The creature continued its slow descent out of Stan, its large claws gripping his shirt in an attempt to tug itself out. Bradley sat there helpless, not knowing what to do or how to help him. He felt as though he were watching a snake shed its skin, but instead, he was watching a parasite shed itself of its human host. The others stood still, watching in horror as the scene continued to unfold. Stan let out a strained and muffled groan as the head began to squeeze itself out. It reminded Bradley of rubber the way it bent itself in order to fit through his mouth.

The bright yellow eyes shone through the darkened sky like spotlights. It wasn't long before the putrid creature pulled itself out of Stan, digging its large claws into the mud to pull itself forward. Its long, snake-like body dragged behind it as it crawled towards the fallen boulder. It used its claws to grip the boulder, pulling itself up and wrapping its body around itself. The body began to harden in an instant, a strange crispy-looking texture forming a protective shell. Bradley realized it was making itself a cocoon.

Stan fell back into the mud, gasping for air as his body began to shake. All power that he once had before was now completely gone. The rain continued to pour on, causing Stan's breathing to worsen. Bradley lifted him up so the rain wouldn't fall directly into his mouth. The rest ran towards the two boys, crowding around them with worried eyes.

"Is it over?" Stan asked weakly, his voice barely audible. Bradley smiled, nodding his head.

"Yeah," he responded softly. "It's over, you did it." Stan let out a small smile himself before coughing.

"Let's get him out of here," Vicky told them sternly. Bradley backed up, allowing Ivan to pick up Stan. The six of them started their way out of the maze, Bradley giving one last look at the strange cocoon before entering the field once more. The mud grabbed at their shoes as they started the trek through the maze, following what was left of the footprints. Bradley kept himself in the back of the group, Vicky leading the front. The rain seemed to lighten up a little.

Bradley felt numb, not being able to properly process what happened, the past week going by in a blur. He was missing school, failing all his classes due to a lack of sleep, and somehow that was the least of his worries. He didn't know what he wanted anymore, feeling as lost as ever. Did he want Stan? Or did he want a normal life? *I might be able to have both now.* He thought to himself, trying to soothe his brain. But something within him felt like it wasn't really over yet. There's no way that's it. Someone would have to pay the price that was due.

The sun was beginning to peek through the clouds once they reached the entrance of the maze, their shoes caked with mud, each step feeling heavier than the last. Bradley let out a deep breath, feeling free now that he was finally out of the maze. Now that he was finally away from that thing. The sun felt nice against his skin, his clothes sopping wet and heavy. He adjusted his glasses, glancing around at the others who were looking up at the sky. The sun seemed to warm them too.

"So where do we go from here?" Annette turned to ask. Ivan stared down at Stan's weakened body, his breathing shallow.

"I'm not sure," Vicky answered, "I think we should all stick together." Jamie nodded in agreement.

"My mom isn't home," Bradley chimed in, "if you guys don't have any better ideas." They all looked around at each other at the sound of Bradley's response, seeming to wait for someone to say something first.

"Why not," Annette decided with a shrug, Bradley feeling a hint of surprise.

"What do we do about your car?" Jamie asked, turning to Vicky. She sighed.

"I don't know, we'll deal with it later," she responded with an exhausted tone. "Right now we just need to get Stan somewhere warm," she said as she started to walk across the street. The rest followed suit, none of them protesting. Bradley walked next to Ivan who seemed to be struggling a little.

"Are you sure you're going to be able to carry him the entire way there?" Bradley asked with a worried tone. Ivan readjusted, looking down at him with tired eyes.

"Don't have much of a choice," he replied coldly. Bradley turned away, knowing he was right. They continued their way down the park and up the street, passing Vicky's car as they did. *Her car is probably gonna get towed.* Bradley thought to himself. The image of Philip Price getting crushed replayed in his mind upon thinking about her car. He shook his head and tried thinking of something else. *Maybe when this is all over, we'll be able to tell everyone what really happened.* Although, he wasn't quite sure if their story would even be believable. It seemed as though everyone who believed had died.

As they continued their way down the street and towards Bradley's house, he got a sick sense of dread. *There's no way it's over.* He thought about the cocoon from before, his heart sinking into his chest. He wanted to talk to someone about it, but he felt as though now wasn't the time. He didn't really feel too close with any of them either. A bond formed from trauma maybe, but not much of a close connection. Even Stan felt distant. *Hopefully, now things can be different.*

They only ever had to pause once to give Ivan a break, making it to Bradley's house soon after. Bradley fumbled with the lock, nearly dropping his keys before unlocking the door and letting everyone inside. The home was quiet, an almost eerie feeling washing over the group. They all took their soaking wet, mud-splattered shoes off, setting them outside.

"Let me go find clothes for you guys to change into," Bradley offered before rushing off toward his room. He searched his closet, pulling out a variety of t-shirts, taking off his own to put a new and dry one on. He wasn't very sure if Ivan would fit any, but he would have to make do. He pulled out a few pairs of shorts along with the bottoms of a few pajama pants. He changed out of his jeans, feeling lighter already. He grabbed the wet clothes off the floor, a puddle soaking into the wooden boards.

He took the clothes into the bathroom, throwing them over and onto the curtain rod of the shower. He searched the cabinets in a hurry, grabbing a bandaid for Stan before going back into his room to gather dry clothes. He brought them into the living room, almost slipping on the wet floor as he did. *Shit, my mom's gonna be pissed if I don't clean this up.* He thought to himself in annoyance.

"Here," Bradley offered while setting the clothes on the coffee table. Ivan had set Stan on the couch, his weakened body giving off a sickly blue color. Bradley could care less if the couch got wet, Stan's well-being was more important than that. He was sure his mom would understand. "The bathroom is in the hallway," Bradley mentioned as they each took their designated articles of clothing. They silently nodded, the girls heading towards the bathroom. Bradley turned away as Ivan and Jamie changed in the living room.

"Where should we put these?" Jamie asked once they were done, pointing towards the dripping clothes in hand.

"When they get out you can just put it on the curtain rod," Bradley responded, gesturing towards the bathroom in the hallway. He sat at the end of the couch beside Stan, touching his hand briefly to see how warm he was. His skin was cold, but he was warm. Ivan and Jamie headed over into the hallway, presumably waiting for the girls to come out. He wondered when Stan would wake up. He looked completely drained, Bradley figured it would be a while before he did.

"Hurry up in there," Bradley heard Jamie say in an annoyed tone, knocking on the bathroom door as he did.

"Suck it, Anderson!" Annette shouted from the other side. Bradley rolled his eyes, turning his attention back to Stan.

"I'm sorry this happened to you," he whispered as he gently put the bandaid over the cut on his cheek. "But you're okay now, it's over." He stared down at his pale emotionless face, a longing feeling overcoming him. Deep down he knew. Even if the moon revolved around the sun, the two would never be able to touch without destroying one another. He looked away, feeling the light within him die a little. The bathroom door opened, Annette and Vicky heading out as Jamie and Ivan went in.

"Hey," Vicky greeted as she entered the living room. "How is he holding up?" Bradley looked down at Stan once again, not sure how to answer.

"Same as before," he replied, grabbing a blanket from the back of the couch and covering Stan's cold body with it. Vicky nodded, sitting on the loveseat beside the couch.

"How are *you* holding up?" She asked softly. Bradley's head jerked up, surprised by her sudden question.

"I could be better," he admitted. "I'm sure we all could, actually."

"For sure," she agreed as Annette entered the room with a yawn. She sat on the arm of the loveseat, rubbing her eyes tiredly.

"I vote we all take a group nap," she mumbled quietly. Vicky rolled her eyes with a smile as the other two joined them in the living room.

"I agree," Jamie chimed in. Bradley got up, stretching as he did.

"I could throw some blankets and pillows on the floor if you guys want," he suggested. They all looked around at each other and nodded.

"That works," Vicky added.

"Okay," Bradley said, making his way towards the hallway closet in search of spare blankets. He found an old one his mother had made him as a child, memories washing over like water as he stared down at the faded and torn fabric. He took it before closing the door with his other hand. He then went into his room and grabbed the rest of the blankets and pillows off the bed, struggling to carry them all back into the living room. He tossed them all to the floor, bending down to spread them out and make the area more comfortable.

Annette plopped herself down before he could even finish, tucking herself in as she rested her head on a freshly fluffed-up pillow. Vicky shrugged, following suit and snuggling up to Annette. Jamie laid himself next to Vicky, the two facing each other with sleepy eyes. Ivan politely sat down on the other side of the three, looking as though he were debating on whether he should lie down or not. Bradley laid down next to him, back turned towards him. He felt Ivan shift behind him, presumably lying down and getting himself comfortable.

Bradley closed his eyes. For a moment, there was peace. Nothing out to get them, the force of the weather at bay with no arguments. Just a simple nap shared between friends. For once, Bradley felt as though he belonged. He felt safe. He knew that as soon as summer started, they would go their separate ways once again. Maybe that was for the best. He thought maybe in the future they may bump into each other, exchange hello's, and be on their way once again. Maybe that was all he needed. To be acknowledged.

He was sure he would still remain friends with Stan, the two having a trauma-induced connection. A small part of him thought they might all remain friends because of this reason. It was always possible of course. Bradley thought anything might be possible now. He didn't think he would ever fully be able to comprehend what happened in the summer of 1987. He didn't think they would be able to either. What happened sounded like a story you would tell your children when they're being naughty. Like some sort of sick book. He knew no one would ever believe him, but that's okay because they would. He had a connection, and that's all that mattered.

Bradley heard what sounded like Annette begin to snore softly. He felt Ivan begin to toss and turn, and he wondered how he truly got here. It didn't make sense to him that these people would get together and attempt to get along for anything. It felt alien to him. He felt as though he were suddenly becoming aware, reality sinking in and hitting him like a brick. The feeling made him wide awake. It didn't help that Ivan's arm would randomly jerk, hitting him in the back occasionally. The feeling made him dive even further into his thoughts. *Despite everything, we're still here, still fighting this together.*

He took off his glasses, setting them on the carpet somewhere. He flipped onto his back and stared at the ceiling, his sight blurry. He listened to the soft breathing of those around him, all of them slightly different. It felt nice to have this sort of warm connection, something so different from what he was used to. He knew he would never be the same after this, and he didn't think the others would either. They were all so exhausted, it was hard to understand why he was so awake. He felt so close yet so distant at the same time.

He closed his eyes, attempting to allow his mind to rest. He knew it would be a while before he could fall asleep, but he didn't mind. He would milk this moment of softness, this moment of calm and peace. He would allow himself to enjoy this moment they would all have together, thankful that the one in the maze wasn't their last. He flipped back onto his side, facing the couch. He felt his mind begin to rest as his breathing began to slow. The sleepiness was starting to cradle him in its arms, the soft lullaby of his companions breathing lulling him to sleep.

John Charles

His eyes widened in the darkness of his room. John Charles felt a strange shift in the air, a shift he wasn't sure he could trust. He jolted up, his old bones creaking in protest. He pulled his curtains aside, light pouring in, causing him to squint his eyes. Not a soul in sight on his lonely street. He was out. He had got what he wanted and now he was out. God dammit. *God dammit!* Stanley had given him exactly what he wanted.

He slammed his bedroom door open, searching for his shoes as he stomped out. He wasn't going to play this game. He knew of the resting period and he was going to make sure this ended tonight. He wouldn't let anyone get in his way. He slipped on his boots, tying them tight. He wasn't going to allow anyone else to fall victim. Not this time. He made sure to grab his shotgun before leaving the house. It was all a free game now. *My turn, Huxley.*

The first step of this plan was to find out where he was resting. In order to do this, he would have to find the boy who started it all. He marched down the street, making his way towards the unstable house. He felt his heart wanting to beat out of his chest, but he kept himself calm. A stray cat darted across the road, running for the treeline as John continued on. He quickened his pace as soon as the house came into view, his eyes narrowing as his grip tightened on his shotgun.

He stomped towards the house and up the stoop, knocking loudly a total of three times. He waited there with his gun behind his back. A disheveled-looking woman answered the door, with cracked lips and shaky eyes. She definitely was not sober.

"What do you want?" She asked as her words slurred together.

"Where is your son?" He asked in more of a command than a question.

"How would I know? He's a teenager," she retorted with a sneer. She closed the door on him before he could reply. Fuming, he turned his head back up the street and towards his house. *The Moore's.* He had a feeling he knew where the kid might be. He backtracked, going back up the street and towards his house. More importantly, towards his truck. He kept a good pace despite his old legs wanting to give out. He would not allow his body to give out on him, this was far too important.

He sat his gun in the passenger as he started up his truck, backing out of his driveway before tearing off down the street. There wouldn't be much time, lord knows how long he's already been resting for. He was lucky no one was outside. It seemed that Linfort had become too dangerous for its inhabitants to go out and enjoy. John supposed it didn't help that it was storming earlier either. Nonetheless, it didn't matter. This would all be over soon. He would make sure of it.

He made it to Bradley Moore's in less than five minutes, adjusting his big dirty truck on the curb beside his house. He put the truck in park and left it running, knowing it wouldn't take too long here. Slamming the driver's side door closed, he made his way up the sidewalk and towards the door, knocking three times just as he did earlier. He waited a few moments before knocking again, a little louder this time. He was feeling his patience begin to dwindle before a very tired-looking Bradley Moore opened the door. He didn't have his glasses, but he seemed to know it was John Charles anyway, his eyes widening at the sight of him.

"What are you doing here?" Bradley asked in shock.

"Where is he?" John questioned without hesitation. He peeked his head around the corner, noticing the group of teens sleeping in the living room, a few of them waking up a little due to the commotion.

"Where is who?" Bradley asked, squinting his eyes as if that would help him see better.

"Stan," he answered strictly.

"He's on the couch, but I think he's still unconscious," Bradley explained. John pushed him out of the way, stomping towards the couch. At this point, everyone was awake except for Stan. He lifted the boy by the collar of his shirt, slapping him in the face.

"Wake up, boy!" He shouted.

"What the hell are you doing?" He heard Vicky holler behind him. He dropped Stan and whirled back around to face the group of teenagers.

"Do you all realize what you've done?" He asked angrily, "You've given him exactly what he wants, and now we're all going to pay unless we kill him now."

"What are you talking about?" Annette asked in a dazed sense of confusion.

"While he's resting, we can kill him. He's vulnerable," John hissed between gritted teeth. He returned his focus back to Stan, who was still lying on the couch like a dead fish. He hoisted the boy onto his shoulder like a fireman, whisking him away and out of the house. Although old, John still had a bit of strength left in him.

"Where are you taking him?" Bradley asked frantically as he went out the door.

"To finish what he started," John grumbled back. The rest of the group followed closely behind, Bradley running back inside to grab his glasses. John passed Stan to the tall one, motioning for him to go into the bed of the truck.

"One of you get in the passenger seat and tell me where Huxley is," John commanded. The rest were already in the bed of the truck, leaving Bradley to be the navigator. He sighed, hopping in the passenger seat, eyes widening at the sight of the gun.

"He.. He's in the maze, in the center with the rock," Bradley stuttered out as he attempted to get himself buckled. John didn't say anything, just tore off down the street and towards the maze. He knew exactly what Bradley was talking about. He didn't feel his foot leave the gas pedal the entire time, his eyes narrowed and cold as he stared at the road in front of him. He faintly noticed Bradley eye up the shotgun with anxiety. It was almost as if he had never seen a gun before. John pressed on, not caring if he was scared or not.

He swerved his truck to the side, parking on the curb beside the maze. He quickly turned the ignition off before grabbing his gun and hopping out. The rest made their departure as well, quickly jumping out of the truck and following John. The tall one held Stan in his arms, carrying him as they made their way through the maze. Bradley kept in front, staring down at the muddy floor, seemingly following the muddy footprints below. They all walked at a brisk pace, not wanting to waste any time.

"Guys, he's waking up!" He heard Jamie shout from behind. John immediately paused, turning around to face them. Stan began to stir in the tall one's arms, causing him to set him down. His legs twitched twice before his eyes shot open. They all surrounded him, allowing his eyes to travel to each of their faces. He slowly sat up without saying anything, his eyes wide and bloodshot. He looked around a few more times before standing up, everyone stepping back to give him space.

"Stan, are you alright?" Bradley asked with worry.

"I'm fine," he replied coldly. His eyes traveled to John. At that moment, John could tell that he knew what they were back here for.

"C'mon," John said calmly, "we don't have much time." Bradley nodded, going back up to the front to lead the way. The rest followed behind until the clearing came into view. A large bulbous cocoon attached itself to the boulder at the bottom of the hill. The group slowly made their way up to it, John no longer being able to control the pace of his heart. The cocoon was a disgusting brown color with a tint of red and yellow, veins covering it as it pulsed against the boulder. The cocoon itself seemed to be alive. Liquids seeped from the bottom, pooling out and around the ground, the scent of the contraption resembling the smell of rot.

John Charles raised his shotgun towards the cocoon, squinting one of his eyes as he did.

"Stop!" Vicky shouted. John sighed before turning towards the scared girl.

"Give me one reason I shouldn't kill this thing right now," John hissed.

"Because he said we'd be free now, shooting him will only make him angry," she pleaded. "We shouldn't risk this, not when we're so close." John shook his head, wanting to burst out in laughter at her stupidity.

"Are you kidding? Do you really think he would let you go like that? He doesn't care about us," he snarled while pointing at himself for annunciation. "We're just human scum to him, our lives are worth nothing."

"He's right," Annette noted while stepping up next to him. "How could we trust someone who kills children for their own gain? He doesn't care about us." The rest looked at each other with worry in their eyes. Jamie shook his head.

"I'm not risking our lives just for the chance of taking his," Jamie spoke with a slight shake in his voice.

"I'm not either," Vicky agreed while stepping back. Bradley stayed silent, looking at Stan for a moment.

"If we show him our peace, he might see it as a sign of worship and leave us alone," Bradley added nervously.

"I don't want to fight anymore," the tall one spoke quietly while putting his head down. John felt his eyes drift over towards Stan. The two made eye contact, Stan's eyes feeling like daggers. He stepped up once, his eyes never leaving Johns.

"I want him dead." He stated coldly. The rest looked at him in shock. He stared at them with his dagger eyes. "We are nothing but pawns in his game and I want him dead." He walked up to stand beside John. "I'm done playing his games." Bradley looked at him with astonishment.

"Stan, you could live a normal life, please don't do this," Bradley begged.

"I've never lived a normal life," he snapped. "Normal doesn't exist and never will, especially if we let this dick live." He pointed at the cocoon with an angry finger.

"We're wasting time," John Charles stated before turning around to face the disgusting contraption. He raised his gun, unloading it on the flesh-like nestle. The veins on the outside popped, brownish blood seeping out. *I'll just tear him out from the outside.* He stomped up towards the wounded cocoon, ripping at the fleshy surface. He could feel the mix of flesh and what felt like soggy skin get underneath his fingernails as he tore through. Blood began to spill, covering his arms in a stinky fluid. The liquid had a light burning effect, the same feeling you get when pouring alcohol on a wound, except worse and all over his arms. He gritted his teeth as he continued to search for a body within the flesh prison.

A sudden hand grabbed his. Long, spindly, black spider-like claws gripped him, pulling him inside. He felt the claws dig underneath his skin like needles, making him scream as he was pulled inside the cocoon. His mouth was immediately filled with an embryonic-type liquid, causing him to choke. He opened his eyes as his lungs tightened, searching for a way out. The only thing he saw was a skeletal-like creature with razor teeth. Its eyes a glowing orange set below horns similar to a ram. It cocked its head slowly, its jaw turning into a sick sort of smile.

"Let's see if the death I planned for you will be as poetic as the death you planned for me," Huxley hissed with a gravelly tone, his voice being clear despite John drowning in the liquid. He felt himself begin to panic as his body desperately fought for some sort of air, being met with nothing in the end. He felt the needle-like claws dig into his sides, squeezing him tightly. He screamed in pain again, instinctively going back in for another breath of air. He felt the fluid travel down his body, coughing and sucking in more liquid as it did. His heart exploded in his chest, fear gripping him as his body fought for life. His lungs felt as though they were on fire, his body weakening as it struggled one last time. *And for tonight, as they say, the leaves will cross one last time before the last of the blood is faded.*

Jamie Anderson

Jamie watched in horror as John Charles got sucked into the cocoon, the outside of it closing him in. Annette fumbled with something in her pocket as Stan was frozen in place while watching the cocoon change its form. She pulled out what looked like a lighter, going over to the puddle of fluids that connected to the cocoon. She bent down, flicking at the lighter vigorously before setting the puddle aflame. The liquid seemed to be just like gas, a bright flame traveling up and onto the cocoon, inhuman screeches of pain emitting from the inside.

She ran back towards the group once she was satisfied with what she had done, her face red and full of fear.

"We need to get out of here, he's angry," Vicky urged in distress. They all looked towards the cocoon, the veins writhing like snakes. Jamie couldn't believe what was happening. The gravity of the situation setting in, he could feel himself begin to panic.

"And lead him into town?" Annette asked, breathing heavily as she did. She looked a lot different from the girl Jamie was used to. Her usual long, well-kept hair was in a tangled mess as mud smeared her face. "We need to kill him now while he's still in there."

"How?" Bradley asked desperately. It seemed as though everyone was giving up hope. A final screech sounded out around the field, causing the group to go silent. The cocoon suddenly burst, the steaming rot-smelling, liquid spilling everywhere. They all jumped back, keeping themselves at a reasonable distance away from it. Huxley's new form stood before them, his legs long and lanky, along with his arms and dark, spindly claws. His ribs practically poked out of thin grayish skin. His face was elongated and skeletal, with ram horns atop his bare head. One of the horns split in half, presumably from coming out wrong. He had small, beady eyes, a deep orange color glowing within them. He had a very tall stature, his appearance quite haunting.

His jaw clicked together, causing an eerie snapping sound. He opened his mouth to speak, pausing a moment before any noise could even come out.

"*You have proven to me that this world is covered in rot. I will cleanse your people from their filth, and I will rebuild, avoiding the mistakes they have made. I was wrong to trust you to be my prophets, humans always fall for their own selfish reasonings.*" He turned his head towards Stan, cocking it to the side as he did. "*My respectable host, oh how I adored you. You could have been perfect. You could have been everything. But instead, you had to betray me and show how you are just like the rest. I would pity you, but I have erased myself from human-like emotions.*" He lurched forward, leaning towards them. "*I will eliminate you all, fix this world that you destroyed.*" His voice was deep yet gravelly, goosebumps popping up on Jamie's arm. He could feel himself wanting to hyperventilate.

"What makes you think you could fix the world if you couldn't even fix us," Stan hissed. Huxley looked taken aback for a moment, his small beady eyes narrowing.

"*If I were your creator, you wouldn't have even been broken in the first place.*" He stepped closer, clicking his teeth together as he did. Jamie found the sound to be very disgusting, forcing him to turn away.

"Right, if you were our creator we would be a whole different type of fucked," Stan remarked. Huxley let out a snarl, swiping the air in front of them, causing them to jump back. *We have to get rid of him somehow.* Jamie thought desperately. He stared up at the tall figure, having no clue how they would make that possible. The whole situation felt hopeless and dreamlike. He squeezed his eyes close. *Wake up! You don't know this thing or these people! Wake up now!* His thoughts were completely useless. He opened his eyes, finally coming to his senses. *We need something to fight with.*

He looked around the surrounding area, finding nothing to work with. They would have to leave the maze. Jamie took in a deep breath, knowing what he had to do. He darted for the exit, hoping the others would follow suit. He kept his eyes toward the ground, watching and following the old footprints. He was able to hear the rest follow from behind, making him feel relieved. He zig-zagged his way through the maze, his short legs moving surprisingly fast. He knew where he had to go, but he wasn't sure if they would make it in time.

They exited the maze soon after, the group darting across the street as the large creature chased from behind. Jamie weaved right, leading them to the local cop shop. Huxley couldn't hide anymore, especially from bullets. He noticed as the others caught up with him, Annette running a little ahead. Huxley was beginning to catch up as well, seeming to not care about being seen anymore. Jamie could feel his heart begin to pound in his throat as his mouth dried up. *We just gotta make it through the park.* He thought as he felt himself slow down. He suddenly wished he was more in shape.

"C'mon, Jamie, keep going!" He heard Vicky shout as they entered the park. He pushed on, feeling a little more energy within himself to continue. They raced against the creature looming above, the police station able to be seen from across the street. The sight of it helped him continue to run, his legs going a little faster. The others seemed to know where he was heading, speeding ahead and towards the station. Annette was across the street when Jamie felt himself get knocked off his feet.

He fell flat on his back, all the air being knocked out of him. He looked up to see Huxley staring down at him. His teeth continued to gnash together, the familiar black goo from before dripping down on him like drool. All Jamie wanted to do was cover his ears to silence the grinding sound.

"*What do you choose, Jamie? You're a very complex boy, I can see, but did you even want to care in the first place? Or did their presence force you?*" Huxley asked with a cocked head. "*Or would you rather drink your problems away instead of facing them, instead of facing what you really care about,*" Jamie said nothing, just stared up at the creature in fear. He tried backing up, but he felt frozen in place. He felt cold.

The sudden sound of gunshots filled the air, causing Huxley to raise himself and back up. Jamie turned his head to see Hudson unloading his pistol on Huxley, his face full of shock as he did. Ivan ran up to Jamie, dragging him away while Huxley was distracted. Huxley let out a disgusting, inhuman scream, the strange liquid from before spewing out of the bullet wounds. Once Jamie was able to regain his footing, he rejoined the rest of the group. They stood beside the nervous Hudson who was running out of ammo. Annette ran back inside the station, leaving the rest of them to watch outside.

Hudson unloaded the last of his pistol on the squealing figure, the gun only being able to produce a series of clicking sounds.

"Shit," he spoke under his breath as he desperately pulled at the trigger. Huxley stood still for a moment, a steaming liquid spewing from each wound. He took one step forward with a shaky leg, eyes staring menacingly at the group. "Get inside," Hudson urged, pushing them towards the door. They did as he asked, scrambling inside the station. He slammed the door shut as they all huddled behind desks and tables. Hudson turned the lights off before taking his own place in hiding. A dim glow from the computers softly illuminated a small chunk of the surrounding area, providing just enough light for them to faintly see.

The sound of a gun having its safety taken off could be heard in the darkness somewhere, footsteps quickly approaching. Jamie felt a shift beside him as Annette squeezed herself between him and Vicky. She held a Beretta pistol out for them to see in the limited light they had.

"This should do him in," she whispered to them carefully.

"And if it doesn't?" Vicky whispered back with a wavery voice.

"Then we'll figure something else out," she said. The building creaked above them, causing them all to look up. Jamie suddenly felt flashbacks from the diner, his heart racing as the creaking continued. To his surprise, however, the creaking suddenly stopped. They waited there in the darkness for something to happen. Jamie held his breath as his heart pumped wildly in his chest. His ears desperately searched for some sort of noise that indicated what was happening outside. He squeezed his eyes shut, praying that he was going away.

The door suddenly slammed open, the teeth gritting together once again. Annette broke from her position, unloading the pistol on Huxley as he began to scream in agony. Jamie crawled out of the way, heading towards the back of the station. The rest seemed to stay in place as Annette continued to fire. Huxley tried to protect his face with his thin, clawed hands, screeching with each bullet. Soon the pistol began to make the same sounds Hudsons did, an empty click. Annette threw the pistol to the ground, going for the lighter in her pocket.

Huxley went silent, his wounds closing in a little. *It's gonna take a lot more to kill him than a few bullets.* His eyes zeroed in on Annette, who was still searching her pockets for her lighter. He raised one large hand, slashing her face with his needle-like claws. She fell back, blood rushing from her fresh wounds. She cried out in pain, reaching for her wounded face with shaky hands.

"Annette!" Vicky shouted, running for her. Huxley went in for a second blow, grabbing her like a damaged doll. He held her up in the air, staring at her for a moment as she struggled. He cocked his head, as if he were studying her. She pounded her fists against his large claws, wiggling around in a desperate attempt to free herself. Everyone watched in horror as she cried out for help, knowing there was nothing they could do. Jamie held his breath, his heart beating in his chest rapidly. He wanted to look away, but couldn't bring himself to do it.

Huxley watched her squirm, seemingly enjoying it, before using one large spindly claw to penetrate her in the lungs, throwing her to the ground like trash afterward. She lay there on the ground, coughing blood out of her mouth with eyes wide open. Vicky rushed over to her, holding her head up so she wouldn't choke on her own blood. She sat there in shock, her body violently shaking as she held onto her dying friend.

"Please stay with me," Vicky pleaded, her eyes welling with tears. "You have to go home." She held her there, hugging her frail body. "We were supposed to take you home," she cried. Annette took one of her bloody hands and held it up, holding Vicky's face with it.

"Vick, I don't wanna die," she croaked hoarsely. "Please don't let me die here." Vicky looked down at her with a teary face, holding her closer.

"We're going to get you out of here, just stay with me," she weeped. Her tears mixed with the blood on Annette's damaged face, the watery blood drops dripping down onto the floor. Jamie watched as the hand slowly reached down for Vicky. He scrambled his way over, attempting to pull her away from Annette. "No, we can still save her!" She cried out, holding onto Annette's dying body. "We can't leave her!" Ivan jolted up from his spot, scooping up Annette while allowing Jamie to tug Vicky out of the way. The rest departed from their spots as well, running towards the back of the station for the door. Jamie held onto Vicky's hand, leading the grieving girl through the darkened hallway. Bradley fumbled with the lock before opening the door, letting the sunlight in and the group out.

They scrambled outside, practically tripping over each other as they did. Hudson shut the door behind them, acting as if that were going to do something. Stan looked up at the sky for a moment, squinting his eyes from the sun.

"What time is it?" He asked frantically. Jamie didn't ask questions, just took a glance at his watch.

"About one twenty-two," Jamie responded, huffing as he did in an attempt to catch his breath. Stan nodded his head as if he were approving the time. Huxley burst through the door, their heads shooting towards the police station.

"Perfect," Stan said.

Stanley Morris

Stan broke off towards his house, knowing exactly what he needed to do. The rest followed behind him, Bradley speeding up to run by his side.

"Where are we going?" He asked breathlessly. Stan turned to face him for a moment before returning his focus to the path ahead.

"Train tracks, trust me," he explained. Bradley nodded, keeping his speed. Stan was feeling exhausted from running all day, he was sure the others were too. They wouldn't be able to keep this up for much longer. The dark clouds from before had returned, thunder rumbling in the near distance. They continued to push on, Huxley following closely behind. Stan supposed this was like a game to him, playing around a bit before really getting to business. He was allowing them to escape. He continued to run, ignoring the sinking feeling in his stomach. He'd finish this today so he could rest tomorrow. So they could all rest tomorrow. *Except for..* He shook that thought away, not wanting to be slowed down by his grievances.

He watched as the treeline came into view, knowing the train tracks would be just a bit further. He continued on, running across the street on fast feet towards the woods. He felt the first few drops of rain fall onto his warm skin, lighting striking the air above followed by the sound of thunder. He could feel his legs wanting to give out, but he persisted nonetheless. His shoes soon quickly kissed the grassy pine-embedded floor, the feeling allowing him to slow down a little. He turned his head, wondering if the others were still keeping up.

The group was still close behind, Ivan in the rear cradling Annette's limp body as he ran, her blood soaking his shirt. Vicky and Jamie ran side by side. It seemed as though the cop never followed, presumably staying back in the station. Huxley was nowhere in sight. Stan slowed to a walk, his head darting in every direction.

"Where is he?" Stan asked Bradley frantically, his eyes wild and full of fear. Bradley adjusted his glasses, looking around himself to see if he could spot Huxley.

"I dunno," he marveled in awe. Stan took in a deep breath, the rest of the group walking up to the two. Vicky sniffled, pointing upwards as she did. They all turned their heads up except for Annette, whose head hung low. Huxley was in the trees, his large body slinking from branch to branch. His eyes never left the group. Stan narrowed his own eyes, stomping off towards the tracks. *Fuck you, I won't let you win.* He didn't have to look to know that the rest were following behind. He felt more raindrops escape the shelter of the trees, dropping onto his face in fat plops.

"Stan?" He heard Bradley ask meekly. Stan turned his head but said nothing. "You know what you're doing, right? Like we're all gonna go home?" Stan turned his head away, not being able to face his pleading eyes.

"I'll make sure of it," he mumbled quietly. The tracks were finally in view, the group walking up to them in quick steps. Stan glanced up at the trees, Huxley's watchful eyes staring back at him. Ivan set Annette down and against a tree, Vicky immediately rushing to her side. She held her lifeless hand, whispering things to her as she did.

"He's still up there," Bradley noted with wonder as he stared up at the trees.

"Yeah, well he needs to come down," Stan seethed. He cupped his hands to his face, taking in a deep breath. "GET DOWN HERE YOU PUSSY!" He screamed, causing birds to flee out of the trees. More rain began to drop down from the sky, along with the blood from Huxley's bullet wounds. They were running out of time. He took in another deep breath. "A GOD WITH NO BELIEVERS MIGHT AS WELL NOT EVEN BE A GOD AT ALL!" He yelled into the trees.

This seemed to get his attention, his eyes narrowing as he climbed down the tree like a cat.

"*And a boy without a brain might as well not even be alive,*" he hissed back in a retort. Stan walked backward, placing himself on top of the tracks. The rest of the group backed up, huddling themselves around Vicky and Annette. Huxley slowly made his way towards Stan, his long legs moving in large strides. Stan backed up as the large figure stepped up on the tracks across from him. The two locked eyes, Stan standing strong. He thought back on the time. He would only have to distract him for a little while longer.

"Look at you, stripped of everything including your own skin. How does it feel to be below? How does it feel to have never once heard the truth?" Stan rambled.

"*I've heard it all before you were even born, even without skin, mine is still thicker than yours.*" Thunder rumbled from above, the rain falling down in thick drops. "*You think I am below? You must think the sky is the very ground you walk upon,*" he bellowed. "*The truth bleeds thicker lies than deception itself.*" The rest watched quietly as this strange scene unfolded.

"Then tell me, can you hear the truth without even hearing at all?" Stan asked. "Silence your hearing and read my lips, only then will you *hear* the truth."

"*I would never believe something so foolish,*" he hissed. Stan could feel his heart begin to pound in his chest. He needed this to work.

"Then stay living in your false reality and never hear what's meant to be heard," Stan retorted nonchalantly. Huxley grumbled as if deciding with himself on what he should do.

"*Fine, but you must stay where you are and only move your lips.*"

"Deal," Stan agreed. He could feel the tracks begin to rumble beneath him. He was right on time. Huxley covered his hands to his head, signaling his silence. Stan held up his finger for a moment as Huxley watched. The truth must wait.

"Stan get off the tracks," Jamie demanded in a serious tone. Stan held up another finger. The rumbling was stronger now, but Huxley didn't seem to feel the vibration.

"Stan, get off now!" Bradley begged. Stan held up a third finger. The horn signaled, but Huxley couldn't hear. Stan could. He put his fingers down, ready to tell his truth. He opened his mouth slightly, getting ready to speak. "GET OFF THE TRACKS!" Bradley screamed, Ivan holding him back before he could get near. Stan stayed perfectly still, watching as the train began to roll in. He took in a deep breath while listening to the rainfall around him. He realized how beautiful it was to exist for a moment. The smell of the rain, the trees around him. To even exist in the first place was a gift on its own, now it's time to pass that gift on.

"The truth is," he started to say, moving his mouth in a motion that was half recognizable to read. "The things we seek out aren't always meant for us." He looked over at his friends, tears streaming down their faces, blending in with the rain. He wished he could have met them in a different life, a life where he *was* normal. He turned back to face the demon ahead. "Sometimes, we don't even know what's meant for us." He watched as the train came into view. His heart beat quickly in his chest, but he knew he was ready. "I suppose we all find what we're meant for at some point." The train let out one last scream like a lone crow, striking Huxley and pulling him underneath the tracks at rapid speed. He screamed, just as he did the first time he died. The train hurdled towards Stan. It was his turn. He took a deep breath in.

And now that I have found myself, I may rest. And just like that, it was night once again, forever, and always.

About the Author

Lynde Miller grew up in a small town in between Wisconsin and Illinois. She had a passion for writing at a very early age and immediately began to work on books such as "The Stupid Tiger" and "Nutty the Squirrel." Although it was pretty difficult to publish as a seven-year-old, this would just be the start of her career. Once reaching High School, she began working on Spiritual Burden which was arguably a step up from her past work. Spiritual Burden ultimately started as a passion project, but her love for entertainment caused her to publish it. She hopes to write more books in the future!

www.ingramcontent.com/pod-product-compliance
Lightning Source LLC
LaVergne TN
LVHW010600100826
845148LV00014B/2784

* 9 7 9 8 2 1 8 8 7 9 0 9 9 *